A

CONSEQUENCE

OF GREED

Jack Eadon

Eloquence Press
Tustin, California

THIRD EDITION

Published by

ELOQUENCE PRESS
2092 Burnt Mill Road
Tustin, CA 92782
Manufactured in the United States of
America

ISBN 0-9753300-7-1

Library of Congress Catalog No.:01-126944

Acknowledgements

I again wish to thank Eloquence Press and a host of other individuals who helped make this update happen. From text smoothing revisions to typo corrections, I hope you will enjoy this "smoothed" version of my magnum opus, now the result of thirty-four drafts and nineteen years. I dedicate this book to all those who have inspired me regarding GREED through the years and to those readers nationwide who have enjoyed the book.

Jack Eadon

Jack Eadon

A CONSEQUENCE OF GREED

PROLOGUE

Corsicana, Texas   January 10, 1969

The sun was setting as Reginald drove his taxi down bumpy Beaton Street in the secondhand town. He adjusted his glasses again. They were ready to fall off.

How was he going to find his fare when it got dark? *Where is Golf Estates, anyway?* he wondered.

Reginald swerved into the parking lot of an old-fashioned Rexall drug store, next to a running pickup truck with a shotgun hung across its rear window. Fluorescent lights shined through the plate glass storefront. The store was open. He merely looked at his taxi's ignition to turn it off. Then he got out, walked up to the door, and pulled it open.

A big cowboy, about twenty-five, with long chestnut hair, handlebar mustache, and straw western hat charged out, drinking a can of beer. "Hey, watch it,

Fuzzy," the cowboy said. He slammed into Reginald.

Reginald chilled when he noticed the cowboy's eyes as he passed. Where they would normally be blue or brown or green, the cowboy's eyes were only black. Not just dark eyes—pure black. Stunned by what he saw, Reginald straightened his shirt and stroked his crewcut as the cowboy pushed by.

"Never mind him, son," a man drawled from behind the counter inside the store. "Just Coy. One of them tough ol' boys."

"But those eyes—"

"Don't know what you mean, fella," the man said. "What about 'em?"

"That's right, I forgot only I—" Reginald could see many things mortals couldn't. But it was the first time he had seen those kind of eyes in many years. There was no doubt about it. They were pure evil.

"Coy's one of them Klan fellas here in town," the man said. "Better not fuss with him."

"The Ku Klux Klan?"

The man nodded. "What else?"

"Maybe that explains—" Reginald put his index finger to his lip. "He certainly looked a bit flustered," Reginald said.

"Perhaps he's going out to burn some crosses?"

The man shrugged. "Been known to happen."

"Oh, I say," Reginald said. "Where might the candy be?"

"Aisle two," the man said. He looked at his worn old watch.

"Thank you, sir." Reginald picked up a package of Junior Mints, and walked back to the counter.

Reginald felt the man's eyes study his fifties style clothes and crewcut.

"Be fifteen cents," he said.

Reginald reached into the right front pocket of his beige wash-and-wear slacks, pulled out a quarter, and put it on the counter. "Here you go, mate."

"Mate?" The man looked up suspiciously. "Say, y'all aren't from around here, are you?" He scratched his matted, curly white hair and squinted his eyes.

"This is my first time here," Reginald said. "Oh, I need one of these kits to repair specs. Mine are ready to fall apart." He laughed. The man didn't.

"Specs? Hmmm. Help yourself, pardner." The man pointed at the kits and looked away.

"Say, it's a bit of a quiet town, eh?" Reginald said and smiled.

"Yep. Unlessin' you count Oscar Sanchez' annual holiday shindig for all them Coyote Brand folks," he said.

Reginald laughed.

"What's so funny?" he asked.

"Werewolves around?"

"Don't know nothin' about that." The clerked frowned. "Say, you mean you ain't never heard of Coyote Brand Products here in town? Best darn canned chili in the whole world. Everybody knows that."

"No, I'm afraid I haven't," Reginald said.

"Better 'n homemade."

"Perhaps I ought to purchase some," Reginald said. The least he could do for the folks in the office was bring back a souvenir. The "main office" had sent Reginald to Corsicana to "pick up a fare"—jargon for verifying that a soul passes successfully into the afterlife. It was a job Reginald had done for many years, since he had died of a premature heart attack at age thirty-five. He hadn't aged at all since that day.

"There, fella." The clerk smiled halfheartedly and pointed. "Aisle three," he said. "Bet those Yankees go and spoil the damn company."

"Yanks?" Reginald asked and walked over to Aisle three.

The man nodded. "That's what I said, son. Some fancy corporation up there in Chicago bought Coyote about a year ago. Still the hot news around town. Made Mr. James Post a mint, that's for sure."

"Post? Indeed." Reginald stopped and glanced at the name on the small piece of paper in his hand. Then he picked up a can and studied it as he brought it back to the counter. "Coyote Brand? Named after the founder's pet—quite clever."

"Sure," the clerk said stoically. "Be all, mister?"

"Yes." Reginald looked at the scrap of paper again. "Oh, I say, I meant to ask: Where might Golf Estates be?"

"Be $1.05."

"Right-o. Golf Estates?"

"Oh. Be North o' town. Take Second Street to the wooded road with the sign. Can't miss it."

"Turn right or left?" Reginald asked.

"Be a left. Only way you can go." The clerk looked over the top of his glasses at the old cash register. His finger pecked a few keys and the drawer opened with a ring. He looked up at Reginald without lifting his head. "Why Golf Estates this time o' night, son?"

"Oh. My assignment, you see. Gather a fare." Reginald pointed out to his taxi, hoping that explanation would suffice. It usually did.

"Course." The clerk eyed him and the car suspiciously. "Not many cabs around these parts no more."

"Thanks, mate." As Reginald picked up his bag and change, he knew this Texas man was studying him.

"Y'all come back," the clerk drawled unconvincingly.

"Right, mate." Reginald walked out hurriedly whistling "God Save The Queen." He felt the clerk's eyes follow him all the way to his taxi.

He glanced back, spooked by the clerk's cool reception. He unlocked his car door with a look, pulled it open, and got in. He held the steering wheel and stared at the ignition switch. Again, without so much as touching his keys, the car's engine roared. He opened his bag and pulled out the repair kit. He took the little wrench and tightened the screws on his glasses. Then he looked at his watch.

Almost time, he thought. Reginald always got to dislodgements on time. He backed out of his parking place and drove down Beaton Street, bumpy with inlaid brick. He looked around the strange little town: a diner, a Salvation Army store, a currency exchange, and boarded up storefronts.

Smells like rain, he thought. Reginald rolled up his window as he turned left on Second Street, passed the Navarro County Historical Society, drove by a road that led to a cemetery, and headed north to Golf Estates.

Minutes later, across town, the thunder cracked.

"What?" James Post looked up from his desk.

Drip. Drop. Drip. Drop.

Across the hall from his office, in the ancient bathroom next to Mary's coffee stand, the faucet dripped. Alone at Coyote Brand, Post heard the drip echo through the five rooms that comprised the little office building, despite the intermittent rattling of the old heater.

Couldn't someone fix that drip?

The thunder boomed again outside.
As he studied Coyote Chili's sales results,
Post puffed on his pipe. What more was
there to do on a rainy Friday night in
Corsicana? Go to Oscar's damn party?
Instead, as president of Coyote Brand
Products, he had worked late, something
he always did on Friday nights since the
Yankees had acquired the company.

Seeming to ignore the impending
storm, evening birds played outside the
office in the fading orange dusk.
Between the drips and the heater and the
birds, Post fancied he had himself a kind
of symphony. Maybe, for a change, it
would serve as a backdrop for a
breakthrough during one of his Friday
sessions.

The sudden ring of the phone made
him jump.

Now, who's that on a Friday night? He
picked up the phone. "Hello?"

"Hi, Jim?" a low voice on the phone
said.

"Yep?"

"Kyle Burghoff here." It was the Food
Division president at Allied Corporation
in Chicago, Post's boss since the
acquisition. "I've been following your O.

I., Jim," he said. "Still down since just after the sale."

"Damn bottom line?"

Burghoff cleared his throat. "At headquarters we call it Operating Income or O. I. for short."

"Right, I knew that," Post said shakily. He knew Burghoff was in his forties and, at fifty-three, Post resented feeling intimidated by a younger man.

"Seems to be your merchandising spending. Those billback trade deals," Burghoff said.

"Really? Well, shoot. Your man Hickman added 'em right after he became sales manager. But I haven't approved any for a while."

"Funny," Burghoff said. "Our reporting system shows that they're killing your O. I. more than ever."

"I know our bottom line's been shaky, but I never thought it was them deals," Post said.

Burghoff continued, "And, Jim, I thought we agreed you'd advertise some other products, too, like that chili hot dog sauce."

"Wait a second now. How can I do that if Hickman's spending the budget on them billback trade deals?" Post asked.

"Hmmm," Burghoff said, "maybe I can send somebody down to help you trim the deals and revise the advertising."

"Nobody 'round here'll take real good to that."

"Jim, come on. I don't want to get off to a bad start with Coyote. There's this young fellow, Marcus Ramsay," Burghoff said. "Sharp young fellow. You might like him."

"Wait, Kyle. Can't I just sort out this billback thing over the weekend?" Post asked. The thought of surrendering to the Yankees within a year after the sale made Post quiver. *Next they'd be making the damn day-to-day decisions,* he thought.

"Sorry, I'll need to put your last payment in escrow until you turn it around down there. A pretty penny—two million."

"Shoot," Post said.

"Listen, Jim. I can send Marcus down next week. Just for a few days. He can really help."

"Sure."

"He's got a reputation up here for getting a handle on those trade deal expenses."

"Right." Post clutched the phone hard.

"I'm trying to be civil here," Burghoff said. "How about if he got down there late Monday?"

"Fine, then, Monday. G'night." Post hung up. He had skipped Oscar's party rather than to attend his plant manager's predictable holiday bash. That Yankee sales manager, Earl Hickman, would be standing in anyway—quite the social climber—his wife, too, the way she flashed that jewelry around.

Post thought back to how Hickman had started at the company humbly the year before: He drove a Plymouth and wore clothes from Sears. Now, less than a year later, Hickman drove a Mercedes and wore custom silk sports jackets made by some fancy tailor in Dallas—pretty strange. *Did the man had inherit a ton of money?*

And now these billback deals are hurting the bottom line? *Maybe I should check them out. Maybe Hickman's made some mistakes.*

Thunder interrupted Post's thoughts. The lightning was getting closer. He glanced toward the window behind his desk. Strange sounds like metal cutting and gravel scraping came from outside.

He stood and looked out the window, but saw nothing in the faintly lit courtyard.

He walked over to the scratched-up metal cabinet where all of his red vinyl binders were stored. He pulled out the Budgeting Manual, walked back to his desk, and sat. He opened to the "Trade Deal" account, thumbed through a few pages, and studied the rows of numbers. With a flick of his old Zippo, he relit his pipe.

He did a double take at the account ledger. Starting with the Dallas market, Post remembered how the billback deals—paid to each of his sales brokers after they submitted a performance certificate for approval—had begun just after Earl Hickman started.

The first of the deals on the list had been approved by Post himself. He specifically remembered that because they were new. For every case sold on "deal," a per-case allowance was paid. A check was cut by Al and mailed to the broker who endorsed and passed it on to grocery trade accounts like Safeway, Tom Thumb, or Kroger. Post studied the ledger:

DALLAS MARKET

$/case	# cases	product	Approved by	Date
1.50	4,102	Plain Chili	James Post	4/2/68
2.00	3,676	Plain Chili	James Post	5/30/68
2.00	3,011	Plain Chili	James Post	6/12/68
1.50	3,388	Hot Dog Sauce	James Post	7/31/68

Then, still in the Dallas market section, Post noticed that at the end of September, the approval signature changed. Hickman had begun approving the deals without Post's OK. That looked fishy.

$/case	# cases	product	Approved by	Date
1.50	5,086	Hot Dog Sauce	James Post	8/7/68
1.50	6,339	Hot Dog Sauce	James Post	8/30/68
2.00	7,212	Chili w/Beans	James Post	9/10/68
2.50	5,923	Plain Chili	Earl Hickman	9/30/68
2.00	5,016	Chili w/Beans	Earl Hickman	10/7/68
2.50	4,925	Plain Chili	Earl Hickman	10/23/68
2.50	5,128	Plain Chili	Earl Hickman	11/15/68
2.50	5,431	Plain Chili	Earl Hickman	11/29/68
2.00	7,936	Chili w/Beans	Earl Hickman	11/29/68
2.50	7,009	Plain Chili	Earl Hickman	12/15/68
2.50	5,127	Plain Chili	Earl Hickman	12/30/68
2.50	6,203	Plain Chili	Earl Hickman	12/30/68
2.00	4,177	Chili w/Beans	Earl Hickman	1/3/69

All these deals in the last three months? Post quickly flipped to other markets and saw no similar deal activity. He flipped back to Dallas. Hickman had been approving all these deals just for the Dallas market. That was mighty peculiar.

When the allowance per case paid by Coyote Brand was multiplied by the number of cases sold "on deal" in Dallas, thousands of dollars worth of billback deals were being "earned" by the Dallas broker, and supposedly paid to trade accounts once they built end-aisle displays of Coyote Brand chili cans. That was assuming the billback check, approved by Hickman and made out to Frank Benedict, the Dallas broker, was endorsed and properly forwarded to the trade account.

Post had always been suspicious of that loosey-goosey payment scheme, but had never questioned it. He figured it was just more Yankee nonsense he'd have to get used to.

He looked at the list of deals again and shook his head.

Wait a second! How could Benedict's band of salesmen have done such a great job that they suddenly earned thousands of dollars from Coyote for putting up displays? *Frank and his boys couldn't physically set up that many displays,* he thought. With no safeguard to guarantee that the retail trade account was actually being paid, Frank could be pocketing the deal money, or kicking back part of it to, say, Hickman.

Post felt himself flush. He regretted not ever having seen this major loophole. He realized he should have been co-signing the checks to verify that the deals had his approval, but he admitted to himself that he had done everything possible to avoid all that bureaucratic nonsense. *Wait, this could be the explanation for why Coyote's merchandising expenses had been so high!*

Post figured that if Frank and his boys were doing such a great job, sales ought to be way up.

I'll just double check sales, he told himself. That would reassure him that there was no hanky panky going on.

Post looked at the sales chart laying on the desk. He followed his index finger down the overall sales column and found Dallas. Sales were up all right, but only modestly.

Shoot. *This here's pretty convincing proof. All these displays and no change in sales? It all fits!*

Suddenly it was hard not to conclude that Post's long term Dallas broker was somehow in cahoots with Hickman, giving the Yankee a kickback. Sure, it was circumstantial evidence, but real convincing. Post shook with anger and fear at the same time.

Is Hickman capable of this? As Post thought back, he recalled that, since the acquisition a year before, Hickman had taken every opportunity to meet alone with Frank Benedict. And Post had considered that relationship positive!

Now the picture looked completely different. Hickman must've been scheming with Frank Benedict for several months.

Post slumped in his chair. He felt the very foundation of his company crumbling under the Yankees' influence. He admitted to himself that his own relationship with Frank Benedict had cooled over the previous year: short lunches, perfunctory phone calls, and canceled golf rounds. Frank had also attended only one of the quarterly broker review meetings, which he normally never missed. Post had thought all along that the man was just put out because

Post hadn't awarded him the Houston market with all that commission.

Maybe that's why he's been cheatin'! More damn evidence, Post thought.

Wherever he looked, he found substantiation for his fears. It seemed obvious now. Irritated, he sat back and roughly flipped through the pages of his latest copy of "Agent," a local periodical that tracked the real estate market in Navarro County. He had begun receiving the little magazine since he moved into the big white house in Golf Estates.

The cover story got his attention. It explained how the Northern folk moving into Texas were affecting everything. He read how they were diluting the growth of Texas products. How per capita sales for Texas products actually declined as these transplanted Yankees chose not to purchase the same shopping basket that Texans did.

Post sat up. *Lord, that must apply to chili.* To tap into the Yankee population explosion, he would have to emphasize a new product mix and not assume Yankees would purchase the same things Texans would. Maybe Burghoff was right about pushing other products like chili hot dog sauce, a chili with a lower meat content formulated to make great chili dogs.

Shoot, even Yankees must like chili dogs, Post thought.

Come Monday, with or without that kid Burghoff was going to send, Post vowed to himself to reconsider what products were appropriate for his changing customers. Those would be the ones he'd push.

He tapped his pipe in the gold-bordered ashtray that he had received for service to the Corsicana Rotary. He looked outside and watched the darkness spread across the company's parking lot.

Again he heard that scraping noise, then a noise like something sliding through gravel. He glared out the window into the dark but saw nothing. Being alone in the office on Friday nights wasn't usually a spooky experience, but this night seemed peppered with weird sounds. He sighed as he looked out the window again and thoroughly scoured the courtyard. Nothing.

Even though he felt shaken by his discovery of Hickman's malfeasance and the need to change Coyote advertising to adjust for the Yankee boom, Post figured his Friday thinking session had gone particularly well. He sat down and leaned back in his chair, plopped his boots on the desk, and clasped his long fingers behind his head.

He glanced at the orange Grady Davis Garage receipt for new brakes the boy had installed over lunch. Post would certainly surprise Margaret when they drove to church that Sunday with quiet brakes. That darn squeaking had bothered her and most of Corsicana for months! But, not anymore, thanks to Grady. That boy could fix a car better than anyone!

Post sat on the edge of his chair and sorted his follow-up memos into piles. A small, folded page torn from a spiral notebook fell off the pile onto his desk. He picked it up and unfolded it.

Dear Mr. Post,
    You must be careful. This is not a joke.

    A friend

That's odd, Post thought. Are Oscar and Harold playing games? Maybe someone else wrote this.

For a second, he thought about calling the sheriff immediately. On the other hand, maybe he could call tomorrow. Tonight, he would focus on summarizing his revelations, then head for home. Outside the storm clouds blocked the last traces of the setting sun. The birds had stopped their singing, conceding to the beat of a steady drizzle. Suddenly, lightning cracked and lit up the blinds.

Post sat up and reached in his drawer for the impressive silver fountain pen Margaret had given to him for their anniversary. He smiled fondly as he studied the "Dearest J.P. Love, M.P." which was inlaid in black oxide around the heavy barrel. Post pulled out his crystal ink bottle and filled the pen with his favorite royal blue ink. He tested it. Perfect as usual. That pen was the nicest present his little darlin' had ever gotten him. He would treasure it forever.

In sweeping blue lines, Post documented Hickman's likely culpability and Coyote's need to take advantage of the Yankee population boom by pushing hot dog sauce. Having scrawled the better part of a page, he reached for the telephone, buried it in his shoulder for support, and dialed home.

"Hello," a dainty female voice answered.

"Margaret!"

"What is it, James? You sound excited."

"I am, sugar. I am." Post tapped his pipe and picked up the summary he had just written.

"When you coming home?"

"Wait, Margaret, I have news," he said.

"What?"

"For once I've had a wonderful Friday night session. It's that damn Yankee, Earl Hickman." He tapped his pipe particularly hard.

"What about him?"

"I had a feelin' all along and now I'm sure. Looks like the polecat's on the take." He sat up straight.

"My Lord, James."

"Yep. Getting a kickback from them damn billback deals he's always pushing." Post laid his pipe down and adjusted the phone.

"I thought he promised those billbacks would save the day," she said.

"He's in bed with Frank Benedict."

"That Dallas ruffian," she scolded. "Is he still bothering you about handling Houston?"

"Well, he would get a three hundred thousand dollar increase in commission, darlin'," Post said.

"As if the man weren't well-off enough. Shame!"

"Oh, don't fret. Frank'll get tired of hearing no on Houston. Fact, now he'll probably lose all his Coyote business!"

"Why can't he just leave you be and do his job?" she asked.

"It'll be OK soon. I caught both them foxes in the hen house now," Post said.

"I never did like that Hickman, James. Thinks he's a southerner because he's from Baltimore—such nonsense."

"Have to let him go is all." Post picked up his pen and tapped the back end lightly on the desk. "Then I'd cut those billbacks and have enough money to push other products. Burghoff likes hot dog sauce. Thinks the Yankees movin' down would go for it," he said.

"James, why don't you forget about all this nonsense and head home. Henrietta's making chicken. And, I have a mighty big surprise."

"Your tests?"

"I'm not sayin', Darlin'," she said.

But Post heard a smile in her voice. She had just received the results of tests that monitored the status of her cancer. The doctor had been optimistic and ordered the tests to see if the disease had been arrested.

"OK. In a few minutes. Oh, and Margaret?" he said.

"Yes," she said softly.

"I do love you."

"Oh, James, you sweety." She giggled. "I love you, too."

"You bathe in that rose blossom scent today, Sugar?"

"Yes, James." She giggled.

"Good." He smiled. "Be home soon. Just need to jot some notes for the boys."

"You and your silly notes! I swear! You run that place with those notes."

"I'll be quick about it, Darlin'. I promise. G'bye."

They hung up.

Before he left, Post picked up his pen, looked over his revelations once more, and added a few scribbles. Then he reached for his little white notepad. He routinely used it to send instructions to each of his managers so they would take specific steps to improve the company's performance. By jotting the notes, which they all hated, he found he could communicate with each of them in the language that they best responded to. For instance, Harold Buick, the Quality Assurance Manager, had a great sense of humor. So, when the company had experienced a product recall the year before, Post rallied Harold's enthusiastic support by implying that the recall was inevitable since Coyote Chili was such a wild-tasting concoction to begin with.

But Oscar Sanchez, the Plant Manager, was a proud man, so talking about the recall in grave terms, had given Post a certain power over him. It encouraged Oscar to put in the extra effort to save the day.

Post realized that his note-writing bordered on manipulation of the boys, like chess pieces on a board. But he undertook it with the best of intentions so, over the years, he began to view it as his secret weapon for managing Coyote, and he became quite good at the technique.

After he finished his notes, Post stabbed them onto a nail pounded into a four-by-four-inch piece of half-inch plywood. Lenora knew to look there first thing Monday to gather the notes for distribution to each manager.

Post carefully laid his pen back on the wooden carrier in his middle desk drawer, and rose. Large drops spattered the north-facing windows as he switched off the heat and turned out the last of the office lights. Monday, with Puritan's token help, Post would begin to weed out the effects of Hickman and his billback deals. With a little luck, the Ramsay kid could actually help. At least Burghoff seemed to have a lot of faith in him.

Post's boots thumped over to the wooden hat rack. He picked up his black felt hat and stuffed it under his arm. He left the office, pulled the door shut, and locked it.

Outside, rain sprinkled the dust-covered asphalt and dripped on Post's thinning hair. He put on his hat. Suddenly lightning zapped a block away.

He knew that Margaret would want to hear about his ideas for the company. She would be supportive, but would also infuse him with skepticism, gently challenging him as always. Post smiled. He loved his dainty Margaret so.

He looked around the company courtyard, lit only by the eerie blue of mercury vapor light. *Allied Corporation might own this place,* he thought, *but it'll always be mine in spirit.*

Crack! The thunder made him jump.

He stopped and looked up. The stars struggled to show themselves through puffy intermittent storm clouds.

How beautiful this is! Post felt exhilarated by his discoveries. Earl Hickman would get the ax for his fool-ass, money-skimming ways. Cecil, who had been there for a decade, would stay, always mister reliable. Al, the backbone of Coyote, would also stay. Maybe Oscar too, if he could douse his career obsession and focus on his job. Coyote's Dallas sales broker, Frank Benedict, would have to be reassessed.

Man's gotta prove that he and Hickman aren't schemin' together.

Post beheld his massive yellow Cadillac with its cruise control and automatic windows. It sat there, bathed in the blue light. Looking up, he stretched out his long arms, catching the rain drops. The car worked perfectly now that Grady had fixed her up. *Margaret will be so pleased.*

Shoot! His retirement of leisure was only a heartbeat away now. He dreamed of it being an idyllic adventure, maybe even in the South Seas. His thirty years of hard work had finally paid off, and no cheatin' Yankee was going to spoil it. Instead, Post wanted his last five years as president—part of the Allied deal—to be the best of all.

He rubbed his belly, realizing how famished he was after his long day. He couldn't wait to get home to Henrietta's scrumptious chicken dinner. *It sure is nice living in that big white house with the breezy porch,* he thought. A might pretentious, but thank the Lord it isn't one of those boxy tract homes across the field from Golf Estates.

Post opened the car door. He heard gravel crunch. He looked left, then right. Not a sound.

I must be goin' nuts, Post thought as he got into the automobile. Putting his keys in the ignition, he thought about how Collin Street Bakery over on Seventh Street, makers of the world's finest fruit cakes since 1896, seemed to operate successfully year after year, even though Gus Weidmann and Tom McElwee had personally stopped supervising production of the famous Christmas cakes years before. *Maybe things worked out for those boys because*

*they didn't have any know-it-all Yankees
spending their money.* Post decided he
would ask Gus and Tom at the next
Rotary meeting if they ever had to deal
with a Hickman. *Maybe they could give me
some advice.*

A young man suddenly jumped up
from the shadows in front of the car. The
intruder turned and ran out the open
chain link gate toward the field across
Main Street.

"Hey, you!" Post blurted out as he
jumped from the car. He shook his fist at
the escaping interloper. His heart
pounded.

The young man, probably in his
twenties, was tall, muscular, and quick.
Long brown hair flopped under his straw,
western-style hat, which he held as he ran
across the partially lit field, thrashing
stalks of weeds and kicking loose stones.
He sped toward the railroad tracks a half-
block away.

Post stared at the disappearing form.
As the boy passed under a streetlight on
the edge of the field, he glanced back,
revealing an obvious mustache. Post
squinted, but still couldn't recognize him.

His stomach relaxed as the patter of
the boy's boots faded. A distant engine

revved and tires squealed.

Sounds like a truck, Post thought. Then he sighed. The trespasser was gone.

Post glanced back to the distribution wing next to the chili plant. As usual, the large door had been left open. He looked over at the plant, then back at the sales office that used to be the old men's shower building—the same size as the little front office building. They were all lit by the purple security light. Everything looked normal around the compound.

Post got back into his car, closed the door, turned the key, and revved the mighty V-8.

After a dusty exit, he rolled down Main Street through deserted downtown Corsicana. His wipers pushed away the increasing raindrops. He hoped he'd run into the boy at some stoplight. Then he could at least get his truck's tag number and report it.

When Post got home he planned to tell Margaret all of the details of his crazy day. How the strange boy had leapt from the shadows. How that Yankee Hickman had hurt Coyote's profits with the billback deals and was undoubtedly getting a kick-back from Benedict. How the company could push hot dog sauce to take advantage of the Yankees moving in.

He calmed down as his car approached Second Street on the east side of town. As he turned left, passing the road to Pioneer Village and the cemetery, he noticed his brakes were quiet, all right, but they felt mushy. He had to press his foot halfway to the floor before they engaged.

Not good. Better have Grady check 'em out again. Post rolled out of town to the sign that marked the wooded road leading to Golf Estates. When he turned left there, his brake pedal depressed too easily and didn't slow the car effectively. Post gulped.

He pumped the brakes several times before he got a response. He decided he would definitely take the car back to Grady's in the morning.

Unlike that boy to foul up.

Anticipating the winding road ahead and shielded from the rain by the old trees, he lowered his window and proceeded carefully. He whiffed the faint odor of manure. *Fresh country, all right.* Enjoying the moment, Post lost himself in thought.

Then freshly painted lines appeared on the asphalt. It signaled the curving road that led into Golf Estates. The road's sudden changes reminded Post of the way Coyote could now focus on a new future despite being owned by Allied. *Maybe that Ramsay kid can help get things cleaned up.* Post promised himself he'd try to be receptive to the boy's ideas.

Meanwhile, he gently swerved down the winding road. He noticed that with the momentum of each turn, his large car began to rock from side to side, gaining speed uncomfortably. As he approached the entrance to Golf Estates,he saw the long entry marker, a freestanding brick wall. Post pressed on his brakes.

Nothing.

What?

He pushed the pedal to the floor three times. No response. He downshifted and the gear broke cleanly. He was in neutral. Post's heavy Cadillac lurched into the dip just before the entrance and gained momentum. "Holy Lord!" The long wall and the words "Golf Estates" loomed at him in apparent slow motion. He pumped the brakes again. The car swerved to the right, out of control.

"No-o-o!!"

Margaret Post was standing beside Henrietta in the kitchen of the Post home when the explosion rocked the neighborhood.

"Oh, my. What's that, Miss Margaret?" Henrietta asked. They both turned away from the chicken on the stove and ran to the front door.

Outside, Margaret Lassiter Post rushed through the rain to the end of the street. There she pushed through the murmuring crowd. Henrietta followed close behind. Empty eyes and shaking heads greeted them. Margaret approached the bloodied body by the brick wall, surrounded by bits of broken glass. Her James had been thrown from the car. His eyes remained open; his body was deadly still. She dropped to her knees next to him, splashing the mud. Behind her, Henrietta hugged herself as the crowd jabbered.

Margaret closed James' eyes and dabbed the side of his bloodied face with an arm of her housecoat. She traced his cheek with her fingers.

"Oh, my James." She shook, straining to control herself. She leaned over and kissed him, vaguely aware of approaching sirens and flashing red lights. In a broken voice she prayed, "Dearest James, may the Lord keep you."

Then the voices faded and Margaret disregarded large drops of rain that splattered on her own coatless body. "Dream sweetly, my love," she whispered. The first lady of Coyote Brand rose to her knees. Her bottom lip shook uncontrollably as she looked up and saw the silhouettes of what seemed like a hundred heads framing the stormy sky.

Then Margaret's muted cry joined Henrietta's and, with the others' voices, sounded an eerie siren.

At the same moment, barely visible in the faint illumination of porch lights, a taxi was parked down the road. The driver, Reginald Waverly, sat there, eating candy from a little white cardboard box with green letters. He shook his crewcut head. "Too much—this death. The hateful ones need to pay." He popped a little minty chocolate circle into his mouth and chewed.

He scoured the crowd and stopped when he eyed his "fare," lying there against the wall, surrounded by neighbors. At Post's side, his wife Margaret knelt and cried.

Then Reginald gasped as he saw the spirit of James Post suddenly rise from the lifeless body. It grew into a multi-pronged swirl of colored sparkles— beautiful, yet terrifying. "My Lord!" Reginald exclaimed. "I'll never get used to this part!"

The vapor shot from Post's body, flew throughout the area, and surged into the sky. In an instant it occupied all the heavens; in another, it returned and entered all the plants, animals, and bystanders—all living things. As quickly as it had come, the sparkling swirl disappeared.

Reginald clasped his hands together, patted his chest, and sighed. "I say. One of the most spectacular dislodgements I've ever seen." He picked up his pen and recorded a few notes on his clipboard. He popped another Junior Mint and thought about how he loved his job, particularly avenging wronged spirits. He knew he was the best in the office at handling those particular kinds of assignments, so he considered himself lucky when such an assignment came along. "Rest now, spirit of Mr. James Post. In time, you shall have your day." Then, by merely glancing at the ignition switch, his car's engine started. The taxi slowly turned around and headed down the road that led into the woods.

Part 1

the Greed

1

(11 Years Later)

Sheila Hickman lay on the hospital bed as it rolled down the corridor. The familiar row of fluorescent rectangles flashed by on the ceiling above. She could feel the wheels below hitting every little bump in the tile. The orderly who pushed the bed hummed out of tune.

Her stomach felt queasy and she shivered. No matter how many times she was given electroshock therapy, she never got used to it. Going into the procedure, the sheets were always cold, covering her nearly naked body. Even her head felt naked. They always shaved two bare spots, one on each temple where the electrodes would be placed. Because she would be totally unconscious from a general anesthetic, Doctor Lockhart always pointed out she wouldn't feel the shock itself. *But how does he know,* she wondered. *Doctors think they know everything!*

"It'll be fine, honey," Earl Hickman said as he slump-walked next to her to the procedure room.

He hoped that maybe this would be the shock treatment that, once and for all, would scare all the bad memories away. Maybe it would finally be a new start: no depression, no anxiety, no guilt. Maybe she wouldn't have those crazy dreams after this treatment like she normally did.

The hospital bed pushed open the procedure room door and the orderly rolled it through. The lights were bright and the cheery voices of nurses filled the room with community gossip. "Good luck, honey," Earl called. He cleared his throat and stopped as the bed rolled through the door. "I love you," he called.

The orderly rolled her bed next to another. Several nurses gathered. "One, two, three!" they said as they transferred her from one bed to another. Feeling exposed, she quickly gathered her hospital gown around her. A nurse covered her with a sheet and light blanket.

"Hi, Mrs. Hickman," a voice said. The doctor was dressed in scrub-green, head to toe. "I'm Dr. Carter. Remember, we talked last night about your anesthetic?"

He fidgeted. "Hey, doctor, this isn't your first time, is it?" Sheila asked.

He laughed. "Oh, I've done this many times before, Mrs. Hickman, I assure you. I'm just going to put a few of these IVs in your veins and insert another permanent IV in case we need it along the way. Then you'll count backward from ten."

"All those damn tubes. That's different."

"It's just routine, Mrs. Hickman," he said. "You'll be fine."

The Demerol the nurse had given her back in her room was settling in. Sheila felt rosy all over.

"Then you'll be asleep. Simple as that," he said and smiled. He had a friendly manner probably because he was new at Navarro and wanted to make a good impression.

"So, where's Dr. Lockhart?" she asked. "Let's get this show on the road."

"He'll be right down," Dr. Carter said.

The IVs went into her wrists with only a prick. The Doctor taped them down. That hurt, the way he applied the tape. Not like the old guy.

"Is there a problem, Mrs. Hickman?" he asked.

"Just hurts a little."

"Here, I'll loosen them." He pulled off the tape and reinserted one of the needles, then reapplied tape. "Better?"

She nodded.

Dr. Lockhart walked in. "How's everyone this morning?" He barked orders to the nurses like a general. Their relaxed banter changed to a silent, methodical scramble.

From Sheila's left side, the head nurse inserted a small, oval, rubber mouthpiece. She put a headband dripping with wires in place. This was the point at which Sheila always began to feel apprehensive.

Dr. Carter stepped forward and poked a needle into one of the IVs that hung from her wrist. "Now, just start counting to yourself, Mrs. Hickman, from ten down."

Ten, nine, eight, seven . . .

First, Sheila saw black all around. The noises around her faded as people seemed to be talking in a cave. She could feel the band tighten around her head as it was adjusted, then abrasive scraping on her temples, then pin pricks at her temples—the electrodes.

Time seemed suspended for a second. After another few minutes of nothingness,

she began to hear buzzing, then a loud
hum, and again, muffled sounds in a cave.
Each time it buzzed she saw white light in
her mind's eye. Then colored memories
flew by, like pages turning in a catalog.
Sheila drifted back, as if viewing a movie:

Her father. Her son. Her daughter. A
football field. A bar. A cowboy.
Wait. Stop there.
A cool sunny day.
Sheila saw herself driving past the
Navarro County Historical Society in
Pioneer Village into miniature downtown
Corsicana.
The Hickmans had just moved there.
Earl was supposed to finally be getting a
real career opportunity. Sheila felt like
she had no choice but to move her family
to Texas but now she needed to assert
her independence, like the old days when
she was in her twenties and hung out at
the docks in Baltimore.
For two weeks Sheila had made
frequent evening trips to the Cat's Meow,
a rustic old bar just outside of town on the
access road along I-45. There she danced
and danced, but mostly drank with good
ol' boys who downed shots and beers.

"Promotion," Earl had called the move to Texas. Right! The Allied big shots in Chicago were probably putting Earl out to pasture. She sensed it, and she was always right about those things.

The other day Earl had gone on a trip because Cecil convinced him to attend the fall broker review meetings around the Southwest: Shreveport, Houston, San Antonio, Albuquerque, and New Orleans. So, while Earl sipped mint juleps and joked with the bigoted New Orleans broker sales force, Sheila decided it was the perfect day to investigate Earl's real situation at the office. She thought that her daughter Erlene was old enough to take care of baby brother Bryan for a little while, even if it meant she'd have to struggle changing his diaper—good training.

She drove through downtown Corsicana with the car windows rolled down, the cool air rushing against her face. She turned right on Seventh, then turned left on Main Street, crossed the tracks, and pulled up to the chain link fence that surrounded the Coyote Brand compound like it was a prison. The gate was open. She made a slow right turn into the compound.

There were two boxy little buildings on the left, the larger plant building on the right, and a massive warehouse in back, all painted a hideous dirty yellow. She parked next to the plant.

God, what a smell! It was the distinctive Coyote Brand spice odor. She started to wander across the company's dusty courtyard, snickering at the two little office buildings that had been painted over and over until they resembled mustard-colored adobe.

After she took two steps, the screech of brakes interrupted her thoughts. Then a loud, melodic horn cut through the thick air that characterized most late afternoons in Corsicana. A pale yellow Cadillac with sweeping fins, each topped with two tiny lights, rolled through the chain link gate into the compound. Its massive whitewalls crunched over a patch of white gravel. More squeaks brought it to a stop in front of the first little office building.

After a second, a small, elegant lady emerged, wearing a flowery dress in shades of yellow and rust. She carried a frilly, outdated parasol. The woman tossed Sheila a pert wave as she floated on delicate white sandals toward the office door. A tall handsome man appeared at the door. He removed his large black cowboy hat, bent over, and kissed the tiny lady, then ushered her inside the office.

Who are those people? Sheila thought as she straightened her own wrinkled, jean skirt and tucked in her blouse. *Looks like the first thing I need to check out is what that lady is doing here. And does that man work here?*

Sheila dashed to the office door just as a large, jolly woman emerged. "Well, hi there," the woman bellowed as her jowls shook. "What's the hurry?" She crunched her brow and held up a pudgy hand that poked out of her frilly white blouse.

Avoiding direct eye contact, Sheila looked past the chubby woman, into the office. "I'm Mrs. Sheila Hickman. You must be Lenora. Lenora Cooper? The receptionist, right? Earl told me abou—"

"And Mr. Post's secretary, too," the woman said. "So nice to make your acquain—"

"Lenora, who was that woman anyway?" Sheila said and pointed.

"Why, Mrs. Margaret Lassiter Post, of course," she said. "Isn't she just lovely, now?" As Lenora spoke, her stubby fingers poised in praying posture. "The first lady of Coyote Brand."

"How cute," Sheila said sarcastically.

"So gracious an' all," Lenora said. "Why, we all think she's the best of the best, being from Chatsworth, o' course." Lenora nodded.

"That's the kind of role I pictured for myself . . . being Earl's wife," Sheila said. She peeked into the office again. "Introduce me, OK?"

Just then the dainty lady emerged.

"Mrs. Margaret Lassiter Post?" Lenora said and faintly bowed. "Please meet Mrs. Sheila Hickman. Earl's wife."

Mrs. Post's hand felt gentle and smooth when it touched Sheila's dish-pan grip. Sheila tried to mimic the way Mrs. Post propped it in the air, like she was about to receive a kiss instead of a handshake.

"I'm most delighted to meet you, Mrs. Hickman." Margaret Post smiled up at her. "I've heard ever so much about your wonderful husband, Merle—how nice that the Allied Corporation sent him to help James here at the company."

"It's Earl, not Merle," Sheila said.

"Oh, of course, how clumsy of me. I do apologize."

"Sure. Right," Sheila said, wiping her hands on her jean skirt. "So, where do you people live? In town, I suppose?" Sheila fidgeted. *Boy, I could use a drink.* She licked her lips.

"Not in town anymore," Margaret Post said. "After the Allied acquisition, James and I were able to upgrade to Golf Estates. Across the field from—"

"Our house?"

"Why, yes," Margaret Post said. "I remember searchin' for your li'l' ol' home. Three bedroom, two bath ranch, I believe. Best on the market at the time."

"So cozy for me, Earl, my teenaged daughter, and our little baby boy," she said. "You and James live alone, I suppose."

"Why, yes. Almost. You see Emma and Chelsea are away at college in the East. Smith and Radcliffe, you know. Now it's only James, Henrietta, and me at home."

"Henrietta?" Sheila asked.

"Our housekeeper and cook. She makes the most exquisite chicken dishes."

"Really."

"You'll have to come over for a marvelous southern supper some time. Tea and rummy on the veranda." She laughed and bent her wrist as she lightly touched Sheila's shoulder. "A custom at home."

"That would be just lovely." Sheila laughed as she whisked off the spot Margaret had touched and tried to hide a grimace. *So would getting my hands on some of your money.*

Margaret turned as her husband flung open the office door. Without stopping, he carefully laid Margaret's hand atop his forearm. He flicked the front of his black hat with his index and second fingers as if he had met Sheila before, and escorted his diminutive wife to their car, passenger side first.

After Margaret Post climbed in and the heavy door thumped shut, Lenora let out a sigh. "Such a fine lady. Originally from Chatsworth, you know."

"You said that," Sheila said, bored.

"It's the next town north," Lenora said. "Where all the gracious southern ladies come from."

"Lenora?" Sheila asked Lenora as she winced at the Posts' squeaky departure.

"Where's Earl in the scheme of things around here?"

"Scheme?" Lenora watched the large, yellow car squeak intermittently as it crunched across the white gravel, then filled the air with tan dust. "He should get them brakes fixed. Awful noisy for such a nice car." Lenora pursed her lips.

"About Earl?" Sheila asked.

"Margaret's always ridin' the brake pedal, you know."

"Lenora!"

"Sorry, ma'am. Earl? Oh, he's the Sales Manager."

"I know that." Sheila answered in restrained staccato grunts. "Where does he fall in the order of progression? The pecking order?"

"Earl is Cecil's boss," Lenora said.

"And?"

"And Mr. Post is Earl's boss. So Earl's right up there."

"What happens when Mr. Post retires?" Sheila said.

Lenora studied the sky, and thought for several seconds. Sheila puffed on a newly lit cigarette.

"With the Allied purchase, he'll be staying—"

"I know about the five-year thing. What if he, say, retires earlier? Hypothetically, that is. You know what hypothetically means, right? Who would take his job?"

"I guess Earl or Al, or even Oscar might-could be the president then."

"Now who's Al and Oscar?"

She laughed. "Al Bishop's the Controller and Personnel Manager— almost everything 'round here, I guess! And Oscar's our Plant Manager."

"So, Earl could be the next president? If Mr. Post weren't around anymore?"

A squat, man with twinkling eyes, a permanent smile, and swept-back, red hair walked toward them from across the courtyard. "Weren't around anymore?" he called. "What's this all about?"

Sheila blushed.

He walked up. "Ma'am, Earl can be the damn president if he wants. Not me!"

"I'm afraid we haven't had the pleasure," Sheila said uneasily.

"Al Bishop, ma'am. What's up anyway?" He reached out his right hand, squinted over the top of his half-glasses, and pushed his hair back with his left hand.

"I was just trying to understand where Earl fits, Mr. Bisher," Sheila said.

"It's Bishop—sure, you are," Al said. "See, Earl's the first Sales Manager since Stan Mendel. And Mr. Post loved Stan—God rest his soul."

"So? What does that have to do with my Earl?"

"Nothin' ma'am. Just that things have changed mighty fast since Earl come on board. Allied buyin' out the operation an' all," he said. "Don't know about Earl's damn billback deals, neither." He shrugged. "Jury's out, as they say."

"I see," she said.

"Guess I best take that up with Earl," he said. He started to walk past her.

"Of course, Mr. Bisher," Sheila said

"It's Bishop, ma'am." He stopped. "And Puritan's a might pushy, too. Y'all need to talk to Earl if he calls in, ma'am? He's in New Orleans, right?"

"No need. He'll call if he's running late."

"Yes, ma'am."

"Thanks for the info, Mr. Bisher." Sheila waved and scurried to the car.

As Sheila rumbled through town on the inlaid brick of old Beaton Street, she assessed her situation. If Earl would only play his cards right, he could eventually have James Post's job and her dreams might actually come true— perfect sandals, elegant country parasol, custom home, live-in cook, children at Ivy League schools. She could indeed become Coyote Brand's next "first lady," the best she could hope for after being stuck in such a hellhole of a town.

This Al guy seemed like he knew what he was talking about, too. She wasn't surprised Earl was already screwing things up with his hair-brain ideas. He would probably get fired or something. Then he'd never be president and she'd never be anywhere.

Her car bumped over the cobblestone. She licked her lips. *No way is he going to mess this up for me.*

She swung into the old Rexall drug store parking lot and skidded to a stop. She got out of the car, walked over to the old phone booth, pulled opened the door, and dialed home. "Erlene, now take care of little Bryan, OK?"

"I will. I will, Mama." Her daughter had started calling Sheila "Mama" ever since they had moved to Corsicana—a local custom Sheila hated. "It's Mother, Erlene."

"Yes, Mother," Erlene said.

"And make supper for your father if he gets in early. The beef stew's fine. It's in the fridge. I'll be home later."

"Aw, you going out again?" Erlene asked.

"None of your business, young lady! I'll be home later." She hung up and jumped back in the car.

Last thing I need is a helpless teenager!

Sheila sped off and, after driving out of town, turned left onto the access road. Woods were on her left, Interstate 45 on her right. She skidded to a stop in her usual parking place at the Cat's Meow.

The rustic wooden building sat on a lot that was carved out of the woods. There was large, grassy field in back, a dusty, gravel parking lot in front.

Minutes later, sitting at the end of the bar, Sheila breathed a sigh of relief. "Double G and T." She knew the bartenders by name. She also knew some of the cowboy patrons.

Sheila sat on a stool at the end of the bar, sipped her drink, and pondered her situation. Earl was in a good position at Coyote Brand, she thought, and so was she, if they could hold out until James Post's retirement. But that was five long

Jack Eadon

years away and by then Earl could mess
everything up. Even get fired. He was
already pissing off this Al Bisher guy. So,
Earl getting the president spot wasn't a
shoe-in. And Bisher said that Allied was
already pushing for better results, too!
Greedy bastards. Bound to get Earl in
trouble. Big fancy corporations always
did that. That's what she remembered
from the novels she'd read.

As Sheila puffed her cigarette and
sipped her drink, she looked across the
room at some noisy cowboys starting up
a two-step. She cringed as she pictured
dancing the precise little dance while she
was drunk. Tonight, instead of dancing,
she wanted to figure out how to fix her
cruddy life.

"Howdy ma'am. 'Member me?" A tall
cowboy with a permanent scowl,
handlebar mustache, and long, wavy,
chestnut-colored hair grumbled low into
her ear. "Lemme buy your next one?"

"Huh?" She pulled away. "Who are
you?"

His perfect mustache reminded her of
someone. He looked like he was in his
late twenties, maybe thirty. His hair fell
from under his straw cowboy hat. Then,
she noticed his ugly scar. Now she

remembered that she had danced with him the week before.

"Let me buy," he said.

"Now I remember you," she said. Her head was already spinning. "One more, I guess," she said, "under the circumstances."

"Circumstances, ma'am? You're lookin' mighty down, sittin' over here all alone. Somethin' wrong?" He straddled the stool next to her.

"Oh, nothing special. My life is only fading away before my eyes. You're too young to understand." She sipped.

"You're one helluva pretty lady to be talkin' all negative like that. Most ladies around here would love to have your looks. Your body, too, if you don't mind me sayin' so."

"Watch your mouth, son," she said.

"Hey, really sorry, ma'am." He toasted her and smiled. "But you are voluptuous, if you know what I mean."

"What did you say your name was?" Sheila asked the cowboy, who was squinting at her through the smoke from his thin cigar. *He's cute in a nasty way,* she thought. She found herself staring at the scar on his cheek.

"Oh, that's from a fight last year," he said and pointed to it. "Name is Coy, ma'am. Just Coy." He tipped the front of his straw western hat.

"Coy?"

"Yep," he said, "Shelly . . . Cheryl . . . no, Sheila, right?"

"You remember my name after a week? You do know how to flatter a lady. I remember your pretty hair and your mustache, I guess. All spiky at the ends. But it was different last week."

"Tryin' to grow a handlebar. You like?"

"Oh, yeah—this one. The other one looked Chinese."

"I always aims to please a lady. Especially the pretty ones." Coy moved closer.

Tipsy, Sheila wobbled on the bar stool as he stood and pressed his crotch against her hip. "I could solve any kind of problem for a lady like you," he whispered in her ear. "Just name it."

"You coming on to me, sailor?" Sheila said.

"I ain't no sailor, Miss Sheila. Ain't never seen no ocean 'cept down at Padre Island. Saw that once on a trip to Houston. Nope, I'm just a good ol' boy livin' in a run-down shack back o' my mama's. Up in Ennis."

"That's north of here, right?" she asked.

"Right, ten miles up I-45. Mama still lives there with my latest step dad, Paul or Peter somebody. A plumber."

"What you do up in Ennis, cowboy? Punch doggies?"

He snickered. "Actually, I fix air conditionin' mainly."

"And cars in your spare time, right? See, I remember."

As she and the cowboy rocked against each other, Sheila began to drift away. She closed her eyes, listened to the two-stepping music, and leaned against Coy, thinking about Sven the sailor, her first lover and Erlene's real father.

Ah, the docks and old times! She had never told Earl the details. She remembered how surprised he looked when she accepted his first marriage proposal. Child needs a father, she had thought. Not some sailor cruising the seven seas. Then she had picked the perfect name—Erlene—to stroke Earl's ego.

"You're taking me back to another time," she said to Coy, "when I didn't have a care in the world except—" Then she flinched.

"Except?" he said.

"My asshole daddy."

"Why asshole?"

She stared straight ahead and hesitated, took a sip, and said: "He raped me a bunch of times when I was a kid— the bastard."

"Shoot." Coy hung his head. "Sorry to hear that, ma'am."

"Until the night my mom gave it to him," she said.

"Gave him what?"

"She shot him." Sheila felt the smoke stream out of her nostrils extra hard.

"Shoot-Howdy." Coy cringed. "Your mama shot your daddy?"

"Dead. He deserved it." She rubbed her index finger across the bottom of her nose and sniffed. "Although, if I wouldn't have screamed, my mom wouldn't have killed him. I just got fed up."

"No need to blame yourself, Miss Sheila."

She shrugged. "They sent Mom to prison for a few years, but let her out for my high school graduation—big deal. I hardly knew her anymore and they had a cop supervise her visit."

He shook his head.

"To this day the whole thing bugs the crap out of me," she said. "Feeling him slump dead on me like that."

"Don't knock yourself out, ma'am. Sounds awful, but the dude deserved it. That's not your problem now, though."

"No, sir. Now my problems are too tough," she said and sniffed again, "for anybody to solve."

"Wanna bet, ma'am? Just try me. Maybe I can help. Swear," he bragged, hands up, palms open.

"Oh sure. What are you gonna do? Be a tough cowboy for me? Beat up my old man?" She put up her dukes and started hitting his raised hands.

"Ma'am, you are gettin' seriously drunk."

"You just never mind, sonny. You think you can solve my problems? OK. Go ahead, then!" She punched his shoulder hard. "Prove it."

"Like I said, ma'am, I aims t' please. If I can help you solve your problems, you and I'll have a roll in the hay. Fair?" he said.

"We will?" she asked. "You mean *the* hay?" She laughed and poked his long mustache. "You're coming on pretty strong, aren'tcha cowboy?"

"I'm one ol' boy known for bein' straight."

"So?" she said and leaned against him. "Be straight, then."

"Well, I don't mind sayin' you turn me on, ma'am. You really do."

"Hmm." *Earl hasn't said that in years.*

"I really like your bushy blonde hair, too, Miss Sheila. An' y'all gotta a nice bod. Big ones, too."

"Naughty, naughty." She rubbed against him. The room was spinning.

"Is your hair for real?" he asked.

"As real as that pretty mustache," Sheila joshed. She poked at it again.

"Well, ma'am, is it a deal? I help y'all out, we get it on?"

"Ooo, my. I can see I've gotten to you." She looked down at his bulging crotch and grabbed the bar to stop it from moving. Then she blurted, "Aw, what the hell, cowboy. You're on."

It wouldn't have been the first time, she thought. Hell, both my kids! Sheila laughed as she felt herself slipping fast toward fooling around, not an altogether unpleasant place to be, she thought.

"Come on, Miss Sheila, spit out those problems." Coy sat closer to her.

"Well." She hiccuped. "I have two of 'em. Both men." She waved two fingers. "One is my wimpy husband. The other is his boss. He's the only man in this whole damned world who will forever keep my Earl from reaching the peak of his career with me at his side."

The bartender slapped the next round on the bar. She reached for hers and took a gulp.

"Well, ma'am, I don't think I can put balls on your fucked-up husband. What about this boss?"

"Oh, you'll never be able to help me with him, neither." She laughed. "Hell, that man's gonna live at least another five years. Earl'll never get his job. Nope, I betcha Earl'll die a shitty sales manager or get fired trying to get promoted."

"Who might his boss be?"

She watched him sip his latest beer. Then, he tossed back his shot.

She said, "James Pos—"

Coy coughed his shot out with a powerful spray.

Sheila dodged the blast.

"James Post?" He coughed again. He quickly scanned the room and whispered.

"You mean the president of Coyote Chili? The tall, good lookin' gent with the black hat?"

"You got it." She shoved his shoulder. "That uppity cowboy with the fancy-ass car that squeaks. Man thinks he's a god."

"Well, ain't that somethin'," Coy said and grinned.

"Guess everyone knows him, huh?" she said. "Son of a bitch big shot."

"They say he really cleaned up, sellin' out to them Yankees."

"Just fell in his lap," she said.

"Asshole's been top of the heap around here for years," Coy said.

"I heard that." She picked up her purse and pulled out a brush. "But I'm pretty new to these parts."

"Well, fear not, Miss Sheila," he said.

"What?" She started brushing her hair.

A slit of a grin appeared under Coy's mustache. "He ain't no problem."

She stopped brushing. "What the hell do you mean?" She cleared her throat and almost guzzled the rest of her drink. Her eyes watered from his cigar smoke.

Coy stared at her deadpan. "If y'all are having a problem with Mr. Post? Consider him gone."

Sheila pounded her glass down. "You aren't serious."

Coy's eyes pierced through her.

"How?" she asked. "You don't mean—"

"May cost you a little," he said and chewed on his thin cigar. "But I don't mean temporary."

"You're shitting me." She laughed uneasily.

"Ten thousand," he whispered, snake-like eyes darting.

"This is nonsense!" She pounded out her half-smoked cigarette. "Besides, cowboy, Coy, whatever you're name is, I don't have that kind of money." She squeezed out the words between clenched teeth.

"Make it five, then," Coy said in a low monotone, not moving a muscle.

"What?" Her whispers were shouts.

"Come on, ma'am," he said. "Easy does it. After all. My mama needs the money. My stepfather, Peter or Paul somebody, don't make near enough."

"That's not my problem." Sheila fidgeted. "I better go." She started to get up, but wobbled.

"No, you better wait, Sheila baby," Coy said. He yanked her back. She stumbled to her bar stool. "Have a heart, Miss Sheila."

"No." She stood again and started to walk away.

He clutched her shoulder and turned her back. "But, I could solve your problems, right?"

Sheila leaned over and whispered. "Five thousand dollars? That's it?"

"And he's gone. Yes, ma'am. Plus one roll in the hay, too, remember?"

"You shameful boy!" Sheila pulled away. Her eyes flashed around the noisy room and met a few patrons'.

God! Suddenly they were all glaring at her like they could read her mind. She tensed, terrified at what she had the potential to do. She picked up her drink, slurped, and slammed her glass down. "More, Butch," she said.

"You've had plenty, ma'am," Butch said.

"Just gimme a fresh one then!" she said.

Butch shrugged and made her another. "It's your last one, then."

Suddenly, through her numbness, it all became a game. She lit another cigarette and blew smoke. She pictured her future with this tall guy named Post gone from it. She pictured herself as Margaret Post in all of her country elegance, floating across the Coyote Brand courtyard. Sheila could be the first lady of Coyote. She would have the prestige, the club membership, the mansion, the cook, the east coast schools, and even iced tea and rummy on her veranda. It would all be hers, depending on her decision right now. One word is all it would take. Just one.

"Well?" Coy's eyes glared.

Pressure gripped Sheila's heart. *This is impossible!*

One word and the future she had imagined would materialize. All it would take was five out of the seven thousand dollars her mother left for her. "Spend it wisely, " her mother had said. "I swear, you'll push your man to the top of some big company. Not like your drunk pervert of a father."

Sheila sighed deeply. She exhaled hard. With only her eyes she looked around the dark room. *This is too easy! How could I?*

Then, almost involuntarily, like someone else said it, she heard her voice say, "Yes." She clamped her lips shut and swallowed the end of the word. She turned to the cowboy. His eyes were dull and cold. She had said "yes" quickly enough to minimize her connection to the word, yet loudly enough to make her intention clear. She whispered through her smoke, "How do I know you'll do it?"

"Easy. 2,500 up front. The rest after," Coy said. "That's it. Done."

"Shhh!" Like a bird, she shot glances back and forth at other bar patrons. "How would I know?"

"Ask yourself, Miss Sheila. "Is 2,500 dollars worth the gamble? Would you miss it?"

"Well . . . " she said and admitted to herself she wouldn't.

"Besides. You have my word." He stared at her.

She leaned close to his ear and spoke through clenched teeth. "How?"

"You'd eventually find out," he said in a grizzly monotone. "But don't worry 'bout that part, ma'am."

Sheila looked away. Her eyes rolled to the right, then to the left. Shifting, assessing.

"Well, Sheila baby?" Coy Duncan grunted.

"Don't call me that. Daddy called me that."

"Sorry, ma'am. So, what's it gonna be?" he asked.

She glanced around the room. She closed her eyes and took a deep breath. She slapped her hand on the bar.

"Does that mean yes, Miss Sheila?"

Suddenly, Sheila blinked her eyes. The movie stopped, the black became bright light, and sound blasted into her ears. The nurse pulled the saliva-covered mouthpiece out and removed the headband of wires.

"Mrs. Hickman? Time to get up," she said.

Sheila opened her eyes wide. She felt like she'd been sleeping for hours.

"There," the nurse said, "how are we feeling, Mrs. Hickman?"

"Oh, fine," Sheila sighed. "Is it over?"

"Yes, Mrs. Hickman. You did fine."

"Wait," she said abruptly. "Did I talk?" Sheila looked around nervously.

The nurse smiled. "With the mouthpiece it just sounds like mumbles, ma'am."

"Good. Oh, good. Where's Earl?" Sheila asked.

"Still in the waiting room."

Doctor Lockhart walked up. "How do you feel, Mrs. Hickman?"

"I had that same awful dream," she said.

"Not surprised," he said. "Although, remember? It's memories that normally flash by."

"No. In my case it was definitely a dream. Definitely. It's the same one, too."

"Whatever you say, Mrs. Hickman." Dr. Lockhart patted her shoulder. "Just rest a couple of minutes. You may find bits of memories flashing back occasionally. Nothing to worry about."

"I know that," she said. "Damn, I'm exhausted. This one was heavy."

"That's because of your convulsions. You did fine."

"What time is it?" Sheila asked.

The nurse looked at her watch. "Eleven o'clock," she said. "How are you feeling?"

"Better." Sheila stretched. "I feel like mush, though."

The nurse patted her shoulder. "You just lie here for now."

A few minutes later, the nurse came back. "You ready to get up now, Mrs. Hickman? Can I help?"

Sheila sat up and swiveled her legs over the side of the bed. She tried to stand, but wobbled in place.

"Easy does it," the nurse said.

Sheila slipped into her panties, jeans, and top. "God, I feel like I was away for a long time. Some long vacation."

"Strange, huh?" the nurse said. "Had the treatments once myself."

"Whew!" Sheila stretched again. "This was a real kick-ass zap."

The nurse laughed. "First time I heard that one," she said. "Transportation, please!" she called out.

An older man rolled a wheelchair up to Sheila.

"Hop aboard, Miss Hickman," he said. She recognized his bushy gray hair and kindly smile.

"Ernie. It's you," Sheila said. "I don't need the chair, really." She waved her hand.

"Better let me give you a lift, just to the front door," he said.

"Ernie, we always go through this!" Sheila sat down in the wheelchair and put her feet in place. "As long as you won't take advantage of me on the way."

"Might-could, Mrs. Hickman," the old gent said. "You're my favorite, you know."

"Ernie. You're flirting with me."

"I try my best, but I'm an old fart. Couldn't flirt if I tried."

She laughed. Then he pushed her out of the recovery room, down a long hall to the waiting room.

"Sheila!" Earl called, standing, stretching, and tossing a magazine down. "Hi, Ernie," Earl said as he walked up to the wheelchair, leaned over, and gave Sheila a kiss. "They told me you were all set," he said. "Went OK? How do you feel?"

"Real tired," she said. "Had that weird dream again. Seemed so real. Glad it's the last zapping."

"We'll see," Earl said as he helped Ernie turn the chair around.

"What?" she looked up and asked.

"Nothing, let's just get you home," Earl said.

Old Ernie rolled her to the elevator, down to the first floor of Navarro County Medical Center, out the front door, and down the temporary covered ramp to their waiting car in the first parking place.

"Here, let me start 'er," Earl said and ran around to the driver's side of the Mercedes. He got in and revved it up.

Ernie pushed her closer, then held the car door while Sheila got in. "Bye now, lover," he said. "See y'all next time?" He shut the door.

"Won't be one!" Sheila turned to Earl and laughed.

"Depends on how you do," Earl mumbled. "We'll have to see what Lockhart says." He patted her thigh.

"Shit, Earl."

"It might be over, Sheila," he said, "We'll just have to see."

Sheila hung her head for a few minutes and muttered. "Oh, damn."

"I had that conference call with my new boss . . . Childress," Earl said.

"Really?" Sheila said and looked up. "You're the president here. You don't need a new boss in Chicago. What do they know?"

"He says I should replace Stoothoff as soon as possible."

"But Stoot just retired," she said. "Why so fast?"

"Childress is thinking about giving me a sales manager from Chicago, maybe a little younger." Earl stretched and pointed his thumbs to his chest. "Let el presidente kick back and rest a little," he said.

"Terrific," Sheila said. "All we need is some smart-ass Yankee kid nosing around."

That night Sheila lay in bed feeling dizzy from her treatment. As she drifted off to sleep to Earl's snoring, many images flew by, the most vivid were the cowboy and the Cat's Meow:

She slapped her hand down on the bar.

"Does that mean yes, Miss Sheila?" the cowboy asked.

Sheila moaned and tossed in her sleep.

Outside the Cat's Meow, Coy Duncan pinned Sheila Hickman against his rusty old pickup under twinkling stars. He breathed his beer-breath in her face. She had forgotten that promising him her body was part of the deal.

The November night chilled as he pulled up her skirt and pulled down her panties. She kicked them free. He growled as he kneaded her breasts, bared from beneath her peasant blouse. She cringed.

"Nice ones," he mumbled as he twisted her erect nipples.

Uninterested as he fumbled with his jeans, Sheila scanned the dark meadow behind the Cat's Meow. "Hurry," she said.

He hoisted her by her thighs and, balancing her on his bent legs, jabbed his penis inside her. "Ah, that's good," he said.

She closed her eyes.

Again he entered her. "I ain't never seen no lady who don't help or fight back," he said. "Don't moan, don't do nothin'."

"Just do it," she snapped and looked away.

"But that ain't no fun," he said.

"I said, just do it!" She suppressed her struggle and gritted her teeth as she gazed up and watched the stars spin. All the while she felt like she was going to puke. He kept slapping her hips and panting steam, like some dog.

Then Sheila stared ahead, imagining it was over. When he finally climaxed, she felt a little flush, but restrained any other physical response.

After Coy finished twitching inside her, she put her feet down and pushed him to the ground, his jeans wrapped around his boots. He lay there cackling a good ol' boy laugh.

She looked down at the cowboy. "So, when'll you do it? Post?" The snappy breeze chilled her.

"Next few months. Bring half the money here at noon Wednesday. Got it, Sheila baby?"

"Don't call me that, asshole." She wiped herself with the inside of her skirt and staggered away.

Sheila awoke and sat up in the dark. *No cowboy? No pick-up? No fuck?*

"What's the matter, Sheila?" Earl muttered as he rolled over and yanked the blankets.

"Nothin', Earl. Another weird dream," she said. "Go back to sleep." She sighed and slumped back on her pillow.

Barely awake, he mumbled. "Just memories like Lockhart said."

"No way," she crabbed. "Big help you are." Sheila lay there with her eyes open. *The dream seemed so real,* she thought. They always did.

2 *Chicago, Illinois   July 6, 1980*

Marcus Ramsay scanned the faintly lit conference room. Mr. John Childress, the new president of Puritan's Food Division, sat twiddling his fingers at the end of the table, staring at the ceiling. The six empty suits at the table were looking back at Childress. Then, all at once, like tennis spectators, they returned their gaze to Ramsay, standing at the front of the room, flipping the next acetate onto the overhead projector.

Ramsay was sure they were staring through the dark at his scraggly hair. He tried to remember his next line. He cleared his throat.

"Mr. Childress, gentlemen," Ramsay said. He flicked back his hair. "I got real curious, so I dug into it and, as you can see, you can actually cut these markets out of Mama's Pizza's geographic territory and the brand would make money."

Dave Hester, the Food Division's sales manager, adjusted himself in his chair and grumbled.

"What is it, Dave?" John Childress asked.

"Well, I've been Sales Manager for almost ten years and all that time I've used low cut trade deals to move product, and now here comes our friend Marcus Ramsay, who does a fancy little analysis and wants to wipe all that experience away."

"We're not necessarily moving on this idea, Dave," Childress said in a grisly, confident voice, ignoring Ramsay. Childress had just become the new president of the Food Division and he didn't need these skirmishes in his ranks. He wanted to establish himself as king of a peaceful domain and didn't like being challenged by unfamiliar ideas, especially those presented by big shot MBAs like Ramsay.

Besides, the executives at Allied had been trying to make money on the 20 million dollar pizza acquisition for over a decade. Now, in the past two years, Ramsay had come along and shaken things up. He'd analyzed the business, isolated unprofitable markets, and highlighted unproductive strategies, especially the use of Hester's low-cut trade deals. In the process, he had embarrassed a number of seasoned Allied executives, including Dave Hester, who had frequently claimed that saving the acquisition was impossible if it wasn't done his way. Ramsay had just proven them all wrong, so he wasn't very popular with the group at the table.

In his own eyes, Ramsay had merely awakened them to the realities of modern marketing that he had learned at the University of Chicago's Graduate School of Business about a decade earlier. But, Marcus figured that, based on the rumors, John Childress was bound to mark his new turf at any moment.

"Marcus, what makes you so sure the brand will make money next year when the best minds at Allied haven't made that happen? Frankly I, for one, am a little skeptical of your voodoo statistics, if you don't mind me saying so." Childress picked up his bronchial inhaler and glanced at Hester.

The group hushed in homage, like lions waiting for their pack leader to finish dinner. Childress squished his inhaler once in his mouth. He paused slowly. Then he squished again. The lions exhaled.

Ramsay felt himself shake. "It's simple, Mr. Childress. Until just last year, Allied has been using unproductive strategies."

"Say you?" Childress said.

Oh shit, there's the infamous Childress parry. "Say I," Ramsay said. "I guess." He pointed back to his overhead transparency, still projected onto the screen.

"We'll see." Childress pulled at his chin and gazed at the ceiling. "Well . . . " He slammed the table and stood abruptly. "That's it," Childress said.

As if on command, like soldiers, the men at the table stood in unison. *You can almost hear them click their heels,* Ramsay thought. He wondered what was going on. What would happen to his proposal?

Then Ramsay remembered the rumors. This was how Childress did things: power, power, more power.

Without a word, Childress walked out, lighting a cigarette in stride. The ceiling grid of six fluorescents blinked on. Everyone in the small conference room gathered their things and filed out.

Standing alone, Ramsay tapped his papers and acetates together.

"Nice job, Marcus," Each of them mumbled as they walked by him, but their comments sounded perfunctory.

The meeting was over.

Back in his office, Childress sat at his large antique desk and smoked. He sucked in a deep drag, then restrained his hacking. He glanced at Ramsay's position paper on Mama's Pizza with all the graphs and statistics and scribbled a few notes on it. Then he tossed it in his shallow executive out-box. He picked up the phone and pressed the button next to it.

In a second, his assistant Virginia answered.

"Virginia? Get me Burghoff" he said. He set the receiver down, leaned back, and twiddled his fingers.

The buzzer buzzed. He picked up the phone. "Kyle?" he said. "Childress here. So, is this Ramsay some kind of protégée of yours?"

Kyle Burghoff was Childress' boss, his predecessor, and now the executive vice president of all Grocery Products at the Allied Food Corporation. "I've looked after him over the years, why?" Kyle asked.

"Frankly, he's already driving me nuts, all this analysis bullshit."

Kyle laughed. "Pretty sharp, huh?"

"Don't know whether to believe him or doubt him. He's a real cocky know-it-all, too."

"Has an edge to him, I'll admit," Burghoff said. "But you can trust him."

"He's what, thirty-five?" Childress asked. "Don't we have some other spot for him?"

"You mean that doesn't report to you?" Burghoff laughed.

Childress squished his inhaler, hacked, and smashed his cigarette out.

That night Kathy Ramsay watched Marcus fiddle with his pasta. Their stylish brownstone apartment on the very near north side of Chicago was quiet, except for the occasional scampering of Bailey, the Ramsays' Tonkinese cat, perfectly dodging Kathy's Lalique crystal and precious Lladros. "What is it, Marcus?" she asked. "You looked bugged."

"Same ol'. Same ol'. You should've seen it. I'm up there, flashing overheads, presenting the profit maximization plan— you know, I've been working on it for months—and Childress—the whole bunch of them—swallow it like stale bread."

"Silence?"

"Just about. One wise-ass comment from Hester, then Childress basically kills it."

Kathy Ramsay shook her head. "Marcus, you've really got to get out of there. Allied doesn't give any value to what you bring to the table." She sipped her wine and put her glass down. "Don't you see that?" she said.

"I suppose. But shit. I've already put in twelve years there. They owe me a nice product group slot. They really do," he said. "It's only fair."

"Fair? I agree with Daddy. You ought to stop being so idealistic and go to work for him at Demo Corp."

He swiped the air. "That's all I need, getting ribbed every day because I'm the son-in-law of the Operations VP."

"Well, it would beat this insecure macho political garbage at Allied."

"But I know dip about car parts," he said. He twisted his pasta around his fork.

"Well, then why can't you leave and get a product group manager slot at another food company?" she asked.

"If I went somewhere else, I'd have to start all over. I'm afraid, at my age, I'm stuck at Allied."

"Well, I'd make some tough decisions and get on with your career. That's what Daddy always taught me. I think that's fairly realistic, don't you?"

"I don't give a shit what Daddy would say. I know how to run my own damned career, dammit."

"All right, all right," she said.

"Say, could you pass me more of the merlot?" he said.

"Here." She half-filled his wine glass. "Then why don't they put you in a job that utilizes your talents? That troubleshooting instinct you have— you're like a bloodhound. If there's a problem with a business—anything at all—you can sniff it out. What would be a good job for that?" she asked.

"I don't know. "Some kind of business analysis—" He sipped down some wine. "The upper management of a struggling company, I guess."

"See. That's why you threaten the hell out of Childress, I bet," she said. "You have a skill that he doesn't have, so he squashes your instincts and doesn't allow you to prove yourself."

"Hell," he said, "maybe I should've gone to a smaller company early-on and used my entrepreneurial instincts. I wouldn't have gotten stuck in this trap. Jim warned me about this corporate bullshit way back." Jim Hubbards was his first boss, still a lifetime friend and mentor.

Kathy ripped off a piece of her French bread. "You should've started your own company," she said. "Or even opened that studio. You love photography."

"I guess. Maybe someday, in my next life." For a minute he just stared into space and didn't say a thing. "Maybe I'm just getting older and need to find a spot where I can take the skills I have and deliver what they need."

"You're ready to make your mark?" she asked.

"Yeah. Sounds corny, huh?" he asked. "It's like I want to mold the company from clay into art."

"Yeah, sounds right. One reason I fell in love with you was your idealism and that's an example. You're experienced enough to just be yourself, don't hold back out there."

Ramsay smiled. "You know, things have really changed over the last few years."

"How's that?" she asked.

"Now you're the one who's coaching me," he said.

She put both fists on her hips. "What's so wrong with that?" she asked.

"Well, I've always seen myself as the strong counselor for you. Now I feel like the ultimate mush."

"Well, you've helped me a lot. Vòila!" She spread her arms like a circus performer. "I used to be timid and ineffective. You've helped open me up. Daddy has, too."

"But it seems like you don't need me anymore," he said.

"I'm just learning to take care of myself out there."

"Makes me feel real needed," he said sarcastically.

"Well, I'm sorry for needing you less. Maybe I'm just blossoming, ever think of that? Why can't you be happy for me?"

"Sorry, I just told you how I feel. Thanks for listening." He roughly pushed his chair under the table. "I'm going out for a walk."

"What's the matter?" she asked. "You pissed?"

"Nothing. Just nothing." He walked to the door.

"Want me to come with?" she asked.

"No, I think I'd rather be alone tonight."

"Marcus, don't worry, some opportunity'll come along. I'm sure of it."

"I'm glad you're so sure." The door slammed behind him.

Kathy winced as he left. She had seen plenty of the same frustration during the seven years she had worked at her company. People busted their butts in search of some grand reward that never came. Was it really the company's fault when employees complained or was it actually the employees' incompetence showing? She wondered as she watched Marcus stride to the end of the block.

Kathy Ramsay leaned forward and cradled the candle's flame with a shaky hand. She blew it out with a quick puff. It was the same kind of candle that had lit-up their dinners since their marriage eight years before. It was supposed to eventually light up some illusive special occasion Marcus kept predicting. A frustrated tear fell to the place mat.

She hated that drawn look on his face. He obviously needed a change. Things weren't like they used to be when he was a shining star and she was an emerging corporate manager. Now, she was continuing to emerge, but he seemed lost.

She didn't like the way he seemed so depressed or weak either. In fact, she couldn't ever remember him this bad off. He was never recognized for his effort or talent and seemed helpless to engineer his own destiny. Yet, he had always been the kind of man who thrived on a little genuine recognition. One pat on his back would generate enough energy for him to deliver a year of butt-busting. But maybe, despite his energy, he had risen to one level beyond his capabilities.

As Kathy Ramsay finished wiping the table and walked to the sink to rinse her sponge she saw a single bruised glass that she hadn't put in the dishwasher. *Something will come along for Marcus,* she thought. *It better.*

Then she remembered what the marriage counselor had said at her solo visit.

"Welcome to the world of existentialism," the counselor had told her.

"No kidding," Kathy had answered.

"You'll never change him. You may have to find other ways to fulfill yourself, but don't count on his successes to continue at the old clip."

"But marriage was supposed to always be exciting," Kathy said, "and his career always skyrocketing."

"Supposed to be? Skyrocketing? You expect the glamour of his early career to fuel your marriage forever?" the counselor had asked and smiled. "Not likely."

A little over a half-hour later, Kathy hung her head as she watched Marcus shuffle back up the walk. While he seemed to be struggling with his career, she felt professionally capable for the first time in her life. She picked up the bruised glass, pulled open the trash compactor door, tossed it in, closed the door, and turned it on. As the compactor crushed the glass and Marcus swung open the door, she realized something. The time had come for her to find her own personal rewards in life.

3 *Chicago, Illinois   July 13, 1980*

One week later Marcus Ramsay walked fast down the long hall of the Mercantile Mart at Allied Corporation's headquarters in downtown Chicago. Ramsay always walked fast. But today he had good reason. John Childress had called him to his office for coffee, which he never did. "The Rock" might have had a cool reaction to Ramsay's presentation a week ago, but having coffee was a sign that something was different.

Marcus had already been the Brand Manager of Mama's Pizza for three years. In his mind, that was bordering on too long. He had done a good job uncovering opportunities for the Mama's Pizza brand and, before that, he had fixed other broken Allied brands for nearly nine years. So, he figured that this coffee with the Rock was a signal that his wait to join the ranks of senior management might be over.

He turned right at the corner into the Food Division, then a quick left. In seconds, he stood at Childress' door. The Rock looked up.

"Mr. Childress?" Ramsay said. "You
called?" *God, that sounds stupid!*
Childress looked bothered, in the middle
of something. Marcus turned away.

"No, no, Marcus. Come in, sit."
Childress pointed to the chair in front of
his expansive desk.

Ramsay walked in. The place dripped
power: bronze sculptures, numerous
awards, limited edition art—an
intimidating kind of simplicity. Marcus
sat.

"Virginia. Coffee," Childress said
quietly to the air. Ramsay heard her
scurry from her desk outside his office.
She reappeared in three minutes, a
sterling tray in hand.

"I brought you some sugar and cream,
Marcus. I wasn't sure what you wanted,"
she said. Ramsay always liked her voice.
It had an elegant Britishness about it.
Childress must've picked her purposely
to hone the overall effect of his new
position.

"Thank you," Ramsay said.

"Of course." She disappeared.

"Marcus, the reason I called you here,
Childress started. At forty-eight,
Childress' prematurely aged face was
pasty, flat, and stretched with downward

sloping eyes and lips—it had a tired, permanent smirk.

"Yes, sir?" Ramsay pictured getting a product group manager position in the Ready-to-Eat Cereals Group or something equivalent. He held his breath and felt his nuisance of a cowlick pop up on the back of his head. He reached back and tried to press it down without success.

"We need to find a home for you. Bump you up, all that. It's about time, don't you think?" Childress picked up his inhaler, squished it, tossed it down, and leaned back.

"Oh, yes, sir." Ramsay smiled. His stomach jittered. *Yes, this is it.*

"I'm thinking that since you had experience on the Coyote Brand Products acquisition a few years ago, you might be able to help us down there in Texas. They never seem to pull their weight. Heavy merchandising expenditures always hurting O.I."

Ramsay flinched, then sunk. *Corsicana? In the middle of nowhere?* "But, Mr. Childress. I was only there a couple of days and that was ten years ago."

"But I understand you got pretty close to the people in a short time, didn't you?

Good sign."

"I guess. James Post, the president, happened to die right before I went down. Some kind of freak auto accident. I stayed for the funeral. The people in the town were devastated and appreciated people who cared about their loss."

"See what I mean? You'd be perfect. Already have history with them, all that."

"But, Mr. Childress," Ramsay said.

"Now, now. Hear me out on this," the Rock said. "You are good at getting a handle on these trade deals, right?"

"Yes, sir. I guess." Ramsay's shakiness was solidifying into fear.

"I'm thinking that with the Mexican food boom and people flocking to the sunbelt, Coyote Brand ought to be breaking all records. Don't you think?"

"I guess so," Ramsay said.

"But it's not. Listen, Marcus. All I want you to do is go down there for a couple of years, help their president— Hickman, remember him, he was the sales manager back then—max out the bottom line. Our records show he's spending too much on these billback deals they keep running. They're not bringing in proportionately higher sales."

"Earl Hickman's been there all this time?" Ramsay asked and tapped his finger. He had heard Hickman was running Coyote Brand like it was his own little kingdom. "I hear he's pretty well established there," Marcus said.

"Well, the fellow's been president ever since Post died. He's probably locked into some bad habits over the years. Maybe you could go down there, shake things up, all that. They're already tied into the Mart's computer systems, you know."

"But, Mr. Childress. I really pictured getting a product group spot here at the Mart. I've been waiting for years. And moving way down there?" Ramsay felt his eyes wander to the ceiling. He hoped he wasn't coming off too arrogantly.

"I know, I know. This'll get you some general management experience."

"Yes, sir." But Ramsay felt the doubts drip down his own face.

Childress paused for a second. "You know, Marcus, Burghoff and I have already talked on this," he said.

"Really?" Ramsay perked up. He always considered Burghoff his mentor.

"Yes. Yes, that's right. Kyle wants you to assess Coyote Brand's upside, develop a new spending strategy, and move their executive and marketing offices up to Dallas."

"But, why? Haven't they been in Corsicana for years?"

"True. But they need to better utilize their ad agency—it's in Dallas. They also need to make the business more accessible to folks visiting from the Mart by being nearer to the airport, all that."

"Oh, really?" Ramsay liked how that sounded. It meant ongoing exposure that would be good for his career.

"And Kyle wants you to develop a campaign for their chili hot dog sauce. He thinks it's their dark horse product. And he wants you to control those billback trade deals, of course. It's all pretty important stuff. We could use someone with your impressive, uh, seasoning, all that."

"Thank you, sir. Sounds interesting." Ramsay meant it. He liked dark horses.

"Really could be an opportunity, Marcus," Childress said. "I promise you. Only upside."

"Yes, sir. I can see that. Can I think about it, Mr. Childress?"

The Rock smiled. "Well, we've already done the thinking on this, Marcus. We

A CONSEQUENCE OF GREED

want you down there to chat with Hickman soon. See if you two get along. OK?"

"Yes, sir." Ramsay said. "Thank you, sir."

"Then if you get along, we'll talk salary, all that."

"Sounds good, sir."

"Group manager level, you know."

"Really?!" Ramsay said and about fell over.

Childress nodded, flicked a little royal wave, then searched his watch as if it was a crystal ball. That was it.

"Well then, OK sir." Ramsay stood. "Thanks again."

"Of course, of course," Childress muttered and flicked his hand, signaling to Ramsay that his time was up.

Ramsay stood, walked out of Childress' office, and said good-bye to Virginia. He had left his cold coffee behind.

As Ramsay left, Childress sat back and sighed. He would no longer be challenged by Ramsay's fancy know-it-all formulas.

103

Some up-and-coming managers can make you look like a hero. But not Ramsay. His style made himself look brilliant, but it can make his bosses look stupid. Being new to his job, Childress couldn't have that. *Now, Ramsay will irritate the hell out of that Hickman oaf.*

"They'll make a perfect pair," he snickered. *And who knows what garbage Ramsay might uncover.*

Ramsay opened his apartment door that night. Kathy was home, clanging pans in the kitchen.

"Better start packing," he called out. "We're heading to Dallas."

"What?" she asked.

"Texas." He smiled.

"What are you talking about?"

But, then he couldn't help it. As he entered the small gourmet kitchen, pots and pans hanging above the cooktop island, a full-fledged grin emerged.

"Wait. You got it?" she turned and asked. "You really got it?"

"The Marketing Manager's spot at Coyote Brand," he said.

Her smile vanished, her nose wrinkled. "Coyote? What's that?"

"Coyote Brand Products," he said. He put a few pots away. "Puritan's owned 'em since '68. I went down there back then to help out. The president died right before I arrived. Remember? We were dating."

"I guess. Sounds like a real good move," she said sarcastically. "I mean, it's a funny name—Coyote. Furs or meat or what?" She laughed. "Put those pots here, please." She pointed.

"It's chili. Canned chili," he said. "Hey, it could be pretty good. I have to fly down, meet Earl Hickman, the guy who's been president since the other guy bit it. He seemed like an OK guy back then. But I hear he's let the presidency go to his head a little. We'll see."

"The presidency?"

"That's who I'd report to." He puffed up proud. "Think Daddy would approve?" he said as he snuggled up to her.

"Of course, my macho manager. Now get away." She pushed him away. "So, we'd have to move? What about my job?"

"Well, I'd move down first and get started. You could follow a few months later. Try to pin down a job in Dallas before you move or once you're down there," he said.

"Hmmm. Think you'll like your new boss?" she asked. "Earl Whoever."

"Hickman? Don't know. I heard the last president, Post, was real charismatic around the town, probably like my dad. They're undoubtedly playing cards in heaven." He half-laughed. "Hickman sounds OK, though, except I hear he's the Napoleon type."

"Napoleon? Short and stubby?" She laughed.

He held a skillet. "Not really, but he supposedly runs the place like he's some kind of king. Should I put this here?"

"No, over here. Oh, Marcus. You really think this is it, something you can sink your teeth into?" she asked. "Gimme that, you'll put it where I can't find it."

"Sounds perfect for me," he said. "Childress said he and Burghoff need me to go down and exploit the opportunities: control deal spending and advertise other products."

"Better than that South American opportunity," she said "Introducing tampons to Colombian women?" She giggled.

"Kathy, this'd be nice weather, too. No more of this Chicago junk. And guess what? They'd want me to relocate the offices from Corsicana up to Dallas. So we could live there."

"Where could I work?" she asked.

"Bunch of possibilities: Chips O'Lay or maybe Southwest Foods. They own Convenient Food Marts. Also, there's a bunch of restaurant chains head-quartered in Dallas. They'd probably die to have a marketer with your experience."

"You think?" she asked. "Oh, it sounds like it might be a new start."

They hugged.

"Childress wants me to meet with Hickman next week. He said Coyote Brand's a high visibility post, too."

"I bet Childress just wants to get rid of you. He's afraid of you," she said as they rocked in place.

Ramsay pulled back. "Kathy, don't be such a chicken. This feels unfamiliar, so it's a little scary. But, it's also sort of exciting. Don'tcha think?"

"I don't know," she said. Sounds a little funky to me. Coyote. The guy's been there so long."

"Oh, don't be a poop-out. I'm pretty jazzed if you want to know the truth. And besides, I don't know if I have much of a choice in the matter. Childress said they really need me to straighten Coyote out.

Get it under control, then chart a new course."

Kathy slung her arms around his neck. "Not bad, my big shot Texas marketing manager husband."

He cleared his throat. "Equivalent to a product group manager, by the way. So I'll be getting a nice raise, too."

"Really?" She sighed. "Guess this could be the beginning of the rest of our lives." They hugged again.

"Yep."

"Or a huge mistake," she said.

"Aw—" he said. They kissed.

"I admit I do feel a tinge of happiness," she said. "Even though we'd have to move away from Mom and Daddy." They pulled apart.

"I don't know. That might do us good. And we can come back to visit."

"I guess," she said.

"As often as you want, babe," he said. "Say, I'm going up to change clothes." He started to walk out of the kitchen.

"Really? As often as I want?" she said. "They'll like that."

"I swear, darlin'," he called back with a twang. "And it's not like we're walking into a pit of snakes on the other side of the world."

"You're right," she called. "What could possibly be so bad?"

4 *North Central Texas   July 21, 1980*

Less than an hour's drive south of sparkling Dallas, faded green clumps dotted the otherwise tawny prairie landscape and marked the route of the old Interurban Railroad Line.

The original nineteenth century plan was for the line to connect Dallas and Houston, passing through a little city nestled in the junction of the Brazos and Trinity Rivers called Corsicana. The town was positioned 32.08 degrees north of the equator and 96.46 degrees west of the prime meridian, 1228 statute miles from Washington D. C., and 144 statute miles from Austin, the capital of Texas.

But the original plan never worked.

Back in 1871, when the development of Corsicana was first underway, government money dried up, as did the rivers. That killed off the cotton crop which in turn, devastated the the area's economy. As a result, Corsicana never came to fruition. Its development just stopped.

A decade later, oil was accidentally discovered as a man drilled for water—

the city fathers actually refused to pay the man for drilling the well because he had struck oil. They didn't realize it was the first time liquid gold had been found west of the Mississippi.

Soon 1,000 oil derricks dotted the booming little city. There was so much of the black gold that it was used to quell the excessive dust on the streets of Corsicana, but the supply dwindled in less than two years—the field proved to be a shallow one.

Again, the city's development suddenly stopped. What seemed destined to become a bustling little metropolis became a barren town. The city had architecture appropriate for the late nineteenth century, but only a few blocks of it. Overnight the big-time northern oilmen from Pennsylvania took their promises with them and left Corsicana. They offered weak apologies as they rushed to exploit the massive Spindletop Field discovered outside of Houston.

By 1980, Corsicana had spent decades trying to rekindle the economic wealth that oil would have created. While the rest of the country had embraced sophisticated late twentieth century styles, Corsicana's architecture boasted a tattered, barren 1950's motif, reminiscent of old Superman TV shows. Generation after generation, cynicism about Yankees and their promises had woven itself into the fabric of Corsicana: talk at church, late night discussions at the Rotary, passionate arguments at softball games, and resentful muttering over many hands of rummy.

Now, Earl Hickman puffed on his Marlboro as he drove home after a tough day as president of the town's premier company, Coyote Brand Products. He had just interviewed the Yankee smart-ass that Childress had sent him from headquarters. Predictably, the young man had been eager, in that irritating northern sort of way, to show how he had the capabilities that could save Coyote Brand from itself.

Hickman pulled into the gravel driveway in front of his house, modest for Golf Estates, the sanctuary of Corsicana's elite. Sheila Hickman stood on the porch wearing Bermudas and a sleeveless blouse, holding a cigarette in one hand, a sweaty glass in the other.

"So, how was the Yankee bastard?" she called out and caught her balance.

Earl climbed out of the Mercedes, slammed the door, and walked up the porch steps. "Good at the old bullshit interview, I'll tell you that."

"Having him here'll put those Allied spies right up your ass, Earl. Got to be careful." She raised her glass, blew out smoke, and sipped her special iced tea.

Earl pointed. "Sheila, you shouldn't be drinking that, especially with your pills."

She snickered. "It's my first, Mr. President."

"You shouldn't have any."

"So tell me, how's the kid?" Sheila asked. She took a puff.

"Sharp, I guess. Not a kid anymore, though. He's aged in ten years."

"Great." She sipped her drink. "Old enough to be trouble."

"I don't know, he's pretty sharp, I think." Earl shrugged. "A real bloodhound, I can tell—question after annoying question."

"Exactly. Earl, you don't need him down here. Things have been great for ten years. He could make you look bad, knowin' all his contacts up at Allied. I betcha he's their spy."

"Don't be so paranoid. I think Childress wants him for the marketing spot because he had some contact with Coyote before. Hell, Ramsay almost met Post way back. I remember the day Post up and died in that auto wreck. The Ramsay kid showed up the next Monday. Even went to the damn funeral, the brown-nose."

"Whatever. Don't really remember that." She rubbed her cigarette butt in the crowded ashtray that sat on the porch railing. The rising smoke made her eyes tear.

"You don't remember much of anything, do you?" He laughed.

"Damn gabbing," she said. "So don't fucking laugh at me."

"Watch your mouth. I do my best to fill you in on the missing stuff, don't I?"

"Right," she snickered. "Now, that damn Yankee stranger'll come down and go snoopin' around. He'll remember stuff I can't."

"Hmmm." Earl recalled old thoughts long since buried, and fiddled with his jaw. "Guess maybe your right."

"Damn Yankee intruder!" she said. She heaved her glass onto the lawn. It crashed as it landed and sprayed glass everywhere.

"Sheila! Why'd you—"

"Hell, my life's never been the same since the damn zapping started," she said slowly. "Can't it be over for good?"

"Aw, don't worry, Sheila baby. Your speech isn't that noticeable, and the treatments may be over soon."

"Don't call me Sheila baby." She burped.

"Sorry, I forgot," Earl said. He thought about how Ramsay might nose around too much. "Listen, if this Ramsay thing really bugs you, I'll fly up next week to see Childress and see if I can stop it."

"Right, Mr. President." She drew in a deep drag, then hacked a guttural cough. "This is only the beginning, I bet," she said.

Later that same night Sheila thumbed through the latest Orvis catalog as she sat at the kitchen table. Across the house, she could hear Earl snoring away. She spied the cashmere sweater with the country pattern they always had on the front page of the women's section. "Not bad, only 298 dollars" She moved away her empty wine glass, and laid her head down. She drifted off:

She was at Oscar Sanchez' annual holiday party and everyone was a decade younger. Thunder announced a winter storm outside. Sheila eyed Earl as he boomed toasts across the small walnut-paneled den loaded with people at Oscar's quaint party. It was Friday two weeks after Christmas. This year she hadn't particularly enjoyed the holidays. She had a lot on her mind.

She fiddled with her cigarette in one hand and a nearly empty glass of ginger ale in the other. The bad weather was a good reason to attend the annual Sanchez bash, one of the better parties of the year. There was nothing else to do that Friday night in Corsicana anyway.

Earl raised his drink across the room and bellowed a toast to Frank Benedict. Sheila studied Earl's hands waving smoothly through the air, in juxtaposition to the rough resonance of his voice. She imagined Earl as the next president of Coyote Brand Products.

She recalled how her brief meeting with the wicked cowboy, Coy Duncan, in the parking lot at the Cat's Meow had sealed the deal that would inevitably boost Earl to the company's presidency. After all, Oscar was too green for the job, Al Bishop was uninterested, and Cecil was too junior. There was only Earl.

The 5,000 dollars it cost her would undoubtedly fulfill her mother's dreams, too. She'd become the glamorous wife of a corporate leader, even though it was in godforsaken Corsicana. Earl would become the big fish in a small pond. A very small pond. Sheila figured that must've been his destiny all along.

As the sun set, more evening thunder cracked from the evening sky. Sheila saw the lightning illuminate the two dozen faces in the Sanchez' recreation room. Pointing fingers and "ahs" indicated that the conversation across the little room had suddenly and briefly turned to the weather.

Sheila was sure that if any of them looked at her straight in the eye they'd sense what she had commissioned the cowboy to do even though she had taken steps to undo everything. She had delivered her warning note to Post late Wednesday afternoon. That was the best she could do, she thought, to reverse the scheme she had put in motion. Now, it was up to him to read the note, understand her terse warning, and respond by protecting himself. If he didn't, she could hardly be saddled with the blame for anything that might happen.

Earl's ready, she thought, as she analyzed the way the small group followed each of his words from one toast to another. When he smiled, so did the group around him. When his large face sobered, the group mimicked him. Sheila noticed for the first time that, however boorish Earl had been as he developed professionally in Baltimore and at the Mercantile Mart, he was now good at giving a bullshit speech.

He actually looks like a president, she thought. True, he still wandered aimlessly toward the end of each speech, but, with her help, that weakness would be corrected in the months and years to come.

Not bad, she thought, recalling one of Earl's favorite expressions. Earl was the single human being who could boost her to the position of first lady of a division of the almighty Allied Corporation, listed on the New York Stock Exchange.

But wait. There is a problem. Her brilliant last minute note to Post might dash everything.

Sheila began to panic. Now she didn't know what she wanted.

She put her glass down and rubbed her cigarette out. She fiddled with her fingers as she watched the other guests indulge in their drinks more and more heartily. She licked her lips, then lit up again. Since Wednesday night she had snuck only one large glass of wine each afternoon, mostly to calm her nerves from Bryan's yakking. She couldn't risk getting drunk. She might have inadvertently revealed something.

Sheila scoured the room for James Post. Why didn't he come? *Wait,* she thought. *Post will be hard at work at the office—everybody in town knows that—and that bitch Margaret is at home, probably playing rummy and sipping iced tea on the porch with their maid.* Sheila began to seethe as she pictured the elegant woman with the old-fashioned parasol and perfect sandals.

"Looking for someone?" Frank Benedict grabbed her shoulder. The massive hand shook Sheila.

"Who . . . me?" She laughed a laugh that resonated from deep in her chest.

"Y'all know Earl might could be the big cheese around here?" Frank whispered low into her ear. "Y'all know that, right?"

"Who? What?" Sheila gasped. Her eyes darted. She pretended not to notice how Frank had penetrated her thoughts.

Frank snickered. "How about a toast in honor of the great James Post's memory, huh?"

"Well . . . I don't have a drink," she said. Sheila felt herself shiver as she held her head and facial expression rigid to avoid telegraphing any thoughts. Only her eyes moved.

"We'll have to fix that," Frank said as he slumped against Oscar's little bar.

"No, Frank." She touched Frank on the shoulder. "But thanks."

"I'd sure like to be working toe-to-toe with Earl some day," Frank said. "Whatchall think?"

Sheila had heard about Frank's glass eye, but this was the first time she'd seen it up close, wandering slightly askew of the good one.

"Sheila?"

"What?" she asked.

"Whatcha think of me working with Earl?" He grinned at her.

Sheila's body tensed, like a child playing hide and seek, about to be caught. She shrugged.

"Except Post'll probably last the five years," he said. "Then, who knows? Unlessin' he dies first."

She gasped, then nodded slowly.

How could I have done this thing? She wanted to scream.

"Right, Sheila?" he growled like a hungry bear.

"Earl'd be a good one, I guess," she said. She spoke in a deliberately lighter tone to disguise the tightness she felt around her heart. "President, that is." *Shit,* she thought, she shouldn't have used the word president.

"My thoughts exactly!" Frank boomed. He confidently raised his glass to Earl across the room, then back to Sheila. She followed Frank's glass in the air. She wanted that drink.

"So, where is he?" he asked.

"Who?"

"Post, o' course?"

"Not here. At the office, I guess," she said. "He's workin', no doubt."

"Oh, right."

"Say, what are you drinking, Frank?" she asked.

"Scotch, Miss Sheila. Here, you can have it. I have to make a quick phone call." Frank bowed with the slightest knowing smile, then lumbered away, stopping to whisper in Earl's ear.

Sheila raised the drink, sniffing the scotch, clinking the cubes. She froze.

Who the hell makes phone calls on Friday nights from parties except doctors and mothers checking on their kids. Not single men like Frank.

The thunder boomed louder. She paused, then guzzled the drink, crunching the cubes. She glanced at Earl, who was watching Frank leave the room. Earl had a strange, forlorn look on his face as he wiped beads of sweat from his brow and under his nose with his handkerchief. *He looks like a sad little boy,* she thought.

Sheila thought of her own little boy, Bryan, and the prior Saturday when Margaret Post walked him home through the three-foot tall grass that separated their two homes. Sheila's production-built two-story stucco home was in the postage stamp corporate management subdivision. Margaret Post's custom-built sprawling southern mansion was across the field in Golf Estates, at the end of the wooded road off Second Street.

Sheila had felt slightly guilty, but more annoyed when Margaret Post, wearing comfortable jeans and a stylishly-faded Madras blouse, emerged from the field just before lunch, towing Bryan.

"Some day you'll be tall enough to see across the field!" she said.

"I like the ducks. Zoom . . . splash!"

"Such a delightful little boy, Mrs. Hickman," Margaret Post had said. She spoke with a proper southern accent and gently scruffed Bryan's hair, like she was his stately, supportive grandmother. "You mustn't lose him, Miss Hickman," she scolded ever so slightly.

"He must've slipped away," Sheila said.

"No, I didn't, Mama. You 'n dad were fightin' again."

"Bryan! Hush," Sheila said.

Margaret Post smiled at the little boy.

"When can I see the ducks again, Mama?" he asked.

"Thanks, Maggie." Sheila said.

"Margaret, please," she said.

"Sorry. Bryan, get over here before I . . ."

"I had a delightful time with him, Mrs. Hickman; bring him by any time. The big—"

"White house with the wonderful porch, I know. Thank you, but we must go," Sheila said.

Then Margaret had the nerve to ask about Bryan's little bruise, the one he got as Sheila fought with Earl that morning. The kid just got in the way—no big deal.

That nosey bitch. Sheila seethed when she thought of the woman's gracious concern. She contemplated how Margaret would feel without her presidential husband or his company to bolster her comfortable classiness.

That lady's had her turn, Sheila thought, pushing any association with the Posts far away, puckering up just in time to land a supportive kiss on Earl's cheek as he walked across the rec room and up to her. He looked as presidential as she had ever seen him, as ready as he'd ever be.

Sheila jerked awake to the smell of newsprint. Her head had been resting on the Orvis catalog on the kitchen table.

Her forehead was dented and sore. She rubbed it.

Crazy dreams! It's surprising how real they seem. In fact, they're just like memories.

She remembered Earl had a trip to Chicago planned for the following week, and wondered if his silk sport coat was clean and pressed. Anything to impress his boss. Maybe Earl could actually convince Childress not to send that nosy Yankee to Coyote.

5 *Chicago, Illinois   July 28,1980*

A week later John Childress watched as Earl Hickman fidgeted in the chair across the desk from him. "So, how's your wife, Earl?" Childress asked. He observed that, in the same manner as the other times they had met, Earl seemed to sweat profusely about the face.

Earl dabbed at the the tiny puddles with his handkerchief. "Oh, fine, just fine," he drawled. "Back from the hospital. Doin' real good."

"So, how'd you like Ramsay?" Childress asked.

"Grown up quite a bit since I saw him last."

Childress noticed that Earl's raspy, ragged growl matched his own. He wondered if Earl saw this conversation as some kind of a contest between them— maybe he thinks that the person who can talk the lowest is the smartest or most skilled. "You remember Ramsay from his visit ten years ago?" he asked.

"'Course. But John, don'tcha think he's a little advanced for us with all that schoolin'?"

"How's that?" John Childress asked. He squeezed his bronchial inhaler and turned away, already bored. Then he glanced back to see Earl's large face bobbing in space across the desk. His bloodshot eyes, veiny nose, purple lips, and pale yellow teeth made him a real life caricature.

"Well," Earl said, "all his fancy-ass statistics talk'll shake up the folks, don'tcha think?"

Childress eyed Earl's elbows awkwardly spread out on the desk, then looked him square in the eye. "Listen, Earl, he's exactly what you need. He's an expert at all that malarkey. Bet he could analyze the hell out of your business. O. I.'s always been a little behind expectations. Right?"

Earl looked down self-consciously and removed his arms from Childress' desk. "How's he gonna help O.I.?"

"Maybe he'll find something your folks've missed. Got quite the reputation for doing that around here. Might even remember the nuts and bolts of Coyote." He used his inhaler again. "So he'll hit the ground running." Then Childress put down his inhaler, lit up a cigarette, and immediately coughed. "And he knows a helluva lot about those deals, the billbacks, all that."

"Huh? Billbacks?" Earl looked up.

"Your merchandising costs—you know, those trade deals—are way out of line, Earl. He can help you with all that."

"But, John," Earl said. "Things have changed. And he was only there a few days way back. All he did was go to the funeral, so how could he remember anything?"

"I bet things haven't changed one bit in ten years." Childress laughed superciliously and then coughed. "Besides, Earl, Ramsay's a shirt sleeves sort of guy. Creative, too. Trust me. He'll pick it up real fast."

"John, with all due respect—"

"Just hold on, Earl." John Childress hit the desk with his palm. He cleared his throat and pointed his index finger in the air. "Listen, every Allied team we've sent down there comes away with the same conclusion: Hickman needs to get things under control and do a lot more with the damn business."

"But—"

"Earl, Ramsay could help you do that. Burghoff's only allowed the business to dribble along this way because Coyote's such a small part of the division."

"But John, I'll turn it around," Earl said.

"Sure you will. Like you have over the last ten years? Earl, now that I'm the main man in Foods, I plan to show Kyle a turnaround down there. Sooner, not later. Got it?"

"I suppo—"

"Earl, I only look as good as you do, right?" Childress coughed again. "Are we clear? This is your last chance." He used his inhaler again, tossed it on the desk, and looked out the window. "If Coyote Brand's gone, you're gone."

"Right, John. I see what you mean."

John looked back and smiled slowly. "That's better. You feeling OK?"

Earl fidgeted in place, pale. "Sure John, but all I'm sayin' is, I think he's a little young. Our folks are mostly middle-aged and set in their ways."

"Ramsay'll add some spunk down there, then," Childress said and looked at his watch.

Earl nodded. "Makes sense. Makes sense. But what about this Dallas move he talked about? That couldn't mean me, too? Sheila and I just can't up and—"

"Now, Earl, listen." Childress sighed. "Wife or no wife, you need Ramsay. We need a new strategy down there, and Burghoff wants something done with that chili hot dog sauce, all that. If he's successful, Ramsay can do whatever the fuck he wants. Hell, he'll be walking on water. So will you. We clear on this, Earl?"

"Yes, John." Earl, looking perturbed, slumped back in his chair.

"And you'll have to work out this Dallas thing. If it means you and Sheila have to move, so be it. She could use a change, right? Been through a lot over the years. Better hospitals up in Dallas anyway, right?"

"But John—"

Childress looked at his watch again. "Pentrate over in Personnel said something about electroshock?"

"They thought it might wipe out some bad childhood memories. And she's a border line manic depressive."

"Don't they have other ways?" Childress asked.

"Hypnosis and heavy therapy, but Sheila doesn't believe in that stuff."

Childress frowned. "How long's this been going on?"

"Off and on for ten years," Earl said. "Sheila's always in the hospital: gettin' those treatments or breaking down or de-toxin'."

Childress shook his head. "Hell of a life, Earl."

Earl mirrored the actions of his boss. "Yep."

"Listen, you wouldn't want Ramsay running the company up there in Dallas while you were in Corsicana, would you?" Childress asked, squinting at Earl.

"Guess not." Earl cleared his throat. "After all, I am the president."

"Right." Childress grabbed his inhaler and compressed it twice as he breathed in deeply. He stuffed it in his suit pocket and gestured toward the door to make sure Hickman got the hint. Their discussion was over.

The odd-looking man with kinky, graying hair, profuse after shave, and out-dated horn-rimmed glasses hobbled out of the office.

Finally! Childress sat down and shook his head. He despised Earl Hickman for his hunched posture, dumb wit, and deferential demeanor—a

Quasimoto with a "wanna-be" attitude.
He laughed.

If Coyote Brand Products represented
more of the division's bottom line, he
would fire the idiot outright. But what
competent manager could he ever get to
replace Hickman in Corsicana, Texas?
Even Ramsay, a junior executive,
endorsed the idea that Coyote Brand
relocate its main office to Dallas, but that
move was obviously not going to be a
smooth one.

John Childress didn't think highly of
Ramsay either, not for his incompetence,
but rather for his arrogance. A new
division president shouldn't have to put
up with daily garbage from naive,
overconfident, and idealistic managers
like Ramsay.

He pictured Hickman and Ramsay
working together, and he snickered
again.

And Burghoff, Ramsay's mentor, was
too busy with his own career to notice if
Ramsay fizzled in Texas. Childress
reached for the phone and buzzed
Virginia.

"Yes, John?" she said.

"Get me Burghoff."

"Yes, sir."

"Kyle's voice came on the line. "Burghoff here."

"Kyle? John here. I'm sending Marcus Ramsay down to Corsicana to take the Coyote Brand marketing slot, boost O.I. and isolate opportunities. Wonder if you could give him a nice send-off pep talk."

"Corsicana's a pit, John," Burghoff said.

"He'll eventually relocate the offices— executive, financial, and marketing—to Dallas. Your idea originally, remember?" Childress said.

"That's right. Say, we can't let Marcus get lost down there."

"Could you have a chat with him? We want to make him feel like he'll always have a home back here at the Mart," Childress said.

"John, the truth now. You're not just getting rid of him are you?"

"What makes you think that, Kyle?"

Corsicana, Texas

"Done," Earl announced with an unsettled stomach as he walked into the Hickmans' Golf Estates home later that night. He dropped his heavy leather overnight bag by the faded easy chair in the corner.

"What's done?" Sheila asked and burped. She entered the living room giggling, holding a glass, sipping on her special ice tea.

"Ramsay. Hey, you're not supposed to be playing around with the damn booze, Sheila. You've had enough."

"Sounds like you could use a little yourself." She burped again, then covered her mouth.

Earl shook his head. "I got enough troubles."

"Well?" she said. "The Yankee?"

"He starts as soon as he can get down here."

"Damn, I knew it." Sheila sipped again.

"Well, I tried the best I could. His wife Kathy moves down in a few months."

"Shit. They living in town?" she asked.

"No, I'm guessin' he'll eventually settle in Dallas." Earl sat in his easy chair and kicked up the built-in footrest.

"Why Dallas?" she said.

"Does it matter? Now Chicago'll be able to upset our damn apple cart."

Sheila shook her head. "Fuck. A Yankee spy." She lit a cigarette and started pacing.

"I knew this was gonna happen some day," Earl said. He shook his head as he unfolded the Corsicana *Sun*. He hoped Ramsay wasn't as incredible a sleuth as the rumors had implied.

"Let's see," Sheila jabbered, "We need to let him know you're the boss from the get-go." She cackled like a hen. "I got a few ideas." She paced, puffed, pointed.

"I bet you do," he said as he slowly turned a page. He looked up and studied her marching. She really doesn't have a clue.

Part 2

the Spirit

6

Two weeks later, nerves and excitement manifested themselves in a twitch on the edge of his left eye as Marcus Ramsay turned right from eastbound Interstate I-635 to I-45, and headed south to Corsicana. It was a humid Sunday night in August. Marcus sang with Christopher Cross, crooning from the Chevy Citation's little radio.

After years of living in the Chicago area, he now had a new job, a new life, and was leaving the city for the first time. How bizarre. *Why am I doing this?* he wondered. *Is it just to get away from her Daddy?* Or maybe I just want to prove myself and make a difference for the first time in my life and really help these Texas folks. *My dad would've liked that.*

Ramsay turned off the radio. As he penetrated mile after mile of sticky Texas night, he heard the protests of a million invisible crickets, muffled by heavy air that rushed past his partially rolled down window.

A week earlier he and Kathy had chosen a home in east Dallas in anticipation of the office's eventual relocation. The house was just northeast of Dallas' downtown. They wouldn't move into their little house on Crow Valley Trail for ninety days. Until then, Marcus would stay at the Corsicana Holiday Inn and commute home to Chicago every weekend or so.

Kyle Burghoff, as executive vice-president at Allied, had stepped in to make sure his job change went as smoothly as possible. Kyle was, after all, his mentor, and that's what mentors did—hover in the background and look out for you. About Childress, the power monger who was Earl's new boss up at the Mart, Ramsay wasn't so sure.

In fact, the combination of the intimidating Childress he knew about and the crazy Earl he'd heard about was sure to be interesting. Would Childress leave him stranded in Texas, working for a weird guy some said was bombastic but impotent, incapable of parrying Childress' power? How would that affect Ramsay? And if he dug up real business problems that had been buried for a decade, was he likely to get Childress' support as he eradicated them? *Maybe I jumped too soon at this alleged career opportunity,* Ramsay thought. So much for ambition.

By the time he found his way off I-45 at the Texas 287 exit nearly an hour later, the stars glimmered in the clear, fresh Corsicana night. As the moon rose, it started as a large, amber orb near the horizon, but in minutes, became a small, white one higher in the sky.

Ramsay took Texas Route 287 past a barren country club with tattered flags and then past a row of old-looking grain storage silos to Texas 31—Seventh Street locally. He turned right and headed to Main Street. Then he made a left over the tracks into the chain link entry to Coyote Brand Products. He pulled over to the right and got out.

The spooky-looking compound basked in the white moonlight, but the cool light was contaminated by the purple glow of a single security light that rested atop a twenty foot pole next to the front little office building. Beneath it Ramsay stood and scanned his future. During his short interview trip, he hadn't viewed the eerie compound at night. It appeared surreal with its boxy shapes and glowing purple.

It looked vaguely like he remembered it had looked ten years before, like a

Mexican prison. Marcus shook his head as he moseyed back to the car, hands in his pockets. As he walked, he kicked up fine dust. He looked back only once at the boxy Sales Office building where his large, fake-walnut desk dominated an expansive room, empty except for a few chairs, some old file cabinets, and a plethora of red binders. That big office had been his one consolation for taking the Coyote Marketing Manager post in Corsicana.

Ramsay looked up at the stars. Anticipation rushed through him as he recalled his office back at the Mart. There, engraved on the anniversary plaque that he had received from his crew, an inscription read "Don't let the Turkeys Get You Down". To them, "Marcus Ramsay" meant doing things right and overcoming the odds, solving the problems nobody else could, and never, ever, letting the bastards who supported the status quo get in the way. In fact, his overriding goal was always to expose the slackers and roll over them on the way to a some grand solution that he had envisioned. That's what he was good at, that's what he liked to do—he always let his idealism drive him to the solution.

Now that Ramsay was in Corsicana and looking at the Coyote complex, constructed in 1927, his apprehension began to dissipate. He realized that they probably needed him a lot more than he needed them. And, whether Coyote Brand looked like some kind of Mexican prison or not, Marcus had to get his mind geared up for a new mission. If he played his cards right, he'd serve his time in Texas, then get a cushy promotion back to Chicago.

He whisked his hands together, jumped in his rental car, and drove off. On Texas 287 a mile west of downtown Corsicana, the only green neon for miles popped out of the black, announcing the Holiday Inn. Getting there was painless, although Lenora's page of directions had suggested it would be impossible to find.

Maybe she thinks the city boy is just plain dumb or something, he thought.

Ramsay pulled into the front lot of the Holiday Inn and parked next to a vacant taxicab, its motor still running. *Strange time and place for a taxi,* Marcus thought.

He got out of his car, walked into the office, and up to the desk. "Marcus Ramsay here," he announced. "Coyote Brand." It was the first time he had coupled his name with the company's. It did actually sound like he must be selling animal pelts.

"Coyote?" the short, scrawny clerk asked in a high, syrupy voice. He wore glasses with plastic fifties-looking frames. *Must be the lead tenor in his church choir,* Ramsay thought.

"Let's see." The man alternately studied a crumpled three-by-five reservation card at arm's length, then Marcus' navy blue suit with tight pinstripes.

The man's obvious up-and-down gawking made Marcus feel like he was being inspected, as if he were a crime suspect. "Is there a problem?" Ramsay asked.

He cleared his throat with a squeak. "Y'all one of them Allied fellers from up there in Chicago?" the man said and looked over the top of his glasses.

"Yes, sir, I am."

"Y'all sure are comin' down more regular these days," he sung slowly and accusingly.

"Guess so. Why?" Marcus scanned the Lion's Club and Rotary signs nearby. "That a problem?"

The clerk frowned. "Ever been on the TV, son?"

"Can't say I have. That required?" He laughed.

The clerk didn't. "Say, boy. You ever been here before?" The drilling dripped like molasses. He fiddled with his lip and squinted his eyes. "Y'all sure do look familiar."

"I was here ten years ago." Then Ramsay pointed at the reservation card. "Lenora's booked me ahead a week at a time." Marcus stretched his neck. He was tired from his ride and impatient for the interrogation to end.

"Lenora? Now, she is wonderful, ain't she? Been playin' the organ over at the church for years, ever since old Reverend Miller took her under his wing way back."

"Really?" Marcus smiled. Lenora must've been the password.

Suddenly the clerk eased his investigative manner, put on a friendly face, and picked up his pace. "Where might y'all be movin', son? Golf Estates?" he asked. "Like Mr. Hickman? He's over there with his poor wife and the kids. She's back from the hospital again, you know. Poor children, puttin' up with all that electro nonsense. Moved near that sweet Margaret Post. Woman never gets out these days." Then the man drawled slowly again, "With the cancer an' all." He hung his head. " 'Cept she drives over once a week with Henrietta to tend to the flowers on poor James' grave. Sad story."

Ramsay remembered how the death of the former president of Coyote had shaken the town.

"So, where y'all movin', then?" the man asked. "Or did you tell me?"

"East Dallas."

"Right, figgers. That's where all you Yankee folk are movin'. Must be something special up there, that fancy lake near downtown an' all."

"Excuse me, sir, but it's late and I . . . "

After Ramsay finished checking in, he went out a door that passed by the entrance to a restaurant and a large meeting room, the walls strung with Italian lights. As he opened the exit door to the outside he almost ran into a short, stocky man with a crewcut and dated clothes. "Oh, excuse me," Ramsay said.

"Why, hello." The man said in a British accent—odd for Texas. The man waved, smiled, and walked past Ramsay, into the building.

Ramsay walked across the sparkling, dew-laden lawn. He glanced up at the bright moon. Then he saw it, jutting from darkness into the Sea of Tranquility.

An oil well?

Before him, in the small lawn that surrounded the pool, stood a full-sized oil derrick. It must have been as tall as the lawn was wide.

"What the hell is that doing here?" An oil well next to the swimming pool at the Holiday Inn outside of Corsicana, Texas?

Ramsay walked over to the derrick. He had never seen one up close. He read the bronze plaque affixed to the base of the derrick:

The site where oil was first successfully
    excavated west of the Mississippi.

Proudly presented to the people of Corsicana
    by the Navarro County Historical Society:

Wyvonne Putnam, Director

and by industrial leaders of Navarro County:

Gus Weidmann, Tom McElwee
  Collin Street Bakery
James Earl Post
  Coyote Brand Products
B. Vance Limerick
  Limerick Petroleum Recovery
  Corporation
Leonard S. Cohagen
  Supreme Oil Drilling Equipment,
  Inc.
Robert T. Busby
  Superior Drilling Equipment, Inc.

Well, look at this. Old James Post made the list. Ramsay leaned against the rig and looked up at the moon again.

He glanced at his watch as his stomach rumbled a suggestion that it was dinnertime. He heard the door from the lobby swing open and saw the friendly little man with a crewcut emerge.

Suddenly Ramsay felt queasy and wobbly. He staggered in place. In an instant everything went black, but he was aware of his own essence, like he was a tiny dot of existence in the middle of a great nothingness. He looked around in the black as if he was a single microscopic eye. At first he was afraid, then curious. Then, more purposefully, he scoured the dark to find a way out.

At that moment, light rushed back in and Ramsay blinked. He sat on the wet ground five feet away from the oil well. His stomach ached. "Oh," he moaned and shook his head. "What just happened?"

The man with the crewcut ran up, car keys jangling, and helped Marcus stand.

"I must've passed out or something," Ramsay mumbled. He still felt groggy and nauseated.

"I dare say, you'll be fine, sir," the man said properly.

"Maybe I fainted because I haven't eaten in a while." Ramsay wiped the wet grass off his shirt.

"Feeling a bit better?" the man asked as he held Marcus' shoulder firmly.

"Yeah, I'll be fine. Say, it's lucky you came back out here."

"Dropped my keys in the grass." He turned and started to walk away. "Just take care of yourself."

"That your taxi out front?" Ramsay called.

He stopped and looked back. "Why, yes sir."

"What's it doing way down in Corsicana?"

He fidgeted. "Every once in a while things get particularly out of whack. They send me to set it right, you see," he said. "This one is quite a bugger." He smiled.

"I don't get it."

"Oh, begging your pardon, sir. You will." The man smiled, waved, and walked away, whistling.

Then, Ramsay remembered that the taxi had been running out front of the motel. Why would the driver be searching for his keys in the grass? It didn't make any sense unless the man carried two sets of keys. *Very weird.*

Once in room 140, Marcus unpacked, stripped to his underwear, and called Kathy. " . . . That's right, a real live oil well—the absolute first one in Texas, even the whole West—was built right in the middle of these motel grounds. The guy at the desk even called me a Yankee. Then the strangest thing happened."

"What's that?" Kathy asked, sounding semi-interested.

"On the way to my room, I passed out."

"You what?"

"I was leaning against that oil well. The next thing I know I woke up and I was sitting on the ground covered with wet grass and there was this little guy with a British accent standing there."

"Are you all right?" she asked.

"Fine, now. But I looked at my watch, before and after."

"What does that have to do with it?"

"It's funny. Five minutes had passed. I must've been lying there all that time."

"Wow. You sure?"

"Absolutely. I remember looking at my watch before I fainted."

"Maybe you ought to see a doctor."

"Yeah. I still feel a little sick to my stomach. If I feel this way tomorrow, I'll find a local doctor," he said.

"Good."

"And that cabby. That British guy?"

"What about him?"

"When I came-to, he ran up and was talking all this gibberish that didn't make any sense. Man, so far it's been sort of an odd experience here. I feel a little foreign."

"Well. It's what you wanted," she said coldly.

"I thought we both wanted this."

"I was talking to Daddy. He's not sure this was such a good career move," she said. "I sort of agree. Let's face it— Corsicana? Whoever heard of Corsicana?"

"I don't give a shit about what Daddy said. You're always siding with his view of the world."

"Maybe he's right. You always see things through rose-colored glasses."

"I thought that was one of the reasons you married me," Marcus said.

"Yeah, but there's a limit. Corsicana— bright future."

"Listen, Kathy, I better go. I have to get up early. And I'm sure you do, too, for one of those fancy meetings you're having these days."

"Actually, I do," she said.

They hung up.

Marcus wondered what was happening. One minute Kathy had been at his side, the next she seemed to be washing her hands of any association with him or his dreams and only concerned with her own. He felt alone in his new Texas prison.

Minutes later Marcus burrowed under the blanket. He reached out to set the old-fashioned alarm clock. He could imagine its clattering bell announcing first light. He turned the lamp out.

Still thinking of Kathy, Marcus simmered quietly as he stared at the harshly back-lit curtains. The jagged shadow of the oil well stretched across the folds. It was amazing how insignificant he felt when she wasn't being supportive of him. He closed his eyes and rehearsed his routine for the next morning, wondering which tie would make the best first impression.

He heard the crickets chirping outside. Something scurried across the floor. He reached in the dark, flicked the lamp on, and sat up.

"Shit!" Over in the corner sat the largest cockroach he had ever seen. Like an armored monster preparing for battle, it seemed to take aim at him from across the room. He reached for his shoe and pitched it at the bug-tank. The roach scurried laterally a few feet, just enough to avoid the shoe. There it sat, frozen, still looking at him.

"I can't even kill a damned bug." He slumped back in bed and turned off the lights. "What the hell good am I?"

Across town, Sheila Hickman lay in bed next to Earl. She talked while he read the paper. "I still don't think it was such a great idea. That Yankee's bound to wander somewhere he doesn't belong or figure something out." Sheila sipped on a glass of wine and wondered. If Ramsay was the bloodhound Earl said he was, he was bound to make trouble, sooner or later.

Earl flipped a page of the Corsicana *Sun* and said, "You're so dramatic, Sheila. What could he possibly wander into?"

She sat up straight. "Listen, Earl, things have been so great for ten years. Why change them? He's bound to stick his Yankee nose into something. Maybe he'll make you look bad to those big shots in Chicago. Ever think of that?"

"Sheila, now you'll see me at my best." Earl put his paper down. "Gettin' the most outa him while I'm constantly keepin' him off guard, like those office changes I ordered."

"I guess," she said. "The whole thing bugs me, though. Can't explain it."

"You're just bein' paranoid. Now, put down the damn booze and turn out the light."

Back in front of the Holiday Inn,
Reginald Waverly sat in his running taxi.
He picked up the CB radio mike.

"Waverly checking in," he said.
"Over."

"Base, go ahead."

"Verifying Ramsay. I met him. Quite a
personable chap. Hope he won't be too
uncomfortable during the *empowerment*.
After all, it does take a while. The
installation of Post's spirit went smoothly,
though. I still remember the *dislodgement*
from his body—indeed, quite spectacular.
Yes, this is an interesting case. Multiple
parties involved—a bit of a challenge
down the road. Say, I'll ring you
periodically to report on status. Ten-
four." Reginald put his taxi in reverse,
backed up and pulled away, whistling.

7

"Welcome to Coyote Brand," the large woman twanged and smiled brightly.

Marcus Ramsay had just opened the door to the little front office building in the Coyote Brand compound the following morning. "Hi," he said and waved.

"You must be Mr. Ramsay." Her ear-to-ear smile froze. "My word. You haven't changed a bit in ten years. Well, a little."

"Thank you, Lenora. I remember you, too. Haven't changed either."

"Why, thank you." She laughed. "Two kids later is all. Say, you found us OK an' all. And the Holiday Inn?"

"Yeah, but that hotel clerk sure gave me a drilling. Looked like he recognized me, too, after all these years," he said.

She gazed at the ceiling. "Yep. I guess old Hank's been over at the motel that long," she said. "Yep. He might-could remember you."

"The weirdest thing happened on the way to my room."

"What?" she asked.

"I fainted on the lawn. Out for five minutes."

"Five minutes? My, oh my. You feelin' OK?"

"Yeah, feel fine this morning." He shrugged.

"Maybe all the travelin'," she said, nodding her head, crimping her eye brows.

"It's good to be back, though. Guess I missed you the day I came down for the interview," he said.

"Church," she sang and nodded again, as if that explained everything. "I play organ. Have all these years."

"Great," he said and remembered how the clerk at the motel knew that, too.

"Boy, it's like a day hasn't passed." She shook her head and threw a glance toward the office across the hall from her desk.

"Mr. Post?" Ramsay asked.

"Yep."

"You miss him?"

"Like he's never been gone," she said. "Like he could walk right in here. Like you just did. Fact, havin' you here sorta brings him back," she said.

"Boy, the town really came out for his funeral," he said.

"The Lord was lookin' down that day," she said.

Ramsay nodded. "Al still around?"

"Yep."

"Oscar?"

"Yep."

"Cecil?"

"Yep."

"All the same people?" he said. "That's something."

"No, now there's Harold and Willy. The Quality Assurance department," she said. "Harold's from Alabama, Willy's a local boy. Since the recall in '76, we put in a new lab on the floor over the plant. But, most of us are the same."

Ramsay smiled. "Well, I'd better get over to my office. The other little building, right?"

"Yep. Used to be the men's shower in the old days, long before I started," she said and laughed. "Listen, Marcus, anything I can do for y'all." She pointed a stubby finger at the phone. "Just give a holler."

"Thanks, Lenora." Ramsay started to turn.

"So now, you're the one's gonna get us to California," she said.

"California?" Marcus turned back. "What's that?"

"Didn't Earl mention it? His latest project." She sounded impressed, like getting to California was the big deal now.

"Well, good morning," Earl interrupted in a raspy grumble as he walked out of his office, Post's old one. He flashed a wide, yellow Cheshire Cat grin. His shoulders hunched, his belly protruded, his large chin jutted, and his after shave permeated the air.

Marcus noticed that Earl's eyes were like marbles, but devoid of shine and tinged with yellow. They seemed to look several feet beyond Marcus, focused on some imaginary plane.

"Got a second, Marcus? I trust your evening was pleasant," Earl said, as he shook hands politely. He ushered Ramsay into his office.

"Except for the roach." Marcus chuckled. "And fainting."

"Fainting?" Earl asked. "roach?"

"Yeah, I guess there'll be a roach in my room till Kathy and I move to East Dallas. I thought that'd be a good location for the house since we'll be moving the offices up there."

"Shhh!" Earl held his right index finger over his lips. He reached behind Ramsay and closed his office door, blocking Lenora's questioning squint.

"What is it?" Marcus asked.

"They don't know about this office move thing," Earl said. He cleared his throat twice. "Some of them'll go, some won't. You understand."

"When do you plan on telling them?" Ramsay asked.

"There'll be a right time. Meanwhile, don't talk about it, OK? Now, about your office in the other building." Earl cleared his throat again. "We made a few changes. You understand."

"Changes?" Marcus felt unsettled.

"Yep. So why don't you get set up over there. Say hello to Cecil. 'Member him?"

"Sure."

"Then we'll all go for barbecue at Hobert's. Best barbecue in town. Some say Texas."

As Marcus Ramsay kicked across the dusty courtyard to the boxy sales building fifty feet away, he spied a curious plant worker here and there and waved at each of them. It seemed like the friendly thing to do. But when he did, they scurried out of sight, like Indians in an old western movie.

The aroma of the Coyote Brand Chili spice blend hung in the morning air. As Marcus looked at the plant building, he heard the clanging that he remembered came from cans on the assembly line before they were filled with freshly cooked chili. In the background, the steel carts rumbled across the plant floor into the ancient, ten foot tall retort machines that would sterilize the cans after they were sealed.

He met resistance when he opened the door to the little sales office which had been painted mustard yellow over and over like the front office building and plant—apparently swollen from humidity. On the third push it opened.

A squat middle-aged man stood behind the empty reception desk wearing a faded, short-sleeved Hawaiian print sports shirt and jeans. He had long, wavy, red hair, a perky mustache, and untamed, wizard-like eyebrows. A fresh pink scar crossed his exposed upper chest. He quickly put down the phone and looked up.

"Oh, howdy," he said. "Remember me? Al Bishop?"

"Marcus Ramsay." He extended his hand.

"Right, I knew that." Al ignored the hand and glanced at the phone.

"Nice to see you, Al," Ramsay said. "What you up to these days?"

"Oh, still handlin' accounting and personnel, the usual. But since my surgery—he patted his chest—I been mainly putting in the new computer and signing those damn billback checks. He counted the tasks on his stubby fingers. "The computer ties us to Allied up in Chicago now, too, you know.."

"That's a lot." Ramsay pointed to Al's chest. "Your heart?"

"Yep. Cleaned out the old pipes. Quadruple."

"Boy, major deal," Ramsay said.

"Changed my ways since then: diet, exercise—the whole bit."

"Feeling better?"

"Yep. By the by, you'll be meetin' Daisy later. She's your secretary, assistant they call it up there at the Mart. She's at her daughter's school play. It's the big deal of the year for the kids."

"Sure."

"Uh, Marcus?" Al asked.

"Yeah?"

"Ain't none of my business, but Daisy comes on to all the boys, so don't take it personal."

"Sure."

"I swear she dreams some Yankee'll whisk her out of Corsicana. You know the drill."

"I can only imagine," Ramsay said.

"She lived a lot of places up North as a child," Al said. "Still sees herself back there some day, but I doubt that'll ever come to pass." He laughed. "You know what they say: Once in Corsicana, always in Corsicana."

Marcus laughed, a little uneasily.

"Boy, you sure do bring back memories of the old boss," Al said.

"Mr. Post?"

"Yep. I remember you from way back then. You're all growed up now, though."

"Post must've been a good man, the way he made such an impact on you folks."

"Yep." Al nodded. "Things have changed a mite since he passed, though."

"Oh?"

"It's not so good to complain, but . . . "

"What?" Ramsay asked.

"Just that Earl's always proposin' these grandiose Yankee plans. No offense."

Ramsay waved his hand. "None taken."

"Now those damnable billback trade deals," he said.

"How so?"

"I've written more of them blasted checks these last few months than ever. Hard to keep up."

Ramsay nodded. "Really?"

Al continued: "And Earl wants to run even more of 'em when we do this friggen California thing. Says they like the big ideas in Chicago. But you'd know that, I suppose."

"We'll see. That's why they sent me down, sort of reassess the approach and strategy," Ramsay said.

"Good. You have quite the job ahead. We don't advertise on the TV near as much . . . "

As Al rambled on, Marcus half-listened. He pulled open the door to the side of the reception desk. He remembered it was the door to his office. Smoke billowed out.

What's this? he thought.

"Well, howdy! You're Marcus." An old guy sat at a desk, right on the other side of the door. "Nice to see y'all again. Been quite a while."

"Yes, sir. Cecil, right?" Ramsay asked.

"Yep. Ten years." The older man had a tanned, craggy face and swiveled in his wobbly desk chair toward Ramsay, a Marlboro slung loosely from his lips. The front of his worn little desk was flush against the front of the desk Ramsay remembered had been earmarked for him.

The older man motioned to the larger desk. "That's where y'all are gonna sit." He waved two half-fingers.

What's going on? Why two desks in my office? Marcus walked behind the larger desk and sat down in a tipsy, green vinyl chair that had stuffing hanging out of a slit in the back. He swiveled it around and found himself staring across both desks into Cecil's pale blue eyes.

"Mighty comfy, huh?" Cecil said loudly.

"I guess," Marcus said. "But, you don't have to yell."

Cecil pointed at his ears. "Sorry, hearin' ain't so good."

Al laughed from the other room.

"Say, maybe you can see old Margaret," he said. She met you back at the funeral, right? By the limos. I remember."

"Yeah, that's right. Boy, you have a good memory."

"Seemed taken by you, I remember." He gazed into space. "The town really came out that day."

"Like Woodstock," Ramsay said.

"I suppose."

"Cecil, what's the deal with the office arrangement?" Marcus pointed to the two desks crunched together. "I thought this whole room was supposed to be mine."

"Couldn't figger it. Earl called over the last minute changes yesterday," Cecil said, scrunching his gray brows together. "We worked like the dickens—Daisy and me—all day. You and I share the phone, by the way. Don't know how that'll work out. You get line one, being the boss an' all. I get line two." He shrugged.

"Really?"

"Sorry. Helluva way to welcome y'all."

Even if this desk thing bugged him, Ramsay couldn't make a big stink out of it because he wanted to be seen as a team player. "Oh, it's OK for now, Cecil. Really."

Ramsay recalled his breakfast at the Mart a month earlier with Kyle Burghoff. He had just become executive vice president. "Coyote Brand has to be brought into the twentieth century, and you're the one to do it, Marcus," Burghoff had said. "Childress and I are counting on you."

Ramsay was inspired by that challenge, especially from Burghoff. It was clear that his mentor expected a lot from him. Having a personal challenge like that was a young executive's dream.

"You OK, son?" Cecil said.

Ramsay looked at Cecil's craggy, concerned face. "Oh, don't worry. We'll make it work, Cecil," Marcus said. He reached across the desk to offer Cecil a handshake. In the process his gaze lingered on Cecil's right hand.

"Oh, the stubs?" Cecil said and held up his right hand, two adjacent fingers had been cut off at the middle knuckle. "Hell, that happened a few years ago when I was opening a case o' produc'," Cecil said. "Doesn't hurt my golf game one iota! I even use these two fingers to hold my cigarette. Looky here." Cecil pulled out a Marlboro, proudly mounted it between his two little stubs, and lit up.

His gleaming teeth popped out of his leathery tan as he smiled.

Marcus laughed.

"Say, can I have one of those cigarettes, Cecil?" he asked. "I need one. I just quit smoking and started running." He looked around at the office configuration. "Obviously, it was bad timing."

"Know how that goes," Cecil said loudly. "Dorothy's been after me for years."

"So, you're a golfer?" Marcus asked.

"Just started. Frank Benedict, our Dallas broker, got me goin'. He thought these fingers might even help my grip a wee bit. Sure did!"

"Frank Benedict's a good golfer?" Ramsay said. "Most sales brokers are."

They laughed.

"Well, it's true," Marcus said.

"Yep. But he's entitled to a few days in the sun," Cecil said. "He sells over seventy percent of Coyote Brand Chili. Has for years."

"Seventy percent? You'd think I would've met him back then," Marcus said.

"Guess he didn't go to the funeral. Damnedest thing. He hired a limo for poor Margaret, but never showed up himself. I wondered about that for years."

"Hmm," Ramsay nodded.

Cecil continued, "Frank's loaded, too. Even more since they made Earl president and Earl gave Frank the Houston market. Another three hundred thousand in commission. Dallas and Houston—Coyote's two biggest markets."

"Really?" Ramsay asked.

"Yep. Frank was always pushing Mr. Post," Cecil said. "But James wouldn't budge. Too much leverage to one broker, he always said."

"A man of principle, huh?"

"No kidding." Cecil's face saddened, reflecting obvious respect for the icon. "James was a wonderful man. Like a minister. Sweet but firm."

Ramsay stared into space, reminiscing.

"Say, you OK boy?" Cecil leaned forward.

"It's nothing," Marcus said. "My dad was a minister, died when I was a kid. The folks in my town always looked up to him, he was always helping."

"Sorry about that, son. Sounds like he was special."

"Well, this Post stuff reminds me of Dad a little. The town really missed him after he was gone."

"Know how that is. Mr. Post was somethin' special around here, too. Only one of them comes around every generation, I guess. Or two, includin' your dad an' all."

"How's Post's wife doing? Margaret, right?" Marcus asked.

Cecil nodded. "OK, I guess. Up there with Henrietta in that big ol' house in Golf Estates. Near Earl's place."

"The clerk mentioned her last night," Ramsay said. "Cancer?"

"Yep, Margaret, she got sick a ways back," Cecil said. "Then it went away. She was gonna tell James on the night he died, they say, but he never got the news."

"Sad," Ramsay said.

"Now it's comin' back with a vengeance," he said.

"That's awful."

"Yep. Looks pretty bad," Cecil said.

They both bowed their heads for a second.

"So, after Post died, Earl became president?" Ramsay asked.

"Yep. He was the Sales Manager. But Allied gave him the boot upstairs."

"Perfect timing?" Marcus smiled.

Cecil waggled one of his stubs. "Hey, hey. That's not nice. Never thought of it like that."

They laughed.

"Earl got the nod after Frank put in a good word for him with the Chicago brass," Cecil said. "Then Earl went and gave Frank Houston."

"By the way, what's all this about a California expansion?" Ramsay asked.

"Another one o' Earl's highfalutin' ideas. Sellin' Coyote out there on the West Coast. He gets his brainstorms whenever Sheila goes into the hospital. Must be real hard on those Hickmans, all that electro gobbledygook."

"Sheila? Electro?"

The ancient rotary phone rang between them. Marcus answered. It was Earl. Time for barbecue down at Hobert's.

The discussion over lunch was all about California. Earl's latest plan was to expand out west first, then around the country via Puritan's network of pet food plants. Chili and dog food, both sold by Allied, required canning. Thus, the opportunity.

After having added as many different sizes as possible to the Coyote line, Earl explained, the only way to expand the business was geographically. The group had obviously heard his spiel before.

"Not bad. Chicago'll buy it, don'tcha think?" Earl looked right at Marcus.

"They're interested in a new strategy, the office move to Dallas, and an advertising campaign for hot dog sauce. They won't necessarily support this California deal unless we can show them how it'll bump operating income."

"What move to Dallas?" Oscar asked.

Earl jumped in. "Nothing. Just speculation"

Ramsay pulled at his chin. "But Earl, what about regional competition out there in California? There must be other brands."

Most of the Coyote managers grumbled.

"And you have low per unit profit margins on canned meat, right?" Ramsay persisted.

"Twenty-five percent," Earl said. "Why?"

"I thought I remembered you telling me that. A decent level of introductory advertising out there would kill your profits."

"Well, we were actually planning on expanding with billback trade deals," Earl said and smiled.

"No advertising?"

"Exactly." Earl smiled knowingly. "You should see our billbacks. Pretty effective."

"Billbacks can't replace advertising. You have to educate your consumers to stimulate trial—that's what advertising can do." Ramsay shrugged and sipped some iced tea. "No offense, but I've seen quite a few introductory programs that were under-advertised and they fail."

"Huh?" Hickman threw down his napkin, apparently miffed.

"I'm sorry, Earl, if I'm killing your plans," Ramsay said, "but they do want me to come up with a new strategy for Coyote. This is an example of pointing out some possible pipe dreams."

"Pipe dreams, huh? Well, they make some sense to me," Earl said with a slow, condescending drawl. "I know that from my days up in Chicago years ago."

"You were up there?" Ramsay asked.

"Before all the days of the fancy MBA marketing. We did pretty good."

"I'm sure, but that's my up-front thinking on California, at least," Marcus said. "I'll have to look further."

"What does the, uh, newcomer say about the taste issue on the West Coast?" Earl boomed in a haughty, resonant tone. He surveyed the group one at a time as if to say, I got him, now.

Ramsay responded, "Well, actually, Earl, California is made up of a mixture of different regional tastes, not like other areas of the country. We researched the same markets for Mama's Pizza. California was our number one market. But I'll have to look at your data to be sure. You do have data, right?"

"Well, I guess," Earl said. "Some." He cleared his throat.

"We can talk about it," Marcus said. "I'll need to do some analysis before we confirm California's a good way to go. OK?"

"Oh, we do, do we?" Earl grumbled.

"Of course," Marcus said.

"Well Marcus, I forgot to tell you," Earl said. "I'll continue to handle California till you get your feet wet. You understand."

"What?" Ramsay asked.

"Sure. You can help Cecil run the numbers for the annual broker-trade parties around the Southwest. Dallas is the biggest one and the first, comin' up in the spring."

"But—"

"I think I mentioned it at your interview. We present the annual results to each of the broker sales forces."

"Dallas is a big fancy shmancy deal up in Dallas at a hotel," Cecil said.

Earl held his glass up with two hands. He slowly sipped at his tea and looked over his horn-rimmed glasses at Marcus. "Assume y'all are up to handlin' the number-crunching." He put his glass down and smiled. "Childress said you were good at that stuff."

"California, here we come!" Frank Benedict boomed over the phone to Earl after lunch.

"Yep," Earl said. "Got our new Yankee marketing guy running some numbers."

"Yankee marketing guy?"

"I told you about him—Ramsay? Don't worry, Frank. That'll keep him busy. Shouldn't be any trouble."

"Better not. I closed the damn deal this afternoon. Just bought majority interest in California Brokerage Company for a mill. Not much to pay for a company with principals like Clorox. Add Coyote to that and I'm one helluva rich son of a bitch."

"One . . . million . . . dollars?" Earl asked, coughing, "I couldn't be happier for you, Frank."

"There's no trouble with this marketing guy, is there, Earl?" Benedict growled. "California's on, right?"

"Solid gold," Earl said. "Just like I've been saying."

"Better be."

Earl hoped nothing more would be said. When the conversation ended, he took a Gaviscon for his jittery stomach, put the phone down, and dashed off a quick note to John Childress, indicating he was even more convinced that the California expansion was a winning idea for Coyote.

After lunch, Ramsay kicked across the dusty courtyard, upset by his cool reception thus far. He pushed opened the sticky door of the Sales Office to the sound of typing.

"Howdy! Y'all must be Mr. Ramsay. Now, how was your barbecue?" The typist swung around fast in her chair, exposing a sudden dose of shapely leg. Her smile was a white island floating in an ocean of torrid red.

"Well?" she said.

"Hmmm . . . the barbecue was great."

She shook her long amber hair and smacked her gum. Her accent dripped heavy Texan. She drawled her words precisely. "Well, how are you? Marcus Ramsay, right? I'm Daisy. Daisy Duncan."

"Nice to meet you, Ms. Duncan," he said.

"Oh, you can just call me Daisy." She smiled.

"Fine . . . Daisy." He looked back at the door, recalling his lunch. He shook his head.

"What's a matter, Marcus? You've known me less than a minute. I couldn't be all that bad," Daisy laughed, looking down at her legs. "You look like somethin's up."

"Well, I'm sensing you folks aren't crazy about having me around," he said.

"Nonsense! " Daisy said. "What makes y'all think that?"

"Well, I thought I was getting my own office." He pointed to Cecil puffing on an after lunch cigarette. "And at lunch, Earl said he wants me to run numbers for those broker-trade parties coming up. Not exactly how I pictured my first day."

Daisy wrinkled her perfectly plucked eyebrows. "Oh, Marcus. You'll be fine when you get the hang o' things."

"Gotta ignore ol' Earl," Cecil called.

"But I thought you guys would be willing to look at some new thinking," Ramsay said.

"Marcus, don't you worry your li'l' ol' head off," she said. "Besides, now you've found me." She threw back her hair. "I'm guessin' bein' from Chicago you might-could be a symbol of disruption to Earl is all."

"Might-could?" Marcus said.

Cecil laughed. From the back room, Al did, too.

"Oh, Marcus. That's just how we talk. Don't be such a damn foreigner!"

"Thanks for making me feel so welcome, Ms. Duncan," he said sarcastically.

"You're bein' a mite sensitive I'd say. Y'all just have to ease up a little."

Ramsay leaned forward, squinted analytically, and whispered, "You know, Daisy, you sure talk a lot faster than everyone else." She had a great mouth, too, her ruby lips accurately cradling every word as she chattered away. They looked velvety, and curved upward at each end, forming an automatic smile. Marcus caught himself staring at her mouth, forgetting his troubles, and not listen—

"You starin' at somethin', Mr. Ramsay?" Daisy asked and smiled.

"Oh yes, I mean, no. I'm sorry." He stood. "It's your mouth. I don't want to presume or anything, but I was noticing your lips and teeth. They're beautiful. I shoot photographic portraits as a hobby. So, I notice these things."

"Sure you do," Cecil laughed.

"Boy, that's a whole lotta Yankee bull," Daisy said.

"No, honest." Ramsay put up his hand in the Scout Sign and laughed as he looked back and forth at Daisy and Cecil. "Photography is my true love. I can show you my portfolio."

"Oh, nonsense," Daisy said, slightly blushing, "I'm complimented, and y'all don't need to apologize. But we might-oughta turn our attention to sellin' some damn chili." She smiled.

Ramsay stared back, for a few seconds unable to shake his gaze. It was then he knew he had an ally at Coyote. For an instant, he tried on a future where he and Daisy would become soul mates.

"You know what I'm sayin' ?" She winked at him, not in a flirtatious way, but in a deeply familiar way that surprised him.

At that second, despite their different cultural backgrounds, he found himself imagining a day when their hearts stirred for each other in some infinite way, like rustling leaves on a mature oak—never coming to rest, no matter how still the air.

Long after Daisy went home to her husband—"the bully," "Roy Rogers," and "the asshole" were three of her descriptors—and their outspoken, four-year-old daughter, Shannon, Ramsay repositioned himself in the darkened front office, sitting in front of the new computer terminal.

He had skipped the Holiday Inn's meat loaf dinner. Instead, he lugged Cecil's old, red sales history binders and the "Deal Expense" book to the front office. There, through Coyote's remote IBM terminal and the phone line, he planned to log Coyote's history directly into Puritan's mainframe computer up in Chicago. Then he could use *Statpure,* Puritan's system for interactive statistical analysis, to automate his number crunching to prepare for the trade parties and, at the same time, analyze past sales to cultivate a new strategy for Coyote.

He sipped a Coke and puffed borrowed Marlboros as he sat next to the desk where Mary Frampton had processed orders by hand for almost 35 years. Marcus contemplated the paradoxical location—he surveyed the red binders filled with hand-tabulated data that surrounded his computer terminal like toy soldiers. A suspended fixture of two, four-foot fluorescent bulbs glared down at him. He figured he would eventually be the Yankee spoiler of all that had been sacred to Coyote.

Here goes nothing!

After dialing the old rotary phone line to the Mercantile Mart and logging onto

Puritan's operating system for marketing databases, he entered one number at a time until his eyes grew heavy. With each entry, Marcus imagined he was building a new Coyote Brand. It would be such a mighty transformation! From an old-fashioned company steeped in tradition to a modern corporation fueled by discovery.

He laughed and admitted to himself his tendency toward self aggrandizement. Then he looked around at the rows of binders and thought about how unlikely it would be that he'd find anything exciting among the plethora of red.

Outside of the Coyote complex a taxi sat near the light cast by the lone security light. Reginald Waverly sat in the glow of his dashboard lights, talking into his CB. "Right, Waverly checking in. Our chap Ramsay is getting settled quite well. He's already putting in extra hours, trying to uncover something—little does he know! He'll be a good point man for us as my plan unfolds. The Post installment will soon begin to affect him. Ten-Four."

8

Corsicana, Texas   August 28, 1980

For the next two weeks Ramsay stayed late every night and got to work by seven each morning. He skipped the dinner specials and hearty breakfasts at the Holiday Inn.

He even gave up visits home to Chicago for the following two weekends. Kathy's interest in her own corporate career had suddenly blossomed. She seemed constantly busy, preparing for this meeting or that presentation. She didn't seem to miss him or need his counsel anymore and for that he felt empty and useless.

Their nightly calls, skipped with increasing regularity, were peppered with bickering about "Daddy" this and "Mother" that. He thought he heard her yawn at his joking reference to "this strange land they call Corsicana." Several times she sarcastically reminded him that working for Coyote Brand had been his career choice all along, never hers.

Meanwhile, having worked all day and evening, Marcus slumped into bed late each night, too tired to care if Henry the roach scurried through the dark. It quickly became a routine: during the day, he absorbed the idiosyncrasies of Corsicana culture as Cecil and Daisy taught him the basics of the chili business, and at night, he entered more sales and trade deal data into the computer as he listened to the songs of night birds and crickets outside the front office windows. Then, exhausted, he'd make an occasional call to Kathy.

Whenever Cecil was traveling among the company's network of brokers across the Southwest, from Phoenix to New Orleans, Marcus played the role of mentor for Daisy, trying to convince her it wasn't normal to accept the violence in her marriage to the man she cynically referred to as Roy Rogers, the "bruiser."

One day, when Cecil had flown up to Oklahoma City, Marcus and Daisy talked again. "But, he should never beat on you," Ramsay said and threw his pen down. "Up North that's just not acceptable."

"Oh, Marcus. It's just his way. Our way." She shrugged as she sat across from Ramsay at Cecil's desk. "'Sides, he's just lettin' out steam after a tough day."

"Fixing air conditioners?" Ramsay said. "Must really tie him in knots."

She folded her arms across her chest.

"Why don't you just leave him?" he asked. "For good. Find someone who'll respect you."

"Sounds so simple, don't it?" She laughed. "Shoot. Down here we have kids and stick it out. No way I'm leavin' Shannon's future up to some ol' judge."

"Well, you could keep her," he said. "The mother usually keeps the children."

"Well, maybe so. Maybe not." She hung her head. "Never can tell."

"Bet ol' Coy lays that logic on you, doesn't he?" he said, leaning forward, squinting. "That's called control."

She looked down. "What y'all mean? How do you know all this, anyway?"

"He has a real grip on you, Daisy," he said. "It's obvious."

"Never you mind." She looked away.

"Ah hah. That's how he does it. The man's playing with your mind?"

"More Yankee nonsense, I guess." She stood and walked to her desk. "High falutin' bull."

"Nope. I think I'm right on the money," he called.

She popped her head back into his office. "Just keep your Yankee nose to yourself."

"Excuse me for caring a little," Marcus said. "I'm just trying to help." For a second Ramsay thought back and realized that he was expounding the same holier-than-thou attitude his father used to. "Hey, Daisy, listen, I'm sorry if I'm upsetting you. I just get on my high horse once in a while."

She slowed her pace and sat back down at Cecil's desk. "No. Wait-wait-wait-wait. Just wait a second here." She half-laughed. "Are you sayin' that you really care?" She leaned across the desk and asked. " 'Bout me?"

"Well . . . of course." He fidgeted with some papers. "Sure."

"More Yankee bull, I guess—carin'," she said. "Stickin' your nose in is more like it."

"Daisy, I'd be cruel not to care."

"Wait." She sat straight. "You're just like the rest of them know-it-all Yankee bastards. You're sayin' how bad Corsicana is and promising there's a way out. Then, when push comes to shove, in a manner of speakin', y'all up and disappear and head back north. Ruth Ann says it always happens and she's my best friend, too. I seen the same thing happen around town."

He shook his head. "Daisy, that's more Coy jive, too, I bet. You've been watching too many movies," he said. " I swear you guys are stuck in the fifties here in Corsicana. It's almost a black and white world out there." He pointed out the window.

"What y'all mean, black and white?" she asked.

"T.V.?"

"Funny, funny. We all got color TV. Have for a while. And anyway, smarty, what about Kathy?" she asked.

Marcus looked away. "What about her?"

"Come on," she said. "Its your turn. Things ain't so great in the young professional marriage either, huh?"

"Could be better, I suppose," he said and fiddled with his ring. "Lotta stress now. All the moving."

Daisy said, "I'm sorry. I didn't mean to butt in, unlessin'— Say, what is it, Marcus?"

"Oh, nothing. Just nothing," he said.

"Really? Come on, what is it?" she said. "You can share it with ol' Daisy. I can tell there's somethin'."

Marcus looked down as he talked. "It's just that I'm down here in Texas helping you folks and she's up in Chicago, suddenly into her career. I feel like she doesn't need me anymore."

"What's wrong with that?" Daisy said. "Us women are independent nowadays."

"I don't know why she's suddenly acting like that."

"I bet you just like helping her out too, being the almighty king. That's it! Being the savior, like y'all act around here." She laughed. "I got you pegged!" She nodded as she patted her heart. "The warm and fuzzy fatherly type, that's why you're so concerned 'bout me, right?" she asked. "Helpin' me makes you feel good about yourself. Powerful maybe?"

"Maybe you're right. But she sure doesn't seem to care what the hell's going on with me either."

"Oh, Marcus. She's just excited about her own life, can'tcha see that?"

"I thought we were a team, though. I like being a team," he said.

"Little like my Coy, I guess. Guy stuff."

"I guess," he said. "How so Coy?"

"Oh, he's always going out with his buddy, Larry Calhoun, carousing and hunting over at Holler's Woods and that. Besides seein' me as his kid's mama, I'm just his cook and sex slave. Even made me do it with another man once."

"Sex?" he asked.

She nodded. "Whilst he was watching. Then, o' course, he joined in." She smiled shyly, but peeked at him with a little twinkle in her eye."

"My God! Daisy. You proud of that?"

"I guess not. Sorry," she said. She leaned forward and fiddled with his pen holder. 'A little rough for you Yankees, I guess."

"Let's not talk about our mates anymore," he said.

"Oh, what you want to talk about, then?" she said. "Us?"

"I didn't know there was an us," he said.

"Might-could," she said, and smiled her perfect ruby smile, fluttering her eyelashes.

"Don't tease me, Daisy," he said.

"What's a matter? Gettin' to you?"

He half-laughed. "I guess you are, a little." Ramsay looked around. "Yeah, I guess."

She laughed. "You might-could be part of my plan if y'all get off your high horse a little, show me what you got."

"You Corsicana she-devil, you," he teased back. "Let's not go pushing it."

She slashed at him like a tiger. "Grrr! Better let my nails get longer," she said.

"No, they look pretty good already," he said.

"Why, thank you, Mr. Ramsay," she said and preened. "Don't believe anyone told me that lately."

"There you go fluttering those lashes."

"Can't hep it," she said. "Help it." She laughed.

"Well, I can't hep it if you're getting to me—a little, say." He put some loose pens back in the pen holder.

"Boy, that's a whole lotta Yankee bull," Daisy said. "Shoot."

"No, really," he said as they exchanged a speculative look.

Lenora showed her concern for Ramsay whenever he went to the front office building to get coffee. "Y'all not lookin' too well, Marcus. Workin' too hard?" she always said.

After Ramsay left the office, Earl snapped at her under his breath, "Leave him be, Lenora."

"I'm just concerned, Mr. Hickman," she whispered. "He's lookin' worn out."

"Do as I say," he barked.

Every time Marcus passed Earl's office, his boss sat up straight and flashed his used car salesman smile. Meanwhile, Lenora kept typing away, trying to mind her own business.

On his second Wednesday, Marcus sat at his desk, unable to see Daisy. But he heard her adjusting the blinds of the window that faced the courtyard.

"Marcus. Lady Sheila's over there at the office," Daisy said.

"Who?" he asked.

"Earl's wife," she called. "Here for her Wednesday visit."

"So?" he said.

"Haven't you noticed how she parades around here like she's the big shot?"

"Not really."

"Wait!" Ramsay heard her slap the blinds closed. "She just walked out and she's lookin' over here," Daisy said in a loud whisper.

"Daisy, what are you doing?" he asked.

"That's weird. She's just standin' there starin' and fiddlin' with her fancy bracelet. She's wearin' a new pair of shoes, too. She gets a new pair every week, you know, then gets 'em dusty walkin' accrosst the grounds. It's like she's thinkin' 'bout whether she wants to visit us," she called.

"Daisy, you're making this into a soap opera," he said.

"Wait. Wait. She's walkin' over to her car!" she called. "But lookin' back here every once'st in a while—with a scowl, I guess."

"Must not like us," he said and laughed.

"Marcus." Ramsay heard Daisy leave the blinds slapping against the window. She appeared in the doorway of Ramsay's office with a queer look on her face. "If you'd watch her, you'd know what I mean. She's lookin' sorta spooky-like."

On his third Thursday morning at Coyote Brand, Marcus sat at his desk unshaven. He squinted at Cecil with tired eyes. Though he was dragging, he couldn't contain his excitement. "I'll finish tonight," he announced.

"Finish what?" Cecil's blunt responses had already become familiar. At first, the Texan had sounded like a gruff father. But then Cecil had warmed up when Marcus laughed at his south Texas guffaw or when the man peered comically over his little reading glasses. It also helped that Marcus always listened intently to Cecil's endless anecdotes about the grocery "bidness".

"What's 'bidness' anyway?" Marcus always asked.

"You know, bus-i-ness," Cecil said carefully.

"So, why do you call it 'bidness'?"

"Don't know. Just a short cut."

"I guess." Ramsay laughed. "So, do I have to say it that way, too?"

"Yep. We're gonna take the Yankee outa you yet," Cecil said.

Marcus continued his announcement. "I'm almost done putting Coyote's sales and deal data into the computer." He scratched his five o'clock shadow. "Then, at last we'll have a database all the way back to 1927."

"1927?" Cecil slurped his coffee. "To be honest, I don't give a tinker's dam about that blasted machine or the old days." He put his cup down.

"Hey, Cecil," Ramsay said.

"Yep?"

"On the surface I noticed that sales per capita—you know, per person—looks like it started a long-term decline back about the time I came down to visit, ten years ago, even a little before."

"Can't say nothin' about that," Cecil said.

"I guess I'll have the computer sort out the trends."

"Shoot, Earl'll just love that," Cecil laughed and sipped more coffee.

"Why wouldn't he?" he asked.

"Well, a decade ago was about the time he became president," Cecil said. "Yep, quite a ruckus, I remember. Then James died an' all."

"Well, like I said, I can confirm that timing once I put all the data in the computer."

Cecil waved his stubs and smiled. "You don't have to explain any more about that blasted machine, whiz kid. I'm sure it'll be just fine. Here, have a smoke."

Marcus laughed and waved it off. "You know, this could actually help you guys if we learn something we don't already know."

"I suppose." Cecil stared at the window above Marcus' head as he half-rose. "Say, isn't that a mighty hefty Blue Norther blowin' up out there?" Cecil pointed.

Ramsay looked out at the dark sky. "Wow. Blue what?"

The thunder boomed.

"Norther," he said. "A storm that scoots real fast from the North across the plains. No mountains and such to stop it. It gets mighty big by the time it gets here. Bet this one here's gonna be a real doozy."

"How can you tell?" Marcus asked.

"Oh, lots o' ways: wind, color, smell, darkness. Mostly you get a funny feelin'. Folks 'round here hate them Northers."

Later that day the storm had passed, settling the brown dust that coated the lot's patchy asphalt. The air smelled fresh like spring and replaced the heaviness of late summer. Looking out the west facing windows of the front office, Ramsay saw the orange sunset behind the flat roofs and crooked smoke stacks of the shanty five blocks down Main Street, home for most of the seventy-four black Coyote plant workers and their families.

He went to the IBM computer terminal in the front office. The rest of the lily-white office staff—and Ted, a Filipino and Earl's token man of color in the office—had gone home. In a few hours, via phone, Ramsay would finish entering Cecil's entire Coyote Sales History and the Deal Expense History into Puritan's massive mainframe computer in Chicago. He would then have a workable database to determine, among other things, whether the proposed California expansion idea made any sense at all; especially if the introduction was only supported by Earl's sacred billback trade deals.

With this database, Ramsay could also verify that chili sales per capita were actually slumping. If so, it would prove that pushing products Yankees would like, items other than chili, would be a good idea.

As remnant summer thunder rumbled through Navarro County, Ramsay lit up a Marlboro that he'd borrowed from Cecil, then sipped a Coke. He continued a set of repetitive movements as he entered the last of the data: Sipped his Coke, typed in the data, puffed on his cigarette, and checked off the entry in his notebook.

After two hours had passed, he sat back in his seat, threw his legs on the desk, and sighed a long sigh. "God, I'm famished!" The last of the numbers had been entered. He typed "Save" for the last time.

Marcus Ramsay clasped his hands behind his head. He knew Coyote Brand was about to enter a new era filled with computers, progress, and discovery. A chill ran up his spine as he toasted the celebratory moment with his Coke.

He put his feet down, took a deep breath, and typed a few lines to transfer to the programs that would analyze the data.

The machine flashed back the *StatPure* ID. A big, pale blue Allied logo appeared on the screen. Then Ramsay was prompted for his password. "Thunder," he typed. The name had come to him one lonely night at the Mart while he was preparing the Mama's Pizza presentation.

"Hello, you turkey!" popped on the screen. The personalized welcome had been added by Kevin Archer, the head of Puritan's Grocery Products Marketing Research. Kevin had been Ramsay's best man when he had married Kathy.

"You're the turkey." Ramsay smiled back. He missed the easy banter that he had shared with his old friends at the Mart.

With a few more keystrokes, the opening screen appeared for *StatPure:* "*Statpure* by the Allied Corporation: a system for interactive statistical analysis created by J. Blair, K. Archer, R. Krupa, C. Joseph, and G. Spitzer."

"Now , let's see," Marcus said, tapping his chin.

He puffed. He sipped.

Ramsay had never failed to expose a pattern if it hid in a particular set of data. Time and time again his colleagues brought him apparently random numbers. In each case, he reported back to them that there was this or that underlying trend. Usually they were stunned and happy after his analysis for, no matter how much of a surprise it might have been, they knew Ramsay would uncover the truth.

"Ah hah," he thought, stroking his lower lip. "Let's print out sales per capita first, a simple transformation of sales divided by the burgeoning Texas population. There we go!" He slapped the return key. The AUTOSTAT program chugged away.

Ramsay heard scratching at the window. *What was that?* He jumped up and almost knocked his chair over. He dropped his pen as he weaved through the old file cabinets and messy desks toward the rear office window. He scoured the infinite black, but saw nothing.

His heart thumped as he returned to the computer terminal. He looked back at the window, then sat. After a few more keystrokes and several more sips of Coke, a series of summary numbers flashed: "m = -14.5."

What's this? he thought. *A negative average trend since before the Allied purchase?* His hunches had been right. This was significant support for pushing other-than-chili products, particularly those that northerners might like since they were becoming a larger and larger proportion of the Texas population.

Next, Ramsay compared the Operating Income he had entered in the database from Al's records with Cecil's deal expense data on the billbacks.

A series of numbers flashed: "$r = -.92$" An almost perfect negative correlation? As billbacks went up, O.I. went down.

Then he looked at the screen: "$R^2 = .846$"

The R^2 statistic meant that a change in the billbacks was responsible for 84.6% of the change in operating income. It was pretty compelling evidence that the billbacks were the likely cause of Coyote's slumping bottom line.

Then Ramsay glanced back at the raw data on the screen. The billbacks had started coming on strong back in 1970, about the time Earl took over as president. He pulled up the results, market by market.

"Uh . . . " He heard a voice outside the window.

Ramsay looked around. He definitely heard a voice. It was a muffled human grunt outside, but nearby. He ran to the nearest window and peered out. He didn't see anything unusual.

He looked out another window. Still nothing. Ramsay was getting concerned about the odd sounds. What could they be? Maybe they were from raccoons that lived in the patch of woods next to Main Street, near the tracks. He returned to the terminal, convinced he had deduced the explanation for the groaning. He settled back into his analysis.

He noticed then that, given its population, the Dallas market had a disproportionately high amount of the billback money paid to its broker, Frank Benedict, for distribution to trade accounts.

That's odd. By midnight, Ramsay's head drooped. The decline in per capita sales was irrefutable. The market skew of the billback payments toward Dallas was strange. *What does it mean?*

Marcus Ramsay decided to pack up his paperwork and head for the Holiday Inn. He turned off the air conditioner, walked out the front door, and locked it behind him. He walked across the gravel toward his car.

"Uh . . ."

That's definitely a man's voice. He turned around and looked toward the sound. A man was crawling on the ground under the front office window, close to the wall. It was the sound Ramsay had been hearing. It was no wonder he had been unable to see the source of the sounds. Marcus rushed to him.

The disoriented man, probably in his forties, smelled drunk and was nearly unconscious. When Marcus rolled him over, his eyes widened. The man's face was scarred and his mouth twisted. He stuttered at Marcus incoherently.

Ramsay cradled the man. "Easy does it, buddy," he said.

The man stammered, unable to get a clear word out. He wore unkempt, oil-stained clothes.

"Sir, I can't understand you," Ramsay said. "Just relax."

The man grabbed Ramsay's shirt at the chest, lifted himself up, and mumbled more.

"Just relax. Lie down. I'll get help." His heart pounding, Ramsay lowered the man to the ground and rushed inside the office. He dialed the emergency number that he found inside the front cover of the phone book.

Minutes later a blinking red light sped toward the Coyote compound. It bounced across the nearby railroad tracks. Ramsay cradled the smelly, stuttering man in the purple glow of the security light as the ambulance pulled through the chain link gate. "Just relax, sir," Ramsay said to the man. "Help is here."

"I ch-checked the brakes for him!" the man blabbered.

"Who?" Ramsay said.

"Post!" Then he passed out in Ramsay's arms.

"Post?"

The ambulance slid to a stop in the granite and a young paramedic hopped out. "It's just Grady Davis," he said.

"Will he be OK?" Ramsay said. "Smells awful."

"Been tyin' one on again," one paramedic said to the other, "This is the worst I seen him. Always looks like he's seen a damn ghost."

The two paramedics loaded the man into the ambulance as the other prepared to check his blood pressure. Then one of them passed a clipboard to Ramsay. "Sign here, sir," he said.

"Thanks for coming so fast," Ramsay said.

"Anytime. Thanks for callin'." The blinking red light flashed in Ramsay's face as the ambulance sped away.

Back in his room at the Holiday Inn, Ramsay undressed, pondering all he saw that night: the drunk, twisted man; the sales per capita decline; and the increase in billbacks coming primarily from the Dallas market that coincided with a decrease in profits.

He thought it was too late to call Kathy. She would probably only remind him of his list of things to do: buy new appliances, call the realtor, find a local map, and get the real estate paperwork they'd need for taxes. She seemed to enjoy playing the role of big corporate guru, the way she ordered him around. Then they'd probably have a fight about some stupid thing. Or she'd talk about what Daddy thought was best for his career. Or she'd lay out one of her own diatribes about his crooked path to the upper echelon of corporate America.

Ramsay felt empty and frustrated. *Maybe I'll finally stop smoking tomorrow,* he thought.

After Marcus pondered his computer discoveries and recalled the stuttering

drunk outside the Coyote office window,
he dozed off sitting up.

9

Corsicana, Texas   August 28, 1980

The next day Ramsay awoke with a jolt, rubbing his stiff neck. Beams of early morning light shot through tiny holes in the plastic curtains and filled his spartan room. Minutes later he sang "On the Road Again" as he showered. After his shower, he had no trouble resisting the temptation to puff on a pre-breakfast cigarette. Instead, the excitement of reporting his discoveries propelled him through a cup of tea and an English muffin with orange marmalade. He pulled into the Coyote Brand compound even before Lenora made the lunches for her kids. He made the first pot of strong coffee before Daisy finished brushing her hair twenty times in the Duncans' double-wide trailer. He sat at his desk, sipping coffee, before Cecil passed Ennis heading south on I-45.

When the old Texan walked into the Sales Office, Marcus jabbered about his statistical findings: "Cecil, it looks like operating income started declining—"

"Whoa!" Cecil held up his hands and laughed. "Bottom line down? Since when?"

"Look at these printouts," Marcus said. "They show when it started. About ten years ago."

"Lemme see." Cecil studied the papers. "1969? It looks like the same time Earl started, all right. We started doing all those damnable billbacks."

"Look here. For several years before that, chili tonnage per capita was heading down, too," Ramsay said and displayed another computer page. "About the time the Northerners started migrating to Texas in a big way. To this day it's still declining."

Cecil held his hand up. "But Marcus, we have the best darn chili there is," Cecil said. "Everybody knows that."

"Maybe we do," Marcus said, "but our consuming public is obviously changing. A lot of it is northern folks."

At eight-thirty, Daisy appeared at the door. "Well," she teased. "Don't you boys say good mornin'?"

Marcus rose. "Later, Daisy. Gotta see Earl. Remind me to tell you about the drunk guy last night," he said as he dashed past her and yanked open the sticky door.

Cecil started his own analysis the minute the Sales Office door closed: "Marcus has some fancy notion that profit started headin' down years ago on account of the billbacks, and chili sales per person is slumping 'cause of the Yankees. If y'all ask me, we don't need that kind of help around here. Earl's right. That blasted machine is more trouble—"

"Now, hush, Cecil Evans," Daisy called from her desk. "We might-could use some truth-telling around here instead of all the dreaming. Dreams don't sell chili."

"But Earl's not gonna like it one iota," Cecil said and went back to his record keeping.

Minutes later Marcus returned from Earl's office. He sat down at his desk.

Daisy got up and ran into his office. "Well?"

Marcus was looking through his printouts. He looked up. "Earl's getting an award this morning at some Rotary function with his wife."

"He's doin' more of that these days," Cecil said. "Miss Sheila sure does push him to play the Corsicana big shot bit."

"The way she marches around here on Wednesdays," Daisy said. "Like she owns the damn place."

Ramsay stacked all his papers together. "What's the big deal? Aren't those speeches part of Earl's job?" he asked. "Community involvement?"

"More 'n Margaret ever pushed James, I'll tell you," Cecil said seriously. "And James use to figger it was his duty, too. Margaret didn't have to push him."

"Boy, you guys are really enamored with this Post guy," Ramsay said. "Like he was some god or something."

Cecil looked over the top of his glasses. "So? What of it?"

"Never met the man personally." Daisy appeared behind Cecil, arms tightly crossed. "But folks around town loved him like a father."

Ramsay held his hands up. "Hey, I'm sorry if I offended you all."

Daisy spit out a laugh. "Marcus, I do believe that is the first time y'all ever said y'all," she said. "Or at least a wimpy Yankee version of it."

"Well," Cecil chuckled, "it's a start."

Daisy said, "I do believe we're makin' progress with Marcus, even if Earl isn't takin' so kindly to him."

"I guess," Cecil said and smiled, "even with all this computer mumbo jumbo, James would probably approve of Marcus."

"Think so?" Marcus said. "Thanks, Cecil. That means a lot."

"But I'll tell you, James'd hate Earl giving all these fancy shmancy speeches and gettin' all these blasted awards. That is, if Mr. Post could see all this malarkey."

Just then Ramsay stood, grabbed his gut, and buckled over in pain. "Shit!"

"What is it?" Daisy asked.

"My stomach! It's really been bugging me lately."

"Should I call Doc Hopkins?" Daisy asked.

Hours later a new voice called out from Daisy's desk. "So, where is he, Daisy? I want to take him to lunch." The nasal voice spoke in a strong Hispanic accent.

Seconds later, the voice appeared. A dark man in his early forties peeked into

Marcus' and Cecil's office. He had a twinkling smile and a small self-conscious wave. "Remember me, Mr. Ramsay? Oscar Sanchez. Plant Manager?"

"Colombia," Oscar said to Ramsay as they munched on onion rings during their barbecue lunch at Hobert's. "Then, after living in the U.S. for several years, I begin to work here at Coyote. I want to run a big Allied cereal plant up north some day."

"Think you will?" Ramsay asked.

"Don't know. They made me a lot of promises. It all depends on who I get to know, I guess." Oscar winked at Marcus. "May I ask for your help, sir?"

"Just call me Marcus, Oscar. But don't expect too much help from me," Marcus said.

"But I been waitin' for help from someone. Never comes through."

"Oscar, I'm really not the right contact for you. You should make yourself a known quantity up in Chicago."

"I thought I was doing that." Oscar winked again.

"Not really, I'm not in Operations and I'm not at the Mart anymore." Ramsay shrugged.

"Aw, you're just like all them other Yankee liars," Oscar said.

"What do you mean?" Marcus asked.

"Nothin'. Just nothin'." Oscar said and sipped his barley soup.

"Oscar, I'm sorry, but it's true. Can't we talk about something else?"

"Like what." Oscar pouted and crunched his crackers, spewing them on the table. "Shoot."

"I know. Tell me about Mrs. Hickman and all this hospital stuff I keep hearing about," Ramsay said.

"What about it?" He swept all of the crumbs into a pile, then onto the floor.

"What's the deal with her?" Marcus asked.

"Well, lemme see. Years ago, the day after she threw a party for Earl gettin' president, she went crazy. Nobody could figger why. She was under a lot of pressure, I guess."

"Pressure?"

"Lotta things happening back then: Miss Erlene's rape, Mr. Post's accident, and Earl gettin' promoted."

"Wow," Ramsay said. "I didn't know the Hickman's daughter was raped, or that it happened around the same time that James Post died."

"Yep. Sheila was on the bottle, too. She went into Navarro Medical's de-tox, then to the loony bin over there."

"Seriously?"

"Oh, yeah." Oscar nodded. "For months at first. Gettin' off the booze, gettin' shocked. She's been back lots of times since, too."

"For shock treatments?" Ramsay asked.

"Yep. She has a real patchy memory. Everybody laughs about the blank spots. We're always introducin' ourselves to her, over and over to tease her. She hates it."

"That's too bad. What a mess." Marcus shook his head. "And all that stuff hit her at once, huh?"

"Yep. Earl don't never want to talk about it. He gets weird when she goes over to Navarro. Writing all these memos, orderin' everybody around—nervous-like."

"Must be the Napoleon bit they talked about up at the Mart."

"Huh?" Oscar flashed a confused look. "Might-could be."

"Or," Ramsay said, "maybe he's just upset whenever Shcila's in the hospital?"

"It's more like he don't have her to coach him," Oscar snickered in a whisper, looking around the room. "So, he gets all bossy. Kinda lost. When Sheila's around, she helps him by playing the big shot."

"Really?" Marcus asked.

"He closes his door when she calls him every afternoon. You can never get to see him for an hour."

"Well, that's normal, calling your wife."

"For so long?" Oscar said. "And there's more."

"Like what?"

Oscar looked both ways and lowered his voice again. "Earl always treats the Chicago brass like they're kings while they're here, then he laughs at 'em when they leave," Oscar said and snickered. "Like he's playin' with 'em, provin' how stupid they are and how smart he is.

"Really?" Marcus said.

"Yep. Impresses all the other Coyote folks, that's for sure. You just watch. He's always playing big shot 'round here."

"I'm sure it's not as bad as you say," Ramsay said.

"Maybe it's worse." Oscar shrugged. "Marcus, maybe you can help me get out of this crazy place."

Ramsay shook his head. "Like I said, Oscar; I really don't think I'm the right contact for you."

"Well, you are from Chicago, right? The Mart? Like Burghoff, Childress, and them?"

"Oscar, there're 2,500 folks up there," Ramsay said. "The best folks to help you with your career are still up there. But, I can get some names for you."

"Sure!" Oscar suddenly slammed down his glass, splashing iced tea on the table. "Thanks, cowboy!" He stood up. "We gotta get back."

"But—"

"Earl's expecting us for the meeting." Oscar threw down a few crumpled dollar bills.

"What meeting?" Marcus asked, stood, and quickly wiped his mouth with his napkin.

"On California," he said. "Or, maybe you weren't invited."

In the all-white Quality Assurance lab at Coyote Brand, a short, freckle-faced man in a lab coat approached Ramsay and extended his hand. "Howdy. Harold Hudson," he said in an unfamiliar twang.

Ramsay offered his hand. "Harold. Hi. Say, you don't sound like you're from around here."

"Good ears! Actually, it's Alabama." He reached in his lab jacket and presented his business card to Ramsay.

"Lenora told me."

Ramsay saw other new faces in the sparkling lab. Earl spoke in a low, breathy tone to a large man in the corner. A pudgy-looking young man wearing a white lab coat stood in the opposite corner. Al Bishop mumbled to his assistant Ted Calivarpio, who had a friendly, round Asian face. Oscar leaned against the back wall by himself, picking at his fingers. The entire Coyote management team was in attendance.

Ramsay walked over to the boss. "Earl, what's this meeting about?"

Earl turned, eyebrows raised in surprise. "Oh, Marcus. Found the place, huh?" Earl said over the rumble of conversation.

"Well, actually I'm a little confused," Ramsay said. "You forgot to invite me."

Earl flushed. "Daisy must've left it off your schedule." Small beads of sweat appeared under his nose.

"I guess," Ramsay said. "With all the meetings we have—"

"Now you can meet Frank Benedict, our Dallas broker." Earl pointed to the large man who had been talking to him.

"Hi Frank. I've heard a lot about you." Marcus shook the man's large hand.

"Shit!" Frank bellowed. "So you're the guy that was down here way back, huh?" His eyes floated out of sync with one another.

Ramsay looked at them curiously.

"Oh, the eye?" Frank said. "Got me a glass one. Football injury. I missed my assigned tackle. Shucks." He bellowed.

The folks in the room laughed.

Marcus looked directly at Earl, then Frank. "So, Frank. Why are you at a meeting about California if you're our Dallas broker?"

"He's a sharp one, Earl," Frank said and turned to Marcus. "I just bought a share of the California Brokerage Company to sell Coyote out there. Guess the big keep gettin' bigger. Right, boss?" he said to Earl. Frank and Earl laughed at the apparent inside joke.

"Great, Frank," Marcus said. "I hope you have some other accounts out there.

You may not have Coyote. I have some issues on the expansion."

"Issues?" Frank said. "You just got here. How could you possibly have any issues?" He turned to Earl. "Well, Boss?"

Earl jumped in, as if on command. "Let's get this meeting going now that we're all here. Now, y'all've met Marcus Ramsay, our brand new marketing manager, green as can be, and Frank Benedict, our longtime Dallas Broker— sells seventy percent of our bidness. We're here to talk about California."

Bidness. That annoying colloquialism again. Ramsay sighed as Earl reviewed the same points he had talked about at the barbecue lunch meeting.

"And now that we have a broker in place, we should be able to get on with the expansion," Earl said. He smiled and posed, hands outstretched, almost as if he expected applause.

Ramsay raised his index finger skyward. "Excuse me, Earl, but having Frank broker us out there won't necessarily guarantee our success. Sorry, Frank."

"What is it now, Marcus?" Earl asked, his eyes turned skyward.

"Well, I've gone through the data, all the way back to the twenties," Marcus said, "and I've found several underlying problems over the years."

"Problems? Like what?" Earl said and laughed. "We're selling more every year. True?"

"True. But we're not keeping up with the growth of the Texas population. It looks like we began a long-term decline in sales per capita about a decade ago. And O. I.'s sliding, too. But you're probably aware of the effect of the billbacks."

They mumbled louder. Al and Ted nodded and looked at the floor.

"The decline in per capita sales started not long after James Post's death," Marcus said.

"Wait a second. You trying to say something here?" Earl asked, crossing his arms in front of his chest, crumpling his sport jacket.

"Well, the data showed—" Marcus said.

"Say, wait, that's how long I've been here," Earl said and looked around the room.

"What Mr. Hickman's trying to say, Marcus," Harold Hudson said, "is that he's really improved Coyote's relationship with the brokers over the years. Those trade deals have become a regular thing now. They just love the billbacks. Right, Frank?"

Frank nodded. Earl nodded. They all nodded except Al. "You can have 'em," he said and swiped his hand at the air.

"We're certainly not selling as fast as Texas is growing." Marcus said. "You hear on the news about how Texas is growing by leaps and bounds every day, right?"

There was silence.

"We're not keeping up," Marcus said.

Earl cleared his throat. "So?"

Frank followed. "So?"

Harold said, "So, what's your point, Marcus?"

Ramsay inhaled. "Well, we can advertise chili, but we also need to push other items to please the northerners who are moving down," Marcus said.

"Humph," Earl said.

"And, those billback trade deals are killing our bottom line, too. We have to end our dependence on them."

Earl laughed. "Right," he said cynically. "You're for that one, aren't you, Frank?"

"No way," he said.

"We've been doing the same thing for years," Earl said to Ramsay. "Since I've been here, at least."

They all nodded and looked at Ramsay.

"Exactly my point," Ramsay said. "You've been doing the same darn thing and it's killing your O. I."

Several eyebrows were raised as the staff gawked at Earl.

"Yet, you want to expand?" Ramsay said. "Make the same mistakes on a grander scale?"

"So?" Earl said.

"That's risky. Eventually you're bound to lose money. Lots of money. California's huge."

They hushed.

"Shoot," Frank said. "California's like solid gold, huh Earl? Don't sound like it to me." He yanked open the lab door and stormed out, grumbling.

Earl turned to Marcus. "Well. From your display here today, I assume you've finished running those numbers for the Dallas Trade Party," Earl said and glanced at the door. "Coming up in the spring, you know. Got to get the information on slides an' all."

"But, Ear—" Ramsay said.

"I can handle California from here," he said and lit up a Marlboro.

Just then pain shot through Ramsay's stomach. He buckled over. "Man, that hurts."

"Say, are you all right?" Earl asked.

Ramsay nodded. "Yeah, I think there's something wrong with my stomach." He righted himself. "Daisy made me an appointment with Doc Hopkins. Might be the water."

"In the meantime, if you can, you better drop this California thing and get to work on those numbers for the Party, son," Earl said. He tossed a haughty grin around the room. "Stop using that machine to cause problems and solve a few."

Some of the group smiled at Ramsay.

"Oh, by the way Marcus, thanks for your ideas," Earl said. "Real enlightening."

"Right. Sure. Dammit!" Marcus held his gut and suppressed more jabbing pains.

Meanwhile, the plant's break whistle blew as a pretty, young blonde woman

walked across the courtyard to the main
office. Daisy sat at Lenora's desk,
covering for her while she was at organ
rehearsal. The door opened.

Daisy looked up. "Welcome to
Coyote, I'm Daisy," she said. Then she
squinted.

The blonde giggled and put her hand
to her mouth.

"Wait. Are you Erlene?" Daisy said.
"Earl's girl?"

The blonde nodded. "And, you must
be the Daisy Daddy always talks about,"
Erlene purred.

A lilac fragrance drifted across the
receptionist's desk. "I sure heard of you,
Miss Erlene, but I don't think I ever met
you," Daisy said to the Scandinavian-
looking girl.

Erlene giggled.

"I've been here for months, but I just
see your mama on her Wednesday strolls.
Where you been hidin'?" Daisy asked.

Erlene is beautiful, Daisy thought. Her
blonde hair flowed straight down to a
blunt cut across the shoulders. Her old
fashioned, hand-tailored clothes fit her
willowy figure perfectly. Her skin glowed
through very little makeup. Long, curly
lashes framed dark brown, almond-

shaped eyes that popped out of her milky white complexion.

"I'm picking Mr. Hickman up today is all," Erlene said shyly.

"I heard you were cute," Daisy said, "Ever do any modeling, child?"

"No, sir." Erlene covered her mouth with her hands. "I just go to junior college over at Navarro. Takin' all the basics. And, I read a lot, too."

"No fellas?" Daisy said. "Bet there's a lotta nice fellas over at the college."

Erlene looked at the floor.

"What'd I say? Well, you oughta start coming around, hear?" Daisy laughed. "Maybe even get out and meet yourself some nice boys."

Erlene looked away. "I help Mama a lot, too."

"Mama?"

"Yep. She hates it when I call her that."

They laughed.

"She likes to be called Mother," Erlene said.

"Who, Miss Sheila? Well, I do declare." Daisy prissed and tossed her hand.

They laughed.

"When Mama first got sick after her comin' out party way back—I bet you heard the stories—and she started goin' to Navarro Med Center, Dad and Miss Kelly needed me to help with little Bryan," Erlene said.

"I guess they did," Daisy snickered. "But, he's a big boy now, idn't he?"

"Yes, ma'am. Whenever Mama's not at Navarro, I go with her to church, chili cookoffs, the Rotary, and when Daddy's gettin' some award."

"I'm sure," Daisy said. "Say, maybe we should go shopping some time over at the Hollywood Shop. Get y'all some nice, grown-up clothes. Would you like that?"

Erlene toyed bashfully with the Peter Pan Collar on her dress. She looked up. "Mama's at the club today. So, she sent me to pick up Daddy. I mean Mr. Hickman."

"Why do you call your dad Mr. Hickman?"

"Daddy at home, Mr. Hickman here— Mama's idea."

" 'Course." Daisy saluted.

They giggled together as Erlene glanced outside at the sound of flying gravel.

"That there's Mr. Frank Benedict." Daisy motioned with her head toward the courtyard. "You heard o' him, I guess."

" I met him awhile back. Mama and Daddy think he's a nice man." Erlene glanced out the front door. "Doesn't look like he's changed much."

"Still got that 450 SL with those Longhorn covers," Daisy said. "Looks like he left the meeting in a huff. He's real rich, girl. Divorced for years, if you're interested."

"Hmm . . . ." Erlene shrugged and blushed.

They giggled.

"You look a little interested, girl. He's a might older'n all those good ol' boys around town, idn't he?" Daisy said.

Erlene stopped her giggling abruptly.

"What is it, girl? What did I say? What's wrong with the ol' boys?"

"Nothing. Just nothing," Erlene said in a monotone.

"Listen, honey," Daisy said, "why don't we go out and crash the Men's Club tonight."

"Men's Club?"

"You know, they used to call it The Men's Club. Now it's Scotty's. Open to us girls. I'll call Roy."

"Your husband's Roy?" Erlene said.

Daisy nodded. "No honey, I just call him Roy Rogers. He hates it." Daisy smiled. "He can pick up little Shannon from tap class."

"Is Shannon your child?" Erlene said.

"Yes, she's my sweety. Four going on fourteen."

They laughed.

"She just loves the dancin'," Daisy said. "You should see her."

Just then Earl pushed open the front office door, back from his meeting. His face was flushed. "Humph. Oh, you two meet up finally?" he asked and darted looks at each girl.

"Daddy, can I go out with Daisy tonight? Over to Scotty's?"

"Well, I guess I could get a lift from Harold," Earl said. "You should get out more these days, anyway." He looked at his watch.

"You OK, Daddy? You look upset," Erlene said. "You feelin' OK?

"Oh, yeah. Nothin' to worry about. Just a tough meeting up there. Two drink limit, hear?" he said. "Daisy, keep an eye on her." Then he walked briskly into his office and slammed the door.

"Ooo." Erlene shook her hand like it was wet.

"Yes sir, Mr. Hickman." Daisy saluted. "Yes, sir."

10 *Corsicana, Texas   August 28, 1980*

Daisy and Erlene giggled as they entered Scotty's, Corsicana's only real night club—formerly the Corsicana Men's Club—now its sole bastion of female liberation. A handful of women, mid-thirties and up, were sprinkled throughout the large, dimly lit center serving area. The old juke box played Hank Williams, Jr. The stench of cigarette smoke filled the room.

The only other patrons besides the women were a few small groups of grumbling men and grown up good ol' boys hunched over drinks. All were older than Erlene and Daisy, who were carded by a perky waitress with a blonde, pixy haircut. Her name tag said Vicki. She took the girls' order with a bright smile, then walked away.

"Jeez, happy, huh?" Daisy said. "So, Erlene, why haven't we met till now?" Daisy asked. "You been hid away for months."

"Actually years." She giggled. "Started with Mama's illness. Back then I was helping Miss Kelly with my little brother, mostly. That is, till he got real big."

"Sad about his accident," Daisy said.

"Yeah." Brian Hickman had been Corsicana High's star quarterback until an accident on the field permanently disabled his right arm.

Vicki returned with their drinks. "Run a tab, honey?"

"Be fine," Daisy drawled. "So, Erlene, everybody's heard about your mama."

Erlene fiddled with her straw.

"But what about your life? You must've been around I guess," Daisy said, sipping on her peach Daiquiri.

"Born in Annapolis, moved to Chicago, then Corsicana. What about you?" Erlene asked.

"Corsicana, upstate New York, Pennsylvania, LA, then came back to big C. My daddy followed the drilling equipment business. Then four years ago I had to get married," Daisy said.

"Had to?" Erlene said.

"Long story," Daisy said and sipped her drink.

"Tell me about him."

"Roy Rogers? Oh, he met me and right away pestered me about gettin' married. Talked about how he was planning on getting a double-wide mobile home on five acres off I-45, near Holler's Woods. Finally one night whilst we line danced at the Cat's Meow, I cuddled him a little. That was it."

"That fast?"

"Yep. We ended up doing it that night," she said.

"You don't have to tell me all the details." Erlene sipped.

"That's OK. It was wild. Out in his truck. Before you knew it, little Shannon was a-coming. I love her like the dickens."

"Must be nice, having a child," Erlene drawled.

"His mama didn't even come to the damn wedding, if you can believe it. Never met the lady to this day. It's like she disowned him. Strangest family, those Duncans."

"That's weird," Erlene said.

"She lives with a plumber up in some old house in Ennis. It was almost hit dead-on when the Perris twister came through. The Lord was watchin' out for them, that's for sure."

A CONSEQUENCE OF GREED

"Still, that's scary."

"Been a bad life for my honey, lousy family and such. Mine's pretty screwed up, too."

"I just couldn't imagine having a family all messed up like that. Us Hickmans are pretty together. Havin' trouble must go along with bein' underprivileged or somethin', huh?"

"Underprivileged? You callin' me underpriviledged?" Daisy suddenly sat up straight and squeaked her chair back. "Why underprivileged? Miss prissy president's daughter? Ain't you got any skeletons lying in your closet?" Daisy suddenly barked at the girl.

Erlene turned stone quiet, then blushed.

Heads turned.

Daisy caught herself. "Shoot." She covered her mouth. "God, I am so sorry, Erlene. There I go, shooting my foul mouth off again. Every oncest in a while—"

Erlene bowed her head, hiding from a few spectators' glances. Then tears started to drip onto the table in front of her.

"Oh, honey," Daisy said and leaned forward. "I am so sorry. I just get crazy sometimes. Comes from livin' with that crazy bastard o' mine. I didn't mean that prissy bit."

"Tough cuss, your husband?" Erlene sniffled.

"Oh, yeah."

Erlene wiped her tears with a napkin. "I can get pretty weird sometimes, too."

"Boy, I might-coulda rattled one of your skeletons, I guess," Daisy said. "Can you forgive me for losin' it?"

"Yep, but—" Erlene looked trapped. She looked around anxiously, unable to speak.

"What is it?" Daisy asked, patting her shoulder. "Girl, listen. You can tell your old friend Daisy. Honest. You need to talk somethin' out? Least I could do is listen after being such a damn bitch."

Erlene forced a laugh. "No, it's nothing. Really."

"You're safe with me, child. Honest." Daisy raised a hand. "Not a word'll leave this table, not even to Ruth Ann—she's my bestest friend—and I promise not to get crazy on you ever again. Tell me 'bout your skeletons."

"Well . . . " Erlene struggled to talk. "Me and this cowboy met whilst we was dancing at some bar I shouldn't have been."

"A cowboy, huh?" Daisy stroked Erlene's hair nonchalantly. "That's OK, honey. Just take your time."

Erlene adjusted herself in her chair. "It happened when I was almost fourteen." She sighed deeply, held her chest. "Seems like yesterday."

"Oh sugar. Fourteen? My word," Daisy said, remembering her own exploits as a young teen.

Then Erlene began to rehash the circumstances of her first sexual experience—a rape. As she talked, she slobbered her words and sighed deeply between each sentence. With the help of two more rounds of Daiquiris, she was sharing everything she remembered about being overpowered by an older man when she was a teenager.

"Go ahead, baby. Spill it," Daisy said.

Erlene trembled. "Well, then . . . he just did it."

"Oh, my dear!" Daisy said.

"He rammed at me, damn him, hooting and hollering. Then he just finished and laughed."

"Men can be such pigs," Daisy said as she reached out to touch Erlene's hand.

"He said it was gonna feel good."

"Damn him."

"Liar. I bled all over," Erlene said and wiped her nose. Then he walked away and left me outside, back of the bar, lying there in wet leaves. I'll never forget the smell of them leaves." Erlene whimpered into Daisy's shoulder, embarrassed.

"It's all right, sugar."

"Oh, I'm sorry, Daisy. I feel so stupid. You probably think I'm some kinda slut."

"There, there . . . that bastard," Daisy said through clenched teeth. "They ever catch the monster?"

"No. I shut out his name over the years. Some good ol' boy name, I think."

"Boy," Daisy said. "that narrows it down. Lotta bastards like that around town, huh?"

Erlene sniffled and pulled strands of hair out of her eyes.

"Say, maybe you should hang out with that big, cuddly brute, Frank Benedict. That'd be safe," Daisy said.

That encouraged a tentative laugh from Erlene.

"You been thinking of that?" Daisy asked.

"Oh, Daisy. If I could just see that cowboy . . . " Erlene said. "From a distance. That sure would help things, you know? Help me let it go."

"Or maybe just flare it up all over. The bastard's probably married now and raping his wife every night. Why can't men be gentle for a change?" Daisy said. She stared blankly for a minute, thinking of her marriage.

Erlene grabbed her hand. "Oh, Daisy. What is it?"

"Oh, it's OK, sugar." She picked at her cuticles. "Say, how's your mama, anyway? Been back to the hospital lately?"

"Yep. Went in not too long ago," Erlene said.

"She seems OK when she comes by the compound wearing those frilly dresses and fancy shoes on Wednesdays. Lotta different shoes, I guess. And all that jewelry."

"Mama went seriously crazy one night years ago," Erlene said. "Day after I told her I was pregnant—that's when they committed her the first time."

"Oh, shit, Erlene. You got pregnant from the rape?" Daisy asked.

"Yep." Erlene nodded.

"Shoot." Daisy said. "Abortion?"

Erlene nodded again. "Since my abor . . . tion, Mama's been going to Navarro to get shocked. And I can't ever have any babies."

"Oh, Erlene. I'm so sorry." Daisy pulled Erlene close to her.

"Now I'm going to the junior college to get my grades up. Mama wants to send me to one of those fancy colleges back East. When I'm not at school, I just stay to myself a lot. And Bryan's in high school, but you know that."

"Yep. Thanks to the sports page of the Sun. He sure is a handsome fella."

"And Daddy's always at work," Erlene said.

"Your mama meet Mr. Ramsay yet?"

"Nope. She gets weird when Daddy talks about him, though. Yankee wise-ass is what they call him at home. But, don't tell nobody."

"I promise. You know, he's real smart. Cute, too," Daisy said. "Gonna change Coyote, I bet. The man works incredible hours. Never sleeps."

"Maybe that's why mama and daddy say he's taking over," Erlene said.

"S'pose, but you know, the man can't be all bad with a hiney like that," Daisy said.

Both women giggled.

"Maybe that's a Yankee hiney!" Daisy said.

They laughed again.

Daisy continued: "Cecil even likes the man. And Cecil never likes anybody. I think it's 'cause Marcus went to James Post's funeral way back. Cecil says Margaret Post ought to meet him some day, he's so much like Mr. Post."

"I heard she's dying. Some kinda cancer?" Erlene said.

"Yep."

"Supposedly stopped, then came back?" Erlene asked.

"I might oughta give her a call," Daisy said, finger on lip.

"Mama acts like she's gonna lose her membership at the club just because of Mr. Ramsay."

"Naw. Marcus is more out to save the day. Like he's on some kinda mission," Daisy said.

"I don't get it, then. What's the big deal?" Erlene sipped on her empty drink.

"Don't ask me. Only thing strange is how hard he works tryin' to change things. Must be because he's a Yankee."

"Mama hates Yankees. She hates everybody. Her and daddy are real prejudice, but don't say anything. Daddy even goes to the meetings oncest in a while."

"The Klan meetings?" Daisy asked. "Ooowee. Roy Rogers and his buddy Larry Calhoun go, too."

"Your husband and the sheriff?"

"Yep." Daisy shook her head.

Erlene nodded. "When Daddy goes, he doesn't wear sheets or nothin', but it's real secret. Mama says he meets with the Klavern council once and a while because he's so important in town."

"What's wrong with this town?" Daisy said. "Can't they get past the damn Civil War? They're even having the regional klavern rally right here in town. This year."

"No kidding?" Erlene asked.

"But, I never knew about ol' Earl." Daisy said.

"You won't say nothin', will you, Daisy?"

Daisy patted her shoulder. "Shoot, no. Don't want to have 'em go whoop my butt, and they would, too."

"Then there's Mama's drinking," Erlene said, crossing her arms and shaking her head. "Think she'd learn; been through de-tox and everything."

"Heard o' that."

"Yep," Erlene said. "She even drinks with her medicine."

"No kidding," Daisy said. "That can't be good."

"Daddy hates it, but she keeps doin' it."

The new confidants talked until two o'clock in the morning. When the bar closed, they hugged like old friends.

"Daisy, you helped me open a door that's been closed a long while, no thanks to my crazy folks," Erlene said.

"You're such a sweety. A breath o' fresh air," Daisy said. "So, you think Frank'll ask you out some day?"

"He is a little old, don'tcha think?" Erlene asked.

"Nope. I hear he goes for the young ones. You're about right, I think."

They laughed.

"Boy, Mama would hate it if I dated him," Erlene said.

"Maybe not. He's so rich."

The girls chattered like old friends as they pushed open Scotty's swinging barroom doors and walked into the dark.

The next Monday after work, Ramsay sat with Harold and Oscar at a different table at Scotty's.

"It's not that you're wrong, Marcus," Oscar said. "It's just that all this talk about sales goin' down—"

"Per capita," Ramsay corrected. "The Texas population's changing, and now it includes more northerners. So, on average, each person doesn't buy as much Coyote Chili as in the old days."

"Whatever you say," Oscar said.

"You're coming on little too strong with all this stuff," Harold said.

"Yeah. Earl hates change," Oscar said. "And most of the Coyote folks been here a whole lotta years, too."

"I haven't changed anything," Marcus said. "I just want to do what I was sent to do. Get you guys out of the dog house with Allied. But, you're all giving me so much shit."

"I think your population idea is bull," Harold said. "I bet Earl's plenty afraid of it. And, you being down on the billbacks: That's like melting down our golden calf."

"But it's the truth," Marcus said. "They're killing our profits. I feel like Earl's a little unrealistically suspicious, not just because he doesn't like change or Yankees."

"Maybe 'cause he's a C.O.D.A.," Harold said and shrugged.

"A C.O.D.A.?" Marcus said.

"A Child of Deaf Adults," Oscar said. "Just think of growing up with two deaf parents. Must be weird. Makes you grow up not trustin' nobody."

"And Sheila's always whispering in his ear, too." Harold said. "Pushin' him, riling him, you know. Feedin' his doubts."

"I guess any of those things could make him act like that. So, why did he want me here in the first place?" Ramsay asked.

The men smiled at each other.

"What?" Ramsay asked.

"Truth is, he didn't," Harold said. "You were picked by Childress. That's what Earl said."

"What?" Ramsay said.

"Earl said the man was just dumping your Yankee ass down here to get rid of you."

"Nonsense," Ramsay said. "Where would Earl get that idea?" But he looked away, wondering.

"You just got to watch out for Lady Sheila," Oscar said.

"She acts like she rules the roost around here," Harold said and snickered.

Marcus looked at his watch. He felt like heading for the Holiday Inn, roach or no roach.

"She comes around every week like a queen," Oscar said. "You seen her?"

"Sheila? I saw her once," Marcus said. "At least Daisy did."

"If you go to Earl's anniversary party, she'll be there," Harold said. "Coming up in a couple of weeks."

The three rose and walked to the door. Outside, a misty halo surrounded the street light at the corner. A fuzzy, pink neon ring surrounded the lit, broken clock atop the Corsicana National Bank building a block away. They stepped out onto the inlaid brick on Beaton Street.

Marcus felt something under foot. He stepped again.

Crunch. He looked down. *What the hell is that?* Hundreds of bugs swarmed around his feet. They looked like grasshoppers, but they were coal black.

"Crickets!" Oscar said and laughed. "Welcome to late summer in Corsicana."

"Crickets?" Marcus said. "They're huge! Up North we have little guys, not these monsters. These are like black grasshoppers."

Oscar and Harold laughed.

"Hey, Marcus," Harold said. "Remember, y'all are in Texas now. Everything's big down here."

"So, tread lightly, hear?" Oscar said. "Or you'll mess up those fancy shoes. Understand, Yankee?"

11 *Corsicana, Texas   September 19, 1980*

On a Friday night in September, the party room across the hall from the Holiday Inn Restaurant twinkled. Draped like garland on a Christmas tree, Italian Christmas lights were attached with layers of masking tape to each of the walnut-paneled walls. The Coyote employees in attendance jabbered at three tables of ten. They were there to celebrate Earl Hickman's presidential anniversary.

Marcus watched Earl hold the buzzing, old-fashioned, chrome-plated microphone.

"It's nice to have y'all join me for my celebration." The mike squealed.

Marcus scoured the group of office folks, managers, and spouses, all required attendees. Not one of the seventy-four black plant workers was there.

Marcus picked up on Earl's speech, just as it drifted from grandiose accolades of a Coyote gone by to the present.

"Let me make a special comment to those who have recently come here from the North," Earl said.

Who else, Marcus thought. He looked around and felt studied by the gawking group.

Earl continued: "We'll never change the way we sell Coyote Chili. And we'll be in California by next July!"

The Coyote employees and their spouses applauded enthusiastically, as if on cue. Marcus cringed. He realized they probably believed that he was the Yankee intruder who was there to infiltrate and destroy a monument built over the prior decade by Earl Hickman and his wife, that the Coyote people had worshipped and grown to depend upon.

They applauded again when Earl squashed the rumor that the executive, financial, and marketing functions would relocate. "Malarkey!" he boomed into the mike. "Who do you trust anyway? Rumors about some Dallas Office bull or me?

Why is he lying to them? Marcus wondered. Just then he caught Frank Benedict leering at him from across the room.

At Frank's half-filled table for ten, Sheila Hickman half-listened to her husband as she puffed on her cigarette. She pushed back when her daughter nudged her to join in the celebratory applause. "Erlene, don't you think I know when to clap," Sheila said.

"Mother, you shouldn't be drinking. I saw you take a pill before we left. You should cut back on smokin' too."

Sheila sipped her wine. "Leave me alone. Just clap for your father if you're so smart." She inhaled deeply, exhaled the last drag of the cigarette, and crushed it into the ashtray along with eight other lipstick-adorned butts. She laughed to herself when she noticed that the butts lay in a row like graves in a cemetery. Each of the cigarettes represented ten minutes of time she had smoked her life away in Corsicana, relishing her role as the first lady of Coyote Brand—right.

"I think Daddy's bein' rude to Mr. Ramsay is all," Erlene said. "He should be thankin' him or welcomin' him, don'tcha think?"

"How would you know, smarty? Yankee's just a troublemaker, Erlene. Over there in his fancy suit—"

Ramsay watched as Earl droned on. Just then the speech of Coyote Brand's president became disjointed in its logic. Earl threw all sorts of seemingly unrelated thoughts together: the positive growth of sales; the significance of the California expansion; and the value of Frank Benedict. Most of the crowd remained piqued as he rambled on about his masterful ability to "control Chicago" who occasionally visited Corsicana to "butt in."

Ramsay took the Yankee jabs personally. Especially the ones that implied that the "intruders" from the North intended to harm Coyote Brand with fancy new ideas. Angry, Marcus Ramsay only felt comforted when he saw Daisy across the room shaking her head at Earl's comments. She was his only real ally in Corsicana.

When Marcus looked back at Earl, he met cool eyes.

"Now let's have the newcomer from Chicago say a few words," Earl challenged.

When Ramsay looked away to avoid his boss' stare and scoured the room, he

saw the entire Coyote Brand family—
employees and their spouses—smiling at
him with cold, empty eyes and pasty
white faces. As he rose to speak, they
hushed. He seized the only thought that
might help win them over.

"Hello. I'm Marcus Ramsay. You
might remember me from when I visited
ten years ago, after James Post died. I
attended his funeral with all of you."

There was a small gasp.

"I want to honor his memory by
helping you rebuild a great business and
help it address a new marketplace. With
years of heritage and lots of caring
employees like you, Coyote Brand can
become better than ever by introducing a
new strategy, providing a new advertising
focus, and moving to a new office—
making it easier for the folks from Allied
to visit us and see that we're doing quite a
job. Let's do it together!"

When Ramsay looked around the
room, waiting for the expected applause,
he heard nothing, just indistinct
mumbles. He noticed Earl, Sheila, and
Frank Benedict sitting together. Of the
three, Sheila, a weathered blonde woman,
stared at him in between puffs on her
cigarette and sips of her wine. Ramsay

continued his speech, responding to the silence. "Thank you. I want to add my congratulations to Earl on his anniversary."

Ramsay met Sheila Hickman's eyes. She squinted back at him as if she had forgotten her glasses. The squint only accentuated her haggard look. He continued: "Now we must springboard off of this celebration into revelation, looking at Coyote in new ways."

Across the room Sheila leaned over and whispered to Earl, "I remember Ramsay being a young punk. He seems pretty smooth to me."

"Just a fancy talker—" Earl said. "Older, too."

"I'm sorta feeling dizzy in my head, Earl. Maybe it's the food."

"You having flashes, Sheila? Remembering something?"

"For a second everything went foggy. I was up half the night last night, thinking about meeting this Yankee scum bag."

"Maybe he's just stirring up old memories: the parties you used to have, the funeral, James Post."

"Wait. He's dead, right?" she said, confused suddenly.

"Post? Of course." Earl laughed. "His funeral took the town over. Remember? You were there, cryin' like the rest."

"Oh yeah. I remember . . . I think." She reached for a memory as it flew by in her head, but it was too faint to grasp. She glanced back at Marcus.

"So, in the future we will honor those who came before us, like Mr. Post," Ramsay said, "and make all the advances he would have endorsed."

Some halfhearted applause rattled through the small room. Sheila's arm flinched and she missed the ashtray. She stared at the young executive. "Such bullshit," she said.

"I thank you all for coming tonight." Ramsay bowed. "And, again, congratulations to you, Earl."

The employees politely applauded, quickly stood, and chatted as they dispersed.

Cecil, blew his nose as he walked up to Ramsay with his wife in tow. She was a prim-looking woman in her fifties. "Marcus, this here is Dorothy."

He shook her hand.

"I can see why Cecil thinks y'all are gonna change things around here," she said. " 'Bout time."

"Thank you, ma'am," Ramsay said. "Cecil says you're a teacher?"

"Fifth grade."

"Ah, an important year. The beginning of a lot of changes for kids."

She nodded. "Oh, yes."

Cecil said, "Marcus, your speech was mighty fine. Kinda what James used to say."

"Really?" Ramsay said.

"Yep," Cecil said. "Machine or no machine, it's time we heard those kinda words. Been too long."

"Thanks, Cecil. But looks like I have a pretty high fence to climb if you know what I mean." Marcus motioned at the dispersing crowd.

"Yep. You got that right."

"Excuse me, Cecil," Marcus said, "but I better say hi to Mrs. Hickman. Nice meeting you, Dorothy."

She smiled.

Ramsay thought about what Cecil had just said and felt good, like his presence might eventually be appreciated at Coyote.

He walked over to Sheila. As he approached he noticed her gaunt appearance. Her powdery make-up had settled into her wrinkles and failed to obscure the effects of middle age. But, she displayed a stylish, country club chic with her tailored culottes; brassy blonde hair tied with a dangling silk scarf; a crisp, tailored blouse with a raised collar; and an array of gold jewelry. He thought back to his days as a caddy at the club in the classy suburb back home. Sheila looked like the rich ladies whose clubs he used to carry as they tried to emulate much younger women.

Sheila eyed him suspiciously as he approached.

He flashed a smile and extended his hand.

She shook it, then quickly pulled hers away to scratch her neck. "So, you're the famous Marcus Ramsay, huh?" Sheila asked. Her eyes were glassy and bloodshot, and she wobbled in place.

"Yes, ma'am. Nice to meet you. You have quite the influence around Coyote, I'm told," he said.

"So? What about it?" she said and burped unabashedly, then covered her mouth.

"I'm confused," Ramsay said. "In what capacity?" He couldn't imagine her having serious influence over anything.

"Young man, I happen to advise Earl, your boss," she said and eyed Marcus. "Wait. I think I do recall you from way back."

Ramsay brushed back his hair. "After ten years, ma'am? Not bad. I don't believe we met at the funeral. Maybe after."

"Yep, I was bawling a lot that day," she said. "Have they explained about my hosp—"

"Yes, ma'am," he said.

"That's why I talk so slow."

"Yes ma'am. Don't worry. Blends in with the accents of everyone I've met here."

She spit out a little laugh. "That noticeable?" She blotted her forehead with a napkin.

"Not really, Mrs. Hickman. It doesn't show, really. Say, you OK?"

"I'm feelin' a little shakey, is all." She turned away, looking confused. She turned back quickly. "Oh, by the way, when do I meet your lovely wife? Carol or Kathy is it?"

"Kathy. She moves down in November. We're moving to east Dallas."

"Ah, near Lake Hubbard an' all? Nice. I like that lake. Long commute, though."

"We'll see." Ramsay remembered that the word on the Dallas move wasn't official yet, so he didn't say anymore.

"I'm looking forward to meeting her, maybe at the Christmas bash," she said. As Sheila wobbled away, she threw a small, inconsequential wave and awkwardly tripped over a young lady who caught her.

"Sorry, Mama. Oh, Mr. Ramsay . . . Marcus," Erlene said as she glanced downward. "I'm Erlene Hickman," she said shyly. "What you said was real nice."

"Thank you, Erlene. I'm glad somebody liked it," Ramsay said.

She looked around, then whispered: "You know, Daisy's quite taken by you." She pushed her long hair out of her eyes.

"I think she's great, too," he said.

"We talked about you late one night at Scotty's a few weeks ago. "She really likes you. I can tell." She giggled and put her hand over her mouth.

"Really? You know she's married, right? A mother, too," Marcus said, looking around the room for Daisy. "And I'm married, too."

"Still. She's right over there." She pointed.

"With her husband, the cowboy," Marcus said.

Erlene turned and looked into the shadows. "Yeah, guess that's him. Looks a little familiar. Musta seen him at church."

"Coy? He looks like a real heavy duty good ol' boy, that's for sure."

Erlene flinched. "Wait. What'd you call him?" She squinted into the shadows. Daisy's husband was manhandling his family out the side door of the party room.

"Boy, Daisy said things were bad at home," Ramsay said. "But that's a little rough." He looked back at Erlene. "Hey, you OK?"

"Just now. What'd you call him?" Erlene asked urgently.

"What? Good ol' boy. Why?"

"Is that what you said, Marcus?"

Marcus nodded as he watched the Duncans disappear, then looked down at Erlene's hands. Her fists were clenched, her knuckles white. "Say, what's wrong?"

"Nothin'. Had me a bad situation once is all. Them good ol' boys look alike, don't they?"

"To me they do. Especially if they're wearing that kind of straw hat."

"They all have names that sound the same, too, don't they?" she asked nervously.

He laughed. "Yeah, I guess, especially if there are two of them: Billy Bob, Tommy Joe . . . "

"Good." She sighed. "Say, maybe I'll see you at the Christmas party," Erlene said.

"I guess so," he said. "Haven't heard much about it."

"Oh, it's the big deal every year."

"I see."

She giggled. "Guess I better go." But, as she started to walk away, she lingered and lowered her voice. "Hey, Marcus?"

"Yeah?" Ramsay said.

"This is so hard. Oh darn. I'm only gonna say this once, OK?" she asked.

"What is it?" Ramsay asked, curious at her secretive demeanor.

She hesitated, then whispered, "Up north do the girls ever ask the guys out?"

"More and more," Ramsay said. "Why?"

She blushed. "Well," she said. "I was thinkin' about askin' this guy out. He won't think that's weird, will he?"

"Naw." Ramsay smiled. "Nowadays, I think he'd be complimented," he said.

"What about if he's an older guy?" she asked.

"Oh, I don't know," he said. "I think it depends on the people involved, don't you?" Ramsay said.

"Sure. Oh, good." She smiled and rubbed her hands together. "Say, thanks." She twirled and walked away.

"Good luck," he called.

She turned back. "See ya then—Christmas."

On their way home Sheila Hickman chattered. "Kid's bright, Earl. Ambitious, too, I bet. Gotta make sure he's on your team."

"Oh, Sheila. Now that you met him, he's even worse than you pictured."

"Just don't show him your back," she said. "He does bring back some vague memories, I guess."

"Maybe he'll help you remember more, dear."

"Just what I need." She still felt a little high.

"From the Post days," he said.

"Earl, I don't remember anything except what you tell me. And those damn dreams." The last one had spooked her. It had pulled her to a blurry new place: night time, a large car, thunder, and rain.

Earl turned left on Second Street, then made another left on the curvy road that led to Golf Estates. In minutes their home came into view, the fourth from the long entry wall.

"Here we are," Earl said, as the car rolled up their stoney driveway.

All this talk about Ramsay made Sheila think of Mark, Bryan's real father. Now, Mark, originally from Baltimore—where she had known him and loved him—was happy in Minneapolis with his wife Doris and lots of kids, no doubt. Meanwhile, at that very moment, Mark's son Bryan Hickman, now lame-armed and unaware that Mark was his real father, was out with his rowdy football buddies cruising through Corsicana.

That Yankee Ramsay has the same kind of style as Mark did, she thought. *If only Earl was more professional when he was young instead of roaming the high seas in*

*the Merchant Marine with Sven, or
cruising up and down the Shore on his
Harley. At least Earl ended up the
president of a corporate division and her
position as its first lady came true.*

Just then Earl jerked the car to a stop.

"Earl, watch it!" Sheila said.

"Sorry."

Erlene said from the back seat, "I
really like Mr. Ramsay, Mama. Marcus."

"What, you and him on a first name
basis now?" Sheila asked. "And call me
mother."

"Well, it sounds like he really cares
about improving Coyote. So what if he's a
Yankee? He's sweet."

Sheila unfastened her seat belt and
opened her door. She turned to Erlene.
"What could you possibly understand
about some Yankee smart-ass making
your father, the provider for your family,
look bad. Fancy-ass computer, Yankee
ideas—he's bound to be a troublemaker,
right Earl?"

"Whatever you say, Sheila." They all
got out. The doors thumped closed.

Sheila rambled: "Stopping California,
per cap whatever, killing the billbacks?
He gives me the creeps, Earl. I say he
goes."

"Yes, dear."

Later that night Sheila stayed awake after Earl drifted off. She sneaked downstairs and drank for an hour, then returned to bed after taking her bedtime pills. As she drifted off, she mumbled. It was a new dream:

Earl and Sheila Hickman sat in a church pew with pretty Erlene and adorable Bryan. She had dressed them both in their Easter Sunday best for James Post's memorial service.

The Corsicana Community Church never looked so colorful. The Post memorial service was planned to dramatically pay tribute to its unfortunate, but well-loved guest of honor. Flowers were everywhere: springy ones, lilies, seasonal flowers and daisies—all of them overflowed the front of the sanctuary and cascaded down the center aisle. Hardly bleak, this funeral service had a wedding look about it.

At precisely 11 o'clock Reverend Miller stood next to his chair beside the pulpit. He turned the pages of his Hymnal. "Will you all open to Hymn number Twenty-three."

After the larger-than-normal congregation's boisterous singing delighted him to the point of smiling, Reverend Miller walked up the stairs to the elevated pulpit. He launched into his eulogy. Within minutes, Lenora sobbed. The packed church listened politely as Reverend Miller said all the right things about James Post, including references to the "Coyote Brand family" and his faithful secretary, normally the organ player for the church.

Sheila looked around at all the sad faces. Sorrow poured through the small church, then out the open stained glass windows onto the lawn, where the overflow crowd had parked their pick-ups. Moms and dads and kids and quilts speckled the grounds of the Corsicana Community Church.

When Reverend Miller finished his comments, he motioned to Al Bishop to come up and give his eulogy. Al squeaked the microphone into position. "James Post certainly was a great industrial leader, the best one Corsicana has ever seen. He was a genius the way he solved problems. There was the time . . . "

Everyone could tell from his verbosity that Al truly loved the man and had shared many memorable times with him.

"Thank you, Al." Reverend Miller reached up and bent the microphone's flexible neck away from him.

Next was Oscar. "He showed me the way . . . " Oscar mumbled self-consciously from his crumpled three-by-five cards. He seemed to be holding back tears as he offered his eulogy with a deadpan expression and monotone delivery from between two tightly pursed lips. Then he put down his cards. As he finished with a few extemporaneous words, he wiped his eyes and his voice broke. Tears began to flow freely throughout the Corsicana Community Church. Oscar sniffled repeatedly as he climbed down from the pulpit.

Then there was silence. A lone chime rang into the open windows from the Lutheran church across town. Earl stood and hobbled to the pulpit. The crowd murmured. He stood there for a moment, checking his notes. Then his resonant voice thundered into the mike: "Mister James Post is gone!"

His voice rang through the sanctuary and outside. His hands waved gracefully.

All heads faced him. Sleepy mourners opened their eyes.

"Today is our day to grieve . . . ," he continued.

The power of Earl's delivery gave Sheila chills. "We all feel grief for a great fallen soldier taken from us before his time by the cruelty of an accidental death!"

Sheila knew better. She saw people cringe at the way Earl had said the word *death* and how it reverberated through the sanctuary. She watched him pause dramatically as he scanned the small church. The small loudspeakers, hung haphazardly from a few open church windows, sent his words echoing across the lawn.

Then Sheila glanced one row back. Her eyes met Coy Duncan's. He leered at her through snake eyes.

She looked away from Coy and back to Earl, whose oration took a twist: "It is so sad to think that his death was caused by those squeaky worn brakes."

Sheila glanced back at Coy. He made a snipping motion with two fingers. It was an action only she could decipher. Then he smiled a slit of a smile and rubbed his index finger and thumb together. He wanted the rest of the money. She looked away, back at Earl.

"You see, he was just too busy caring about his company to have those old brakes replaced," he boomed.

When the congregation answered, "Amen" out loud like Mountain Baptists, Sheila felt they were yelling an accusation at her.

"Day after day, he rolled into the Coyote lot with his car squeaking. He had no idea that the simple squeakiness would ultimately cause his death," Earl said.

Sheila glanced back at Coy. He was gone. Now she realized that Post's well known procrastination with brake repair had made it easy for Coy Duncan to disguise his evil deed. He had found Post's weakness.

Sheila felt sick. Post's brakes failed as a result of her scheming with the cowboy. She had said yes to him while she was in a drunken stupor, surrendered her body, and would pay for the deed from her secret savings.

"Oh, Lord have mercy . . . " Earl continued.

Sheila flushed. She realized her own husband's flowery oration had unwittingly disguised her guilt.

"Few of you may know that on the day of his death—during his last lunch hour, in fact—he arranged for a special surprise for his loving wife, Margaret." Earl looked down at diminutive Margaret Post. The eyes of the congregation followed his. *Who cares about any old lunch hour,* thought Sheila.

"I'm sorry we will never know what that surprise was, for he only talked about it in general terms with the rest of us. Margaret, I'm sure he'll have it waiting for you in heaven."

Garbage! Please stop, Sheila thought.

Earl looked down at the dignified little lady who mourned behind a black veil. The crowd wept at the tender simplicity of Earl's story, the gentleness of his movements, and the slow cadence of his delivery.

Meanwhile, Sheila's heart pounded as Earl's words pierced into her.

"Once we have wept for James," he continued in an elongated, mournful drawl, "we will continue to remember this loving man in our hearts forever."

Sheila clutched her chest as Earl looked directly at her. She looked around at the congregation. They appeared mesmerized as he finished softly. The people of Corsicana would always revere James Post and continue to talk about his funeral, as well as the unusual circumstances surrounding his death, thanks to Earl's eloquent guidance.

Leave it alone, Earl. Enough is enough. She wished the service was over.

The church choir began singing "Rock of Ages". The unsynchronized vibrato and tearful strains encouraged nose-blowing throughout the sanctuary as Reverend Miller's tenor voice rang above the parishioners'.

Margaret Post's two college-aged daughters, Emma and Chelsea, sat on either side of her in the church. With her veil hiding controlled tears, Margaret had sat with dignity and grace, quietly patting and consoling them, throughout the eulogies. She had been the perfect widow: serene enough to make the mourners comfortable; grief-stricken enough to earn their empathy. Sheila was relieved and awestruck at the woman's composure.

But suddenly Margaret Post let go. She shook from heart wrenching sobs that seemed greater than her small frame could handle. Her grief spawned even more throughout the sanctuary.

Sheila Hickman had wished this moment would not come. From around her, waves of sadness crashed into her ears. She was surprised to feel her own tears slip down her face as she watched Margaret Post weep.

When Sheila darted looks around the church, she didn't feel alone in her tears. She saw other sorrowful faces, some weeping, some sobbing, and some clenching tightly closed eyes.

An ugly young man with dented scars from his own terrible accident, sitting two rows back, erupted into tears and looked directly at Sheila. She felt conspicuous because of his pointed glare. She looked away, but everywhere she looked someone else looked back. If these people knew of her culpability, she thought, they would have stoned her on the spot.

Earl climbed down from the pulpit, shook Reverend Miller's hand, and, as he hulked back to his seat next to Sheila, wiped his eyes. He had been so moved by his own grand oration.

Reverend Miller ascended into the pulpit and tapped the microphone. "I want to assure you that James has passed through the great tunnel of light. He is now with his Lord and would want you all to be comforted knowing that. So, go in peace . . ."

After the minister finished his benediction, the mourners exited the sanctuary, row by row. Sheila watched two ushers properly escort Margaret Post to the flashy black limo ordered by Frank Benedict, who had failed to attend the event. *The rich bastard,* Sheila thought.

A second car waited for Emma and Chelsea Post, who walked to it weeping and hugging each other.

After everyone had settled in the cars, the doors closed. They glided away from the church and proceeded to the grave site in the old cemetery next to Pioneer Village for final good-byes.

"Hurry up, kids," Sheila Hickman said to Erlene and Bryan. They all walked across the gravel to their Mercedes and climbed in.

"Can we go to McDonalds yet?" little Bryan asked.

"Shut up, Bry'," Erlene said and adjusted her hat. "Don't you know we go to the grave first?"

They closed their car doors.

After the graveside service, the Hickmans drove through bumper-to-bumper traffic on Second Street. Hundreds of mourners walked by, carrying babies, blankets, and coolers, hurrying home to beat the late afternoon rain.

Sheila Hickman, riding in the front seat, composed a question as she puffed nervously on her Winston and craved some form of stronger fortification. *God, I need a drink!* Finally, she spoke in a shaky voice, trying to mimic Margaret Post's elegant southern demeanor. "So, Earl, what is going to happen with the company now, my dear?" she asked, flicking her ashes haphazardly out the car window.

"They'll be sending someone down to put together a new management team, I guess," Earl said with a shrug.

"You mean you don't know?" Sheila asked, her southern dignity vanishing.

"Why are you so interested, Sheila?" he asked.

"Well, aren't you?"

"I guess, but let's put the man in the ground first."

" 'Course, but you need to make sure of your next move," she said. "Call the right people, make yourself a player, don't be a dummy . . . " she chattered.

"What the hell you talking about?"

"Getting the man's job, of course," she said.

"What?"

"Becoming president," she said.

"Can't wait to move in on the big prize, can you, Sheila?"

"How dare you!" she said.

"Well."

He had nailed her. Raindrops splashed on the windshield. The pressure grew inside Sheila's head as she glared back at Earl. As the rain outside echoed her tears, she raised her middle finger and jammed it in the air at Earl. "Stuff it, sludge!"

"What?" Earl said and shook his head. "Jesus."

"Mama, Daddy," Erlene said, "Please don't fight."

"Oh, hush." Sheila couldn't catch her breath as she recalled Coy Duncan, the Cat's Meow, Margaret Post, the Post girls, and now a townful of mourning Corsicanans. "If it wasn't for your fucking incompetence!" she screamed at Earl.

Later that night, after her family went to bed, Sheila Hickman, alone and tormented, returned to the dining room. She drank scotch straight from the bottle until she collapsed on the floor, bruising her forehead on the hutch and vomiting all over the carpet. She futilely tried to clean it up, rubbing the carpet fiercely with paper towels that only disintegrated in her hands.

Now, in bed, Sheila awoke and sat up. The clock said 2:15. She expected to find vomit all over her hands, encrusted in her nails, and the smell of it everywhere. Instead, Earl lay beside her snoring in a predictable cadence amidst clean sheets. The air conditioners cycled on and off.

She rolled over and stared into the dark. She didn't want to sleep and dream those hideous dreams that made her out to be a murderer, hiding her crime from all of Corsicana. *Why do I have them?*

She quietly rose and found her way to the crawl space beneath the kitchen. Pointing with a flashlight, she pulled aside the wooden doors and crawled in, pushing and shoving boxes this way and that, searching for the money that her mother had left her. She was sure she had left it there in one of the boxes. If she could find it now, then she would know all her dreams were nonsense. She shined the flashlight on box after box.

Minutes later, Earl appeared at the crawl space opening. "Sheila, what the heck you doing down here now? Are you crazy?"

"Shit, Earl! You scared the hell outa me," she said.

"Sorry. What's going on?" he asked.

"Nothing, I guess I was doin' some crazy sleep walking. You know, the drugs and all."

"Well, best we both get back to bed," he said.

"I guess." But Sheila wondered if the money was still hidden in one of the remaining boxes, or if she had actually given it to that slithery cowboy. She searched her mind, but couldn't remember.

"Come on, baby," Earl said as he motioned her out.

After Sheila had crawled out, Earl reached for the Makita drill that was hanging on the pegboard over his work bench. Then he sunk eight three-inch drywall screws around the circumference of the crawl space doors. "There, this oughta discourage anymore nighttime antics."

She studied his thorough job. "But what if I ever need anything?"

"Aw, Sheila, when was the last time we ever needed this stuff? Except the Christmas decorations, right? Better we get a good night's sleep, don't you think? If you need anything, Bryan or I can get it for you. OK?"

"Right. Sure," she said. "Whatever you say."

Marcus Ramsay lay in bed across town, holding his stomach. Doc Hopkins had checked him out and thought everything looked fine, though he had recommended an upper GI to rule out an ulcer.

Suddenly Marcus felt like he needed to vomit. He got up and ran to the bathroom. He positioned himself over the toilet.

"Shit!" He retched once, then twice, then a third time—all dry. Then he retched a fourth time. Bright yellow bile-looking drool mixed with a little blood dripped from his mouth.

God! What the hell is going on? he thought.

He felt like a virus was taking him over. He kneeled over the toilet for another half-hour, heaving unproductively three or four more times.

Then, in the middle of the night, drained and sore about the rib cage, he lay awake. He thought back to the night he had arrived in Corsicana, when he had fainted by the oil well at the Holiday Inn and the taxi driver helped him. Marcus wondered if he had contracted some strange disease during his trip to Corsicana.

Part 3

the Empowerment

12 *Corsicana, Texas   October 15, 1980*

One month later Marcus Ramsay sat
at his desk with a Coke as the late
afternoon sun shone through the window
behind him. In the next room Daisy
waited to type corrections to his analysis
of the California expansion idea. Ramsay
thumbed through the latest draft of his
six-page document.

"So, how's it look, Mr. Ramsay?" Daisy
called.

"Looking real good, Ms. Duncan.
Cecil'll have to read it when he gets back.
He might even buy it." Ramsay turned
the page. "Earl's just gonna die, though."

Daisy walked in and sat across from Ramsay in Cecil's desk chair. She flopped her legs in a crossed position over the arm of the chair. "Yep. I agree. He's jus' gonna up an' die."

Ramsay continued to read the document intently. He looked up. "Do you have to do that?" he asked. "Your legs?"

"Why? Bother you?" she said and smiled.

"I'm just trying to concentrate here," he said.

She stroked her legs. "They're not all that bad, are they?"

"Hardly." Marcus Ramsay lost his concentration somewhere between the ineffectiveness of billback deals and the need for new advertising on non-chili products. He sighed audibly and turned another page. "Yeah. California's just a bunch of dreaming," he said. "This analysis'll put the frosting on the cake."

"Frosting? Mmm," Daisy said and slowly pulled the end of her tongue across her lips, "What might frosting have to do with it?"

"Do you have to make everything an innuendo?" he asked.

"Oh, sorry, boss." She smiled.

"Don't get me wrong, but a guy can get excited, if you know what I mean."

"Hmm. What do y'all mean?" she asked.

"Well, that blue dress with the buttons all the way down the front . . . ," he said.

"Drives the plant guys wild, don't it?"

"Bet it does," he said.

"Lenora and Mary talk like I'm some kinda whore," she said.

"I bet," he said.

"They forget I have a young child. And I get my clothes at the Hollywood Shop in town, same place they go," she said. "I don't buy 'em from the old lady side of the store, though."

"What's Coy think about how you dress?" Ramsay asked.

"That's a whole other story." Daisy's voice sank, her head hung.

"I saw him rough you up at Earl's party," Ramsay said.

"Once in a while I actually hit the bastard back," she said.

"All that violence is stupid," Ramsay said.

"Ol' Coy can't get enough. Hell, he goes out hunting Saturday mornings at Holler's Woods, the swamp near our place? Let's it out on the damn ducks."

"No offense. The guy sounds like an animal." Ramsay shook his head.

"Thanks for concernin' yourself over it," she said. "My daddy always roughed-up my mama, though, and Coy's granddaddy always roughed up his grandma—Coy always says that's the way married people act. Then you come along and talk different—gentle-like. You ain't one of those queers are you? That's what Coy'd say." She put her leg down and leaned forward.

"No, Daisy, hardly."

Her hand drifted across the desk and grabbed Marcus'. She squeezed it and their eyes met.

Marcus looked away for a second, unsure.

She yanked away and leaned back. "Shoot."

"What?" Ramsay said. "What'd I do?"

She stood and pushed away Cecil's chair. "Now I need my damn boss to hold my hand."

"Daisy, what the hell's going on here?" Ramsay asked.

"Lord, don't you know frustrated when you see it?" she said.

"Frustrated?"

"Yep. You care more about me than Roy does," she said.

"I thought I was just being civilized." But inside he secretly enjoyed Daisy's labeling him her knight in shining armor, poised to vanquish any threats.

"You mean you don't feel nothin' towards me?" she asked. "I mean, in particular, that is?"

"Actually . . . ," he said.

"So, you're holding back?"

Ramsay wondered: If he said yes, he'd be admitting how close he felt toward her. If he said no, he'd be lying. No matter what he said, he'd lose. "I . . . guess . . . Oh, I don't know."

"Shoot." Daisy marched out of his office to her desk and grabbed her purse. She yanked open the sticky door. "Night, Yankee," she called and ran out into the blustery warm October evening. "I thought Yankees were real straightforward-like!"

Earl was reading for the first time the final document on the efficacy of the California expansion two days later. Ramsay had already had it delivered to key Allied personnel at the Mercantile

Mart, including John Childress and Kyle Burghoff.

"Is this document really already gone, Lenora?" Earl stood at his desk and asked, angry and beet-red.

Lenora nodded and winced.

"Is he gone, too?" Earl asked.

"Yep. Doing some stuff for his new house up in east Dallas. Why did he buy up there, Mr. Hickman? Seems silly, don't it? All that commute."

"Uh . . . couldn't imagine." He cleared his throat. "Lenora, get Harold and Oscar over here, pronto."

Minutes later Earl's right-hand men sat before him. They acted like kids, punching each other on the shoulder. Earl glared at them, then asked for their ideas on Ramsay's California Report. Earl's beige fifties rotary phone rang loudly behind him. Earl jumped and glanced out at Lenora, who intercepted the call. She talked warily under her breath.

"You want ideas?" Oscar asked. "Just do California any way you want. You are the President, Earl."

Earl glanced out at Lenora, who cradled the receiver in her hand. Then she looked back at him with concerned eyes.

"Mr. Hickman," Harold Hudson sang in his sly Alabama drawl, "if it's a good idea, you oughta support it, and if it's not—"

Lenora bellowed importantly through the old-fashioned com line, "Mr. Hickman! It's Mr. Childress, The Mart, line one."

Earl felt a pang in the pit of his stomach. He inhaled deeply, then raised the phone and spoke in his lowest, slowest, friendliest voice. "Yes, John. How are you today? Oh, yes, I agree. I think it about nails California." He paused. "Billbacks?" He sat up straight. "They're in there, too?" Earl shuffled the pages of Ramsay's California report. He hadn't read that part. "Turn the bidness around . . . I understand . . . yes, John, makes sense to me . . . new campaign ideas, other products, of course . . . talk to you soon, John. Bye."

Earl put the phone down. He felt shaken. He looked at Harold and Oscar. "Shoot howdy, that man can talk," he said, relieved the call was over.

"Well?" Harold said. "What'd he say?"

"Whew!" Earl sighed, then mumbled profanities as he lit the cigarette in his mouth, jiggling Sheila's old Zippo. "He's OK with Ramsay's report. Even the billback part."

Earl leaned back in his chair and took a few short drags. He wondered what to do next. He cleared his throat, thought about what Sheila would say, and how their lives would change . . . or if they'd have to.

"Well, Mr. Hickman?" Harold said. "Whatch'all think?"

Earl cleared his throat roughly. "Not good, Harold. I'd say not good at all."

Later that day, Frank Benedict slammed his mug down on the old butcher block table at Scotty's. He had called an impromptu meeting with Earl and driven down from Dallas. "So, Earl, what the living hell is he up to?" Frank asked. As he splashed his beer, the bartender grumbled.

"Frank, I don't know what to say," Earl said. "The Yankee put the lid on California faster than I—"

"This is fucked, Earl."

Earl felt scolded. "Frank, we've talked about this before. Now that Ramsay's here, I just don't know."

"I don't give a flying fuck about Ramsay!" Frank said. The bartender turned toward them and put his index finger to his lips. At the same time Earl waved his hands in a downward signal at Frank. He hated wild talk: from Frank, from Sheila, from his parents' angry mumbles—from anyone. "Listen, Ramsay's dead set against the billbacks, too. He just might get his way, Frank, especially if Chicago keeps razzin' me about the O.I."

"Wait." Frank grunted like a grizzly. "That doesn't mean we have to take it lyin' down." His glass eye floated out of sync.

"Humph?" Earl puffed his cigarette and sat straight, trying to mimic Frank's confident air.

"We could," Frank said as he slowly sat back in his chair and slung his elbows over the arm rests, "get rid of him."

Earl almost spit out his drink. "What? Murder?"

"No, dumb fuck, I don't mean murder," Frank laughed, ignoring the bartender's gaze. Then he whispered to

Earl, "I thought we had enough of that way back. Eh, Mister President?"

"Right. Then, what do we do?" Earl asked.

"Shit, I don't know, fire the bastard?" Frank sloshed down the rest of his beer and looked at his diamond-studded Rolex.

"Shoot. Sheila'd be for that I'm sure," Earl said, then lowered his voice. "Her damn dreams about the Post thing are givin' me the willies. It's like she thinks she did it."

"Right!" Fred roared. Then he flashed a steely stare at the bartender. "What are you lookin' at, shithead?" The bartender turned away.

"But Frank, I can't just up and fire the fellow if there's no reason. He can sue nowadays, can't he? That's all I need."

"If he sues, then we'll murder him!" Frank laughed.

Earl froze. He never particularly cared for that solution, even though Frank considered it a viable business strategy.

"Hell, Earl, get creative. You could fire the Yankee pisshead, double the billbacks, and increase both our takes. I can unload my share of CBC for a mill and just be out points, which you'll split

with me 'course, you asshole. They're all
a bunch o' flakes out west anyway, eatin'
all that fag food. Chili'd be too manly for
them." They laughed, Earl less easily
than Frank.

Earl cleared his throat repeatedly.
"So, Frank, why on earth you come down
tonight, anyway? Just for a beer? This
CBC thing?"

"Hardly! I got me a date with one
pretty young lady I met at the cook-off
last week," he said. "Yep. Marty and the
divorce are a distant memory, that's for
sure."

"Pretty lady?" Earl asked. "Young?"

" 'Course boss," he said, "you know
that's how I like 'em."

"Maybe Erlene knows her then," Earl
said.

"Hmm. Don't know if they'd run in
the same crowd. She even asked me out.
She's as pretty as can be, tell you that."
Frank rose. "Yep, she's real pretty . . .
and tight, too, I bet. Know what I mean,
Mr. President?" He growled and grinned.

"Too bad you're busy, I was gonna ask
y'all to dinner over at the Ponderosa with
Erlene and Sheila," Earl said.

"Maybe next time, boss. " Frank
looked at his watch again. "Whoops.

Gotta git. Keep in touch regular, huh?"
He stood and bounded away, ignoring the
bartender's watchful eye.

"So, where's the kids?" Earl asked as
he walked in the house several hours
later.

Sheila looked up quickly from her
glass of red wine.

"You shouldn't be drinking with your
damn pills, Sheila. You know what
Lockhart told you," he said.

"It's my first glass, smart-ass," she
said. It was really her third.

"You're not supposed to have any," he
said.

"Screw Lockhart. He just wants to zap
me. Say, where the hell you been?" She
coughed deeply and patted her upper
chest.

"Out for a beer with Frank, then did
some mail at the office. I'm yours the
rest of the night, though," he said.

"Right." She hacked a laugh.

Earl shook his head. "Where are the
kids?"

"Erlene's out with her new boyfriend.
Bryan's with his buddies."

"How's Erlene's fellow? We don't want her getting in trouble with one of those cowboys again," Earl said.

"He didn't come in. Ain't no good ol' boy, though," she said. "Had some fancy car. Must have money."

"Good," he said. "But, I'd like to meet the fella."

"At least she's dating, Earl! He's older, I guess, so we won't meet him till we all go to dinner someday, maybe up at the City Club. That'd be nice."

"How old is he?" Earl asked.

"Don't know. No cowboy is all I know," she said.

"That's good. I lost on California, by the way." Earl poured himself some wine.

"Shit. What's that mean?" Sheila puffed on her Winston.

"They liked Ramsay's report in Chicago," Earl said. "Say, does this work OK?" He brought his dinner over and put it in the deluxe Amana microwave, Sheila's latest purchase from the Navarro Mall.

"You letting that Yankee smart-ass kid whoop your hiney, Earl?" Sheila's eyes were trained on his as she took a big gulp. Then, when he looked away, she snuck another. "We don't want him getting his way too much or you're out of a job and we're out of a life. Ever think of that?"

He turned back to her. "Nonsense. He's only thirty-something."

"Still, he makes me feel out-of-kilter every time I see him: at your party, on Wednesdays, at the cook-off last weekend. It's the way he looks at me."

"Oh, Sheila. You're so dramatic."

"Well, everyone treats him so special. Even though he's a fucking Yankee."

"Watch your language. Sheila. Maybe it's because he takes 'em back to the old Post days, the way he talks so high and mighty."

She exhaled smoke hard through her nose. "Post, I swear. It's like that man's come back more and more, the way his name keeps popping up."

"Goody-goody, two-shoes," Earl said. "Who?"

"Post."

"Why?"

"He worked so hard. Even after the Yankees came along. Who the hell was the man trying to impress?"

"Sounds just like your goddamn Yankee." she said. "Except Post's dead and gone."

Sheila looked confused.

"Remember, Post died in that spectacular accident," Earl said. "What a way to go."

"The car thing?" she asked.

"I've told you before. The crash, right down the block."

"You know how my memory fades in and out," she said. The microwave beeped. Sheila jerked.

Earl removed his dinner from the microwave and left the kitchen.

"So, where you going now, Mr. Big Shot?" she called.

Earl didn't answer. He shuffled across the living room and up the carpeted stairway.

She took a big sip as she watched him wobble away. She hated his stooped posture. "Going to hide away, Mr. President?" she asked in a normal voice. "Just don't let the Yankee push you around! Hear me? The kid's spooky." She gurgled down the last of her wine and shook the bottle. "Already gone?" She held it up to the light. She lit up another Winston, took a deep drag, and coughed hard.

The bedroom door shut upstairs.

Jack Eadon

"You better not blow it, Mr. President," she said through clenched teeth. She looked up the staircase as the muffled TV went on. Smoke seeped out her nose. "Now I'm even dreaming about Post and the Yankee—fucking weird." She tossed the bottle in the trash and sat at the kitchen table, scanning a few of her favorite mail order catalogs till her eyelids sagged.

The same night, across town, Marcus Ramsay lay in his room at the Holiday Inn, back from meeting with his realtor in east Dallas. Even at this point he had his doubts about Texas. Maybe Kathy's instincts had been right all along. He felt so unwelcome, constantly undermined by Frank, Earl, and even Sheila, the company's queen-in-residence. His only support came from Daisy, and, to a certain extent, Cecil.

By nailing the California proposition, he felt he had shoveled away some of the bullshit Earl had spewed on Coyote for years.

Besides the personalities, his intuition told him there was still something strange about this whole experience. It felt like he was looking through the dark at the tip of a very large iceberg. Maybe his vague imaginings had been out of proportion, but maybe they were real, and the base of the berg was still out there somewhere.

Just then he felt that gnawing inside his stomach. "This is too much!" He held his gut and gazed at the irregular shadow on the vinyl curtain of his little room. The oil wel—

"Uh!" he moaned as pain shot through his stomach. His forehead, arms, and head were covered in sweat. He doubled over in pain as a mild state of vertigo threw him off balance. *What the hell is going on?* he wondered.

Just then, Henry, the roach, scurried across the room. Marcus breathed heavily from the disorientation and pain he felt. Then, anger and frustration flashed through him. "Goddamn!"

He reached down and grabbed his shoe as the pain subsided. But the vertigo was still there. He looked across the swaying room at the old, hairy roach. He tracked the bug's progress as it dashed toward the safety of the floor moulding. Ramsay wobbled, then flung his shoe from ten feet away.

Squish! Yellow blood squirted from the roach. "Yes, I got it!"

Marcus walked over to inspect the bug's twitching body. He examined it closer. Forget decades, this roach had probably lived a thousand years, so dull and ancient was his armor. He grabbed his shoe and slammed the heel down hard on the critter, still struggling as if its tiny movements might help save its life.

"I finally got you," Ramsay said. Again and again, he flailed at the bug till there was only a flattened corpse—motel kill.

Marcus scooped it up with the thin Corsicana vacationer's guide, opened the motel room door, and tossed the dead roach into the Corsicana night.

He walked to the bathroom to wash up before bed and looked in the mirror. His eyes widened at the sight of bright yellow mucus and tiny drops of blood dripping from the side of his mouth.

13 *Corsicana, Texas   December 10, 1980*

Several months later, a horn honked outside the Hickman home. Sheila was in the kitchen, tipsy from testing her special pre-holiday eggnog.

"It's probably for me, Ma," Erlene said.

"Don't call me Ma," Sheila said, "and when are we going to meet your new beau?"

"Christmas, I guess," she said. "And I told you, he's not a beau, he's a man," Erlene said.

"Whoop-dee-do. Our teen angel has grown up," she said.

"Shut up, Mother!"

"Y'all just sad 'cause your idol died."

"You wouldn't understand, Mama; John was a big part of my life."

"Never understood that Beatle bull: yeah, yeah, yeah. Nothin' like Elvis. So, when do we meet your fella, your man?"

"Maybe, if you're nice, I'll introduce you," Erlene said.

"Is that a promise or a threat?"

"I'm going now." Erlene's satiny voice faded into the night. The door slammed.

"Don't be late, you hear?" Sheila ran to peek out the window, then returned to the kitchen. "You little tramp."

Minutes later Bryan bounded down the stairs. "I'm goin' now!" he called. The front door opened, then slammed behind him.

It seems so quick that both kids have become independent, Sheila thought. Bryan was healthy and strong, except for his right arm. He could have been the starting quarterback at SMU, that is, until the accident.

And then there was Erlene. *Earl and I never got as mad as we could have about her gettin' raped,* she thought. *We were more concerned about lookin' good around town, keepin' things under wraps. It's amazing Erlene's worked it out on her own.*

"And Bryan's arm . . . ." Sheila reached for a new bottle. It didn't matter which brand, Cutty was fine.

It was another one of those nights Earl read his meaningless mail at the office, she thought. He was always catching up, it seemed, while she was smoking, drinking, and sulking at home. *The first lady of Coyote Brand? Ha!*

Sheila sipped and thought more about Earl. He seemed to be losing his spark, if he ever had it. He had controlled the local idiots at the company for years, but what's to control? She laughed. *Now this Yankee kid shows up and in a few months is takin' over the damn place.*

Half a bottle later Sheila slipped into a fitful nap at the kitchen table. After her cigarette had burnt down to the filter line, she woke, confused at the vivid dream.

Ramsay becoming Post on a rainy night?

"Never been so clear," she said. Now the dreams were persistent and more vivid every time. They had been vague at first, but now they were coming into sharper focus. She wondered what they meant. They were so gruesome. They couldn't have been recollections of real events like Dr. Lockhart said. *Me, a murderer? Fat chance!* she thought.

And undoubtedly, her money, originally stowed in the storage closet, had simply been moved somewhere else, maybe her hope chest. Someday she'd run into it. Sheila lay her head down, slipped into a solid sleep, and began her dream.

But Earl jarred her out of it when he came shuffling in about ten. Erlene and Bryan were still out. Earl pointed at the bottle and ashtray. "You've got to stop this garbage, Sheila. You're gonna get hooked again. Wanna go through another de-tox?"

"No way, Earl."

"Zapping?"

"No fucking way."

"Let's just go to bed." Earl hobbled out of the kitchen.

After he walked out, Sheila cuddled up at the table and snuggled into her arms. She recalled the bright fall day, just a year before, when Bryan lost the use of his right arm. Corsicana was playing its arch rival, Highland Park, a prissy, rich kid's school. "Here I am!" she had yelled at Bryan from the bleachers. She saw him distracted. In slow motion he scoured the stands in her direction, microseconds before HP's massive defensive line crushed him without mercy.

Instantly, because of one vain moment on her part, her son would never again sign his beautiful signature. Instead, he was destined to hulk around with an arm that made him look handicapped and weak, like his father; not strong and invincible like a Viking god, like Sven, her first lover and Erlene's father.

"Shit," Sheila Hickman mumbled. Head in hands, she drifted off again. Events flashed by: her father's death, the football game. Then Post and Ramsay. A car. A rainy night.

Her heart raced. She shook herself awake and sat up. It was so real. She clutched her chest, short of breath and sweaty. Sheila closed her eyes, but her head spun as she tried to conjure the image again.

Meanwhile, outside the Hickman home, a taxi parked in the shadows between street lamps. By courtesy light alone, Reginald Waverly hurriedly took notes: "A flowing pen . . . smooth lines."

Then he thought back to his training. To properly orchestrate balance during Ramsay's empowerment, and elegantly avenge Post's death, he would need to take hints provided by the mortals. "Save the Queen!" he said. "I think that flowing lines bit, and Post's love of writing notes, is the beginning of a grand idea."

14 *Dallas, Texas December 14, 1980*

Marcus Ramsay parked on the quiet street in front of a restored Victorian House in the near-north section Dallas called Turtle Creek. It was quarters for Cherry-Black, Coyote Brand's advertising agency. Ramsay walked up the stairs to the front door and rang the bell.

The ornate maroon door opened. "Well, hey, howdy, I'm Bob Cherry," the bald man said. "You must be Marcus Ramsay." A grin spread from ear to ear on his elfin face. His small features made him look more Danish than Texan, Ramsay thought. Bob Cherry was one of the agency's two principals.

A young-looking fifty, probably because of his boyish good looks and lack of gray hair, Bob explained over coffee how he had been in the ad business for two decades. At one time, his larger accounts had been several Allied brands, something he was still obviously proud of. But, after he had played the big agency game for years, he sold off his interest in a large agency and took on a few smaller clients, one of them Coyote Brand. He opened a smaller agency that operated out of the old house in Turtle Creek.

Ramsay had stopped at the agency on his way to sign additional papers at the realtor's. Kathy was flying in and planned to meet him at their new home in East Dallas that evening.

"We're glad a regular marketing guy is in the Coyote Brand saddle. I can tell you that," Cherry said as he ushered Marcus past the small reception lounge.

"I'm afraid you might change your minds about that," Ramsay said.

"Why's that?" Bob's brow crinkled. "Carol! Can y'all bring in some coffee?"

"We need to do some serious talking on Coyote," Ramsay said.

"Wait." Bob Cherry held up his index finger. "Hey, Steve!"

Scruffy, dark-haired Steve Causte entered the room, shirtsleeves rolled up.

"Need your AE here," Bob said. Steve was Coyote's Account Executive. They shook hands.

The three sat in a cozy conference room. Paneled in rich mahogany, the walls were plastered with colorful ads.

"So, is there a problem, Marcus?" Bob's grin disappeared.

"First, I gotta say I'm happy to finally be working with you guys directly," Ramsay said, "and I'm looking forward to moving the office up here."

"When's this?" Bob said and looked at Steve, shrugging his shoulders.

"Earl hasn't told you? They promised it within six months of when I took the job. My house is up here, so I can stop in often."

"Right," Steve snickered. "Dallas office? I'll believe it when I see it."

"Steve!" Bob said and shook his head.

Carol brought the heavy coffee tray in and set it on the table, her petite frame barely up to the task. "Y'all think I'm a trucker or something?" she asked. "Got your cream and all, too. I'm only doing this on occasion, right, Bob?"

He nodded. "It's a new world."

"You got that right." She nodded and walked out.

"Don't mean to be stepping on any toes, Marcus," Bob said and sipped, "but your boss doesn't play it up front all the time. We've gotten used to that. If I were you, I'd nail Earl down to a moving date ASAP."

"Hmmm. I'm sure he's told you about the status on the California expansion,"

Marcus said.

"What about it?" Bob asked. His forehead wrinkled.

"It's dead. In the final analysis, I found out we couldn't make any money doing it."

Bob stroked his chin. "That's something. Earl called me last week and specifically said it was still on. Golly, you can't ever tell what's smoke or fire."

"Maybe he just forgot," Marcus said. "Although I've heard Earl brag about how he controls Allied with mirrors. Maybe smoke and mirrors are the same thing—control."

"Shoot." Bob shook his head. "I wasn't gonna say, but that's what we see a lot. We never know which way is up."

Steve asked, "Marcus, you've met Sheila, haven't you?"

"Oh, yeah. Down there they call her Lady Sheila."

Steve laughed. "How is she these days?" he asked. "You should've seen her at the last commercial shoot. Satin hot pants, matching boots, and every piece of jewelry she owns."

Marcus snickered as he poured more coffee. "I can imagine. She likes to play

Queen Bee at Coyote. Man, was she drunk at Ray's party, too."

"At the shoot she was constantly drunk, hanging on the lead actor like he was some Hollywood star," Bob said. "Sad to say, but the only time she's not stickin' her nose into Coyote stuff is when she's in the hospital."

"And she's about due soon," Steve said and laughed.

"That's not nice," Bob said. "Though I have to admit, it's difficult at times dealing with the Corsicana syndrome."

"I guess," Marcus said. "I've been down there a few months and I'm getting to know what you mean. It gets a little trying, but things'll change, I think."

They smiled.

Have you guys heard about the billback deals?" Ramsay asked.

"What about them?" Bob said. "For years Earl has pushed 'em instead of TV. Used to do a lot of TV. He's almost put us out of business."

"Well, I looked at all the old data, from 1927 till last month, and found that the billbacks went up like crazy right after Earl started ten years ago. Continued more and more. Especially in Dallas."

Steve put his hand over his mouth. Then removed it. "I don't want to say what I'm thinking," he said.

"What? Your theory again?" Bob asked and shook his head.

Steve nodded. "This sounds like proof."

"What theory?" Marcus asked.

"Well, I wouldn't be surprised if Earl was getting some kind of kickback or something," Steve said. "From Frank Benedict, maybe. I mean, look at the way he dresses and the car he drives. I've always wondered where he gets all his money, like he owns a stake in some oil well."

"Well, let's not jump to conclusions," Marcus said. "Kickbacks? I mean, we are talking the eighties here, right?"

"Ever hear of cash?" Steve said accusingly. "It works for the Mob, right? What if Frank sends his billback performance certificates down to Coyote, Earl OKs them, and Coyote cuts a check to Frank. But, instead of paying the trade accounts, Frank pays Earl back in cash— nothin' to trace."

"I guess it's conceivable." Marcus considered the possibility.

Steve continued, "Sure. Everybody knows that right after Earl was made president, he awarded Frank the brokerage contract for Houston. Worth three hundred thousand a year, I've heard. A little obvious."

"Naw, Earl's not that smart," Marcus said. "Or is he?"

"Don't know." Bob shrugged.

"Seems like a savvy move to me." Steve crossed his arms and grinned.

"Hmm. On a lighter note, I do have some good news for you guys," Marcus said.

"Really?" Bob asked.

"I have an endorsement from the top of Allied to run some new programs," Marcus said. "They want to see a campaign for hot dog sauce."

"Hot dog sauce?" they asked. "They've never done anything on that product before."

"Exactly. From the numbers, it looks like there's a lot of potential with all the northerners moving down and eating chili dogs. If we can hype the Coyote name, the campaign'd help chili, too."

"Makes sense," Bob said. "What media you thinkin' of?"

"Gormel owns the tube, so I was thinking of a mix of radio and outdoor," Ramsay said. "First we could test it in Dallas, then rollout the program. That's if you guys can come up with an exciting concept. What do you think?"

"Sounds good. We'll give it a shot," Bob said. "Say, Marcus, could I talk to you for a sec' in my office?"

"Sure." Marcus stood and followed Bob into his office.

Bob sat behind his antique desk and Marcus pulled up an upholstered chair across from Bob.

"What's up?" Ramsay asked.

"Well, you seem hell bent on flying a new flag down there in Corsicana."

Marcus smiled and nodded. "Yeah, I guess I've made it my mission to turn things around. Even got Burghoff on my side."

"That's great, Marcus. Really. But I want to tell you something that may sound like a bit of a let-down, but it's meant to be helpful. Honest."

"Fine. What is it?"

Bob sat back in his chair. "I learned this lesson a long time ago, especially when it comes to Corsicana. Now, I'm passin' it on to you."

"What is it?"

"Well, you can help 'em, but you can't fix 'em," he said.

"What's that mean?" Ramsay asked. "I thought that's what I was doing—helping."

Cherry's eyebrows raised and he shrugged. "I don't know. We'll do a bang-up job on this hot dog sauce campaign, but it's not really gonna fix anything down there. Neither is you killin' the billbacks or movin' the offices. Or uncoverin' who's payin' off who. Not gonna fix a thing, you'll see."

"I don't get it," Marcus said. "What's the point in continuing then?"

Cherry looked down and half-laughed, "Oh, you'll get it sooner or later. For now, let's just say y'all care too much and it's distortin' what you can really do for 'em. You'll never make 'em over: Corsicana folk is Corsicana folk. Just think on it. Believe me, I have for a long time."

By the time Marcus drove up to his new house, it was seven o'clock. A brilliant, orange sunset lit up a few puffy clouds. Kathy had flown in earlier, signed the remaining papers, and unpacked some kitchen things. Barnum and Bailey strutted around the house like two southern gentlemen, meowing about their new surroundings.

"Babe!" Marcus tried to give her a big hug.

She held up her hands. "Wait. Did you stop and sign the papers?"

"Of course, why?"

"Just checking," she said.

"You're always just checking. How about a little affection mixed in with all the checking. We haven't seen each other in two weeks."

"Once we get settled." She looked away and kept banging pans.

He shrugged. "Hey, we are married, Kathy. It's almost Christmas, too. You'd think we'd be in the spirit!"

"We'll celebrate when I get my new job," she said flatly. "Why were you late?"

"Had to stop at the agency," he said. "I think I have some problems."

"More weirdo Corsicana stuff?" She kept banging.

"Yep. Earl's been telling the agency his own reality."

"What does that mean?" she asked.

"Well, he didn't tell them the California expansion had been canceled and never mentioned that I discovered the billbacks were hurting O.I."

She turned toward him and winced. "Marcus, this whole Texas thing wasn't such a good idea."

"But Burghoff himself wanted this," he said. "I thought we did, too."

"Well, actually, you did. I barely made it here, if you remember. And Daddy always had his doubts. You've conveniently recollected only what you want to."

"Shit! You and Bob Cherry are casting doubts like we're just wasting our time. Screw it!" He shook his head and walked away. To Ramsay, Cherry's fatherly talk was nothing but words from a man who seemed to have given up on the Corsicana folks years ago.

Well, Ramsay wasn't about to give up, even if Kathy denied part ownership of what he had thought was their joint decision to start a new life in Texas. "Don't worry," he called back as he walked toward the bedroom. "It'll be much better when the office moves to Dallas." He paused and pictured contemporary offices and systems. It would be a new Coyote devoid of tan dust, red binders, and provincial ideas. Then he recalled his dismal talk with Bob Cherry that afternoon. "But, I guess that's another Earl story," he called.

"I can't hear you!" she said.

In a normal voice he answered. "Maybe it's better."

"He's been misleading the agency," Marcus said to Cecil the next day in Corsicana. "Up North we would call it outright lying."

"Nonsense!" Cecil said. "Besides, he is the president and maybe he had a mighty good reason."

Daisy walked in from the reception area, folded her arms, and slowly shook her head as she stood behind the craggy old Texan. "Earl should've at least told our Marcus the truth," she said.

Cecil turned. "Now, Daisy Duncan, nobody asked you," he said.

Her hand whisked the air. "Well, at the least, he might-shoulda clued Marcus in on what he was doing. The right hand's gotta let the left hand know what's going on. Am I right, or am I right?"

"Daisy, I happen to think you're right." Marcus rose, walked around

Cecil's desk past her, yanked open the sticky door, and huffed out.

The president of Coyote Brand was engrossed in his US News magazine when Marcus walked in. "What can I do you for, Marcus?" he asked politely.

"Several things, Earl."

"Oh, by the way," Earl said, "Lenora tells me you're quite the photography buff. Can you take a portrait of me for the inside front cover of the Rotary directory?" He continued turning pages slowly, looking at his magazine. "They're installing me as president next year. Might even put a statue of me on Beaton Street. What do you think of that?"

"Terrific," Marcus said. "But the reason I want—"

"When?" Earl said. "The photo?"

"Earl, the reason I need to talk to you is that I found out you're not being totally straight with the agency."

"Oh?" He sat up. "And who told you that?" Earl asked.

"Doesn't matter. We have to play it straight if were going to work effectively together and turn around operating income."

"You don't think Coyote is the best brand out there?" Earl asked.

"Our sales per capita have been falling for years, basically because of the Yankee invasion. We can't hide that anymore. Allied wants me to help you turn that around. So, I'm doing my damnedest. Part of that is testing a new campaign on hot dog sauce."

"What makes you think our slipping—assuming we're slipping—has anything to do with the Yankees movin' south. Sounds stupid to me. Of course them Yankees'll like us!"

"And the new campaign on hot dog sauce?" Ramsay said.

"New campaign? Hot dog sauce? Why don'tcha do some other marketing magic, like expand to California?"

"Earl, listen. Burghoff's been behind the hot dog sauce idea for years. Yesterday I asked the agency to put together a campaign idea. We'll see it after we move into the new place."

"Burghoff? You did what?"

"If it works in a Dallas test, we can roll the program out across the Southwest."

"Dallas? Southwest?"

"And, by the way, when are we moving the offices up to Dallas? I'm getting moved into the new house up there. I can't do a two-hour commute forever. You'll be moving up there, too. Right?"

Earl looked out at Lenora, whose raised eyebrows showed that she'd heard the question. He stood up, walked to the door, slammed it shut, and scolded, "Nobody knows about this move thing yet, Marcus."

"But, Earl! It's been almost six months. I assumed somebody was working on it."

"We are, we are. Just haven't found the right building," he said.

"Which realtor you working with?" Ramsay asked.

"Well, uh, we don't actually have one picked. These things take time. You understand." Earl spoke slowly, gestured gracefully. Sweat pooled under his nose.

God, I hate the way he says, "You understand," in that condescending voice, Ramsay thought. "No, actually, I don't understand," he said. "Listen, I'd like to handle the move. You don't have a problem with that, do you?"

"Uh . . . no, I guess not." Earl started shaking. "Oh, by the way, Marcus, is your Kathy joining us at the Christmas Party on Friday night? It is this comin'

Friday night," Earl said. "Got my speech all ready. You?"

"Hardly," Ramsay said. "This is the first time you've mentioned it to me."

Ramsay watched the sweat under his nose. Ray's upper lip caught it, then the moisture fell to the floor.

Ray smiled. "Love to see you there," he said as another drip splattered on the magazine on his desk.

"Thanks for the notice," Marcus said. "I wish you'd see I'm just trying to help Coyote." He turned and walked out of Earl's office.

Ramsay passed Lenora's desk, sending a few pieces of paper flying, and opened the door to the courtyard.

Earl watched Ramsay's exit and pulled a folded handkerchief from his pocket, patting it under his nose. He walked around his desk to his office door. "Say, Lenora, Marcus looked a little perturbed, or am I imaging things?" Earl asked.

The phone rang; Lenora picked it up. "Earl, it's Miss Sheila. Line one."

The next day after Cecil had left for his Dallas appointment at the Benedict Company, Marcus Ramsay called from his desk into the air, "What a hell of a day." He stretched back in his squeaky green vinyl chair and groaned.

"You in a testy mood again, Mr. Ramsay?" Daisy called out from her desk in the next room. "You've been in a fuss all week. Going to the party, aren't y'all?"

"Yeah. Just finished my speech," he said.

"The speech stuff is tradition, you know."

"Whoop-dee-doo," he said. "Hope the company folks respond to me a little more favorably this time."

"Oh, Marcus. You bein' harsh?" she said.

"Actually, my speech is pretty good, I think," he said.

The wind whistled and the courtyard darkened. All of the Coyote Brand employees had gone home early the day before the party. It was part of the tradition.

"You bringing Kathy?" she called.

"Yeah. Roy Rogers and Shannon coming?"

"Just Coy. He'll insist on coming 'cause he knows y'all will be there. It should be a good time if Earl doesn't talk too long."

They laughed. She walked into his office.

"Where's the party?" he asked.

"Where else? The Holiday Inn."

"Do those Italian lights hang on the walls all year long?"

" 'Course. Oh Marcus, there's nothing wrong with the ol' Holiday Inn's li'l lights or the oil well outside. Folks in town are mighty proud of all of it."

"Ms. Duncan, you know I love the way you talk," he said.

"Say what?" She sat in Cecil's chair.

"Hey,you got 'say what' from me," he said and smiled, emotion welling up in his voice. The day, the week, the last few months had worn on him. "Daisy, you've been such a wonderful help, so supportive through this, really. I don't know what I would've done without you."

"Aw," she said as she walked into his office and stood behind Cecil's chair. "Honest?"

"Really. It's almost been five months," he said. "Do you realize that?"

"Actually seems like a year." She laughed and sat.

"Really, you've always been there for me. And nobody else has besides maybe Cecil."

"Oh, Marcus," she said. "You been pushin' so hard."

"You're always saying 'Oh, Marcus' too."

"Really?" she asked.

"You oughta get me a western belt with 'Oh, Marcus' on the back."

"Maybe next Christmas," she said. She crossed her legs and hung them over the arm of Cecil's chair.

"Daisy?" he asked.

"Yep?"

"Come here." He felt spontaneously reckless emotions stir inside him.

"Say what?"

"I think it's time we do something to celebrate."

"Celebrate what?" She slowly stood.

"Christmas. Progress. Us."

"How might that be?"

"We might-could have a little Christmas kiss," he said. "Just a little one."

"Might-could. But, we ain't got no mistletoe."

"Ain't got?"

"Oh, Marcus, it's just the way we talk. Don't be such a damn foreigner."

"I remember you called me that when I just started. Those were almost your first words to me."

"Great. Well, can we proceed with this li'l ol' kiss idea ASAP?" she asked. They stood.

"I do believe ASAP are my words, Ms. Duncan." He stood.

"Exactly. Perhaps we just mixed-up our words, Mr. Ramsay," she said.

"Now, how do we undo that?" he asked.

"I guess we might-could put 'em back in each other's mouths where they belong," she said. They both laughed, a little shakily.

"How do we do that?" he asked, and walked to the side of Cecil's desk.

"You know, Mr. Ramsay. The damn kiss," she scolded. She smiled and stood poised by Cecil's desk, six feet away from him.

"Well. I'm waiting," he said. "I can only wait so—"

But as the words left his lips, he caught himself. He thought about previous first kisses and wondered if this was such a good idea. If it was a boring little kiss, he would be unaffected, able to continue carrying on his normal day-to-day routine with this lady—his secretary and friend—but with less of the attraction that had tugged at him for months.

On the other hand, if it was an electrifying kiss, he would be tempted to pursue Daisy further. He knew he should consider the fact that Daisy was married. He was, too, albeit to a woman who checked him more than she hugged him. Ramsay was confused.

"Marcus?" she said, arms outreached. "You know."

It was too late, the seed was planted. "I don't know," He hesitated.

"You *do* know, Marcus." She kept smiling. "Y'all want this and I do, too. Now, I'm a-comin' to get it. You better not let me down."

Her mouth, he thought. What would it hurt? Just this once. He held up his arms.

She threw her hair back and flew to him from the side of Cecil's desk. She floated toward him until her face was a foot away. She grabbed his shirt at the chest with her right hand.

"So forceful, Ms. Duncan?" he asked softly.

"Y'all may be gentle an' all, but there might-could be a time and a place . . . " As he felt her long nails take hold of his shirt, she slowed her movements. She had moved so gracefully to him, as if her approach had been planned for months; a prima ballerina finally executing flawlessly on opening night.

"You like it, Mr. Ramsay?" she asked.

"Might-could."

"Too much talk, Marcus," she said.

"You think?" He pulled her until she was an inch away. Their foreheads touched.

"My-oh-my," she said slowly, the mys sounding more like ahs than ever before.

He felt her chest against his and warmth below his waist. He watched her out-of-focus eyes dart around at different points on his face. Ramsay weakened as she easily hung on his shoulders. "Your breath is so sweet," he said.

She pulled him closer with a jerk. "Marcus, I know I shouldn't do this, but I've been wantin' it so bad."

He gulped.

"Well, Yankee," she said, "come an' get it."

They both closed their eyes. His lips touched hers for the first time, giving way easily. Their eyes opened, then closed again. He felt the tip of her tongue between his teeth.

He hesitated, then responded with his. Then, just lips again. They both pulled away.

"Now wait a second, Ms. Duncan." He sighed. "Perhaps we should stop right there."

"Yankee tease," she moaned. "Just go with your heart, man."

"You sure?" He gasped into her neck.

"Oh, Lord, this is the first time anyone has ever called me Ms. Duncan and kissed me in the same breath. You can't stop now."

"Oh, Daisy," he said.

They paused a second, then melted into one another. Daisy moaned passionately as she kissed Marcus. Her tongue explored every tiny crevice of his mouth carefully and completely.

Their eyes opened on occasion to catch a glimpse of the other's. Minutes passed as they enjoyed each others' pleasure.

Marcus pulled away. "I knew this kiss would be good, but not this good."

Marcus felt tingles course through his entire body as he hungered for more than kisses.

She pulled away. "Happy Holidays, you Yankee bastard."

"Shit," he said, flustered. "Ease up, OK?"

"Why?"

He gently kissed her neck. "Just let it be gentle for a second."

"I'm just not used to . . . You hold me like velvet," she said.

"That's right. Just relax."

"Wait!" She yanked away. "My daughter is expecting me to pick her up from dance. Besides, if you knew everything about me, you'd . . . "

"What everything?"

"I'd better go." Daisy turned her head toward the door. "This gentle stuff makes me crazy." She opened the door to the courtyard.

"I guess I should head north, then," he said, confused.

"You'd better." She pivoted and ran out, across the courtyard to her Pontiac Sunbird, bathed in mercury vapor light. She looked back and flashed an empty smile that he had never seen on her before, like an angry little girl abandoned by her parents on the first day of school. She got in her car and slammed the door. The engine roared, the tires spun, and the dust flew as she sped away.

Marcus Ramsay stood there licking his puffy lips and sniffing her lingering fragrance. For the next hour his obsession to help the business soar to new heights set with the sun. He sipped a Coke as he sat at his desk, pondering the good and bad of what he had just done, and how it might affect his mission.

15 *Corsicana, Texas   December 18, 1980*

The walls of the party room at the
Corsicana Holiday Inn sparkled with
Italian lights on the Friday night before
Christmas as the Coyote Brand
employees gathered for their company
annual holiday party.

The male employees wore the same
dated suits that they wore whenever
Allied management visited from Chicago.
Their wives wore simple cotton dresses
and stubby heels from some indiscernible
era. Each female employee wore a
wristlet corsage reminiscent of prom
days, a tradition that prompted giggles
from small groups of ladies around the
twinkling room. Their reluctant
husbands wore crumpled jackets and
wash-and-wear slacks, each futilely
pressed with irons and towels at the last
minute.

Several dresses contrasted with the
others: Kathy Ramsay's long, sparkling
silver-on-black gown, Linda Hudson's
contemporary, bright yellow dress with
puffy shoulders, and Daisy's long, clingy
blue knit dress with rows of shiny beads.

The three women found each other and shared a drink and chitchat until Al Bishop's glass chimed, signaling all to sit.

Within minutes, the garden salad was served. Kathy Ramsay commented to Marcus that the plates looked like miniature flying saucers as they glided out of the kitchen in the hands of the part-time waiters who carried them shakily to the handful of tables-of-ten.

The salads were barely on the table when plate after plate of roast beef was paraded into the room. From the group's comments and spare applause, Ramsay gathered each course was the traditional fare at these celebrations. Kathy Ramsay quietly chuckled about the oddity of the event, elbowing Marcus repeatedly.

"Hey, cool it," he said. He looked around and realized that Harold, Linda, Daisy, Coy, Kathy, and he were the only people under fifty, outnumbered by an older contingent who seemed much more interested in discussing the mediocre food than in other stimulating conversation.

Ramsay also noticed that all seventy-four of the black plant workers were absent from the party. That is, except Jesse Evans, who had just been promoted to the position of distribution manager (to meet a Allied mandated quota), and his shy, overwhelmed wife. The Evans couple were the sole representatives of their race.

Just then, Earl Hickman stood and, after getting a ceremonial peck from Sheila, cleared his throat loudly. The group hushed. He walked up to the old microphone atop a small podium that said ROTARY, stationed at the front of the room. "Now, testing, testing," he said, tapping the microphone. It squealed. "Before I start, I want to say that it's a testament to my time here at Coyote that my little girl is old enough to skip this event and go out with her fancy new boyfriend from Dallas."

The crowd laughed.

"Whoever he is!"

Like an applause track, the crowd laughed again.

"I'm also sorry to see that Frank Benedict, our fine Dallas broker, was unable to make it. Maybe he and Erlene are going out together!"

"Ooo," they said.

"S'pose that'll be the headline in the *Sun* tomorrow."

The crowd murmured.

"Speaking of news, 1980 has been a helluva year for Coyote Brand and I'll tell you why," Earl said and paused. "It's been the year that we've all worked together to bring our fine product to the great state of California."

Marcus Ramsay perked up and looked at Kathy. *No. Not California again,* he thought. *This is crazy.*

Earl continued. "Now, there might be some who would come to Coyote from the North and, after being here only a short while, think they know what's best for our little company. But, make no mistake about it, after ten-plus years, I think I'm finally getting the hang of it!"

Applause rang through the little party room.

"Ain't nobody gonna lay down no fancy new ideas 'round here."

Earl waited for the cheers and whistles to subside.

"Now, we got our new computers that Al's putting in, all right, but we're taking one step at a time. That means we're not changing our advertising and promotional programs anytime soon. No-o-o how. And, as your president, I will lead you to California, then beyond. No matter what Chicago says."

They cheered and applauded.

"Ain't no Allied folks gonna invade our little company. . . " Earl looked around the room and stopped at Marcus. The rest in the room followed his gaze. " . . . and change it. No how."

The crowd clapped. Some hooted.

Invade? Change? Marcus looked back at the homogeneous wall of empty, smiling eyes. He couldn't believe Earl had singled him out as the Yankee intruder once again.

Then, Earl waved at Marcus to stand up and address the crowd.

Oh great. Helluva introduction, Marcus thought. He stood in place, staring at the odd assemblage, and wondered how his words could possibly inspire them after Earl's critical preamble. He glanced across the room and saw Daisy heading toward the door where Erlene had just entered, apparently back early from her date. The two women exchanged a girlfriend hug and turned to listen to Ramsay, whose stomach gurgled.

He flapped his papers and started. "I don't know what to say, except that I appreciate the welcome and hope that we all can work together during the coming year to do great things for Coyote Brand.

Together we'll conquer all the roadblocks that would otherwise prevent our progress! It is truly the dawn of a new decade . . . "

He continued the speech he had worked on for hours, designed to rally the cynical Corsicana troops. But, as he spoke, they only replied with glares and random claps. The more eloquently he delivered his prose, the sleepier their response seemed. Finally, as he finished, they just stared at him like they hadn't heard a word.

He had talked about all the changes the little company had been through over the previous six months—analyzing trade deals, canceling California, reorienting the Cherry-Black Agency—and how he was there to help them adjust to inevitable changes in the marketplace. But having finished, Marcus Ramsay stood, stranded, and looked dumbly at them.

"I don't feel so well," he said. The room spun and his gut tossed. He saw Sheila Hickman blabbering away and laughing, flailing her hand at him between swigs of wine and saying, "Yankee go home!"

Then Ramsay wobbled in place, lightheaded. He nearly stumbled as he tried to sit.

"Marcus?" Kathy asked, "Are you OK? You look pale as a ghost."

"My stomach. I feel queasy," he said.

Daisy came over. She said, "Maybe it's all the changes since y'all moved and such. And these ungrateful folks might-could be getting to him. He hasn't looked so good lately, workin' so hard."

"You're probably right, Daisy," Kathy said. She dabbed a wet napkin on Marcus' forehead. Marcus shook as she applied it, but felt a little better.

As he inhaled deeply to quell the nausea, the crowd's prattle returned and glasses clinked. "Wow," he said. "Really crept up on me."

"You'll be OK, honey," Kathy said. "Your color's coming back."

"Yeah, but we're going now," he said. After a few minutes he stood. "Just excuse me," he said to no one. "We have to go." Without hesitating, he pulled Kathy behind him toward the side door of the party room.

It was the kind of scene that might have evoked applause had it been a senior baseball player's last game as he succumbed to the rigors of his sport. But casual conversation and laughter at the tables continued. They completely ignored the Yankee's departure and his wife's smirk as she held open the exit door. It was like his leaving was merely an expected part of some grand plan, his presence in this place that birthed the first oil west of the Mississippi, a mistake all along.

Erlene chatted with Daisy, who watched the Ramsays leave. "Poor fella. Might-coulda been what he ate," Erlene said. "You think?" Sensitive Yankee stomach, she thought.

Daisy laughed. "You think? Holiday Inn food? Then we're all in trouble."

Erlene looked over at her mother, sloshing another glass of house red as she blabbered at the nine other people at her table. Erlene shook her head. "Damn Mama."

Then Daisy's husband, sitting nearby, rose and squeaked his chair back.

"Lotta beer. Huh, Coy?" Daisy razzed him as he clunked forward in his boots, his head awkwardly drooped, his long chestnut hair resting on the shoulders of his checked western shirt.

"All full up," the tall cowboy with the mustache grumbled.

After Erlene eyed him for a second, she froze. "Wait. You called him Coy? Is that his name?" she asked, suddenly piqued. "Coy?"

Daisy nodded. "Yep. Good ol' Coy. You know that, darlin'."

"No, sir," Erlene said. "That's the first time you ever called him by his real name. Always been cowboy or Roy Rogers or some such."

"So, what about it, girl?" Daisy asked.

"Coy, Coy, Coy," Erlene said, finger to lips. She listened to herself say the name. She studied the man swaggering closer to her, now in better light. His features, the color of his hair, mustache, and that scar were similar to the cowboy who had raped her a decade before!

Erlene backed away, gripping her fists so tightly her nails broke the surface of her skin and drew bits of blood. "He's the one," she gasped, barely able to get the words out. She pointed at him with a single finger. He looked up and kept coming.

"Who, honey? Who?" Daisy asked and searched beyond Coy for some evil person Erlene had just noticed.

"Coy! It's your Coy," Erlene said as her finger wavered in the air.

"What's the matter with him?" Daisy reached for Erlene, who pushed her away.

"No, no. It's really him!" Erlene screamed, one hand on her mouth.

Coy lifted his head and looked at her.

Sheila watched from across the room. She moved around her table, now realizing why her daughter had cried out, "It's him." The way Erlene had said it could only mean one thing to a rape victim's mother.

"You rapist!" Sheila yelled loud enough for all to hear. "I see you, you rapist. Everybody look. Coy Duncan is the rapist!"

Sheila bounded across the room. She felt her eyes bug out of her head. She held a cork-plugged, half-empty wine bottle high. It was the same asshole cowboy she had dreamt about recently, along with Ramsay and Post. She breathed heavily as she felt pressure in the veins of her neck. Old memories flashed by, too quick to catch.

"Sheila, wait!" Earl said. He raised his hand, but she pushed past him.

Erlene sobbed and Daisy held her. Coy shrugged as Sheila got within striking distance. "Hey bitch, now you leave me alone," he said and raised his hands.

Sheila raised her bottle like she had her tennis racket so many times at the club. She began to swing it forward. But, the cowboy stepped forward and thwarted her near the top of her swing and pushed the bottle back.

Then Earl marched over and, with great effort, pulled Sheila to his side. He puffed his chest and turned beet red. "Young man, I think you better go now. You hear me?" he roared.

She saw Coy Duncan wink at Earl. *The nerve,* she thought.

Sheila swiped the bottle at Coy's body. "I swear I'll kill you with my bare hands!"

Earl held her back. "Now! Out," Earl said. "You hear me, boy?"

Most of the Coyote employees froze. Ten years earlier the rape of thirteen year-old Erlene Hickman was the big

news around town. But, it had become a
dead issue until this moment.

Coy strode toward the fire door. He
flashed back a cocky sneer at Sheila.

She broke free of Earl's hold and ran
toward Coy. Just feet from him, through
the thickness of his beer stench, Sheila
heard Coy growl, only loud enough for
her to hear. "She was better'n you, too,
Sheila Baby."

"You asshole!" Sheila yelled. She held
onto the neck of the bottle and cracked it
against the nearby walnut-paneled wall. It
exploded, sending red wine and green
shards everywhere. The Coyote Brand
families moved away. Some scurried
through the other door.

"You bastard!" Sheila flung the
remnant of the broken bottle end-over-
end at Coy. The cracked edge slashed
through Coy's shirt. Blood dripped from
his arm.

"Shoot!" As he knocked away the
bottle, he cut his opposite hand. He
pushed open the fire door and left,
cradling both wounds. The fire alarm
started wailing.

People screamed and scattered.

Daisy held her chest and cried over
the alarm, "Erlene, I just don't know what

to say. Oh baby!"

Sheila walked up to her. "You've said enough, sleaze! Go home and tend to your rapist," she said.

The alarm continued.

"Daisy, you better go home," Earl said. "Do you need a ride?"

"Maybe, if Coy's gone," she said. "Mr. Hickman, I just don't know what to say."

"Nothin' more to say." He shook his head in disbelief. "It's been one tough evenin'."

Miles away, as Marcus Ramsay drove past Ennis on the way to their new home two miles northeast of downtown Dallas, off of Central Expressway down Walnut Hill Drive, a few blocks from Lake Hubbard, Kathy slept on his lap. Drained by another cool reception from the company and the sudden, dizzying sickness that had overcome him, he felt weak and out of breath. He cleared his throat involuntarily three or four times. It was like something was stuck in there.

He looked around for a Kleenex, but found none. Kathy adjusted her snoozing position. When something came out of the back of his throat into his mouth, he wiped his lips with his shirt sleeve and looked at the bit of saliva. But it wasn't saliva.

Sticky yellow drool?

16 *Corsicana, Texas*   *February 12, 1981*

A month or so later, after news of Coy Duncan's role as a rapist had been ignored by his buddy, Larry Calhoun the sheriff, and was all but forgotten by the Corsicana townfolk who were afraid of the local Klan boys, including Coy, Marcus and Daisy were talking in the little sales office. Ramsay was still wondering about how to theme his presentation at the Dallas trade party coming up in the spring.

"Marcus, maybe things'll seem clearer when we move to Dallas," Daisy said. "That is, assumin' we ever do. In the meantime, I think this book I got from Wyvonne Putnam down at the Navarro County Historical Society might help you about now." Daisy struggled as she raised the thick, brown book, then thumped it onto his desk. "Whew!"

"You need to work out, Ms. Duncan," he said.

"Say what? I'll have you know I'm in splendid shape, Mr. Ramsay. This damn book is just heavy."

Ramsay thumbed through the book. "Daisy, why didn't you tell me about this Wyvonne Putnam and the Navarro County Historical Society before?"

"Lady's devoted her life to gettin' the history of Navarro in print," she said. "Shoot. Somebody's gotta do it."

He fiddled with his chin. "Hmm. That gives me a great idea for my presentation," he said. Marcus turned through pages of the brown book. "This is great! It tells the whole history of Coyote Brand, Corsicana, and chili."

"Yep. Wyvonne and her friends did quite a job," she drawled. "Navarro County history from the 1800's till now."

"Incredible," Ramsay said.

"I wouldn't give you a bum steer, would I, Yankee?" she said.

He flipped more pages. "It tells about the floods during the late 1800's, the cotton crop, the oil boom, old Lyman T. Davis, Post's uncle, and even Lyman's Model A chili delivery cars—all of it."

She folded her arms proudly. "If it wasn't for Wyvonne, we wouldn't have much of a history 'round here. Bless her li'l' ol' heart."

"This even tells about James Post's memorial service," he said.

"You happy I brung you that?" she asked.

"Are you kidding? Here's a photo of the service, right here in Corsicana. Remember this, Daisy? I was there, you know," Marcus said.

"Good for you, Marcus. And, just think, James Earl Post was the guy who got Allied to buy Coyote in the first place," she said.

Ramsay laughed. "So, if it wasn't for him, I wouldn't be here banging my head against the wall trying to help you guys?"

"Guess it's your destiny, Marcus," she said. "To hep us, if we want it or not."

"If you believe in that destiny stuff," he said.

"I don't know," she said, "Haven't you ever noticed how the bad guy always gets it in the end? That's destiny, idn't it?"

"I guess you're right, or is that Karma?" he said.

Daisy's face lit up with an idea. "Say, Marcus, ever think maybe Margaret Post'd be up to giving you some ideas for the Dallas show?"

He stopped thumbing. "Boy, that would be cool," he said, "if you could arrange it."

Two months later, in the front office across the courtyard, Earl sat at his desk. His phone rang.

"I'll get it, Lenora!" he called. "Hickman, here."

"So, what's the Yankee doing now?" It was Sheila's regular afternoon phone call. "Just drawing a salary, I suppose," she said. "The troublemaker."

"Guess he's putting together the Dallas show. Cecil's showing him how," Earl said. "Takes a lot of time, all those numbers an' all."

"Why not just fire him for good, Earl?" she asked.

"So I don't have to do all the work! It's about time I kick back a little." He leaned back in his desk chair.

"As long as he doesn't walk away with your job, Mr. President," she said.

He laughed. "I'm still giving the Dallas presentation. He just doesn't know it yet. He's just doing all the work; making it pretty good, too, according to Cecil."

"Well, I'll let you get back to work. Oh, Earl? You might want to know your daughter's started seeing Frank

Benedict. I found a pretty juicy love note."

"I figured that," he said. "I saw them running around like kids at the cook-off last week."

"I guess she could've done worse. Man's rich, after all. Say, how'd he get so damn rich?"

"Commission, I guess. Six percent idn't bad. Lotta ways to make bucks in the brokerage bidness." Earl stared empty-eyed into space.

The next day Daisy wandered into Ramsay's office reading his final outline for a new Dallas Trade Party slide presentation. "I got to say, this is real different. You got your cowboys and range cooks. Then Lyman T. Davis starts canning his chili and delivering it in those funny-lookin' chili cars, then James Post takes over and gets Allied to buy the place . . . not bad. It all rings," she said. "Like a movie."

"I can't wait to present it," he said.

"Wait, smarty. Aren't you missing something?" she asked.

"Like what?"

She put the stack of papers down. "One surprise that oughta blow your socks off." Daisy stood in front of Cecil's desk and held her arms behind her back.

"What is it now, Daisy?" he asked. Ramsay stood and walked around the desk. "Well, my Corsicana lass?" He held out his hands. "Gimme."

"No, Yankee. You owe me. Now, you come and get it." She didn't move.

Marcus walked over, tossed her hair back, and kissed her neck.

She shivered. "Ooo. A real magic mouth, you are, Mr. Ramsay." She fluttered her eyes and fanned herself.

"I assume that kiss pays the appropriate toll," he said.

"Mmm. Might-could," she said. She pulled a small scrap of paper from behind her back. She laid it in his hands. "You like, boss?" She fanned herself more. "Whew!"

Ramsay unfolded the paper. His eyes popped. "Daisy, you are truly incredible!"

Sheila woke suddenly that night, sweating. She had seen the rainy night, a large car, a long brick wall, and an older Marcus Ramsay turn into James Post. It was so vivid, yet fleeting. She had just had a new version of "the dream".

As she sipped a glass of wine at the dining room table to help her get back to sleep, Sheila tried to recall the nightmare's details. No matter how she strained, she couldn't hold onto a single thought. "Shit!" She slammed the table.

When she returned to bed, Earl mumbled, barely awake. "What is it, Sheila?" he asked.

"Nothing, Earl. I don't know anymore. It's like all this stuff gets planted in my damn head. These weird dreams . . . "

"You think it's time for Navarro?" he mumbled.

"Zapping? No fucking way! That'll only make things worse," she stuttered. "See, I can't even talk right." As Earl dozed off, Sheila Bradley Hickman sat up in bed in the light of the full moon with her eyes wide open, thinking back to her times at Navarro. I feel so confused. These damn dreams seem so real. I wish I could just cry.

As the moon cast hard shadows across the room, her thoughts spun and her hands sweated profusely. She rubbed them together, then on her pillowcase until it was damp.

Please make this sick feeling go away, she thought.

She stuffed her hands between her legs, but that just made them sweat more. When she finally dozed off, she dreamt she was in church:

It was that nippy January day and glowing space heaters were situated around the Corsicana Community Church sanctuary for James Post's funeral service. The whole town was sitting in the pews or on the lawn outside.

As Sheila sat alone in a pew, sweat dripped from her hands. Suddenly, it inexplicably turned to blood. She futilely rubbed her hands on her flowery, white dress, but the red liquid continued to flow.

Meanwhile, Earl walked up to the pulpit. It seemed that his words boomed through the mike directly at her, "You'll never forget him. You'll never forget him . . ."

Gawkers, young and old, looked at her. "It's Sheila. It's Sheila Hickman," they murmured.

An ugly, crooked man who had been sitting several rows behind her, stood up, pointed at her, and stuttered an accusation, "You're the o-one. Not m-me."

Reverend Miller walked up to her. He whispered, "Come with me, Mrs. Hickman. I'll help you find peace." He took her arm and escorted her down the aisle, out the front door, and around to the side of the church.

"Oh, thank you, Reverend Miller," she said. "I so need peace." Once outside, he directed her to stand with her back against a ten foot windowless stretch of church wall.

Why should I stand against the church wall? she thought.

"May the Lord bless you and keep you," he whispered into her ear. Then the old man patted her on the shoulder and stepped aside.

About twenty feet away, a row of Corsicanans scowled and held stones. They began throwing them at her, first little ones that only stung as they hit, then bigger ones that really hurt.

"Ow!" she yelled and tried to dodge them, but no matter where she stood, they kept coming. In a few minutes they became a shower of black cannon balls. They pummeled her until all feeling disappeared. Then she was engulfed by an infinite, black nothingness . . . and peace.

Sitting in his taxi, parked under some trees just outside the Hickman home, Reginald mused into his radio, "I knew it would slowly make sense," he said. "That pummeling. I say, I do like the pummeling. It's something else to use in my plan. I knew as time went by, the method of Post's spirit's revenge would unfold quite naturally." He took some notes.

Ramsay dodged weeds as he drove up the stone driveway of the large white house. The plants were untended. The grass was long. The flowers were withered and dying.

He pulled to a stop and got out. He crunched across the gravel driveway to the tattered porch and walked up the wooden steps.

He rang the rusty doorbell next to the screen door and looked back as he waited for an answer. The spacious porch overlooked an amber field that separated

Golf Estates from a neighborhood of smaller tract homes. His journey to the Post place had taken him just north of town, up Second Street, and through the woods, past a stone Golf Estates marker.

"What's the occasion?" Kathy Ramsay had asked him that morning. Ramsay had ignored her and straightened his tie. Later, as he drove down I-45, he was excited, like he was about to visit an old girlfriend. He wore his best suit and stopped in Corsicana for daisies at Margie's Flower Shop, one of the few independently-owned stores still open in the shabby shopping area. Daisy said that everybody knew Margaret was partial to that particular flower. This day, Marcus Ramsay knew he would talk with history.

"Mr. Ramsay?" A middle-aged, black woman answered the door.

"You must be Henrietta?" he said. "You talked to Daisy Duncan about my visit."

"Sure did. Miss Margaret's almost ready, Mr. Ramsay," Henrietta said. She eyed Ramsay's daisies suspiciously, then his yellow legal pad. "Why don't you come on in, then. Now don't be spending

too much time with her. She needs a lot
of rest these days."

He followed Henrietta in. While the
porch had looked worn, the entry hall
was immaculate. It was decorated with
neatly framed black and white pictures:
the 1966 Coyote Brand baseball team,
Margaret and James visiting the Tyler
Rose Festival during their courting days,
and James Post's monumental funeral.

Then, there was an array of
photographs of James Post.

"Marcus Ramsay?" A dainty female
voice called.

He turned and saw her.

"Why, I think I do remember you,
son," she said. "You introduced yourself
at James' funeral, I do believe." A frail,
petite, middle-aged woman with sparse
hair accused him affectionately.

"Yes, ma'am. I remember you, too,"
he said.

"Well, I swear. It's been ten years.
But my hair . . . " She held her hand to
her mouth.

"Don't worry about that," Ramsay
said.

"I even remember the driver that day,"
she said. "He borrowed James' beautiful
silver pen to sign the receipt. When he

gave it back . . . well, I can't explain it . . . I just felt relieved, I'd say, like everything would be all right. He was a strange young man with a British accent and one of those short haircuts. Never saw him before or since." She coughed.

Henrietta stepped forward. "Miss Margaret? You OK?" she asked.

"I'm feeling fine. Now, leave us alone. Mr. Ramsay?"

"Please, call me Marcus."

"Marcus. I'm not so good a day or so after those awful chemo treatments. I've started them up again, you know. Truly awful." The delicate woman shuffled toward him wearing a long, quilted satin robe and muted pink slippers. She primped at what hair she had. Her eyes sparkled.

"I'm quite amazed. You haven't changed one bit." She smiled brightly. "Thirty-five now? Maybe forty?"

"About right, Mrs. Post," Ramsay said. "Been tired lately, though. So nice to see you." He reached out his hand to the stately woman, who held hers in the air for him.

He paused, not knowing what was expected, then awkwardly kissed it.

She nodded and smiled approvingly.

"You have a wonderful home," Ramsay said, and looked around.

"Henrietta keeps it just beautifully. Doesn't she, Mr. Ramsay?" The woman gently pointed around the room.

"Yes, ma'am. Please, Mrs. Post. Just call me Marcus."

"Oh, that's right. Now you just call me Margaret. Please call me Margaret." She coughed.

"Of course, Margaret," he said.

She closed her eyes and sighed. "Margaret. No one has called me that in years. It's always Mrs. Post this, Miss Margaret that."

Ramsay flushed. He hadn't noticed he was still holding on to her frail hand. He gently let it go.

She smiled. "Marcus, would you like some of Henrietta's homemade iced tea or lemonade? Either is but a simple nod away." She reached for his hand again and cradled it as she walked him to a small love seat across the large drawing room. As she sat, she motioned for Ramsay to sit in the adjacent wicker chair. In it lay an old stuffed animal.

She pointed to the wicker chair, then smiled fondly. "Sit here, please. James' favorite, you know. His little toy coyote."

Ramsay had heard from the rumors that this woman was an eccentric recluse. *Impossible,* he thought. He scooted the toy aside.

"Ma'am, I want to say first that I'm truly honored you would give me some of your time," he said.

"Nonsense. I'm more than willing to offer you any advice or background, as you call it, on my James. Just seeing you brings back memories of him. Call me silly, but in a way it's like an angel of some sort has come back to visit. But your accent?"

"Chicago," he said.

"Of course." She gazed at him, about to say something. "No. I'll wait." She sniffled as he prepared his pen and opened his notebook. "Mr. Ramsay, uh, Marcus, my James was a great man. Respected and admired for his contributions to the company and Navarro County. You know about his Uncle Lyman and the cars?"

"Oh yes, Ma'am. I'm pretty well up on that."

She smiled, then motioned to his yellow notepad. "What is it you need to know?" she asked.

"I'd like to know about your husband from your perspective, ma'am."

"James was not one to mince words. Got right to the point. Like you, my dear boy."

"Yes, Margaret. At least that's what I've been told."

A single tear fell past her affectionate smile when Ramsay said her name. "He was funny, too, my James," she said. "Always teasing."

Marcus wrote on his pad.

"He was such a visionary, always had the big ideas. But at the same time he was silly . . . with his little notes." She tossed a hand at the air.

"Notes?"

"My James always sent everybody at Coyote little white notes telling them what to do. He liked to manage them, is what he used to call it. Like he was some kind of puppeteer." She giggled, then coughed.

Ramsay wrote a summary of Margaret's note-taking stories. "Machiavellian?" he asked.

"Yes, I guess that's what you'd call it." She smiled. "He was so funny how he'd come home and tell me about his notes."

Then she eyed Ramsay inquisitively. "My dear boy, there's something about you."

"What?" Ramsay looked up. Just then he felt jittery, as if he had arrived home from a long trip on a bumpy road. "Margaret . . . " He shook his head to ward off a sudden nausea.

"Oh, Marcus. What is it, dear?" Margaret asked and leaned forward.

"Nothing. I'm feeling a little odd is all." Some yellow phlegm slipped from the edge of his lips. He wiped it awkwardly.

"Henrietta," Margaret called, "Get the boy some water and a tissue."

Henrietta scurried to the kitchen and returned.

"My word. I hope you're not coming down with something," Margaret said.

"I think it's just that I've been working so hard—nights and weekends."

"I'd say so. Sounds like my James," she said.

He wiped his mouth, sipped some water, and handed the glass back to Henrietta.

"There, now," Margaret said. "I hope that's better."

"Yes, ma'am," he said. "I just felt a little woozy there for a second." Henrietta walked away.

At the same moment, on the road adjacent to Margaret Post's gravel driveway, Reginald Waverly was parked in his taxi, clipboard poised. "Smooth, flowing lines," he recalled from his nighttime visit to the Hickman's, plus those little white notes Margaret spoke of. He grinned. All at once a complete idea sprouted in his mind's eye. Now he could see how he could create a design for his assignment: he might use Sheila Hickman's guilt, James Post's Machiavellian tendencies, and Marcus Ramsay's desire to help.

Back inside the Post home for the next hour, Ramsay asked questions and scribbled thoughts onto his yellow pad, which Margaret Post seemed to speak to directly as she hugged one of her spindly arms with the other.

Then Ramsay noticed he had begun transferring her thoughts effortlessly to his pad, gliding his pen along in a single squiggly line. But his squiggles materialized as perfectly legible words.

He looked down at his pad. *What kind of weird stuff is this?* he thought.

Occasionally, Ramsay glanced up and lingered in Margaret's moist hazel eyes. Then he returned to his pad, always surprised he had written so much.

"You know I'll be with you in spirit, young man," Margaret said, "when you present your program." She smiled fondly at him, then coughed and cleared her throat. "Like some more iced tea, Marcus?"

"No thank you," he said. "You've been so kind. It must have been terrible to lose your husband so unexpectedly in the prime of his life."

"Yes. But, Marcus," she looked up squinting, studying the sky, "there was not a more blessed day than when all of Corsicana said good bye to my James. Thousands, yes thousands. Remember it? Quite the spectacle." A small tear that had lingered on the edge of her right eye silently dropped to her lap.

"Yes, I remember," he said. "People were everywhere, like Woodstock."

She sniffled.

"Oh, I'm sorry, ma'am," he said. "I think I'm stirring up too many sad memories. I'd better go."

"Nonsense, young man. You mustn't go," she said.

"Why do you want me to stay, Mrs. Post?"

"There's more to tell." She looked up at her housekeeper. "Henrietta thinks I'm quite crazy, but I do believe there's a reason you came today. It was your destiny."

"My destiny?" *Why is everybody saying this experience somehow has to do with my destiny?*

She continued. "That's right. Just like it was James' destiny to complete so many wonderful things in his life, for the company, for the town, and for his family. But his life was cut short. It was queer that . . . " She hung her head.

"What was queer, Mrs. Post?" he asked.

She repositioned herself. "No. I shouldn't."

"Please, go ahead. What is it?" he asked.

"The way he left us was such a shame. Poor James died when his squeaky old brakes failed—supposedly."

"Why supposedly?"

She looked at him anxiously and spoke. "You're the one I must tell. I know I can trust you, unlike the rest over there at Coyote or up in Chicago. Even Larry Calhoun, the sheriff."

Ramsay was puzzled. "But ma'am, you've just met me."

"Regardless," she said and smiled. "James always said I had the gift, you know. And I do feel close to you." She patted his knee. "I know you're the one."

"Gift? The one?"

"The gift to tell a good person from a not-so-good person," she said.

"Thank you, ma'am," he said. "But, why haven't you shared your thoughts on this with anyone?"

"I started to," she said. "But, they treated me like I was just a nutty old woman."

"Tell me, then." Marcus leaned forward, readying his pad and pen.

"Well. Not more than four days after my James passed, Grady Davis, a friend of the family and our fine mechanic, came to see me."

"Grady?" Ramsay wrote and thought back to the drunk he had helped outside the Coyote offices one night. "Grady Davis?"

"Yep. He did all of James' auto repairs, you know. Poor Grady thought he made a mistake fixing James' brakes that day. He swore he'd always feel responsible for James' death, the poor boy."

"But, ma'am, I thought Mr. Post's accident was caused when his old brakes failed."

"That's precisely my point. Remember I said supposedly? Grady told me he replaced James' brakes on the day he died," she said.

"So, Mr. Post's car had just gotten new brakes the day he died?"

"You see the problem, then?" she asked.

"So, the legend's wrong," he said.

She nodded. "How could James have perished in his car from a brake malfunction when they were brand new?" She began to get flustered, twisting her handkerchief over and over. "It just doesn't make any sense."

"Maybe this Grady installed them incorrectly," Ramsay said.

"Nonsense. He might stutter, but he's a fine young mechanic. Corsicana's best, even after that ruffian cowboy beat him up years ago."

Ruffian cowboy? Ramsay wrote furiously.

"The brakes worked well enough to get James back to work from the garage without incident, didn't they?" Mrs. Post fidgeted.

"I see." Marcus wrote. "Didn't you bring this information to the attention of the authorities?"

"Actually, yes. I told Larry Calhoun. He was the new sheriff at the time. He was such a nice young man, but a mere child. He's still the sheriff after all these years, you know. He said he'd let me know if he ever found anything. Never did."

Larry Calhoun? Why does that name sound familiar?

Margaret spoke to the pad. "And there was that dreadful Benedict ruffian."

"Benedict? " Ramsay stopped. He looked up.

"Frank Benedict," she said. "The broker in Dallas."

"Of course." He wrote more, but slowed his pace.

"Yes, indeed. That pushy man had just started back then. Quite the up and comer, they said. Slick and rough, too."

He wrote more.

"Frank was badgerin' James, tryin' to get the selling responsibilities for Coyote down in Houston. He wanted to boost his commission a pretty penny, I'll tell you," she said. "But James wouldn't budge. He was a man of principle, you know."

"Mrs. Post, are you saying you suspect foul play here?"

"I have been praying that I'm just dreaming all of this," she said. "I can't believe that this sort of thing is possible in beautiful Navarro County. Oh, my James . . . . " Margaret Post wept into her hanky.

Just then Henrietta returned. She stood quietly behind Mrs. Post.

"Margaret, I promise I'll look into this," Ramsay said.

"I feel so embarrassed." Margaret Post dabbed her tears and reached for Ramsay's hand. "Henrietta thinks I'm crazy, but I feel like James has visited me today. I know you'll hold his name in the highest regard in your program."

"Of course. And I'll keep my eyes open on this Benedict thing, the brakes, and Grady. I'll get back to you."

"You're not shooin' me off like Larry Calhoun did?"

Ramsay smiled and patted her hand. "No, ma'am."

Margaret Post rose with some difficulty, signaling the end of Ramsay's visit. She waved Henrietta away as Ramsay stood and helped her right herself. Then she reached up and gently touched his face. "Remember, Marcus. It is your destiny. I know this is true."

Ramsay was unsure what the little lady meant. He was spooked at the way she had said it, but was encouraged by her spirit.

Her eyes twinkled. "Listen carefully to me, dear." Then, although she spoke to him in a delicate, formal tone, another more intimate communication passed between them, transmitting an energy that seemed to suspend time.

After a moment, he shook his head, breaking out of his trance. "Whew!" He suddenly felt drained. Then a small bit of yellow sputum slipped from his lips. He reached for the wad of Kleenex he had set aside, and wiped his mouth. "Oh, I'm so sorry," he said. "All of a sudden, I didn't feel so good again," he said. "I must be coming down with the flu or something."

"Henrietta, please get Marcus some more water," Margaret called. "Don't worry, dear. James would want you to persevere through this to find the truth."

"Yes, ma'am, I understand," he said. "I think."

She smiled and nodded.

Henrietta hurried in with a pitcher of water. She filled Ramsay's glass and he sipped it.

"I really should go now," Marcus said and wiped his forehead. "I've had a lovely visit today, Mrs. Post."

"Indeed." She reached for his cheek again. "Poor boy. Are you feeling better?"

"A little. Thanks." He sipped again and handed Henrietta the glass.

"That's better," Margaret said. "May you dream sweetly tonight." She stroked his cheek with the outside of her soft hand.

Henrietta sniffled noticeably. Ramsay glanced at her, and then looked back to Margaret. "That's a wonderful thing to say," he said. "I've never heard that."

"It's something James and I used to say to each other. Much nicer than sweet dreams, don't you think?" Then Margaret Post broke down.

Henrietta hurried forward and led the fragile lady away.

17 *Dallas, Texas   March 11, 1981*

Earl Hickman and Marcus Ramsay scanned the huge ballroom of the Dallas Hilton. Earl said, "Who did Cecil invite, anyway? The world?"

"Yeah. Quite a crowd."

"Bigger than usual, I'd say," Earl said.

"Are you well rehearsed, Earl?" Marcus asked. Ramsay loved every word and note of music of his new Coyote Brand Dallas trade party production, but now it was out of his hands. The day before, Earl had surprised him by announcing that he was planning on presenting the program to the members of the Dallas trade himself.

"Presidential purgative," he had said. "You understand."

Now, as Ramsay watched, Earl broke away to hobnob with an old buddy, the mayor of Dallas. Ramsay was both angry at and nervous for Earl. He scoured the echoing, old ballroom. Broker salesmen and trade buyers were trading war stories and toasts, especially regarding Coyote, their host for the evening.

During the previous week, for twelve hours a day, Ramsay had worked with Daisy, Cecil, and Audio Visual Resources (AVR) to fine tune the breakthrough slide show. Intermixed with live narration, now Earl's, it would begin with a sepia-toned young cowpokes on a cattle drive, the first consumers of chili. Then it would spin through an impressive pictorial review of James Post's contributions, including his masterminding the company's sale to the Allied Corporation. Finally it would illustrate how that acquisition would inevitably bring prosperity to Corsicana and Navarro County.

The show would end with a brief summary of the most positive Coyote Brand sales statistics for the year. Punchy and exciting, it was designed to coax any new or lazy trade buyers to order Coyote Brand Products again and again.

Earl finished his conversation with the mayor and, clearing his voice repeatedly, walked back to Ramsay. "He's gonna give me the key to the city, you know. Old friend from the grocery bidness—you understand. Used to head up Tom Thumb Food Stores in the old days."

Bidness again, Ramsay thought. "Earl, you look awfully pale," Ramsay said. "Are you OK?"

" 'Course."

With that, Marcus walked to the podium at the front of the room to introduce Earl. "Attention! Attention!" he said into the mike. He glanced at Earl, who pulled away when Frank Benedict patted him on the shoulder. Meanwhile Erlene, who seemed to be ignoring her father altogether, stood beside the AVR operators at the slide projector. At the spouse's table nearby, Sheila Hickman chatted with Cecil's wife. Kathy Ramsay was not in attendance.

In his opening comments, Marcus explained that commitments of years past were being re-evaluated, especially regarding expansion to California. Now, company resources would be focused in Coyote's strongholds, like Dallas—a comment that sparked the evening's first applause.

After Ramsay introduced Earl, applause erupted as Earl approached and Marcus left the dais. The two men executed a well-rehearsed, mid-aisle handshake and Earl took command of the podium, a spotlight reflecting off his shiny forehead. He looked around like a bird as he waited for the western music to cue him to start.

Just then, Tanya Tucker's recorded singing echoed through the hall. Introductory slides, projected onto a ten-by-ten-foot screen behind the speaker's platform, explained the roots of chili heritage. Warm-toned images of cowboys flashed on the screen as a friendly, prerecorded announcer explained Coyote Brand's roots. Earl fidgeted in place.

When the famous Coyote Brand Chili delivery trucks appeared on the screen, the crowd applauded. The announcer described Lyman T. Davis's Model As and how they had first delivered what ultimately became the Southwest's number one canned chili. Earl smiled and tipped his head to the crowd as if he had invented the contraptions or the Chili or both.

Ramsay seethed at the arrogance of the man. *Who does Earl think he is? He has prevented real progress at the company rather than ever encouraging it,* Marcus thought.

Earl began to sweat beneath his nose, a sign Ramsay had learned meant his boss was nervous or about to stretch the truth. Just then James Post's image filled the screen, wearing his familiar black hat, his arm dangling on Al Bishop's shoulder. From the rear of the photo Oscar looked on with a pouty gaze. The prerecorded announcer explained Post's many accomplishments and how he had died *mysteriously* in 1969.

"Huh?" Earl asked, caught off guard. The "mysteriously" part seemed to throw him off guard just when he was about to begin his speech. With bright spotlights in his eyes, Earl scanned the audience and stopped at Sheila, as if she held his first lines. She rose, a drink shaking in her hand, but said nothing. Then she urged him with her free hand, like a palsied orchestra conductor.

The crowd in the ballroom quickly fell quiet. After a second, just when they began to mumble, Earl burst out his first line: "And Coyote Brand has forged forward since Mr. Post's time . . . "

Sheila sat, shaking her head. The microphone squealed. Just then, Earl froze again, shrugged his shoulders, and looked for her.

Sheila stood and flapped her hands at him like a young mother cuing her child at a kindergarten play. Earl looked at her and cupped his ear, as if he was listening for her cues. When she didn't respond and glasses began tinkling across the room, Earl cleared his throat and rattled on about how California would be a sterling future for Coyote. Then, he talked about how the company's sales had been better than ever that year. All the while, like a seasoned conductor, he waved his arms gracefully.

Marcus looked at the floor and shook his head. *Oh no,* he thought. *Earl is rambling as usual.*

"Shoot!" Frank Benedict said to Marcus from across the table. "Ramsay, look at him. He's dying up there."

"I should've known this would happen," Marcus said. "With the script and all, and the music."

"And what's all this *mysteriously* bullshit?" Frank whispered harshly. "Post's old brakes failed. He crashed into a fuckin' wall and died. Period."

Ramsay leaned across the table. "Frank, it so happens that James Post actually had his brakes fixed on the very day he died," he said. "So, how could they have failed?"

Frank froze. His good eye darted left and right, askew of the glass one. "Bullshit!" One brow crunched. "Now how the hell do you know that?" Frank asked.

"Sources. We haven't found the evidence yet. But, if there is some, we will."

Frank's good eye glared. "Sources? Evidence?"

"Yes."

As Earl Hickman brought the presentation to a bumpy end, Daisy walked from the AVR table up to Marcus.

"Whew! Weren't that something?" She giggled, leaned over, and whispered into Ramsay's ear, "We're still going for a drink later, right boss? Erlene wants to come. Fit in and all. OK?" she asked.

"Sure, I guess," he said.

"I assume y'all can handle both of us," she whispered and kissed him quickly on the ear.

"You tease," Ramsay laughed.

"Hey, y'all are comin' over to my place in my fancy-ass car, aren't you?" Frank asked the girls.

Just then, having completed his bows, Earl walked over. Tentative clapping filled the hall. "Damn," he said. "All those fancy slides and music. Never again."

"Earl, you did a great job despite the slips," Marcus said. He joined the obligatory applause.

"Humph. I think you ought to ease up on that *mysteriously* crap when you go on the road to present this show to the other brokers. You make it sound like Post's death is some kind of unsolved crime. Have some respect for the man."

"Sorry, but it's beginning to look—"

Frank barged in and handed Earl a Perfect Manhattan. "Earl, you need a stiff drink about now. So, y'all are coming back to my place for a drink later, right? Tradition?" Frank said.

"No, thank you, Frank," Cecil said. "'Fraid not this year. Dorothy and I are heading straight home. I'm feelin' a mite tuckered after this last week."

"No thanks, Frank," Marcus said, "The ladies and I are going to the Double Tree."

"Daisy? Erlene?" Frank lunged forward, looking at the women. "Y'all are comin', right? It's a tradition."

"You aren't jealous, are you, Frank?" Daisy laughed.

Erlene shrugged. "Don't be mad, Frankie."

"Wait. Going out with the Yankee ain't no fun," he said. "Come on, we can squeeze into my little Mercedes."

Daisy laughed. "Mr. Benedict, I must say your urgency is most appreciated," she said, "but Mr. Ramsay, Erlene, and I already planned to hit the piano bar."

"I guess we're all set with wheels, Frank," Marcus said. "Maybe next year."

Daisy and Erlene grabbed Ramsay's arms. He shrugged at Frank. They pulled him away, giggling. "Sorry, Frank!"

Earl was the only one who had taken Frank's invitation to come back to his place in North Dallas for a drink.

"These are enough for a small army," Earl said as he studied Frank's shiny gun collection, from a small machine gun to pistols, displayed in the polished mahogany cabinet in his great room. "Must be worth a small fortune." A tiny spotlight accented each of the shiny firearms.

"Thousands, I'm sure. It wouldn't take much to start, though. Didn't know you liked weapons."

"Got to show my Texas machismo, right?" Earl said.

"That's the spirit, Earl. You're gettin' there."

"See, I really don't like shooting," Earl said. "Except trap once in a while. Or is it skeet? Say, let me see that one."

Frank opened his cabinet. "See, in Texas you gotta show you're a real man. This is one way, Earl. Besides, they really are beautiful, you gotta admit." He reached for a handsome pistol and handed it to Earl. "It's Italian. A Beretta

9mm. Perfect for you, boss," the big man said.

"For what? Murder?" Earl said.

"Thought we had enough of that," Fred said.

"Really."

"Keeps comin' up though." Frank laughed uncomfortably. "You know, Post only thought he was a big shot," he said.

"Yep," Earl agreed. "That's for sure."

"He was just lucky gettin' his mint. Listen here, I'm whatcha call a real big shot," Frank said.

"Now why's that, Frank?" Earl asked.

"First, I made my own millions," Frank said. "Didn't drop in my lap one day. Especially from some Yankees."

Earl slapped the Beretta into his left hand repeatedly.

"Say, be careful, Earl. It's not loaded, but you never know."

"Oh, sorry." Earl stopped.

They laughed.

"So how'd you start collecting?" Earl asked.

"In the service," Frank said. "Was a damn Sharpshooter. With the right weapon I coulda nailed Kennedy easy." Frank laughed heartily.

"I better stay on your good side, then," Earl said.

"Oh, you been stayin' on my good side over the years: Post, the billbacks, Houston."

"Say, Frank," Earl said, "There's something important we need to talk about. Something that's bugging me. Not bidness."

"What, partner?" Frank laid the Beretta back on its stand in the gun cabinet.

"It's Erlene," Earl said and fidgeted.

"What about her?" Frank asked.

"About you seeing her, what else?"

"Earl, she's a great kid. Really," Frank said.

"Least you'd protect her from that Duncan asshole."

"What about him?"   Frank crunched his nose.

"Thought you knew. I guess you weren't at the Christmas party. Everybody saw Erlene recognize him as her rapist."

"What?" Frank's face contorted more and flushed. "That asshole?"

"Yep."

"I'll kill that son of a bitch," he said with his teeth gritted.

"Easy does it, Frank. That was a long time ago."

"And I wasn't datin' her then."

"Frank. 'Stead of killin' Duncan, you might want to think about gettin' married again. Stop datin' all these young girls," Earl said, "and settle down." He patted Frank's shoulder.

"We'll see," Frank bristled. "Duncan raped her? Once an asshole, always an asshole. I love Erlene to death, too."

For the next hour Earl and Frank talked over brandies and cigars. Earl tried to adjust to the idea that this burly, middle-aged brute was dating his sensitive, naive daughter.

After eleven, Earl turned to leave. Having had a few too many drinks, Frank staggered after Earl to the door. The wobbly bear grabbed Earl's shoulder. "Fuck—"

"Y'all better sleep this one off, Frank," Earl said.

"I ain't never gonna sleep this one off, buddy. Ain't been this drunk since school." He didn't release Earl's shoulder.

"Hey, Frank," Earl said and pulled away.

"Oh, sorry." Frank's good eye filled with emotion. "Say, I never told you this, Earl."

"What's that?" Earl asked.

"You're a old buddy, really. More than just the business bullshit, all the heavy shit, the money."

"Say thanks, Frank," Earl said reaching out to shake Frank's hand. "Comin' from you that's pretty special. 'Course, you're drunk as a skunk, too!"

Frank threw his arm over Earl's shoulder, tried to steady himself, and let out a deep sigh. "Shoot, I'm so sick of this rat race, boss. If I could get out of it, I would."

"You sure are telling me a lot of personal stuff tonight, buddy. I guess the booze is loosenin' you up some."

"Well, shoot, Earl, you could say we're damn blood brothers. It's about time we acted like it."

When Earl got home, he found Sheila at the kitchen table. She looked drunk, too.

"You OK?" he asked.

She looked up. "Feeling a little confuscd."

"You're always feeling confused these days. More dreams?"

"Fuck you, Earl," she said. "Just flashes."

"Well, you ought to see Lockhart."

"He'll just zap me," she said.

"Maybe it's best," Earl said.

"You're being stupid about Ramsay, Earl," she said.

"Sheila, I swear you're obsessed with him."

"Earl, if you don't watch your ass, he'll have your cherry wood desk before you know it. I'm gettin' sick of dreaming about him, too."

"Ramsay?"

"Who else? And Post. They're getting to be nightmares, Earl. Damn nightmares."

"It's your damn booze and those pills."

"The rain and the Post's old Cadillac. You wouldn't believe me if I told you. Damn psychedelic, it is. It's a rainy night, and I'm in Post's Caddy with Ramsay. At least I think it's Ramsay. But he's older. It's like he becomes James Post. Oh, shit!"

"Sounds crazy." Earl said as he walked away. "Go to bed."

"But, Earl . . . " she said.

18 *Corsicana, Texas   April 8, 1981*

Sheila tossed in her sleep. The drinks and pills hadn't helped. For a month since the Dallas trade party, she hadn't slept through a night without having the dream. All Earl kept saying was that she needed another trip to Navarro.

"No way," she always said, anxious that the dreams seemed more and more real. "Lockhart'll just say they were memories."

"Then stop bitching all the time," Earl said.

"Fuck you. You don't care." That was the typical exchange between them. Now she moaned in her sleep. The dream was especially vivid:

Ramsay popped into her mind. She was at the Coyote Brand compound at night. She floated across the gravel pad to the large yellow Cadillac with sweeping rear fins. Each fin had a pair of little round lights glowing bright red. The driver's side door opened. Marcus Ramsay called to her in an echoing voice from the sales office door. He wanted another ride.

Not again, she thought.

He approached the car in slow motion. She looked down and saw the rapist Coy Duncan lying under the car just outside her door. He looked up, smiled, and made a snipping action with his fingers.

"Sheila Baby. Give me a lift?" Ramsay asked as he climbed in. His deep echoing Yankee voice seemed far away.

"Don't call me that." She noticed that Ramsay apparently couldn't hear or even see Coy under the car. She kept glancing down, afraid the rapist would be discovered near her. *What would the good people of Corsicana think?*

Ramsay got in and they closed their doors, quieting Coy's laughter beneath the car, laughter only she apparently could hear. Sheila turned the key and revved the Cadillac's engine. The car rolled out of the Coyote Brand lot, crunching gravel.

"Looks like rain," she said to Ramsay.

As they left the lot, Margaret Post floated transparently before them, wearing a wide-brimmed hat with a frilly little autumn dress, and carrying her lacy parasol.

"Stop, Sheila!" Ramsay said. He grabbed the wheel from the passenger side. "You'll hit her!"

"Hands off, Yankee!"

"Just trying to save her," he said.

"She didn't come to Oscar's party, the snot-nosed bitch!" Sheila said.

"But, Sheila Baby," he said. "That's not very nice."

"Don't call me that. My old man—"

"You must have loved him very much," he said.

"Shut up, Yankee."

Sheila drove through the ethereal image of the former Coyote first lady, who motioned with a glass of iced tea in the hand carrying the parasol and pulled a vision of bruised baby Bry' along with the other.

Sheila turned to Ramsay. "Why, Marcus, I have to admit you are handsome—for a Yankee, that is. A real smart-ass you are, too," she said and laughed. "Both Earl and I think so."

"Thank you, Mrs. Hickman. Why are you driving so fast?" he asked.

"Get some air, Yankee." She lowered all four windows with her power controls. "You like?"

"Sure. Just slow down, please," he said.

The yellow Cadillac lurched and groaned as it rolled through deserted downtown Corsicana, weaving from side to side. Then, like a machine gun, it rumbled over the cobblestone on Beaton Street.

She laughed. "What's a matter, Yankee? Too fast?"

Sheila laughed as her bushy blonde hair flew in the breeze. She approached the entrance to the Navarro County Historical Society on Second Street and waved to Wyvonne Putnam as she passed, ignoring the stop light that glowed red in the mist. Sheila sped past crowds of sobbing people who huddled alongside the road, carrying babies, blankets, and coolers in light rain.

"Slow down, please? ," Ramsay said. "This is getting dangerous."

"You chicken?" She flew down Second Street, out of town, and turned left at the large wooden sign. She sped through the dark woods and curvy road that led to Golf Estates.

Now, from Ramsay's seat, a guttural voice with a proper Texas accent growled at her. "Mrs. Hickman, I must say! This driving is absolutely unacceptable!"

"Huh?" she said. She looked to her right. James Post sat in the passenger seat now, where Ramsay had been only a second before! He tipped his black felt cowboy hat and smiled.

The massive Golf Estates entrance marker loomed ahead.

"Sorry, Mr. Post." She glanced ahead. "It's for a good cause, you know," she said.

"What cause might that be, ma'am?" he asked.

"Me!" she said and drove on.

"Yes, of course, ma'am. I'm sure Margaret will understand. Also Emma, Chelsea, Coyote, all of the citizens of Corsicana, and even some people beyond the greater Navarro County area," he said. "Why, actually, all of them will never forgive you, Miss Sheila. Never!"

"Fuck forgiveness!" she yelled.

"Then the guilt will have its way with you, ma'am."

"You think so!" Sheila laughed out loud.

"I know so," Post said in a calm voice. "Yes, I know so."

Sheila's heart pounded as rain spattered on the windshield. She drove faster, aiming at the huge stone monolith.

The car crashed. Smiling Mr. Post, tipped his hat as he shot through the windshield. Glass sprayed everywhere. As he flew in sitting position, he called back to her, "I warned you, Mrs. Hickman. I am so sorry," he said. "May your soul—"

"Sure," she said. "Right."

Then the gas tank behind her exploded into a brilliant fireball, lighting up Post as he hit the wall. Blood spattered everywhere.

"My God!" Sheila looked around. "What have I done?"

The leader of Corsicana industry lay in a lifeless heap against the wall. Screams erupted as feet trampled nearby lawns. The fireball blossomed.

In a few minutes the heavens hurled rain. Margaret Post pushed people aside as she scrambled through the assemblage. Behind her, her delirious housekeeper wailed.

Sheila forced open the wrinkled car door and stepped into the mud. She watched Margaret Post approach and kneel in the mud, gently kissing her fallen husband.

So sweet—you bitch!

After a brief hesitation, the little lady moaned into the night. "May you dream—"

Under the car Coy Duncan laughed.

How did he survive this? Sheila wondered.

Coy's snicker echoed through the clearing in the woods. He stood up, pulled the door open, and yanked Sheila out. He pressed her against the side of the car. No, wait, it wasn't a car anymore. It had changed to a rusty, old pickup. "Y'all remember our deal, Cheryl or Shelly, whatever your name is?" he said.

"What the hell is going on?" she said.

He roughly yanked down her panties, dropped his jeans, and howled. He hoisted her onto his thighs and jammed his erection into her. Sheila panted, angry, finding she was helplessly aroused.

The cowboy manhandled her breasts and pinched her nipples.

"You fucking sailor! You did it! I saw you! You killed him!" she hollered.

"I ain't no fuckin' sailor!" He slapped her hips and hooted. "I'll just tell 'em you hired me, Sheila."

Children and proper old ladies born in Chatsworth gathered around, laughing and throwing stones as Coy raped Sheila. Coy ignored the stones, but Sheila felt each one as it pelted her body, then her head.

"You better stop that!" she shrieked back at them. "I'm Coyote's first lady, ya know." Then Sheila stared across the tops of their heads as their jabbering faded.

"It was worth it," she moaned when it was over. "It was worth it, I swear."

The laughing cowboy dropped to the rain-soaked grass, coated with wet leaves, his pants crumpled around his ankles. "That'll be twenty-five hundred now, Sheila Baby. The rest later," he said in slow motion. The flames lit up his face. "And, I get your daughter's little twat, too."

"Asshole!" she screamed and threw a wine bottle at him, but it merely bounced off his shoulder.

Then Sheila reached into the car, pulled out her purse, and turned to the smiling cowboy. He lay there, cackling like a hen. The crowd hushed in anticipation.

"Take your damn money!" she said. She tossed twenty-five hundred dollar bills at him.

"Thanks, bitch!" His voice echoed inher in slow motion.

"Remember, he raped Erlene, too," little Margaret Post said properly as she wagged a finger and approached the rusty pickup. "But, it is wonderful that your Merle is helping James at the company."

"It's Earl. But call him Mr. Hickman, you bitch!"

"Welcome to Coyote Brand!" Lenora floated by in the rain, umbrella in hand. "Earl's right up there, I guess."

"Will you shut up, you fat cow?" Sheila said.

"Why are you nosin' into that, Mrs. Hickman?" Al Bishop appeared, scrunching his nose and squinting over his little glasses. "The old boss can't hear you now. He's dead, lady! But, you'd know that, wouldn't you?"

The crowd started to weep together as the sad, orange-gray dawn finally came.

It wasn't over. Scores of Corsicanans arrived with their kids and blankets. They were joined by a sea of pick-up trucks, strewn across the perfect lawns of

Golf Estates. Reverend Miller, normally a kindly old man, turned into a cruel devil, booming from atop the stone wall. Sheila watched the mourners wail. *Oh, please let this be over,* she thought.

Earl's eulogy was next. Between squeals from an old, chrome-coated microphone, his proclamation rang out. He looked directly at Sheila.

"None of us will ever forget this fallen hero, especially you."

She cringed. Organ music thundered into her ears and echoed across the lawns.

Erlene appeared in the crowd wearing her slinkiest western outfit. "By the way, Mama, I'm pregnant! What should I do, Mama? Abort?"

"Erlene. I'm so sorry," Sheila said.

"I'll just kill the cute li'l' ol' thing, right? And, I won't never have babies again."

"Oh, honey," Sheila said.

"I was gonna name her after you, too. Sheila, the dock-whore. Isn't that what you were, Mama? A dock whore in Baltimore, gettin' screwed by all the guys?"

Bryan stood there, flapping his limp arm wildly. "Hey look here, Mama! My fancy-ass signature's no good no more, but I can still wave. Well, sorta."

"Howdy, ma'am." Frank Benedict stepped out of a fancy black limo. He toasted Sheila with a drink that he waved in the air. "Earl'll be the big boss soon."

Sheila jerked out of her violent sleep. Her hands sweated profusely, she panted, and her mouth cracked dry. She looked both ways, trying to orient herself in the dark, hoping none of it was true.

But it was. She knew it wasn't a dream anymore. "No-o-o!" she cried out. "I know everything!" she cried, angry and teary-eyed at the same time.

Earl jerked up. "What's the matter, Sheila? What do you know?" It was early Saturday morning. Earl shook her uselessly.

"Get your hands off me. I'm already awake," Sheila snapped as she sobbed.

"What is it, Sheila?" he asked. "A nightmare?"

"Real, Earl," she said, "It's all real. Just everything."

"Oh, honey. It was just a dream," he said.

"Holy Jesus, not this time. Shit." She shook her head. She swallowed her tears with the truth.

"Mama, what's wrong?" Erlene appeared at the bedroom door.

"What's going on?" Bryan rushed up, his blonde hair mussed from sleep.

"Nothing, kids," Sheila said. "Now get out. You know the rules."

"Yes, Ma," Bryan said. They slumped away.

Sheila stared at nothing.

"Tell me," Earl said. "What is it?"

"Nothing," she mumbled. "Just nothing." *But it all makes sense now,* she thought. She slugged the bunched-up blankets behind her and flopped down on them.

Once her tears dried, Sheila drifted from anger to a dead gaze that lasted the better part of that day, then the next. No matter how often she tried to wish it, the truth wouldn't go away.

19 *Corsicana, Texas   April 18, 1981*

Ramsay woke up with a start at his office desk, fists clenched.

Oscar backed off. "Hey! Easy does it, cowboy," he said. "Not ready to duke it out yet."

"I must've dozed off. Got here before six," Marcus said in a sleepy voice. "What time is it?" He rubbed his eyes hard and looked at his watch. Oscar came into focus. "Hey, I'm sorry, Oscar."

"No problem," Oscar said. "Gosh, you're always working. Guess that's what Yankees do."

Ramsay shook his head side-to-side like a dog, trying to see more clearly.

"It's eight o'clock. Whatcha doing here on a Saturday?" Oscar asked.

"Packing for the move. You have heard about the office move to Dallas by now, I hope," Ramsay said.

"'Course. Even ordered the van. Be here Tuesday after the meeting. We'll miss you up there in your big fancy Yankee-style offices."

"What meeting?" Ramsay yawned and stretched.

"On new strategy. You called it, remember?"

"Oh, yeah."

"Betcha Earl's never gonna change his mind 'cause of that computer stuff," Oscar said.

"We'll see. It's all for the good of . . . "

"All this mumbo jumbo?" Oscar nudged Ramsay's computer output, sitting on his desk.

Ramsay shook his head. "You guys don't get it."

"Nope. And he'll never buy it, neither. Never."

"Listen, Oscar, a lot of this is fairly obvious. Trust me."

"Trust you? Listen, Earl hates cutting them billbacks and pushing hot dog sauce. Always been our junk product." He snickered. "He thinks you're one crazy Yankee. In Mexico, they'd call you a *loco gringo*."

Marcus shook his head and mumbled, "Man. He's so afraid."

"Been doing things his way for a long time, boss." Oscar folded his arms across his chest and nodded.

"I guess, but what's right is right," Ramsay said.

"Don't know nothing about that, " Oscar said. "But everybody says Sheila's whisperin' to him how you're taking over. What you think about that?"

"Oh, really?" Ramsay asked. "How do you know that?"

"Lenora. One day she overhears him on the phone with Lady Sheila," Oscar said. "She's telling him you'll be the next president if he don't watch it. That true?"

"I don't want to be president, Oscar," Ramsay said. "I'm just trying to help."

"Sure. You marketing guys always get to be the division heads at Allied, right?"

"Not true."

"And they ain't never gave me the big plant they promised," he said.

"But, Oscar—"

"Earl says it's 'cause of smart-ass, MBA Yankees like you." He kicked at the floor.

"Figures," Ramsay said. "That's bullshit, Oscar. Honest. I don't know what to say."

"Not bullshit according to Earl. And he's the president, so he ought to know!" Oscar flushed.

"Easy, Oscar," Ramsay said. "Easy."

"Well," he moaned, "Allied went and destroyed my damn career." He hung his head. "Shoot. I move up from the valley and this is what I get?"

"Hey, listen. That's really too bad," Ramsay said.

"Sure. Don't you get it?" Oscar sniffed. "It's my whole damn life. The kids. The wife."

Just then Daisy burst in the door. "Good morning, y'all." She tossed her purse down on her desk and brushed her hair. "Oscar, what's the matter with you, honey? You look terrible. Where are those bright eyes?" She lifted his chin.

Oscar pulled away from her. "Just missin' you already, Miss Daisy. Up there in your fancy Yankee office."

"Aw, Oscar," she said. "Poor thing. You really gonna miss me?"

"Daisy, better leave him be," Marcus said. "Not now."

Oscar pulled away from Daisy, huffed out of the sales office, and slammed the door.

"Just like Grady Davis," Daisy said matter-of-factly after the door slammed shut. She stuffed her keys in her purse. "Damn boy committed suicide."

Ramsay looked up. "Really? Grady Davis, the drunk? Are they sure his death was suicide?" he asked.

"Might-could," she said. "Everbody around town knows Grady never stopped blaming himself for James Post's death. Although yesterday's paper did say Grady didn't leave a damn suicide note."

"That's odd."

"Oh, Marcus. You make everything a mystery, don'tcha? I heard they found a noose on the floor next to poor Grady, you know?"

"Hmm. Grady Davis commits suicide because he feels so remorseful about accidentally killing James Post, but he doesn't leave a note to explain that. And he hangs himself? Or at least it looks like that. But it seems to me the noose would've been around his neck if he used it to kill himself. Yeah, on the surface it sounds a little strange."

"Hmm, I guess." She looked at her watch. "Well, uh, listen, Marcus, we better turn our attention to some serious packing. Coy's pickin' me up in a few hours, so we better move our hinies. Want some coffee?"

"Sure. You know Oscar really seems down," Marcus called to Daisy as she walked back to the new coffee maker in Al's office. "About his career and the promises Allied made to him."

"Don't he?" she said, fiddling with the coffee and filters. "Always talkin' about it. Just hope he doesn't go off and—"

"Imitate Grady?" he called.

"Or worse." Ramsay heard Daisy say as she poured water.

"What could be worse than suicide?" he asked.

She walked into her office and peered at Ramsay from around the nicked door jamb. "Guess he could take the whole damn place with him."

By ten o'clock, having packed most of the current files, Ramsay started sorting through the old ones. "God, these are easy to toss," he said. "Earl had a lot of ideas, but he's never acted on any of 'em as far as I can see. Has this guy done anything besides dream and write these pretend memos?"

"Hey, he worked on each one of them for a long time," she said. "I know. I typed some of 'em over and over." She opened the top box of a crooked, dusty stack. "Al said we should designate these boxes keep or toss. Lookee here. This old one's labeled JP-1969."

She carefully pulled out a single, crinkly page with yellowed edges from an old spiral notebook and put up her finger as she read. "Hey, wait. Marcus."

"What?" he said.

"This is a goody." Daisy waved the handwritten page. "You won't believe it. This one here's dated January 10, 1969."

He stood, walked over to Daisy, and looked at it. "J. P. January 10, 1969," he read. "That couldn't have been written by the late and great Mr. James Post, could it?" he asked.

"Whoa. This is spooky." Daisy held it behind her back, stretching her tube top. "Come get it."

"Please be careful with that," he asked.

"I'll bet you'll want to kiss me when you read this one," she said. "It's from the night Mr. Post died. Everybody knows that date. January 10, 1969."

"Really?" he asked. "If you're not lying to me, you'll get a big kiss. But only if it's worth it."

"You'll see." Daisy smiled a sly grin and held the old note in the air with two fingers.

Marcus reached out. "Please hand it over, Ms. Duncan."

"You are truly not going to believe this, Mr. Ramsay," she said. She started jumping like a child, waving the old memo.

"What could be so special?" he asked. He held his hand out.

She stopped. "Just take a look at the title. You'll see." She handed it to him as if it were recovered treasure.

Ramsay read the top of the page. "Oh, my God." He walked back to his chair as he read:

From the Desk of: JAMES POST
Date: 1/10/69
  To: My File
  Subj: Sales and deals
  We ought to start looking at our sales on a per capita basis to make sure we're really growing. Otherwise we could be fooled into thinking our sales is growing from the population boom when it's really heading south per person.

  Lots of that population growth is from them Yankees who don't like chili as much as us Texans. We need some new advertising that'll break through to them. Push some of our other items besides chili, too.

  Then there are those damnable billback deals. We've been spending more and more ever since Allied bought this place. That man Hickman's been pushing them down our throats. And Frank's sending the performance certificates straight to Hickman to sign. Something fishy going on there.

  Hickman's been showing up around here with that fancy new car and new clothes. And he always talks about all this new stuff he's getting: a John Deere mower, that Chris Craft outboard, and fancy trips

to Cancun and Hawaii. Mighty suspicious.
Like he's on the take.

Got some changes to think about.

James Post

"Per capita? Billbacks?" Ramsay said.
"On the take?" Ramsay couldn't believe
it. Chills ran up his spine.

"Oh, Marcus. I do believe this means
you just connected with Mr. James Earl
Post," Daisy said, "across a whole
decade."

"Incredible." He read the memo
again.

"Backs up your fancy-ass computer
jazz, don't it?" she said.

"This'll change everything at that
meeting on Tuesday," he said. "Wow."

"Yep. Bound to raise an eyebrow or
two," she said.

"This must've been the last thing he
wrote before he died that night," Ramsay
said. "Man."

"Oh, look here!" Daisy waved a small
orange and white receipt.

"More?" Marcus asked. "What's
that?"

"Lenora must've stored all of Mr.
Post's things back here after he died."

"What is it?"

She handed it over.

"A receipt from Grady's garage?" he said.

"Yep."

Ramsay read. "Shit! This proves Grady Davis fixed Mr. Post's brakes on the day he died. Margaret told me everyone's always thought Post's old brakes did him in; new ones couldn't have."

Daisy put her hands on her hips and gazed out the window in thought.

"Hey, Daisy. It says here that Grady road-tested the new brakes for five miles outside of town that day," Ramsay said. "They worked fine the whole time. The guy couldn't have blown the installation."

"Hmm," she said and shook her head. "Lord, almighty."

"What is it?"

"Nothing."

"Can new brakes fail hours later?" he asked.

"Don't know," she said slowly, shifting her eyes back and forth. "Coy would, though. Yep, Coy would sure know."

"Something wrong, Daisy?" he asked.

"No, nothing." But Daisy looked antsy, even a bit angry, as she walked back to her desk, mumbling.

About eleven o'clock, Ramsay called Margaret Post to schedule a follow-up meeting. On the sixth ring Henrietta answered, noticeably out of breath. Ramsay scheduled a brief meeting with Mrs. Post for the following Tuesday afternoon.

"Gee, I hope nothing's wrong," Ramsay said after he hung up.

"Why do you think that?" Daisy asked.

"Henrietta sounded upset," he said.

"Boy, she's been with Mrs. Post all these years."

"I have to tell Mrs. Post about this memo stuff." Ramsay sat in his chair and threw his head back. "Man! This packing is tough on the old back." Daisy walked over behind him and massaged his shoulders. "There, how's that?"

"Right there, a little harder, plea—"

The sticky sales office door lurched open. "Daisy!" It was Coy Duncan. "Daisy, you back there?"

Daisy pulled away from Ramsay. "Oh, shoot."

Coy walked into Marcus' office. "So, what's goin' on?"

"Why'd you come so early?" She stood there blushing, looking at her watch.

"Just in time, looks like," Coy glared squint-eyed at Daisy, then Ramsay. He slung his pointed boot over the side of Cecil's chair. "Well, well. Lookee here."

Daisy left Ramsay's side. She hung her head and pushed past Coy on her way back to her desk.

"Hey, Coy." Marcus stood at his desk. "I have a technical question," he said to stop an impending fight.

Coy was a tall, muscular good ol' boy. His old scar and dark, squinty eyes made him look like a devil. His voice was low and gravelly. "Oh, yeah? Like what, Yankee?" he asked.

"That's assuming you know anything . . . about cars, that is," Ramsay said.

"'Course I do."

"Maybe you can help us untangle a little mystery."

"Mystery?" he asked.

"Yeah, we just found an old receipt that proves James Post had his brakes fixed earlier the day of his accident," Marcus said.

"Fixed? Receipt?" Coy fidgeted and glanced at Daisy. "Say what?"

"Something wrong, Coy?" Marcus asked. "You know something about brakes, right?"

"What about 'em?" He jangled his wad of keys hand-to-hand. "I knew about that. New brakes on Post's car. So? What about it? Everybody knows that." He glared back in Daisy's direction.

She called from her desk. "You sure, Coy?" she asked. "Is that all you got to say?"

"Now leave it be, Daisy," he said sternly. He cleared his throat repeatedly, like a large object was stuck deep inside. She stood and walked over to the door jamb.

"Well?" Marcus said. "The entire population of Corsicana has been under the impression that Mr. Post died of squeaky old brakes, not new ones. But you say, 'What about it?' Sounds a little funny that he died from new brakes, doesn't it, Coy?"

"Jesus, you knuckle head." She shook her head. "Good ol' Grady's the best, you always say. Even after you went and whooped him."

Coy shot a glance at her. "Shut up, bitch!"

Ramsay looked up. "And isn't it true that Grady Davis and Mr. Post would've been the only ones who knew the brakes were brand new. Right, Coy?" he asked. "That's unless you somehow saw 'em later."

Coy froze.

Daisy fidgeted. "Shoot."

Coy wiped his forearm across his face. "Grady Davis was nothing but a stuttering ol' drunk lynched by his own noose." Coy cleared his throat as he continued to fiddle with his keys.

"Wait, Coy. Enough's enough." Daisy stood there, hands on hips. "Noose? How the hell'd you know about a noose. You never read the *Sun*." She squinted curiously.

Duncan swallowed. "Say, Daisy? Let me talk to Marcus, here, for a second."

"No way," she said. "A certain cowboy might-could put his boot into a certain Yankee's mouth."

"Just got some ideas for y'all's mystery and such." His voice shook. He pointed to the front door. "Now get out, bitch! Or I'll up ya one side of the head, and you know how that can sting."

"Whatever you say, Roy. Shoot. Be nice, now." She quickly yanked the door open and slammed it behind her as she walked out.

"Damn bitch," Coy said after she closed the door. "Y'all know how they can be." He laughed.

"So, what's the deal, Coy?" Ramsay asked. "You know something about this Post thing? The brakes? Grady?"

Coy clunked past Cecil's desk, over to Ramsay. Marcus remained standing.

"Let's just say you might-oughta forget all this shit, Yankee. If y'all know what's good for you. You might end up like Grady, never can tell. Or maybe Post. He was nothing but a piss-ass Yankee at heart anyway. So, better watch it."

"Coy, when I see something fishy, I dig a little deeper," Ramsay said. "And something doesn't ring right here."

"Wouldn't be so good for your health, ol' Marcus. Certain people wouldn't be too happy neither."

"Boy, that sounds weird," Ramsay said. "Someone put you up to this?"

There was a pause.

"Hardly, Yankee," Coy said. "Uh . . . I don't need no fuckin' rich bastard or drunken bitch to take someone out. I can do it fine myself. So better just leave it be, you Yankee pussy. Hear?" He didn't move. "Shoot," he whispered. Coy looked at Ramsay like he had just said too much. Only his eyes shifted left, then right. He jabbed at Ramsay's chest with his index finger. "Just forget we talked. At all. Got it, Yankee?"

"I think you'd better leave, Coy," Ramsay said. "Now."

"Long as you got the message loud 'n' clear." He poked again, this time harder. "Hear?"

Ramsay pushed Coy's hand away.

Coy faked a punch. Ramsay flinched.

"Gotcha!" Coy said. "See, y'all are nothing but another piss-ass Yankee." Coy turned toward the sales office door, snickering. He stopped and looked back. "Oh, and by the way, Yankee, stay away from my woman. Hear?" He spit on the old, wooden office floor. "Only thing good about you is you're white." He laughed.

"Son of a bitch," Ramsay said under his breath.

Coy snickered and clunked across Daisy's office in two steps. He jerked open the door. Daisy spilled in.

"Thank God you boys are done," she said. "Looking like rain out here."

"Hey girl, you better not be late. Got it?" Coy said. He poked her in the shoulder twice. "Dinner on time or else.

And keep your goddamn mouth shut."
She backed away from his hand.

"Yes, sir," she said and saluted. He
shoved her aside and stormed into the
sprinkling rain.

She talked without stopping to breath
as she rushed back into Marcus' office:
"What did Roy want now? You look
shook up. You OK? Did he hit you?"

Ramsay shook his head. "He just
threatened me big time. About talking to
you, and about looking into Post's brakes.
And, it sounds like he probably helped
Grady Davis hang himself."

"What? My Coy said all that?" she
asked, looking flustered and angry.

"Yep. He said Grady Davis was
getting drunk, talking about this Post shit
too much," he said.

"Shit, Coy—the dumb ox," she said.

"Maybe I should call the Sheriff."
She laughed.

"What's so funny?" he said.

"You mean Coy's old hunting buddy,
Larry Calhoun?"

"I knew that name sounded familiar."

"Yep. They've known each other since
they been boys. Might as well have a
party in the swamp by the tallest tree in

Holler's Woods. That's where Coy and Larry shoot ducks Saturday mornings."

"But it sounds like murder here," he said.

"The ducks?" She nodded. "Guess you could call it that."

"No!" he said. "I mean Post . . . and Grady."

Daisy fidgeted with her fingers.

"What's the matter?" he asked.

"Nothing," she mumbled. "Why doesn't he just keep his fool mouth shut?"

Ramsay continued, "He mentioned a rich bastard and a drunken bitch, like somebody else put him up to it. Maybe they hired Coy to kill Post, and Grady, too," he said.

"My Coy said all that?" She paced back and forth, flailing her hands. "The stupid idiot blabber puss."

"What can we do now?" he asked.

Daisy looked both ways. "Wait. We can't panic. Gotta remember he's just a big-mouthed ox and likes to push his weight around. Probably don't mean nothing."

"But, Daisy! You can't suppress this. This is bad shit," he said.

She walked up and fiddled with his tie. "Oh, Marcus. Can't we just go out on the access road for a little bit, forget all this bull? Please?"

"At a time like this? We should be calling somebody, not kissing."

"We should be kissing more'n ever now—to calm down." She returned to pacing and fanning herself.

"I don't know," he said. "Why are you so flustered anyway?"

"I'm just nervous about all this murder talk. Say, I really do need that kiss, I swear. You owe me, Mr. Ramsay. A hug, too. 'Sides, I got something important to tell you."

Just off the I-45 access road, Daisy's Sunbird sat empty, its rear wheels sitting in a growing puddle of mud. A Blue Norther was soaking all of Navarro County. The couple huddled in Ramsay's Citation for almost an hour as the rain poured. They wrapped up together, reeling from an historic memo and a good ol' boy's threats.

"Why would he say all that? Is he just stupid or what?" Ramsay asked. "He's really a racist, too."

"He might-coulda got flustered is all. Mighta let loose with something he didn't mean. You're lucky he didn't smash you right there. He and his buddies from the Klan can get carried away."

"The Ku Klux Klan?"

"Yep. Them ol' boys are always throwing their weight around and such. This year the regional klavern of the Klan'll even throw its meeting here in town. They say it'll be on the national news and everything."

"Jesus," he said.

"What?"

"I had a feeling things were a bit racist down here. That explains a lot. You folks hide it well."

"Marcus, we're going to have to ease up on our times together, so he doesn't get the boys together and whoop your pretty little hiney," she said.

"You know, it really looks like your husband could be involved in the damn brakes thing. I wouldn't be surprised if Coy meant Frank Benedict when he said rich bastard," he said. Who else would you expect? Aren't many around here, right?"

"Really?"

"Well, sure. Margaret Post told me James was under intense pressure from Benedict the week before he died.

Benedict could've hired Coy to harass James Post. Maybe even do him in. And Larry Calhoun never really investigated it either. That might've been Coy's cover."

"My Coy do that?" Daisy said. "Naw." But she looked warily out of each window, then looked back at him. "Say, Marcus? I admit I've been lying about something."

"What?" he asked.

"You'll hate me."

"Tell me," he said.

"When Coy's drunk, he still brags about the night he beat on poor Grady years ago, when he heard the man was takin' a liking to me."

"Grady, the mechanic? Grady Davis?"

"Coy beat him with a damn tire iron."

"Jesus Christ," he said.

"Grady's head was all cut and dented afterwards. He had brain damage and almost died. The boy could only stutter after that, but Coy made me swear to keep it quiet."

Marcus said, "That's funny. When I first started at Coyote, I found a stuttering man outside the office one night, drunk as a skunk. In greasy clothes, too. I think the paramedics called him Grady Davis."

"Yep, that sounds like Grady. Hell, he probably thought you was Post all pissed off and comin' back from the dead to do him in."

"Sometimes I feel like that man's taking me over," he said. "From the inside out."

"Who, Grady?"

"No, James Post. Like he's part of me. Some people say you shouldn't ignore a coincidence, let alone a bunch of 'em."

"This is weird." Daisy put her hands to her mouth. "You're sayin' my Coy could've killed James Post. That's a little far out, idn't it?"

"No. Maybe he did it for a drunken bitch and Frank Benedict," he said. "But who's the drunken bitch ?"

"Probably Sheila." Daisy half-laughed. "She's the only female drunk around these parts."

Marcus shrugged. "Even though it sounds like a stretch, she'd have a darn good motive, too. Kill off Post, get Earl promoted."

"And remember, Earl gave the Houston market to Frank," she said. "Coulda been part of the deal."

"Yep. Earl runs the billback deals and Frank kicks part of the trade deal money back to Earl," he said.

"Sounds slick," she said and cuddled up. "Enough of the mystery talk. Marcus, don't you owe me a break from all this? A big kiss, I do believe."

She cuddled closer, grabbed his hand, held it up, and kissed it multiple times. "Did I ever tell you, you have beautiful hands, Mr. Ramsay?"

"I don't believe you did," he said.

She kissed it again.

"So young, smooth, untouched—just perfect. Like you've never been in a fight or scraped 'em up. Coy's are all mangled and such." She fondled one finger at a time, slowly sucking on each, as she stared into Ramsay's eyes.

She pulled up her little stretchy top, exposing her breasts. "See I told you I wouldn't wear much." She pulled his wet hand to her bare chest and rubbed it all over. She groaned. Then she unsnapped her jeans, put his hand between her legs, and pulled up and down in long, slow strokes. "Please, let's do it," she said. "Oh, please."

He leaned over and kissed her. "Are you sure?"

She arched her back. "Oh, pull at my nipples. Please pull 'em."

He kissed them gently.

"No. Pull on 'em hard," she said.

"But, I don't want to hurt you," he said.

"Don't worry, I'll tell you if it hurts."

He cautiously pulled at her nipples.

"Now, suck 'em hard," she said.

He sucked her nipples gently.

"Bite 'em!" she said. "Bite 'em!"

They kissed, sucked, and kneaded each other, and made love as the windows steamed. After an hour they lay exhausted in each other's arms.

When a curious farmer knocked on the windows, they laughed out of embarrassment. A post-rain mist, heavy in the air, surrounded the car.

The rear wheels of Daisy's Sunbird got stuck in the mud when she tried to leave. She looked at her watch. "Shoot, now I'm in trouble."

She got out of the car, half-crying between good-bye kisses and laughs. "What the hell am I gonna do?"

It was near dusk when they flagged down an old yellow-and-rust tow truck waddling down the access road. When the kindly old driver asked how they got caught in such a little square of mud, they giggled like children caught smoking.

Then the tow truck pulled her car out of the mud for free.

As the truck jangled away, Marcus held Daisy, gently stroking her cheeks with the back of his fingers. He said good-bye to each tiny droplet that clung to her face. "I'll never forget this. I promise," he said. Then he whispered in her ear, "I love you, Daisy."

His words floated away on the chilly country fog. She touched his lips with the tip of her index finger. "Oh, Marcus. I love you, too. That was what I wanted to tell you. But you beat me to it, you damn Yankee."

"Can't get anything by us folk," he said.

"You Yankees always think you're one step ahead." She pushed hard at his shoulder.

"No. We *are* one step ahead." He laughed.

"Get outa here, you asshole." She shoved him away.

"Hey, watch it," he said.

"Wait!" She grabbed him by the shirt and roughly pulled him back. "Kiss me one more time, you damn fool."

A quarter mile down the access road, a taxi sat in the mist. The driver, Reginald Waverly, reported into headquarters. "A bit like London, I'd say," he said. "Yes, sir. I'm quite delighted with the weather in this Texas place, sir. Not only was the *installation* perfect, but the *empowerment* is surging ahead of schedule with minimal side effects, just that disgusting mucus and nausea. Everything is in splendid shape for our chap, Ramsay. I'm sure my strategy will run smoothly. Oh, and when he visited her, I'm certain Mrs. Post recognized Mr. Post's essence in the lad! Yes, that was exciting. My design will soon begin to unfold. After all these years, with Ramsay's help, Post's spirit will vent quite nicely. I have quite a clever outcome planned now, too. You'll be so proud—such a tightly woven web."

20

Corsicana, Texas   April 20, 1981

On Monday, Marcus Ramsay waited in the sterile, white QA Lab, and carefully clasped the old Post memo that he and Daisy had discovered the previous Saturday. This was the moment he had waited for. Now, like magic, words from the father of Coyote Brand would support his contentions. Today the non-believers would have to listen.

As usual, when Earl Hickman waved his hands in the air and began to speak, all eyes followed him. "We all must be wary of false promises from the North."

He began spinning the same convoluted logic that had controlled the Coyote Brand family for a decade. Al Hopkins, Ted Calivarpio, Oscar Sanchez, Harold Hudson, and, to a lesser extent, cherubic QA assistant Willy Womack, all nodded like loyal subjects would to their king.

The Coyote Brand president explained how the Company couldn't possibly justify testing any new advertising because doing so would eliminate the sacred billback deals—obviously sacrilege—no matter what any "damn fool Yankee" said. Earl bellowed, "We must maintain our greatness!"

They all nodded. Marcus' stomach grew queasy with pangs of excitement as he waited for Earl to bury himself further in his meandering oratory. When Earl boomed his denunciation of any cretins who would swoop down from the North and promote non-chili products, Marcus Ramsay's hands shook with anticipation. He raised an index finger. "May I say a few words, Earl?"

"Humph?" Earl stopped suddenly, turned, and glared at him. "What now?"

"I need to announce something," Ramsay said.

"Announce? Go ahead, boy," Earl smirked. "If you must."

All of them grumbled.

Ramsay started slowly. "It has come to my attention that I am not the first person to feel strongly about tracking per capita sales and advertising non-chili products."

Ramsay paused calmly. The group hushed, but a few of them murmured inquisitively. Ramsay purposely delayed his announcement for dramatic effect. Then he raised the old, yellowed paper slowly. *Timing is everything,* he thought. "These ideas were first proposed by a man who noticed that Coyote's per capita sales were leveling. He knew that something had to be done to restore the company's declining consumer base. Unfortunately, for us, his speculation never had an airing."

"Huh? What man?" Harold said. A few snickered.

Ramsay continued. "Here are notes written by this man more than a decade ago. As you will see, it happens that his underlying notion is virtually identical to mine. He projected that the profit situation would only get worse unless there was a change. He specifically referenced billback deals and how they had been sucking the lifeblood out of Operating Income. You all know that I've recently explained how that's gotten worse over the years."

Oscar groaned. Other worried Coyote Brand employees' glanced at each other.

"Who is this man anyway, cowboy?" Oscar said. "Do we know him?"

Harold snickered. "And how could an outsider have this inside information?"

His laugh was obviously designed to rally the skeptics. A few nodded. The rest grumbled.

Earl cleared his throat, then waved disapprovingly at Ramsay. "More Yankee hocus-pocus. That damn per capita nonsense."

"The man was not an outsider!" Marcus Ramsay said it loud enough to be heard over the heckling.

"Sure," one of them jeered.

Earl flushed and said, "Marcus, I think I speak for all of us when I say I'm sick and tired of your Yankee nonsen— "

"The man who wrote this warning was none other than James Post!" Ramsay yelled. He held his old memo high.

Everyone was struck silent by Ramsay's shocking pronouncement.

Ramsay looked out the open windows. Even a few people walking from building to building outside froze and looked up at the lab. It was like they had sensed that the spirit of their old boss had come back to visit for a moment.

"Let me see that," Earl said as he walked over. Ramsay held the memo so Earl could read it for himself. Then Earl whispered hoarsely to Ramsay, "This will not be read aloud." He flushed. "You understand."

During the next five minutes, Ramsay stood by the white counter and paraphrased the Post memo a number of times, but only as it applied to the technicalities of billback deals and advertising. Each time he started to mention Earl, the president cleared his throat, interrupted, and changed the subject. He even physically inserted himself in the spot a guardian dog might have, preventing anyone from reading the memo.

But, as the document remained on the table, Coyote Brand experienced a symbolic coup of sorts. The employees in the lab moved forward and clustered around Marcus Ramsay, asking about next steps Coyote might take.

"I bought y'all's points all along," Harold said and smiled.

"Sure you did," Ramsay said, but remained skeptical of the good ol' boy's slick manner.

Ted Calivarpio, Al's assistant, grinned, stepped forward, and shook Marcus' hand. "I'm glad you found this old memo. It clears things up quite a bit."

"This is quite amazing, Mr. Ramsay," Willie Womack beamed excitedly. "What's the plan for hot dog sauce? I always liked it, you know."

"Willie, how 'bout you call me Marcus now. Just Marcus."

Then the Coyote Brand family separated into smaller groups around the room. They buzzed about the memo's discovery as Earl called over Ramsay. "As president, I should show this material to Mrs. Post." He smiled. "You understand." He poked offhandedly at the delicate document.

"Please be careful, Earl," Ramsay said and coddled the paper. "History, you know."

"And Mrs. Post?" Earl asked.

"I'll be visiting Margaret tomorrow," Ramsay said as he stored the old memo in a manila folder.

Earl flinched. "But—"

"I've already scheduled the meeting, Earl," he said. "She wants to hear from me directly."

"She does? I see."

"Sorry," Marcus said.

Earl hunched his shoulders and slunk out of the lab as the others chattered excitedly.

"I don't know if I can handle anymore of this," Earl said that night to Sheila, who was reading a romance novel by the fire as she waited up for Erlene to return from her date.

"What now, Earl? The Yankee again?" she asked and looked up.

"They resurrected a damn memo Post wrote the night of his death," he said.

"What memo?" Sheila said, piqued.

"Nothin' big. About billbacks and advertising."

"Oh? So what?" Sheila said.

"Just bidness stuff," he said.

"Daddy," Erlene said as she opened the door and walked in, "You talkin' 'bout the discoveries?"

"Uh, yes, kitten. I guess you could call 'em that," Earl said.

She took off her jacket. "And about Daisy finding the receipt?"

"Memo? Receipt?" Sheila said. "Will someone please tell me what the hell's going on? Does everyone know what's going on here but me?" She sipped her wine, then dribbled a drop on the rug and cussed.

"Mama, Daisy said she and Ramsay found a receipt that shows Grady Davis fixed Mr. Post's brakes on the day he died. Sort of odd, don't you think? So, they're looking into it."

"What about brakes?" Sheila asked nervously.

"Let's go to bed." Earl slapped her leg. "Let's go, sugar."

"But Earl." Sheila rose hesitatingly. "See. Ramsay's a damn troublemaker. I always knew it," she said. Then she whispered to him, "You might-oughta make a call, Earl."

"Call?" he said and leaned closer to her face.

"The boys," she whispered in his ear. "You know, might be best."

"Oh. Right," he said and stood. He started walking into his home office.

"And that damn Ramsay should be doin' things to sell more chili anyway," Sheila called. "Not solving murders."

"What was that?" Earl stopped and turned.

"What? Solving murders?" she said.

"Who said anything about a murder, Sheila?" Earl said with a shake in his voice. "Between Ramsay's *mysteriously* comment at the Dallas Party, receipts for

429

new brakes, and you calling this a murder, I think you're all crazy. Next, somebody'll be sayin' that you're the damn killer."

That hit Sheila like a rock and reverberated through her foggy memory. Her chest tightened. *And people like this asshole Ramsay are looking into it?* "Shit," she gasped.

"What is it?" Earl asked. "You OK, Sheila?"

"It's nothing. Nothing at all. Just go and make your damn call."

"What call, Mama?" Erlene said.

"Nothing that concerns you," Sheila said. Guilt had continued to gnaw at her since the night she had recalled her managerial role in Post's murder. Now, she felt panicky inside, realizing that those pangs of culpability would continue to preoccupy her, every minute of every day for the rest of her life.

Minutes later, Earl sat at his desk and dialed.

"It's me," he said. " . . . Listen, you boys have to destroy those Post papers, hear?" There was a pause. "Just burn 'em, then whatever else . . . "

He nodded as he listened to the reply.

"Just do it. And, don't waste any time."

Ramsay sat at his desk the next day when the phone rang.

Daisy answered it. "The Mart, Marcus," she called. "For you."

"I got it," he said and picked up the phone. "Ramsay here."

"Marcus Ramsay?" the voice asked.

"Yes. Who is this?"

"Terry Yapp, Grocery Products Accounting."

"What can I do for you?" Ramsay asked.

"We've watched this old liability for years now."

"What's that?"

"The Post Escrow. Way back then, Burghoff decided to withhold part of our acquisition payment due to their excessive merchandising spending and slumping operating income. That was ten years ago."

"And?"

"I heard you were stirring up things down there. The results are beginning to show. Cutting that expansion and killing those trade deals are helping O. I. I'm pretty sure we can release the funds now."

"How much?" Ramsay asked.

"Two million. Plus ten years of interest," he said. "A pretty penny."

Ramsay straightened up. "What did you say?" His old chair squeaked. "Who gets it?" he asked.

"The Post Estate—his wife, I guess," Terry said.

"That's incredible," Ramsay said and sat back. "When do you think we'll know something definite?"

"I'll get this Approval Routing over to Burghoff's desk right away. It should just take him a day or so to approve it."

"That's it?" Ramsay asked.

"That's it," he said.

Later that day, Mrs. Margaret Post lay in her large poster bed. A frilly flannel gown clutched her frail neck. Her eyes seemed to bulge out of their sockets, like she had lost significant weight quickly. Henrietta came to help her sit up, but was shooed away by Margaret's wandering spindly fingers. She coughed. Marcus was surprised at how she had deteriorated in just a few days.

"Now, Mr. Ramsay." She cleared her throat. "I trust you have some interesting news for a sickly woman on a gray Tuesday." She strained to get the words out.

Ramsay sat in the old rattan chair, brought from the drawing room to the bedroom for his visit. The extent of Margaret's decline caught him off guard.

"Yes, Margaret," Ramsay said, concerned but relieved he had made the trip, for her demise appeared imminent. "We found one of Mr. Post's old memos."

"I know, son. And James called me, you know, to go for a ride in the Cadillac, so we better hurry."

"Margaret . . . " He felt himself verge on tears as he watched her struggle.

"Now, what about this . . . memo?" she asked.

"It has already started to inspire a real metamorphosis over at the company. Thanks to Mr. Post, the employees are beginning to get behind some real necessary changes."

She perked up when he said 'Mr. Post', as if the man had walked into the room. "Yes, I believe I know this news. I've read it in the *Sun*."

"Of course." Ramsay continued to speak in a melodic tone, trying to conversationalize the drab details of per capita sales and billback deals that James Post had written about on the night of his death.

"It's so like my James," she said. "He always read his ideas to me first, you know. I vaguely recollect . . . " A faint smile formed on Mrs. Post's face. "Oh, yes, I think I remember." As Ramsay continued, she appeared to be searching, glassy-eyed, for James' voice.

He finished and waited in the silence for Margaret's response.

"And the brakes? The brakes, young man?" She gulped repeatedly.

Henrietta scurried over. "Just spit in this bowl, Miss Margaret."

Margaret leaned over and spat.

"Better, ma'am?" Henrietta asked.

"Yes. Much better," Margaret said. "Thank you, dear. I'm so sorry, Marcus." Henrietta quietly retreated to her chair in the far corner of the room.

"Maybe I should leave," Ramsay said and started to stand.

"No!" Margaret said. "You mustn't. Please."

He weighed the options before him. He wondered if he should raise her hopes about anymore money coming her way, or tell her about the suspicions that had emerged surrounding Mr. Post's death.

He decided as he squeezed her cool hand. "We've found no evidence of foul play, Mrs. Post," he said. "Only news of a mechanic who committed suicide after doing a bad job on James' brakes."

"Not poor Grady." She delicately stroked the air. "You're merely holding back the evil truth, like James would." She coughed. "You sweet boy."

"Mrs. Post . . . Margaret, we'll carry on your husband's legacy with great vigor. I swear." Ramsay cleared his throat, but he couldn't keep the tears from welling up.

Margaret Post frowned and moaned softly as she held her fingers to her cracked lips. "Oh!" Her eyes searched his face franticly for a moment. "I forgot. You must have this, Marcus." With great difficulty, Margaret reached to the bedside table and picked up a small, white box, six inches long, two inches wide, and one inch deep. She handed it to Ramsay. "James wants you to have it. He said so himself."

Ramsay took the gift. "Of course.
Thank you, ma'am. I want to assure you
that if there is some culprit who took him
from you, I'll find out. I swear I will see
that justice is done for you and Mr. Post."
He squeezed her hand again. She was
staring off in a daze.

"Margaret?" he asked.

She looked back. "So, you think
there was another player in this scheme,
then? Someone who undermined Grady's
work? A henchman of that Benedict's, I
bet." She coughed again. "Remember,
Marcus, it is your dest—"

"Just rest, Mrs. Post."

"James, dearest!" Margaret Lassiter
Post called into the air with her eyes
tightly shut, as if she saw her beloved
James. She clutched Ramsay's hand with
surprising strength and infused him with
the last of her fading energy. Then she
was gone with one grand sigh. Marcus
stroked Margaret's soft, still hand,
engraving the sweet lady's image in his
heart.

He sat there, stunned for a minute,
before he finally called Henrietta.

"I'm so sorry, Henrietta," he said,
failing to hold back his tears as
Margaret's old friend sobbed.

Ramsay drove back to the office. He felt shaky and weak after watching Margaret pass away.

When he pushed open the sales office door, Daisy held the phone in her hand. "Here he is now. Marcus, it's the Mart for you. What on earth's the matter?"

"Nothing," he slumped into his desk chair. He picked up the phone. "This is Ramsay."

"Terry Yapp here," the voice said.

"Who?"

"Grocery Products Accounting?"

"Oh, yeah," he said.

"Good news."

"What?"

"Burghoff signed the routing. We can release the funds. Two million plus interest. Somebody over at the Post house is going to be quite happy tonight, I'll bet. They'll sure be celebrating."

Ramsay shook his head, recalling his last few hours with Margaret.

"Marcus, are you there?" He laughed. "They'll be happy, don't you think?"

"Terry."

"Yeah?"

"She's gone. Margaret Post just died."

Two hours later, Ramsay sat at his desk as darkness fell. Daisy had left, so had everyone else. He was alone in the Coyote Brand compound. He put the decade-old James Post memo in a manila envelope, put that in his briefcase, snapped it shut, and rose to leave.

Once outside the sales office he looked up at the starry sky and thought about his tumultuous day. Margaret Post's death had shaken him completely. As he walked to his car, his tears welled up again. Then his gut churned. He wished the persistent stomach upset would stop. He hunched over to accommodate for the pain.

Just then, out of the corner of his eye, he saw two good ol' boys rushing at him from across the courtyard. He quickly looked behind him, but there was no escape. He turned to face the men, whose faces were covered with kerchiefs. They charged him, knocked him down, and tore the briefcase from his hand.

"Hey! What the hell." Ramsay tried to get up, but they pushed him back down.

"Stay there, you Yankee asshole!" an unfamiliar voice said, as a stiff poined boot kicked Ramsay in the chest. The anonymous assailants alternated kicking his face, his gut, his groin, and his back.

"Stop!" Ramsay yelled. No one heard.

With every part of his body aching, Ramsay sat on the edge of the bathtub as Kathy dabbed hydrogen peroxide on a multitude of abrasions. He kept spitting blood. Then she covered the worst cuts with gauze and taped them down.

"Ow! My ribs," he said. "Those cowboy boots were pointed, you know."

"God, I'm sorry," Kathy said and pressed more lightly on the adhesive tape. "Do you think your ribs are broken?"

"If I'm not better tomorrow, I'll go to the emergency room at Presbyterian," he said.

"I knew all along we shouldn't have done this Texas thing," she said as applied more gauze.

"That's the most you can say? Your goddamned husband is sitting here bruised and bloodied and you move into the old regret mode. Incredible." He

shook his head, coughed, and spit. "Ow
. . ."

"Well, just look at you. This is
ridiculous," Kathy said. "You came here
to help these people and this is the thanks
you get? You gotta see this for what it is.
It's the eighties now! We're not living in
the fifties or some foreign country. This
is crazy."

"You sound real concerned. Blame,
blame, blame . . . "

"I'm sorry, I'm just no good at that
concern stuff. I expected much more
from this change. I'd hoped it was going
be a new start."

"You're right." He hung his head. His
throat filled with tears. "This is the last
straw," he said. "I'll call Childress in the
morning and end this nightmare."

Later that evening, Kathy was reading
Newsweek in the den while, Marcus,
covered with gauze and adhesive tape, sat
gingerly at his desk and clicked open his
briefcase.

He pulled out the manila envelope and
looked inside. "The Post memo! It's
gone!"

"What did you say, dear?" she called.

"They took that memo. Why would they want that?"

Then he noticed that the white box he had received from Mrs. Post was still where he had put it. "Oh, yeah. I forgot." He picked it up and opened it.

"Wow." He pulled out a wonderful silver pen, old but recently polished, from its bed of cotton. It had a worn engraving that was partially-filled with black oxide enscribed around the circumference of the cap: "Dearest J.P. Love, M.P.". He jiggled the heavy pen for a moment. He scribbled on the top of his empty legal pad: "James Post, James Post, James Post . . . . "

The man wrote with this very pen! What a wonderful gift, he thought.

Ramsay's stomach felt queasy and suddenly he felt like he was in a long, dark tunnel, looking out at his own surroundings. He looked around at the details in the room, but they seemed removed from reality, much like he had heard happens when someone has a seizure. Coolness flashed over the surface of his skin. After an indeterminable length of time, he shook himself out of the strange trance and pushed the lingering nausea away.

Weird. And, not a second seems to have passed, he thought.

"Marcus, Masterpiece Theater is on!" Kathy called from the den. "What was that noise?"

"I said, they took the Post memo!"

"No, I heard that," she said. "I meant that growling and tearing."

"What growling and tear—" He gaped at his pad and dropped the heavy pen to his desk.

The bottom third of the long pad was shredded vertically, like an animal had clawed it over and over.

"Oh, my God," he said.

Under his James Post doodles and beside a few drops of saliva, beautiful blue script graced the page:

Thy destiny be: Ensure the fate of three.

Most alarming, under the message, a white, three inch square notepad laid cocked at a forty-five degree angle. The little pad looked years old. Discolored about its edges, another message was scrawled in blue script:

Use this as I did.

Recalling Margaret's recollections of her James using a note pad to control his employees, Ramsay shivered.

Part 4

the Revenge

21 *Dallas, Texas   May 5, 1981*

Sheila Hickman hadn't noticed the first page mention of Margaret Post's passing in the day-old Corsicana *Sun*. She had been busy preparing for her move to the impressive, executive condominium on the shore of beautiful Lake Hubbard, in Rockwell, just east of Dallas. The address was on Alamo Road, just a block off of Walnut Hill Drive, not far from where Marcus Ramsay and his wife Kathy had settled in their new home on curvy Crow Valley Trail. Sheila reasoned that the condo's enviable location on the lake shore was certainly the more desirable location of the two.

Since her shocking dream—a harsh recollection of her role in James Post's murder—she drank even more to help numb her perpetual fear of discovery. In addition to her "special" iced tea in the late afternoon, she added a glass of cabernet an hour after she took her lunchtime pills. Each day, with pangs in her stomach, she drifted off to sleep imagining how Ramsay and the rest would eventually discover the truth. She likened them to a band of children playing with shovels near a shallow grave.

This particular afternoon Sheila sat at a table in her great room and wrote a letter to her aging mother:

Dear Mother:

Not much news. The condo's pretty nice. Earl says the new office is only fair. After all, that Yankee has handled the entire move, including the decorating, the queer. Earl says he catches him in a daze once in a while now, must be getting lazy.

Now that Coyote Brand's financial, marketing, and sales functions had finally been moved, the Hickmans had been forced to relocate from the rural royalty of Golf Estates to the sizzling sprawl of Dallas. As she sat among the moving boxes, Sheila Hickman looked up from her letter to gaze across the mile wide lake. Smooth, dark, and shiny, the water's surface reflected the images of noisy Canada Geese as they glided to a landing.

Between sips of her afternoon wine,
Sheila's ragged coughs echoed through
the house. She looked at the sandstone
walkway that separated the two wings of
the condo's stylish layout. It started at
the front door and ended at a sliding patio
door, where a long pier led to Earl's new
toy, the Corsicana—a pale green rowboat
with a trawling motor. He had already
started taking the boat out in the evening
to the center of the lake to sit quietly, an
executive privilege he had explained that
he owed himself.

Sheila's eyes wandered to the striking
ivory upholstered furniture grouped in
front of the stone and moss fireplace to
her right. The modern mahogany cabinet
where Earl housed his growing gun
collection was nearby. Even though she
loathed guns, she added to the collection
on every birthday, at Christmas, or on
special occasions as he requested. Each
time she'd get advice from quick calls to
Frank Benedict. Earl's favorite gun was
his newest, the Beretta pistol. Frank had
given him that one at the going-away
party that the employees threw for him at
the Corsicana Holiday Inn—that's one
place she wouldn't miss.

Sheila continued writing her letter:

Mom, remember the oil derrick in the middle of the the Holiday Inn grounds? They disassembled it for relocation to the new "Petroleum Park," Wyvonne Putnam's latest project. Earl gave one of his bullshit speeches to the Corsicana City Council to get it approved. I always hated that derrick at the motel anyway.

It'll be reassembled on a lot they cleared behind the Coyote Brand property. The plant workers, Al, and the QA Lab are staying at the compound in Corsicana. Now they call it the operations department. Meanwhile Earl, Lenora, Ted, Ramsay, Cecil, and Daisy all moved to the fancy new Dallas offices.

As she looked around, Sheila noted that it was, in fact, a truly beautiful condo, much nicer than her Corsicana tract home had been. *God, how I hated that box of a house,* she thought. She sipped more wine and continued her letter:

Earl says the only weak spot in the Dallas location is Marcus Ramsay's office. He got this ugly modern table desk with chrome legs. It looks cheap compared to Earl's cherry wood. God, that Yankee has no taste!

By the way, the Chicago brass actually agreed with Ramsay's Long Range Plan. Get this! He recommended that Coyote add chili-flavored spice mix in a packet and a hot chili variety in a can—weird. He even got them to agree to the hot dog sauce campaign he's been squawking about.

Earl said he thought the Long Range Plan presentation might have been a way to dump Ramsay if he'd screwed it up, but apparently he came through with flying colors. All the brass congratulated him at the end which Ramsay told Earl would be good for Coyote—but that was just more Yankee bull. It was certainly good for Ramsay, I bet. Earl says the kid's other ideas are pretty useless.

Sheila reflected on the past year's tumult as she alternated between a puff on her cigarette and a sip on her wine.

The rumors had persisted about Grady Davis putting new brakes on Post's car the day he died. Perhaps they always would. But the move to Dallas had distracted Ramsay from continuing his so-called "investigation." *Thank goodness for small favors,* Sheila thought. she continued:

And, Erlene is hopelessly in love with that Frank Benedict. After six months of dating him, it looks serious. Earl hates it when she slips away every weekend.

I hate the way she moans about how she feels safe with her Frankie. I think it's probably his money. He's older but he's filthy rich, too, you know.

Every Sunday night she walks into the condo all flushed from being with that guy all weekend. From the luggage tags she has on her suitcase I can see that Frank's not afraid to spend the bucks, that's for sure.

Sound familiar, Ma? Sheila thought. *At least Frank's taking her around the country instead of down to the dirty old docks like Sven did. Good old Sven.* Every time she looked at Erlene, she recollected how she and Sven had loved together on a hundred dirty old beds to create her daughter.

Sheila sipped her wine again, then squinted as the smoke from her Winston attacked her eyes. She returned to her letter:

Earl used to bring his problems home to discuss them with me. Now, he doesn't even ask me for my opinion and he calls me less and less during the day. I guess my ideas just don't count anymore. He leaves his briefcase at home and carries a *U.S. News* magazine back and forth to the office. He doesn't get bothered by deadlines like he used to.

Sheila went to the counter and refilled her wine glass. *Maybe this is just how it is on the top of the heap,* she thought—*the life of an executive and an executive's lonely wife.* She resumed writing to her mother:

The Coyote Brand crew in Dallas all hang around Ramsay, especially that

Stuart Noyes, the new Brand Manager who looks like my old tennis coach. During one of my visits, everyone hovered like bees around Ramsay's office. It was sickening. There was nothing happening around Earl's office, except for Lenora. She was busy typing his memos as usual. Earl always has another new idea! He loves to put out those memos!

Everything's going great, Ma, she told herself. Sheila quickly sipped the last half of the glass of wine, put her pen down, crumpled up what she had just written, and stretched. "Nap time," she said. She tossed the wad of paper at the fireplace and decided on a rewrite some other day. She went to the sink, rinsed her wine glass, dried it, and put it away. As she glanced out the window, another stately goose glided toward the water, cleanly cut the surface, and barely splashed, raising its magnificent wings as it landed on the lake. Sheila delighted in the simplicity of that skill, so technically perfect, so esthetically beautiful, so peaceful.

Dallas, Texas   May 16, 1981

"Don't blame me," Erlene said two weeks later at the family's leisurely Saturday morning breakfast on the redwood deck, on a small knoll adjacent to their condo. "Daisy told me last night," Erlene said. "What's the big deal, anyway? Hey, Mama, you shouldn't be drinking that stuff. I know what's in there."

Erlene's mother sipped a mimosa and glared through the cigarette smoke. "What do you mean Ramsay's looking into the brakes thing again?" She looked concerned. "I thought he was through with all that bull."

"It's probably nothin'," Erlene said, "but Daisy said that Marcus is suspicious of Coy cuz of something he said in Corsicana. Whenever Daisy brings it up at home, Coy throws a fit and beats her. Don't you think that's weird?" Erlene asked. "She tries to hide the reason for all her bruises, but Mr. Ramsay always pulls it outa her."

"Poor Daisy. Rapist's wife," Sheila said.

"Don't ya see, Ma?"

"No," Sheila snapped. "And, don't call me that."

"Sorry, Mother, but Marcus thinks Coy's coverin' up somethin' about Post's death. Daisy says he's not, but Marcus keeps pushin', you know, lookin' into it."

"What's that mean?" Sheila fidgeted with her drink and cigarette, nearly dropping both.

"Why are you so concerned about all this, Sheila?" Earl picked up on the conversation as he strolled out to the deck with a brown paper sack of breakfast treats. "Especially if that asshole Duncan is implicated in the Post killing. After all, he did rape your own daughter."

"Just leave it!" Sheila snapped. She stormed over to the wrought iron security gate and threw her mimosa, glass and all, onto the wilted, untamed roses growing on the gate. She stood there and flicked ashes, gazing out at Lake Hubbard.

"God, that smoking's gonna kill her yet, Daddy. Just look at her—non-stop," Erlene said.

"Keeps her from drinking too much at least," Earl said.

"Right, like that mimosa doesn't count. What's the big deal, anyway? It sure

looks like Coy Duncan had somethin' to
do with it, don'tcha think? Even with
Daisy playin' it down, which I think she's
doin'—she's just protectin' him."

"I suppose so. And you know your
mother. Always exaggeratin', gettin'
concerned about something. Now it's
this ten-year-old garbage."

"She's sure lookin' upset these days,
don't you think?" Erlene said and shook
her head.

"Typical," he said.

"But, Daddy."

"What Sugar?"

"She looks especially awful, those dark
circles under her eyes and all. She never
had them before," she said.

"Oh, baby. Now you're getting
dramatic, just like her. That's just her age
showin'."

"No, Daddy," Erlene said. "Just look
at her real close sometime."

22

Dallas, Texas   May 28, 1981

"Daisy?" A female voice said on the phone.

"Yes?" Daisy answered as she sat at her desk.

"This is Kathy Ramsay. Is Marcus in?"

"No. Should I have him call you?" Daisy asked.

"Actually, I need to talk to you," Kathy said.

"Me? What forever for?" Daisy adjusted herself in her chair.

Kathy whispered. "I'm concerned about him."

"What About?"

"He's acting funny. Have you noticed anything?"

"He's always been a little loony, if you ask me." Daisy laughed.

"No, really. At home he's staying to himself much more and never want to go out. And, he's quiet, too. Preoccupied."

"Hmm. I'll keep an eye on him," Daisy said. "That is if y'all want me to."

"Thanks," Kathy said.

"I guess he really does need looking after, the way he's workin' so hard," Daisy said.

"I know you take good care of him, Kathy said. "Best assistant he's ever had."

"Thanks. The man's a refreshing change for me, too."

Later, Ramsay sat in his office looking out at Turtle Creek, reflecting on his victory a month before in Chicago. His proposals for Coyote's Long Range Plan had been approved by the Food Division's Management Committee. Marcus thought, as he flipped pages of the plan, that it looked like Coyote Brand Products would finally be saved from its own apathy.

The phone rang. Ramsay picked it up. "Yes? Ramsay here."

"Howdy, this here is Marty Pritchard. Use to be a Duncan. Coy's mama?" She had a husky, rural twang. "What y'all call me for?"

"Thanks for calling back, Marty. I have a few questions."

"What is this? The FBI? IRS?" she asked. "They answered the phone Coyote."

He cleared his throat. "No government, ma'am. Just Marcus Ramsay over at Coyote Brand Chili."

"When I called Corsicana they said y'all moved the offices up t' Dallas."

"Yes, ma'am. Not long ago. I just had a question for you about Coy and James Post."

"James Post. Never a finer man walked on Texas soil."

"Well, this'll be a tough question, ma'am," Ramsay said.

"What?"

"Well, one day down in Corsicana, Coy implied that he might've had something to do with Post's death. I wanted to know what you thought about that."

"What? Impossible. My Coy's crude once in a while when he's doin' the Klan bit, and he hated it when Post went a-courtin' with them Yankees, but he wouldn't never do nothin' ornery to a man. 'Sides, Post died in an accident caused by bad brakes, right?"

"Right. Sorry for troubling you." It was clear the woman didn't know anything, but her confirmation of Coy's association with the Klan reinforced Ramsay's suspicions that Coy could be capable of involvement in numerous odious acts.

"Say, you a Yankee, ain'tcha?" Marty asked.

"Yes, that's right."

"Figgers." She hung up.

Ramsay went back to thinking about his recent victory in Chicago. All he had lost was his capital recommendation to replace the Coyote Brand compound's antiquated sprinkler system. Earl had argued so vehemently against it that the committee rejected the project. Marcus figured they were letting Hickman go home with one clear victory, though it was inconsequential.

Daisy appeared at the door with a worried look on her face. "Marcus, you better get line one."

"Sure." He swiveled around and picked up the phone.

It was Paul Pentrate, the Human Relations VP at the Mart. "Marcus? Is that you."

"Yes, Paul. What's up?"

"Are you doing OK down there?"

"Sure. What is it?"

"I have real bad news, Marcus." He sounded upset.

"What is it?"

"It's Kyle Burghoff. You know he's always been into handball. He was just in that Chicago Invitational."

"So?"

"Marcus, yesterday he was on the court and collapsed. He had a fatal heart attack."

Ramsay gasped. "But Kyle was in such good shape."

"Looked like a congenital problem that reared its ugly head. We were all shocked. I'm so sorry. I know you viewed him as your mentor."

"Thanks for calling, Paul."

Marcus hung up and put his head in his hands. Kyle had always been such a supporter of his. An hour later Daisy came in and Marcus told her the news. When Daisy shared it with Lenora, she pointed out that Earl had gotten a call about Burghoff's death the day before. Daisy reported back to Marcus that Earl hadn't bothered to pass along the news. Incredulous at this, Marcus stayed in his office and stewed for an hour. Then he got up from his desk to open his office door.

"I'm so sorry about Kyle, Marcus," Daisy said.

Lenora didn't say a word. She just stared at him with a tiny smirk, noting his reaction.

Ramsay returned to his desk and pulled out James Post's old silver pen. He stroked the smooth, cool metal. He began to doodle on the discolored white notepad that had appeared on his desk at home the night he was assaulted by the good ol' boys. Minutes later Daisy walked in and startled Ramsay. He looked up and exclaimed, "What?"

"Sorry for scaring you. Thought I'd come in to cheer y'all up. Boy, you should have heard Earl out there before, bragging about how he killed your sprinkler system deal at the Chicago meeting."

Ramsay sighed. "Yeah. He thought it was a big deal meeting, going up there to rub shoulders with Allied management." He snickered emptily. "Except he's scared as hell of them, so he ass-kissed all of 'em. That's the last time I saw Kyle, then I lost on the sprinkler."

"Oh, Marcus. I'm sorry." I thought you were convinced we needed that it down at the plant."

"We do, but you win some, you lose some." Ramsay shrugged. "They loved the rest of the plan," she said. "Earl'll buy into the sprinkler eventually."

"Oh well."

"You're not actin' concerned about it at all. You're feeling pretty down about Kyle, I guess. What you got there?" she asked. "Something for me to type?"

"Oh, nothing." He quickly placed the little piece of notepaper in an envelope and sealed it.

"Why so secretive?" She laughed. "What's that?" she asked.

"Nothing."

"Looks a damn sight neater than the memos you give me," she muttered. "Pretty writing, too. Why the different writing?" she jabbered. "A little love note to Kathy, I bet. Y'all gettin' along better now? Been a little standoffish with me, I'd say."

"It's nothing."

"OK - OK." Her hands went up defensively. "Whatever you say, Mr. Ramsay." She turned away. "You're the boss."

"Hey, Daisy?" he said. "Sorry. We need to focus on the final draft of the Long Range Plan, OK?"

She turned. "I'll say. The new hot dog sauce campaign is comin' up a mite fast."

"That's right. In fact, I already got the test approved in Chicago. They loved the music. Cherry-Black'll be presenting the rest of the elements tomorrow. We're all going over to the agency to take a look."

"I know. The kick-off's Monday," Daisy said. "Cecil had me book the Hilton for one-two hundred."

Stuart Noyes' well-scrubbed face appeared at Marcus' door. An avid swimmer and skier, Stuart was handsome and well-built. He had a head of short, kinky brown hair and looked more like a gym teacher than a brand manager. "Hey, I heard about Kyle. Sorry," he said.

"Thanks, Stuart."

"I heard we're doing the hot dog sauce kick-off at the Hilton. Pretty impressive—Kyle would've approved."

"No kidding. It was his idea originally."

"Am I going with you to the agency tomorrow?"

"Of course," Marcus said. "For today, I need your thoughts on the final LRP, just in case."

"Just in case of what?" Stuart asked.

"In case I have to leave suddenly," Ramsay said.

"Leave?" Daisy and Stuart asked in stereo, then laughed.

Stuart said, "Wait! You better not go leaving now. I came here because the master marketeer, known far and wide, would be my boss. That would be you."

"Well, thanks," Marcus said, "but in business, you never know about these things. You have to be prepared. Just look at Burghoff. He was in great shape."

Stuart frowned. "Hmm." A concerned crease spread from temple to temple.

"Don't worry. Always have to have a contingency, just in case," Marcus said. "Oh, by the way, Daisy?"

"Yes, boss?"

"You said Holler's Woods is where Coy hunts on Saturday mornings, right?" he asked. "Near your place?"

She laughed uneasily. "Yep. At dawn. Why?"

"Just passing on a hunting recommendation. Pretty place, right?"

"You sure are actin' a mite strange these days," she said and shook her head as she left the office. "I know you're no hunter."

"Just passin' on an idea," he called. "Oh Ms. Duncan?" She stopped in the doorway and looked back at him.

"When will I see El Franko next?" Ramsay asked.

"He's out of town now, I think. I know you'll see him at the hot dog sauce kick-off Monday."

He put his finger on his lip. "That's right," he said.

The next day, in Cherry-Black's little board room, the group laughed at a drawing of a bright orange cartoon dog wearing a blue polka dot bandanna as sixties rock music played through bookshelf speakers. The dog held an oversized hot dog heaped with Coyote hot dog sauce. The dog's bandanna gave him a western look, but his sparkling teeth made him look like Walt Disney's Pluto. Bob Cherry removed the piece of paper that hid the headline:

"Taste the Wild Coyote Dog!"

The creative strategy was a good one. The friendly cartoon character would capture the imagination of kids who would gobble up chili dogs, a summer treat that would be as familiar to Yankees as it was to Texans. And, since most of the chili sold across the Southwest was Coyote Brand to begin with, and most of it sold in the fall and winter, summer chili sales would be favorably affected by the campaign. The sixties music would play well with the mothers of the targeted kids.

"You really like it?" Bob asked.

"Man. It's right on the money," Marcus said.

"Won't take much to make Monday," Daisy said.

"Yeah," Marcus said. "We already have the Hilton booked and the broker guys are invited."

"Yep. We're all geared up," Cecil said.

"Ooo-ooo," Daisy sang with the music. She talked loudly. "All we have to do is double-check the order of the slides, hang that outdoor billboard at the Hilton, and set-up the P.A. to play the music. It'll be so cool!"

"Don't forget them flashy sales aid packets I got printed for everyone," Cecil nearly shouted.

"I've ordered boutonnieres for y'all, too. And I'm wearin' a corsage!" Daisy added.

"We're your Coyote Team, Bob. Gotcha covered," Ramsay said. "I think it's gonna come together real well." Then he felt himself slip into a daze.

"Mr. Ramsay? Mr. Ramsay?" Daisy asked. She waved her hand in front of his face. "You're in one of them trances again, like you're not all here." She waved her arms around in front of his face to get his attention. "Hello, in there! You OK?"

"Yeah, sorry." He shook his head. "I guess I'm out of it today. I've been thinking about Coy's wild threats again," Marcus said as he fiddled with his silver pen.

"Your Coy?" Bob Cherry said and pointed to Daisy. "What threats?"

She nodded, then shrugged. "It's nothin'. Just typical cowboy bull is all."

"Hardly, Daisy. Don't brush it off," Marcus said. "Looks like Coy might've had something to do with James Post's death, among other things."

"No kidding?" Bob laughed uneasily. His eyes squinted. "Seriously?"

"And the rich bastard that Coy mentioned down in Corsicana one day? We're pretty sure he might've been talking about Frank Benedict," Marcus said.

"No," Bob said. "Frank? You're kidding."

"Yep," Marcus nodded. "Coy also slipped and mentioned that a drunken bitch might've hired him to do some dirty work on Post's brakes," Marcus said.

"Aw, Marcus," Daisy smirked. "See, Bob, the Yankee's gettin' carried away again."

Cecil stewed. "Yep: Marcus, that dog don't hunt, if you ask me."

"Well," Marcus said. "I'm just looking at the facts as they appear."

Bob Cherry jumped in. "Wait. You're sayin' Sheila hired Coy?"

The group hushed for a Texas minute. They looked back and forth at each other.

"What'd I say?" Bob Cherry asked, hands up.

Cecil blurted, "Shame on you, Bob. You just accused Mrs. Sheila Hickman— in all her glory and them fancy shoes—of planning the murder of Coyote's former president, the great James Earl Post.

Why can't we give that man his eternal rest?"

"Well," Steve Causte, the account executive,asked, "why couldn't Sheila have had somethin' to do with it? She had everything to gain if James Post died, didn't she? Just think of it like a real mystery. It all fits."

Cecil swiped the air. "We've had enough mysteries around here, Mr. Causte," he said.

"Yeah, Steve, and think about it," Bob said. "Sheila with her cowboy boots, hot pants, and all that booze. She's a little on the loo-loo side half the time, too—hardly the murderer type."

Steve stood. "True, but remember, Earl became president right after Post died. Sounds like she had a couple of motives to me—position and wealth." He counted on two of his fingers.

"Wait, Steve. Cecil's right. This whole thing isn't too likely. It would make a great movie, but it's a little far fetched," Ramsay said. "Although," he added as he held his index finger up, "position and wealth would be darn good motives."

Steve pulled on his lip. "I don't suppose she'd be capable in her mental state, though."

"Yeah," Ramsay said. "All that electroshock stuff."

Steve Causte raised his finger and stepped forward. "But, on second thought, y'all know what they say about that electroshock therapy?"

"What?"

Causte stood there nodding, hands on hips. "It sure kills the patient's sense of guilt—that's one thing it does. That could make Sheila's involvement more logical."

Earl and Sheila sat at the kitchen table, talking after dinner. "You don't look so good, Sheila." Earl said. "Should you see somebody?"

"Why don't you just fire the bastard?" Sheila said and hacked.

"Shoot. Not Ramsay again. Say, that cough is murder," he said.

She looked up, then nodded. As she puffed on another cigarette, she recalled how Ramsay had become her nemesis. As her dreams had become more and more vivid, James Post and the Yankee had routinely begun appearing in them. It was almost like the two men were becoming the same person. "Damn spooky, that Yankee," she said. She shook her head, confused.

"Sheila, you just don't understand about Ramsay," Earl said and sipped his coffee. "I'm damned if I do and I'm damned if I don't. Everybody's listening to him, now. And, he's coming up with things I never even thought of. If I get rid of him, I hurt sales and my image up in Chicago. That's bound to hurt you and me, both. I just wonder what he'll come up with next?"

"But, is it worth it?" Sheila asked. "He's taking over and you don't even seem to care."

"Well, at least he keeps Childress out of my hair," he said.

"Yep, but Earl. You've got no pride in your work—no incentive to go to the office. You even had a tough time dealing with Erlene and Frank. And, you leave me out of everything. All because of that damn Yankee."

Earl slumped like a scolded school boy as Sheila listed his problems. "Well, I used to think I was good at my job, but not lately," he said. "Now I need you for advice and Ramsay for ideas. What the hell do I bring to the Coyote table anymore?"

"Oh, Earl," she said. "I'm sorry."

"Shit. I'm going out in the boat for a while. At least I can still operate that," he said. "Maybe I should run away to Mexico and be a fisherman." He stood.

"Earl, listen, I'm really sorry," she said.

"Just leave me be, Sheila." He turned and walked to the sliding door that opened onto the pier.

"Oh, shit. Now I fucking did it," she said.

"Be back in an hour." He turned around. "Sheila, you know I was feeling fine till you reminded me how bad everything was. Thanks."

Three blocks away, in their house on Crow Valley Trail, the Ramsays talked finances at their kitchen table. "It looks like we went way over in the office supplies account," Kathy Ramsay said, studying her notes.

"But you included postage as an office supply," he said. "That was enough to have its own account," Marcus said. "It was never intended to be in office supplies."

"Well, if we gave it it's own account," she said, "it'd still be over budget. You shouldn't—"

"What's all this blaming bullshit?" he asked.

"What are you talking about?" she asked.

"The way you're saying things."

"I'm not blaming you," she said. "It's your fault."

He laughed cynically. "Kathy, why do you always end up proving you're right and I'm wrong? Is that so important?" he asked.

"I've made my point. You went over budget and took what I said the wrong way."

"See! You're blaming me again," he said. "God, I'm sick of this bickering."

"You're wrong," she said. "Really."

He shook his head. "Listen, I'm going out for my run." Exasperated and wondering if those things that seemed so unfixable in his marriage could ever be repaired, Marcus Ramsay stormed outside to run down Walnut Hill Drive toward the lake.

Soon, he jogged past the Hickman condo. He kicked stones as he passed the impressive security gates covered with Sheila Hickman's untamed roses. Earl had mentioned how Sheila had finally consented to moving there because she'd inherit those roses—she liked them growing wild. Then Ramsay recalled talking about Sheila at his meeting that day over at Cherry-Black.

He wondered if Sheila Hickman was really capable of murder. She had always had such a coarse, irreverent nature. *Possible,* he thought. *Naw, she might be a drunken cowgirl, but not a murderer.*

On the other hand, it was true that she had the motives of position and wealth. And the opportunity: Post's brakes. And the means: Coy Duncan.

If she was the so-called drunken bitch Coy had referred to, Ramsay wondered how she must feel now. He wondered how she must've felt for the decade since Post died, especially now that the case was getting renewed attention.

If she had anything to do with it, she'd be nervous as hell, he concluded. She'd have to be worried that she was, slowly and inevitably, being exposed.

He ran on. He almost felt sorry for anyone who had to live with that kind of haunting guilt and fear of discovery. *What would they be desiring most now?* As he ran, he noticed the repetitive pounding of his feet on the pavement, and pondered the question. Then he suddenly stopped.

"Peace." That's what she would want if she was the guilt-ridden culprit. What would bring peace?

He started running. Prison? Maybe. A move to some desert isle? Probably not. What was peace anyway?

Death is the ultimate peace, he thought.

Just then Ramsay saw the Miller's German Shepherd up ahead. It was off the leash again! The dog had bitten him soon after he and Kathy had moved into their Crow Valley home. After that, Ramsay had taken numerous routes to avoid the dog on his evening runs. Whenever he saw the animal, it stood its ground, ready to defend his invaded territory.

Ramsay jogged warily onward, half-thinking about Sheila Hickman and half-worrying about the dog. Then, he saw the dog's eyes glaring at him. It growled as Ramsay approached.

Ramsay stopped. He felt himself growl back automatically at the dog. It was a deep, coarse snarl. God, it was so animalistic! He cleared his throat. *Where the hell did that growl come from?* he wondered.

The dog stopped ten feet in front of him. It cowered, whimpered, and then, after hesitating a second, scurried away; like it had just crossed paths with some horrendous beast ten times its size.

Ramsay was stunned at the dog's timid behavior. Then he felt saliva on his lips and wiped it off. He looked at it. *What is this?* He looked inquisitively at his hand. This drool shit is getting weird. Then he ran on, swearing to himself not to get wrapped up in anymore murder theories.

At the Hickman condo, Earl moored his boat. "Earl! Please hurry," Sheila called in a muffled voice through the partially closed slider. "You need to get dressed for the dance. Come on, you'll feel better."

Earl double-checked the mooring and stowed the oars in the pier-side cabinet. The rowboat bounced in the water at the pier's end, lit by a single, blue safety light.

A big storm was due any day now, he guessed. It was that time of year in northern Texas, Earl thought. He swished the gas can. *Getting low,* he thought. *Just enough to get to the center of the lake. Maybe a little more.*

He stood. "I'll have to pick some up—"

"Earl, hurry!" Sheila yelled from the house. "The dance?"

"OK, OK! I'm coming," he said as he walked in.

23

Dallas, Texas   May 29, 1981

"Coyote Dog?" Sheila smirked.   She sipped her wine at the sparkling table and looked around the large ballroom at the Dallas Hyatt Regency's Celebrity Dance. "That's a stupid name, Earl. Why're you letting Ramsay do this crazy advertising stuff anyway?" she asked.

"It doesn't matter what I think, Sheila," he said. "The agency designed the outdoor billboards. They recorded the fancy-ass radio commercial up in Nashville—stupid sixties rock 'n' roll. The Dallas broker kick-off meeting is Monday at the Hilton. Hell, it'll probably flop."

"But why are you even letting him do it?" she asked.

"He may act like he's the damn president, but his power is only in his head." Earl flashed a grin and waved as a familiar couple danced by.

"Sure, Earl," Sheila said, eyeing the passing guests. She didn't buy Earl's supercilious attitude. "It's not worth having him around is all." She stamped her cigarette out with jerks that clinked the ashtray into her glass. She hacked deeply and sipped again. "Why not just dump him?"

"Sheila, you don't understand the realities. They love him up in Chicago." Earl sipped his Perfect Manhattan and settled into an empty gaze across the room.

Sheila studied her husband's face. The skin under his chin drooped, his graying hair receded more than ever, and he intermittently broke into a tremor. She realized he would always be there for her, totally devoted, for that was how it had been since they met. But, suddenly she felt alone. After all, Earl had always tried so hard, but had never risen beyond the status of impotent corporate mole. And now there was no way his fancy speeches, waving arms, and resonant voice could rescue her from the inevitability of this Post thing.

She recalled how Erlene had said it so casually earlier that day, like unwittingly pronouncing a death sentence, "They're putting it all together, Mama." Then Sheila had shivered deep to the bone and had admitted to herself that her guilt would be discovered, sooner or later.

Now, in the middle of the party's gaiety, Sheila couldn't quite catch her breath. Her chest tightened. It was like an invisible hand gripped her heart, capable of effortlessly snuffing her out at any moment.

"Are you all right?" Earl asked. "You look awful."

"It's my chest," she said. She slapped it. "It feels real tight."

"We really should get you in for a check-up."

She looked around nervously. "Naw. It's just the excitement."

On Monday, while Earl attended the Coyote Dog kickoff at the Hilton, Sheila took her pills, lay down for a nap, then was shaken awake by her own hacking. She went to the bathroom, stood at the sink, and held her rattling chest. The coughs were longer now and rocked her lungs. "Fuck it," she wheezed. Even her first glass of wine hadn't settled her. She stared at herself in the mirror. Her image was surrounded by small spherical lights, most of them out. Her eyes were dark and tired, her skin was sallow. "Earl's right. I do look like shit," she said.

The shower curtain fluttered from the lake breeze and slapped the wall like a wet towel, startling her.

After a few minutes she went back to bed.

Just as she began to doze off, the front door bell rang. *Was that real or a dream?* She struggled to rise, sleep pulling her back, but she managed to stand. "Shit. What now?" she asked.

By the time she got to the door, no one was there. The distant sound of thunder rumbled. Sheila glanced around the front entry.

Only a folded piece of old, white notepaper bounced at the doorstep. It was caught between the door and the little red brick wall that surrounded the planter. She picked it up, carefully unfolded it, and read it. A messenger must have left it.

The note was written on old, crinkly paper, perfectly hand-scripted in blue ink. "In the lake ye shall find peace," it said. It was written in a flowing, elegant blue script that reminded her of Bryan's writing before his football accident. Its message of peace reminded her of the geese she had seen carefully landing on the lake's surface.

She took it to the dining room table, where she read it again and again. She sipped her second glass of wine. Perhaps, now she could sleep. In a way, she felt spooked at the note's message, so logical and simple. It was weird, almost like reading a personalized religious fortune cookie. "In the lake ye shall find peace," she read.

Where did it come from? she wondered.

After she sipped and read for another hour, she lay down and day-dreamed. She figured a religious missionary from some odd sect must have deposited the note on her doorstep while visiting all the lucky homeowners on the lake shore. Then, irked by the strangeness of the delivery, and hoping to discover some faint evidence of whomever was responsible for it, she went to the front door to investigate the area. The way she was carrying on about the note made her feel like she was dreaming, yet everything seemed so vivid.

When she scoured the porch, she noticed a spot of white just under the border of a hedge. She walked over and picked it up. *A boutonniere?* She sniffed it, twirled it, and tossed it into the hedge.

Who would've left a boutonniere? she thought.

At first she hoped the phantom visitor would not return to leave another note. The message might have been beautiful, but it was cryptic as well, and written on such old paper—why? It was even a little threatening—such an odd message about peace in the lake. Then she wished her ghostly guest would reappear, properly announce him or herself, and take leave, promising not to disquiet her again.

Sheila decided to take control of the situation. She would frame the note at some point and display it above the fireplace. She'd go to the craft store soon to get one of those distressed frames. Then having put the note safely in a place of her own design, she wouldn't feel so bothered by it.

She returned to the bedroom to continue her nap. First, to avoid severely creasing the note, she folded it gently and stowed it in the bottom drawer of her jewelry chest. She planned to look around the house for some big books to press it the next day. *Wait.* She sat up suddenly. *Was that whole episode about the note real or a dream?* She wondered frantically and couldn't tell, but after a few minutes, concluded it had been a strange dream.

Across town, the Hilton's large ballroom was a flurry of activity when Earl entered. Sound-men strung wires while a construction crew hung a colorful fifteen-foot long roll of paper high on the wall behind the podium. The Coyote Brand Team, as they had begun calling themselves—Cecil, Daisy, and Stuart—supervised the technicians and hotel staff as they performed a myriad of tasks. It was antlike, the way each of them worked together to perform their duties.

Marcus Ramsay rushed in late, sorted a pile of papers, and tested the microphone on the podium. Daisy ran up to him, straightened his tie, and fussed with his lapel. "So, where is it?" she asked loudly. "I spent all my time getting y'all a nice flower. Then you go and lose it? Look, Cecil's got his and Stuart's got his. I got my corsage. You're not gonna look like you're part of the team!"

The ballroom was filled beyond fire code restrictions. Each of the tables was fully occupied, and more salesmen stood

and jabbered. Frank and Oscar joined
Earl at his table. The room darkened for
the kick-off of the Coyote Dog campaign's
Dallas test market. The audience
quieted to a low hum.

"Why all the melodrama?" Earl leaned
over and asked Frank. "We didn't need
all this schmaltz in our days, did we?"

"Fancy marketing stuff," Oscar said.
"More proof that the Yankee is taking
over."

Just then Ramsay walked up. He
shook hands with Frank, Earl, and Oscar.

"Guess Daisy was giving you a plenty
hard time about that flower," Earl said.

Ramsay snickered and pointed to his
lapel. "Lost it somewhere. Well, at least
she didn't banish me to Holler's Woods
Saturday morning where I could get shot
by Coy. Say, I better git." He turned and
started to walk away.

Frank yelled, "Hey, Marcus! Wait."
Ramsay turned. "What?"
"What did you say about Coy?"
"Nothing. He always hunts at dawn
down at Holler's Woods, north of
Corsicana, on Saturday mornings. Why?"
"Every Saturday?"
"That's what Daisy said. It's a regular
deal."

"Say, Marcus, you got some paper?" Frank asked and fiddled for a pen. Ramsay reached in his pocket, pulled out some old note paper, and handed a piece to Frank.

"Holler's Woods?" Frank asked and wrote it down.

"Yep. Just west of I-45."

"Every Saturday, huh?" Frank wrote hurriedly.

"What is it, Frank?" Earl asked.

"Just making notes for future," he said. "Holler's Woods is near Ennis then, right Earl?"

"Just north of Corsicana," Earl said. "You and your huntin', Frank. Whatcha gonna kill next?"

"Some poor duck, I s'pose," Frank growled. "Maybe a whole family."

"Gruesome," Earl said and shook his head.

Frank shrugged. "Well, leaves none to grieve."

"You aren't hunting with that rapist Duncan are you?"

"Hardly," Frank smirked as he stuck the note in his pocket. Ramsay shook his head and walked toward the podium as the ambient lights faded to darkness.

Earl watched Ramsay stride into the spotlight, put his papers on the podium, and scan the audience. This was the moment of truth for the Yankee's new bullshit ad campaign for hot dog sauce, Earl thought. He secretly wished Ramsay bad luck. Then Earl heard the low hum of background music rumble from the speakers in each corner of the room, now filled with over a hundred excited broker reps from the Benedict Company. "Huh?"

After Ramsay's dry exposition of the marketing logic behind the campaign, a louder rhythm began to emerge from the speakers. Then Ramsay spoke rhetorically into the mike. "Coyote Brand hot dog chili sauce is used to make what?"

Earl snickered. *Fuck you,* he thought. *Yankee mumbo jumbo.*

"A Coyote Dog." Cecil rose and tentatively pointed his stubs at the crowd. A few of the broker salesmen joined him.

Earl looked up at Marcus Ramsay. The Yankee looked disappointed—*good. This is nonsense,* Earl thought. *Sheila should see this.*

Ramsay pleaded louder, "Come on, you can do better than that, can't you?

Coyote Brand hot dog chili sauce will encourage consumers to make what?"

"Coyote Dogs," more of the crowd barked back.

Ramsay smiled. "That response was better, but I'm afraid it's a little on the tame side."

Then the reflections of the spotlights twinkled in Ramsay's eyes. A stronger, deeper voice boomed from inside him. In a slow, dramatic cadence, oozing with confidence, he drawled like a Texas gentleman, "Now that's better y'all. What can you fellas tell me will create the single largest volume increase of any product in Coyote's proud history? And put lots of dollars in y'alls' pockets?"

Where have I heard that voice? Earl wondered and almost dropped his drink. It reminded him of James Post! He looked at Frank, who appeared equally taken aback.

Then Ramsay paused, smiled, and like a preacher, slowly raised his hands. "Come on, y'all. Let's hear it."

"Coyote Dog!" the crowd yelled in perfect unison. Earl sat up. *What's this?*

Then Ramsay's charismatic voice became gruff and raspy, growling at the crowd. Earl looked twice, wondering how the bestial voice could have possibly come from Ramsay. Even Ramsay appeared surprised at his own voice and cleared his throat. *The boy is probably sick from nerves,* Earl thought.

But Ramsay continued, stronger than ever. "Now, listen here y'all!" he called.

Earl shuddered as Ramsay recovered and suddenly became the forceful southern gentleman again. "Together now! And don't y'all be letting me down," Ramsay said. "What are all the little kids gonna be eatin'?"

"Coyote Dogs. Coyote Dogs!"

"That's it! Don't be shy," Ramsay called back.

Then the audience's response swelled to a primitive chant. "Coyote Dog! Coyote Dog!" They clapped their hands, stood, and stomped their feet, making a muffled rumble on the carpeted floor. "Coyote Dog! Coyote Dog! Coyote Dog! Coyote Dog!"

"That's it! That's it, boys!" Ramsay waved his hands. "Let's hear it."

"Coyote Dog! Coyote Dog! Coyote Dog!" In just a few minutes the group had shifted from cheering like school chums to chanting like savages on a hunt.

Ramsay started pounding the podium as his eyes flashed.

Earl sat up straight and combed the throng. *What the hell is going on here?* he thought.

Just then Ramsay waved a hand toward the rear of the room. A professionally-costumed Coyote Dog character with an oversized head bounced through the rear door. Cecil, Daisy, and Stuart followed, passing out bright yellow Coyote Dog sales brochures to each row of chanting salesmen. Earl turned this way and that to take it all in. *Sheila's not gonna believe this,* he thought.

The Coyote Dog character marched to the podium, shook Ramsay's hand with its oversized paw, and pointed at the roll of paper hanging high on the wall. At that moment, the roll unfurled. It was a full-sized Coyote Dog outdoor billboard, accented with spotlights!

"Aah-ooo!" the costumed varmint howled into the mike. Ramsay patted its furry back.

The group applauded as the Coyote Dog character danced on the stage and pointed to its likeness on the billboard. Meanwhile, the Coyote Dog theme song continued to rock from the speakers that were situated around the room.

At once all of the program's elements had coalesced into a jubilant, irreverent Mardi Gras in the Dallas Hilton Hotel. Earl watched the salesmen clap, the music play, and the Coyote Dog character wave its paws.

Frank Benedict even directed his men from atop a folding chair. "I love this, boss!" Frank yelled down to Earl.

"Sure. Sure," Earl said in a shaky voice. "It's something else, isn't it?"

The next morning Sheila fidgeted over her second cup of coffee. Before he went to work, Earl had reconstructed how Ramsay turned the hot dog sauce meeting into a crazed barbarian rite. She trembled as she held her cup, unsettled at the Yankee's apparent power to put broker salesmen, normally a staid bunch, into some kind of frenzy. *Yankee's some weird kinda 'cult guy or something,* she imagined.

"And his voice even sounded like James Post's," Earl had said. "That southern gentleman type."

She had looked up. "What?"

That afternoon, curious at the tranquility the eerie note had brought her twenty-four hours before, Sheila drank her wine, then, after she lay down for a few minutes, got up and retrieved it from the lower drawer of her jewelry box.

She read it over. "In the lake ye shall find peace." At first it had sounded like a silly promise, but now it rang with some kind of spiritual believability.

While she sipped her glass of Cabernet at lakeside, she became entranced by the repetition of little lapping waves. She thought about the note as she felt the wine mix with her pills. Tipsy and a little nauseated, Sheila rose, walked inside, put her wine glass on the dining room table, and staggered into the bedroom for her afternoon nap. She fought sleep for several minutes before she felt herself slip into a dream:

Sheila stood in a dark cemetery. It was the one in Corsicana, adjacent to the Pioneer Village and the Navarro County Historical Society Museum. Dressed only in one of Earl's soft flannel shirts, Sheila wandered among the graves. She smelled the storm clouds brewing and heard thunder booming a muffled alert.

Suddenly an apparition of James Post appeared alongside his large tombstone, wearing his famous black felt hat. "Mrs. Hickman! You do remember me, don't you?"

"Of course I do." She said indignantly, but she shivered from the damp air and the fear that filled her as a result of coming face to face with James Post. Curious, she took a deep breath and approached the floating apparition.

The vision of Post smiled and tossed something her way. It was an old silver pen clipped to a little folded note. Oddly, it looked like the same note she had just stowed in her jewelry chest, the same note she had decided to press and frame, the same note that had been beautiful enough for another inspection that afternoon.

She looked around. The gravestones loomed everywhere and steam floated about. Threatening clouds boomed a few times.

Mr. Post said that he had been writing notes during one of his Friday night thinking sessions and explained how he had delivered the note in person the day before. "It was just for you, ma'am." He tipped his hat.

Sheila trembled, confused for a second at finding the same note here in the cemetery. She thought she'd safely stowed it in her jewelry box. She bent down and picked up the pen and note. She unfolded it and read it again.

"So, you were the one that wrote this?" she asked as she protected it from a few falling raindrops. "Nice handwriting, like Bryan's used to be."

He nodded. "I know. In fact, exactly."

A bell chimed in the distance.

She looked up at him with tired eyes. "I need this pain to be over, Mr. Post."

"I think you knew all along that to get everything you wanted you'd have to pay," he said.

"Yep. But, why me?" She read Post's note again.

"It's merely a consequence of greed. You just took everything, Miss Sheila. You never earned any of it."

Sheila scrunched her brow. "What about everyone else?"

"Their greed, your greed. Y'all's greed."

"But, it's so unfair, me going through this."

"World's not fair, ma'am. Especially to folks like you. You were never capable of earning it, so all you did was take it. That's the nature of greed—you just have to get it even though you haven't earned it or never will." Post smiled with fond reassurance. "Y'all understand that message now?" he asked in a somber, caring tone, folding his hands peacefully in front of him like a funeral director.

Sheila gasped and covered her mouth. She suddenly understood the note's personal message: the lake, final peace. She folded it and stuffed it in the clip of the heavy pen. She tossed both into the daisies at the base of Post's grave.

Then a flood of relief poured over her "I do understand. I hate it, Mr. Post, but I understand," she said. She looked up at his image. "Thanks, sir . . . I think." She felt odd saying that. "It's strange that you're the one that'll help me get rid of the pain, even though I did you in. You're a good man."

"Oh, don't thank me, Miss Sheila. Now you'll pay like Ahab did before you."

"Ahab?"

"Yes ma'am," he said. "He was blinded by his obsession, too."

Sheila didn't understand Mr. Post's reference, but she did know that he had just given her a way to totally assuage the guilt she had accumulated over the years: killing her father; maiming Bryan; and finally, killing the man in front of her and taking him away from those who loved him.

"Thank you," she said. "Is that all, sir?"

"Oh, hardly," Post said and tipped his hat with a bow.

"I can't wait," she said sarcastically. "Always a gentleman, you brown-nose."

"The Yankee is getting mighty close to exposing the whole thing, isn't he?" Post asked.

She nodded and looked down. "That bastard pushed me into this."

"Then we must make preparations," Post said. "After all, it is your destiny."

"I guess so, dammit. I promise I'll make preparations," she said. "Anything for peace." Unlike other promises Sheila routinely broke, she planned to keep this one.

The next night, Wednesday, as the Hickmans ate dinner quietly, Sheila hunched over and thought about how vivid her afternoon dreams had become. She could no longer deny that her dream world had become her reality. It was difficult to tell the difference anymore. "Earl, for your own good, not just for me, promise me you'll dump the Yankee," she said. "Soon?"

"Yes, dear. Sheila, you look awful." He shook his head. "Make an appointment with Dr. Lockhart, OK?"

"Sure," she said, but didn't mean it. She stared into space.

Later that night Sheila shivered in bed. When Earl tried to cuddle her, she pushed him away. "There's nothing you can do, Earl." She stared at the dark.

"I'm concerned about you," he said. "This isn't funny anymore."

"It never was," she said.

That same evening, after a romantic pasta dinner, Erlene cried to Frank about the rape she had experienced as a teen a decade earlier. They were sharing secrets on the cozy couch in Frank's rustic great room.

"My dad has a gun cabinet just like that one! It's filling up fast. Mama gets him a gun on Christmas and his birthdays."

"Now, come on, Erlene, you're stalling. Back to that rape," he said.

"It was just the worst, Frankie." The time capsule of pain opened once again. She cried. "It's like it was yesterday."

"Why didn't you tell me all this before?" he asked.

"I tried, Frankie. Honest. I was afraid you'd hate me or think I was a dirty slut or something." She snuggled her soft blonde hair into him.

"Why didn't you just resist that bastard cowboy, sugar?" he asked.

"I knew you'd ask me that." She pulled away. "Like it was all my fault or somethin'."

"Well—"

"He was just too strong. He just kept whooping me and slapping and jamming at me while he threatened me. It hurt so bad. Sometimes when you and I are doin' it, I think back to that night."

"You what?" He sat up. His eyes flared.

"I do, Frankie," she said. "It's true, I'm sorry."

"That bastard." His jaw clenched.

"Oh, Frankie." Erlene cringed.

"I'll kill that asshole. What else haven't you told me?" Benedict said. "Come on, girl. Spill it!"

"Don't yell, Frankie. I don't like it when you get like this."

"Well?"

"Just that Daisy said something about Coy making a statement about Post's death bein' a murder. And the Navarro County D. A.'s reopenin' the case."

"What? Wait, it's too long ago, Erlene," he said shakily. "They call it the statute of— "

"Ramsay said that the Navarro County D. A. told him there's no statute of limitations on murder," she said.

Frank flinched. "What? Murder?"

"That's what they're calling it now. Coy is the key witness. He's bound to point the finger at anyone else involved, isn't it great?"

Frank looked ashen gray all of a sudden. "Damn fucking Yankee," he mumbled.

"You OK, Teddy Bear?" Erlene said. "You look mighty flustered."

"I'll be fine, Erlene." But he shook his head and looked blankly at his gun collection. "I just got somethin' to do."

That Saturday morning, as dawn shone through the trees at Holler's Woods, Frank slid his Mercedes SL to a halt on an infrequently used gravel road twenty feet from the pond. Minutes later, his large feet trampled the long, green grass into the mud as a mix of invisible morning birds sang. Shoot. *Can't let Duncan open his mouth to no DA,* he thought.

The dampness of the marsh filled his snorting nostrils as he trounced heavily, reticent but resolved. A few steps away from the water, he came to the perfect spot, across the pond from a large tree. A lone goose flew high overhead, looking left, then right, in search of its flock. *Holler's Woods is a hunter's paradise,* Frank thought. He hid in a natural screen of cattails.

Frank stood patiently in the reeds for several minutes. Then his attention was piqued by his target across the pond, a telltale red hunting cap and long chestnut hair.

"Shit," he gulped. He raised his high powered rifle and squinted into its site to verify it was Coy. Then he was sure. He clicked his safety off.

I'm not gonna let no piss-ass fuckin' shithead be the one to bring me down, he thought. *And no bastard's gonna get away with rapin' my woman.* He spit and reconsidered one last time. *You played us all for suckers, Duncan. This'll teach you good.*

Frank squinted through the sight with his good eye. He followed the red and black checked target, predictably bobbing across the pond, just above cattail line. A shotgun rested on Coy's barely visible shoulders.

"One, two, three, four," Benedict mumbled. "One, two, three, four." Then, he exhaled. Then a slow, but decisive squeeze of the trigger unleashed the might of his weapon—*blam!*

A second later, through his sight, he saw Coy's head jerk violently as blood, hair, and scull fragments scattered everywhere. Frank felt the kick go all the way to his groin as hate flushed through him.

The blast faded into the morning chill.

"Done," he said. He inhaled the stench of freshly burnt ammo. For the next few minutes Frank stood there as a handful of geese squawked by. Then he slushed back to his Mercedes. He opened the door and sat on his custom Longhorn seat covers.

He reached in the back seat and picked up a wad of hundred dollar bills which he counted. Earlier that morning, as he drank coffee at home, he had counted the wad over and over.

"I'm history." He revved his engine, pulled away from the pond's edge, and turned around. In minutes he headed south on I-45 toward Houston to start his new life.

24 *Dallas, Texas   June 1, 1981*

The news of Frank Benedict's disappearance hit the Dallas Coyote Brand office on Monday. "Just up and disappeared without a trace," Sheriff Larry Calhoun was reported to have said, according to Lenora, who had heard the Corsicana gossip at church. Tracers had been put out by the Dallas police force since Frank lived in that jurisdiction, but the detective in charge wasn't very encouraging.

Monday morning Detective Mike Adams had patiently explained to the Benedict brokerage staff, then the Coyote Dallas staff, that the incident had followed the profile of an "executive bailout," something he had seen before. Some wealthy oil tycoon would get tired of his daily grind, take a lifetime of cash, catch the next plane to the French Riviera, and disappear forever. The motus operandi could certainly match Frank's—wealthy and marginally fed-up with the life he had so fervently pursued.

"Occasionally my husband's been known to up and stay away after he's been huntin' on Saturdays, but he's never gone this long. I even went and called Larry figurin' he could rustle Coy up," Daisy said on the phone from her desk to Willy Womack the same day after lunch. "But Larry didn't go with him last Saturday. Coy's probably still out there suckin' down beers and shootin' a mess of poor, innocent things."

Marcus Ramsay walked out of his office. He hadn't looked closely at Daisy's face all day. He froze as he studied her.

"Coy's been so preoccupied with this Post nonsense," Daisy said to Willy. "Why, I was telling Erlene just the other night he was plannin' on makin' some kind of statement. Friday he even wrote it all down. Guess they might-could call it a murder now. Then we'll clear this whole Post thing up once and for all. You know Mr. Ramsay said the D.A.'ll reopen the case if there's enough evidence." She listened. "Yep. And if Coy gives his statement they might-could give him immunity," she whispered, then listened. "Well, he didn't do nothin', don't get me wrong, but so many folks are talkin' about his big mouth around town, he could probably use some sort of guarantee so he don't get blamed." She listened. "Yep, I swear it'll come to a head real soon. See, I'm helpin' Coy like a true Yankee would. Pretty smart. huh? . . . "

"What the hell happened to you?" Ramsay interrupted, pointing to her face. He hung on his office door jamb. "Has Coy been beating you?"

She held the phone away and whispered, "Bastard did it Friday night. Makeup didn't cover, I guess." She stroked the not-so-faint purple bruises on her left eye, cheek, and temple, and shrugged. "Roy is still gone. Must be having a good ol' time out there in the swamp," she said. "Cussin' and drinkin' and killin'."

"Daisy, we have to talk." Ramsay motioned her into his office.

"Gotta go, Mr. Womack," she said, "It is sure nice talking to y'all, but Mr. Ramsay needs me."

She entered his office and closed the door.

"What gives with the bruises?" Marcus shook his head. "This is getting serious, Daisy."

"The son of a bitch nailed my Shannon, too," she said. "My little baby." Daisy's bottom lip quivered.

"That asshole," he said.

"After he whoops me a couple o' times, he takes out his huntin' knife. I thought he was gonna kill me. Then he whittles a brand new point on an old pencil and sucks on a beer while he scribbles down a statement."

"Really?" Ramsay fiddled with his chin.

"Well, that's what he said. In fact, he said 'I'm gonna get them assholes' all the time he was beating on us. Then afterwards, he throws a fit lookin' for an envelope, puts the paper in it, and seals it. He shoves it at me sayin' I should give it to the 'Bears,' that's what he calls the Texas Rangers, the smokies."

"Weird. That knife bit scares me. He's gonna kill you some day, dammit," Ramsay said. "Somebody's got to stop him."

She went on, "Larry couldn't make it Saturday morning, so Coy had his coffee and went out by his lonesome to bag some damn ducks. Least he takes part of it out on them."

An hour later Marcus and Cecil talked
in Cecil's office about the impact Frank's
disappearance would have on the future
of Coyote's relationship with the Benedict
Company, or if there would be a Benedict
Company anymore. Earl had left the
office for an afternoon meeting with the
mayor. Just then an unfamiliar, simply
dressed, middle-aged woman glanced
into Cecil's office as she walked by.

"Who's that?" Marcus asked.

"Never seen her," Cecil said.

Marcus walked to the door and
peeked out. The plain-looking woman
was formally shaking hands with Daisy.
"She and Daisy are going into my office
and closing the door," Ramsay said.

"Mighty odd. Looks like some kinda
nonsense going on," Cecil said. "Maybe
an old friend."

"Her mom?"

"No! Coy!" The screams, muffled
only slightly by Ramsay's office door,
shook Cecil's cigarette from his stubs and
onto the desk. Seconds later the woman
scurried past Cecil's office, going the
other way down the hall.

"What the hell is happening?" Marcus
said.

Cecil and Marcus rushed toward Daisy's screams, now louder with Ramsay's door thrown open and Daisy storming out.

"Daisy, darlin'!" Cecil said. "What is it?"

Daisy paced frantically around her desk, shaking her fists in the air. "Oh, my Lord!" she said, sobbing. Lenora tried to hug her, but Daisy pulled away and continued crying.

She turned to Ramsay and said in a hoarse whisper, eyes glaring. "It's Coy. He's been shot! He's dead. My Coy! I knew somethin' like this would happen."

"Should we stop that lady?" Ramsay asked. "What's going on?"

"Hunting," she whimpered. "Don't you get it?"

"What?" Ramsay said.

"Think, Marcus. She said they found the tire tracks, the big footprints, and ammo they think matched a high powered weapon that Frank would've owned. Then he disappears?" Daisy cried. "It's lookin' like Frank killed my Coy!"

"Frank?" Marcus asked. "Why?"

"Leave her be, Marcus," Lenora said. "You can do your investigation later."

"Just trying to help." He shrugged. For a moment Ramsay pictured Coy, beating this woman he claimed to love and beating her young child, even maiming or killing others. Though he could understand Daisy's pain, he was relieved, too. At this moment, he couldn't imagine how Daisy could be so grief-stricken about Coy's death.

"Marcus, don't you get it?" she bawled. "I loved the man!"

Ramsay stepped back, nonplused. It was then he realized the Duncan couple had a relationship far beyond his and Daisy's trivial fling. Maybe the love Ramsay received from Daisy was an illusion all along, and the love he felt for her, misplaced affection.

Daisy slumped into Lenora's arms.

"I'm sorry, Daisy." Ramsay moped back to his office. He turned. "Who was that lady then?"

"That was Marty. Coy's mother," Daisy said.

He nodded. "I should've known," he said.

"They contacted her when they found Coy's body in the swamp at the back o' Holler's." She heaved a mournful cry.

"Man." He hung his head.

Later, as twilight raced to beat what was sure to be a monster of a late spring storm, Marcus closed up his briefcase for an early departure. He heard the thunder bearing down on Turtle Creek.

Ramsay jerked when Lenora buzzed him via the intercom. "Mr. Hickman wants to see you," she said importantly. "He'll be right in."

Boy, that sounds official, Ramsay thought. He neatened his desk for the atypical conference.

Within the hour Earl wandered into Marcus' office and sat in one of the visitors' chairs. He picked up a magazine and started thumbing through it.

"We need to talk, Marcus, but no hurry," Earl said, looking away, stalling. The accent lamp made the moisture under his nose glisten. He fidgeted like someone twenty-five years older.

Ramsay straightened papers. "I'm all done here. What is it, Earl?" Ramsay asked.

Earl turned a page. "I don't know how to tell you this," he said. "Humph."

"What?"

"Well, John Childress wants me to fire you," Earl said.

"Excuse me?"

"You heard me."

After a silent minute, Ramsay stood behind his desk and paced back and forth three steps one way, three steps the other. "Wait, Earl. This doesn't make any sense," he said.

"Maybe it does." Earl cleared his throat. "Your assignment here at Coyote is complete. New this; new that. From new offices to new advertising. And . . . most of it without my consent."

"Wait a minute," Marcus said. "I was just doing my job."

"Oh, really?" Earl shook his head. "More like insubordination, don'tcha think? When I complained to Childress, he said, 'If he's so bad, let him go.' So—"

"That's it? That's only Childress' manner of speech. His style."

Earl mumbled as he huddled over his magazine, shaking every few seconds and flipping pages.

"Earl, look at it this way, you don't have any grounds. All I've done here . . . " Ramsay threw his hands in the air. "You just gave me a great performance rating and a juicy raise."

Earl shrugged. "We never wanted any of it. Including that raise. Al said it about broke our bank, those damn Allied salary guidelines."

"Wait. You really can't do this. It has to be a mistake."

Earl shook his head, turned a page, and snickered, "Hardly."

"Earl? Wait a minute." Ramsay started to believe this could really happen. He marched around, more frantic now. Then he stopped. "Listen, it's really been an awful week with Frank disappearing, and Coy. Why don't we just go home tonight and think about it. We'll talk in the morning. Things'll be clearer then." Ramsay hunched over as deferentially as possible. "Please, Earl?" he begged like a teenager having lost his driving privileges.

Earl glanced up, then back at his magazine. "Humph?" Earl looked up again. He pretended that he hadn't noticed Ramsay's tone.

"Tomorrow, Earl?" Marcus asked. "Then we can sort this all out and have a good talk."

Earl paused, deliberating, then rose. As he hobbled out of Ramsay's office he shook his head like an old man and mumbled vague concurrence.

Ramsay sighed. *It's a reprieve,* he thought, at least until tomorrow.

Minutes later, without looking back, Earl slumped out of his office with his magazine in hand and headed down the hall to Coyote's front door.

Ramsay waited behind. For fifteen minutes he wandered through the Dallas office, one of his contributions to the little company. The thunder roared outside, announcing the impending storm, due to slam Dallas. Then, Ramsay's numbness changed to tears as it sunk in. *Being fired after all I did for the company? For Allied? How could this happen?*

He walked over to the floor-to-ceiling window and looked out at the storm as it moved into Turtle Creek. There was an ominous beauty about how the lightning crashed around the buildings and the clouds hovered so close they seemed touchable. Ramsay felt that jabbing pain inside his gut.

"Ow!" It was worse than ever. He keeled over. Marcus hobbled down the Coyote office hall to the men's room adjacent to the reception area. He walked in, pulled open a stall door, and leaned over the toilet. He felt clammy and sweaty. The urge to vomit overcame him. But as he retched, only saliva and bits of yellow bile dripped from his mouth.

After he wiped his mouth with a small wad of tissue, he left the bathroom and tottered back to the bullpen of desks. But when he looked outside at the hanging purple clouds, now closer than ever, he felt the urge to be sick again.

As he leaned against the large window, mucus dripped from the side of his mouth. He wiped it off with the tissue wad. He felt even weaker. *This is really bad,* he thought. He thought maybe he should call 9-1-1.

Like a giant magnet, the storm pulled at him from through the glass.

As Ramsay became disoriented and felt a deep emptiness inside him, his resistance faded. "Help me!" he cried, feeling he was about to succumb to some serious illness or even death. "I can't stand this anymore!" he called out.

In the next instant, a swirl of colored light shot from Ramsay's chest, out through the window, and into the clouds. For a second, he felt voltage surge through him, but at once it was gone and left him wobbling in place. He felt so weak in his legs that he collapsed to his knees. He glanced out the window at the storm as it crackled a display of blue, pink, and white bolts of lightning amidst the purple clouds.

Across town, Sheila Hickman took out the folded, white note again. She had read its message every few hours as she meandered through the house. Occasionally she glanced outside at gray, choppy Lake Hubbard and the increasing clouds. As the minutes passed she felt a pit in her stomach. The note made sense. She knew her dream visits to James Post and Ramoay had become her reality. She realized it was time to end her pain, but she had to hurry so the foul weather wouldn't spoil her plans.

She gulped down her glass of Cabernet, then proceeded to ceremonially brew some of her favorite French Roast coffee. The kitchen clock ticked loudly once a second, like the clock in the padded cell at Navarro Medical Center.

Slightly woozy, she filled an old thermos with the coffee, splashing some on the counter. Just like during the cemetery trip, she decided to strip herself of everything except one of Earl's old flannel shirts, soft from too much washing. She found the exact one she had worn to the cemetery! It felt so comfy.

She sat at the kitchen table and scribbled a letter listing all the truths she had been suppressing. Writing down the truth would surely free her soul for all eternity. It would hurt people, definitely shock some, but by having made the effort to tell all, she hoped she would eventually earn their forgiveness.

She folded her note and slipped it into the shirt pocket. She walked to the bathroom, picked up her pill bottle, and stuffed it into the other chest pocket.

Then, a little off kilter, she staggered to the end of the pier, where the Corsicana bounced in small, choppy waves. She climbed in, pushed off from the pier, and started the trawling motor.

The clouds lit up and a stiff breeze snapped her messy hair to and fro. Waves lapped against the Corsicana. The boat bounced and sputtered to the center of the lake. Sheila shut off the motor and rocked in the choppiness for several minutes as the purple clouds loomed above her.

Her children and their fathers, Sven and Mark, flashed through her mind. She stood, wobbling in the boat, and looked up at the billowing clouds. "Sven! You'd be proud of me down here—a real sailor. Just like you, you ornery asshole." She coughed deeply. "And Mark, you too. I really made it—the first lady of Coyote! See, I told you old Earl was a good pick. And you doubted it, you collegiate snob!" She cried hysterically as she sat back down.

"And here I am, sitting in a boat called the Corsicana. Figures." She recalled Corsicana, how it had served as a backdrop for her realizing her dreams.

I hope I won't be condemned to Hell, although I probably deserve it! she thought. Was any of the garbage she'd accumulated in life from the shoes to the jewelry to the wardrobe to the condo really worth it?

Her eyes dried quickly in the stiff breeze. Sheila began to feel dizzy. "Who fucking cares?" she laughed through her tears. She sipped on the coffee. Then, with the thermos still half full, she threw it overboard. It splashed and floated away. As occasional rain drops splattered her, she looked up. The clouds seemed to have eyes. The lightning exploded into a variety of colors—it was the first time she had ever seen that!

She half-cried and half-laughed. "Post was right. I guess I do feel at peace. I just don't care!" Now even the vague nausea she felt when she normally mixed alcohol with her pills had disappeared. The thought of Marcus Ramsay and James Post and Coy Duncan and murder and the police meant nothing. Even thoughts of Earl's struggles meant nothing. James Post's promise of peace was materializing.

"Here I am!" Sheila Hickman stood and, thinking of the simple grace of the geese she had seen land on Lake Hubbard, she took off her shirt and stashed it under the boat's bench. She stood straight, holding her arms out like wings, and exposed her naked body to the heavens. From above, light beams shot through the clouds onto her. She shivered as small drops hit her body and caused her to flinch at each cold little splash. She opened the pill bottle to swallow its contents and spread her arms again. This would be peace . . . finally. The thunder boomed. But she stalled.

Suddenly the cold drops shook her to attention. "Oh, fuck!" she called as she cringed. "This is stupid, look at me!" She laughed hysterically. "I can't even take my own life. I deserve to die."

The thunder boomed as she cringed. "Just forget it. Maybe another day." She laughed at herself, relieved. *Tonight I'll fix some fancy-ass dinner for Earl,* she thought. *I hope the neighbors can't see me. I must look stupid.*

As Sheila looked up at the storm, a long, vertical bolt of lightning cracked by the lake shore near her house.

"Holy shit! Look at that!" She turned to start the trawling motor and dropped her pills. "Damn," she said. The bottle bounced away in the choppy waves.

She laughed. "Oh well. I can replace 'em." Then she reached to the back of the boat and pulled the starter rope on the trawling motor. *Nothing.*

"What?" She laughed uneasily. She tried again, but without result. "Shit." She yanked again, harder. *Nothing.* Lightning flashed.

She glanced forward in the boat. "Where are the fucking oars?" She yanked at the motor again. Out of gas. "Earl, that incompetent asshole!" she yelled. Sheila looked up. The clouds loomed.

A clank sound.

What was that, she wondered. "Ow!" It was a heavy thud on her left shoulder bone. Hard, sharp, cold! "My God. Hail?"

She grabbed her arm and felt moistness. A trickle of red dripped from her shoulder.

"Ow!" Another, the size of a small softball.

The clanging paused. Sheila reached for her shirt. That would surely protect her. But another baseball-sized hail ball smashed her wrist.

"Ow!" She dropped her shirt in the water. She reached for it, but it slipped beneath the water's surface.

She scoured the shore, now barely visible. She looked up at the sky. "Oh God."

The storm threatened Earl Hickman's drive home. He celebrated to himself about initiating the act he had dreaded for months. Ramsay was almost gone, tomorrow for sure. Sheila would be so happy.

Then he'd make up with Erlene. She needed a father now more than ever. She was undoubtedly going to have a hard time with Frank's disappearance, let alone the fact that he had killed Coy. But, Erlene could survive without her Frankie, Earl figured. She was a smart, lovable young woman and deserved better than Frank anyway.

Darkness fell prematurely as Earl merged onto the Central Expressway and the traffic crept along. Larger droplets fell. It was the storm Lenora had warned him about. "We might-should leave early today," she had said, referring to the Coyote commuter car she and Ted drove daily from Corsicana to Dallas.

Thank God Sheila's safe at home, he thought. She was probably following the storm's progress on the news. He would certainly stay off the lake that night, and leave the Corsicana bouncing at dockside. He needed to get gas anyway. Maybe he would get to it in a day or so.

This would be a great night for building a fire in the huge fireplace, sneaking a few sips of champagne, and having cheese fondue, one of Sheila's favorites.

The rain drummed harder on Earl's windshield. The green Walnut Hill Lane exit sign popped into view. "Not good," he said as he looked around. In fact, it had to be the worst storm he had ever seen. As he turned off the exit, the sky rumbled and rain pounded the car. A long, thin bolt of lightning shot from the sky far ahead of him. Then the storm paused.

"I hope it won't get any worse. Phew!" he said. Just then, the sky cracked open with a magnificent display of lightning. Earl pulled to the side of the road as brilliant bolts, some colored, pounced on east Dallas.

"Shit!" Then he heard loud thumps pound the car. *Hail?* he thought. The Mercedes reverberated as a volley of baseball-sized spheres bombarded the car and smashed against the windshield for ten minutes, maybe more. Dents were inevitable. Sheila would be so pissed.

As the rain calmed, Earl looked at the hood, now like the surface of the moon. Amazingly, the windshield had not cracked. He drove slowly up Walnut Hill, past Crow Valley Trail, to Alamo Road, crunching new hail balls and dodging freshly fallen limbs. After turning left on Alamo, he saw the lit-up condo on the lakeside surrounded by Sheila's battered roses.

As rain began to pour smoothly like a fresh spring shower, thunder boomed in the distance. Earl was home at last, just as the storm came to an end.

Once inside, he called, "Sheila?" No answer. "I'm home!" Still, no Sheila. *She might be in bed,* he thought. But when he turned on the light in their bedroom, the bed was empty and the bedspread was ruffled from Sheila's afternoon nap. Back in the dining room, a used wine glass sat on the table as usual. She'd been drinking red again, and undoubtedly having those crazy dreams. She needed to see Lockhart again, he thought, or maybe some new doctor at the Presbyterian Hospital nearby.

A strange noise gurgled from the kitchen. Earl rushed in. On the stove, a nearly empty coffee pot perked wildly, spitting steam. He turned it off. "Sheila?" he called. Still nothing. *She must be out,* he thought. *Maybe she went to see a doctor. But in this storm? That doesn't make any sense.*

Then Earl glanced outside toward the end of the pier. The gray sky had brightened several shades. *Where is the Corsicana?* he wondered.

Earl rushed out the patio door into the light rain. Had the boat been stol—

He caved in.

"Sheila! Sheila!" He called out when he saw something familiar rocking in the misty grayness of the lake. Was that the Corsicana out there?

Uniform little waves lapped against the pier. The chill of the lake engulfed Earl Hickman as he squinted through the mist. He rushed back into the house. For the next hour he made calls to multiple agencies and neighbors not-at-home, as if they might be able to help. After he returned to the pier, sirens blared and emergency lights flashed around the house. Soon there were uniformed bodies rushing up the pier to him.

Earl turned, looked out at the lake, and screamed inside. He watched, horrified, as the Corsicana rocked up to the pier.

The morning after the storm, as he drove to work to face Earl Hickman, perhaps for the last time, Marcus Ramsay thought the day looked especially clear and cheery.

The DJ had dubbed it the "storm of the century" on the radio. Across the Dallas metroplex, a thousand homes that were normally dry had sprung leaks. The air was so clear that visibility doubled, and the silver ball sitting atop its perch on the Regency Hyatt Hotel, gleamed in the morning light. That is, except for the tiny, dark spots on the mirrored panels: holes created by the huge hail balls that had pummeled Dallas.

Early the previous evening, Marcus, drained from his emotional day-end meeting with Earl, had run down Walnut Hill Drive through the post-storm dusk. He had trampled on fallen bark, hopped over broken branches, and crushed the remnants of hail balls. Preoccupied with thoughts of his meeting that day, and distracted by the strange chorus of emergency sirens and chain saws that serenaded him for the entire two miles, his run had not been as peaceful as normal.

The announcement to Kathy of his imminent dismissal had hit like death itself. First she'd been silent, then she started jabbering, trying to arm him with the perfect words to save his job. Suddenly she seemed obsessed with the idea of his staying at Coyote.

"I just don't get it," he said over and over as he drove down Central Expressway. "How could I get fired?"

Maybe John Childress would step in to stop the injustice, he hoped. If Kyle Burghoff were still alive he certainly would. After all, they had selected him to come down to Texas and help the little company. And, Ramsay had saved it from itself. In turn, Childress should save him, he thought.

He has to. It's only fair. Ramsay had changed the company into a modern division, just like he had promised. Coyote had been transformed: a new, improved product; new contemporary offices; new spending policy, new breakthrough advertising—new everything. The company would now profit from future generations of Yankees-turned-Texan without having the shackle of billback trade deals.

Losing the new sprinkler system for the plant had been Ramsay's only loss, if you want to call it that, and that decision could be reversed once Earl realized it was just a good safety measure.

Now he should get rewarded, not fired, Ramsay thought.

He drove through the puddles at the Haskell Avenue exit, swerved around two fallen limbs on Carlisle, and pulled into the little Coyote parking lot.

Once in his office, Ramsay immediately dialed Childress' number.

"Mr. Childress' office." It was Virginia.

"Virginia! It's Marcus Ramsay. I need to talk to John right away."

"Oh, hello, Marcus. I'm afraid Mr. Childress is out of town at the annual sales meeting in Phoenix."

"Sales meeting? I hadn't heard."

"Oh, I'm sorry. I'm sure I sent a complimentary invitation to Mr. Hickman two weeks ago. Didn't he mention it?"

"Apparently not. Thanks." Suddenly the timing of his dismissal seem very convenient, if not obvious.

Ramsay hung up and continued his rhetorical questions over coffee as he waited for Earl. Had his boss wanted to dump him all along?

It was ten o'clock before Earl entered his office next door. Ramsay rose and followed him in. Earl stood there quietly hunched behind his desk.

"Good morning, Earl," Ramsay said.

He didn't answer and looked away.

"Well? Feel like talking?" Ramsay asked. *This firing bit really couldn't come true,* he thought.

But there was only silence for ten long seconds. Earl stood behind his desk, weary-looking and ashen. He cleared his throat repeatedly. He looked disheveled—unusual for Earl Hickman. There was no scent of aftershave. The man obviously hadn't slept at all. Ramsay sensed an apology coming.

"You're fard," Earl rumbled in his lowest voice as he continued to look away.

"What?!" Marcus asked.

A long pause.

"Excuse me, Earl? I didn't hear you." Ramsay leaned forward. "Did you say—"

"You're fard. You're fard. You're fard!" Earl broke down and cried. He continued to look away and hold his large face with both hands.

"Earl, my God, what's wrong?" Ramsay asked.

"She's dead." Earl shook as he bawled.

"Who?" Ramsay asked.

"Sheila."

"Sheila? But how?"

"Electrocution," Earl said. "And the hail."

Ramsay closed his eyes, stunned. He tried to conjure a scene. "I don't get it."

"She was out in the damn boat . . . in the storm."

The thought nearly made Ramsay sick. "I don't know what to say, Earl. I am so sor—"

"She wasn't wearing anything," he said.

"Why?" Ramsay asked.

"How the hell should I know?" Earl's voice trailed off as he shrugged his shoulders.

"God, Earl, I'm so sorry," Ramsay said.

"Shoot." Earl's crying continued. Lenora appeared at the door, tears in her eyes, her fingers in praying posture. "Oh, Mr. Hickman."

Marcus Ramsay sighed. He realized he would never forget this pair of events:

his own dismissal coupled with Sheila's strange death. He shook his head, nonplused. He had come to Texas to help these people climb out of an incredible time warp. *Can this be the unfathomable result?*

"Earl, listen. Why don't you just go home?" Marcus said.

"I have to make some calls. An autopsy, the funeral," he said. "You understand."

"Sure," Ramsay said.

"Just—" Earl just stood there, looking away, shaking his head. "Oh, never mind."

"The kids OK?" Ramsay asked.

Earl glanced over his shoulder. "Just go away."

"But, Earl," Ramsay said. "Let me help."

"You?" He laughed. "Help?"

For the next hour Ramsay sat in his office with Daisy, Stuart and teary-eyed Ted. He tried to convince them they shouldn't leave Coyote in protest of his dismissal.

"I have to be the honorable man here," Ramsay kept saying. "And you have to carry on . . . " That night, when he regurgitated the scene to Kathy, she only told him how he should have tried to reach John Childress in Phoenix and confront the situation, not given up.

"At least that's what Daddy would say," she insisted.

"But they're all assholes up at Allied or this never would've happened." Ramsay went out for his run, but he already felt the scarring from the dismissal settling in.

Late that night at the Coyote Brand compound in Corsicana, the mercury vapor light cast an eerie glow across the two little office buildings and the warehouse where new flames flickered through the windows. From across the courtyard, in the plant building, a shadowy figure watched the fire begin to blossom. He shuffled through the plant building, splashing liquid from a can. In one area, then another, through the complicated labyrinth of gleaming Oz-like pipes made necessary by Yankee innovations, the aroma of Coyote Chili spices met the smell of kerosene.

"May the Lord have mercy," the figure grumbled. He splashed more fluid around. He reached in his pocket, pulled out a matchbook, and hurriedly lit a match. Then he tossed it.

Poof! All around him the fumes from the kerosene ignited.

25

Dallas, Texas   June 2, 1981

Lenora interrupted Earl Hickman's morning coffee mid-sip. "Mr. Hickman, Al says the plant's burning . . . or was!" Earl had been sitting at his desk, imagining Sheila's funeral in Corsicana.

"What?" he said and picked up the phone. Al's little voice squawked some of sketchy details. It wasn't an inconsequential fire.

Earl threw on his jacket and dashed out of his office, past Lenora. He said urgently, "Take the day off, Lenora. Whatever. Bye." He ran down the hall. "Cecil, you, too," he called into the man's office as he passed it.

"Everyone OK, Mr. Hickman?" Lenora called after him.

The front door to the Dallas office slammed.

"Shoot, ain't had a fire in a long time." As Lenora reached for the phone, Cecil walked up. "What's all the ruckus anyway?" he asked.

"Big fire at the plant. Hope everybody's OK," she said.

"They'll put it out real quick," Cecil said. "Always do."

"Does it count as a vacation day if we leave?" Lenora asked.

"It will for Stuart and Daisy, I betcha." He laughed. "Hell, they'll be gone all day over at the Rose Festival."

She chuckled. "Maybe we should head to Tyler, too."

"Naw. Too far," Cecil said. "But if I hurry, I can get in nine holes."

"Bet it'll be lonely out there, playin' without Frank," she said.

"Yep. No one to beat me," Cecil snickered as he walked away.

"Yep." Lenora listened to the distant rattling of Ted's ten key adding machine. Then it hit her: Coy dead, Frank gone, Sheila electrocuted, the plant burning. Her tears started.

It was a little past nine-thirty that morning. Heading south to Corsicana, Earl sped past the fields of bluebonnets that bordered I-45. Sheila would've expected him to handle this fire thing like normal, he thought, so he drove on with purpose.

As the Texas 287 exit approached, Earl felt adrenaline in his veins. He looked to his right and saw a billowing, dark gray cloud of smoke. "Humph." It slowly drifted north, pulled by an invisible wind current high in the sky. By the time he reached Second Street, a tame, white smoky plume rose from the same location. He turned onto Seventh and was about to make a left onto Main, when two fire engines rumbled past him on Main heading the opposite way. Saved again. *See, we didn't need that damn sprinkler,* he thought.

As Earl bounced over the tracks, he looked ahead to his right on Main Street. "My Lord," he mumbled. As he drove up, ruins of all three buildings smoldered. Al's pudgy form stood in new mud and waved a little, discouraged wave through the rising steam. Earl turned right, passed through the chain link gate, stopped, and got out of the car. "What happened?"

"It's all over," Al said as he waddled up. He dodged puddles with a shrug. "A bunch of the crew and office showed up, but I sent 'em home."

"No kiddin'," Earl said.

The stench of burnt chili filled the air. "It didn't take long, I guess. Poof." Al's eyes squinted. "Pretty ugly." He pointed to the burnt-out buildings. The ochre paint was charred, a black vertical smudge above each window rising to the roof line.

"We should've got that damn sprinkler system," Al said, shaking his head. "Coulda saved the place, they said. Too expensive, remember?" He snickered. "Say. I'm sorry about Sheila; Lenora told me."

Earl hung his head.

"Real sorry," Al said. "No time for jokes."

As if he ignored the comment, Earl waved his hands around. "So, this is what a burning chili plant smells like?" He squinted. "Anyone hurt?"

"You won't like this," Al said. "Man."

"What?" Earl asked.

Al shook his head. "Oscar."

"Hurt?" Earl darted his head around, looking for his plant manager to magically appear.

"He was in there, Earl," Al said. "He's gone."

"What?" Earl pointed to the plant with a questioning look. "There?"

"Yep."

"Oh, my Lord. This is too much."

"Jesse heard him hollerin' and swearin' in the flames. It was awful. They took Jesse to Navarro. He was in shock. I called Maria to tell her about Oscar. I told her I'd go over to her place later."

"Why was Jesse here?" Earl asked. "They were supposed to be off today."

"Just came in to check on everything, like always. He got here not long after it got a-goin'."

"Good old Jesse," Earl said. "I always said he was reliable for a black man."

"Yep. You sure did," Al said. "Fact, he called in the fire, but by the time they got here the place was . . . well, look at it. They're pretty sure Oscar started it and got caught in the middle."

Earl looked at the ground. "Poor Maria."

"And the kids," Al said.

"Oscar was that upset?" Earl asked.

"Wasn't your fault, Earl."

"Sure."

"He was a mighty angry man, especially at Allied. I'm going over and see Maria," Al said. "We were close."

"Maybe I should. I am the pres—"

"Naw, Earl. I better," Al said. "Really."

"Yep . . . I understand."

"There's nothing more we can do today. Or ever." Al sloshed through the swamp of water, charred bits, and mud. He stopped and turned to Earl. "Damn thing's not our problem anymore, Earl. Let Allied worry about it. It's theirs, right?"

"I guess I better call 'em."

"Already did."

"What'd they say?"

"Sending a team down. "

"Figures—Yankee bull. God, now I gotta cater to them one more time. That's somethin' I feel like," he said sarcastically.

"Sorry, Earl. What're you gonna do now?" Al asked.

"Without Sheila, the company? I don't know. All I have left is the kids. Never thought I'd be leanin' on them."

"Say, call me if you need anything," Al said. "I'll be at home in a few hours."

"Thanks." Earl pointed around. "Sorta reminds me of *Gone with the Wind* and Tara. That was the name of her house, right?"

"Yep."

"But I think this is worse."

"What made Sheila do that?"

"Dunno. She burnt up just like Coyote, except it was from the damn lightning." Earl Hickman sniffled and pulled out his handkerchief. By the time he finished blowing his nose, Al had reached his old, olive green van, decorated with faded chili cook-off decals.

"When's the funeral, by the by?" he called back.

"Service at Corsicana Community at ten Friday, then over at the cemetery here in town after.

"Right. See you then."

"I'm just gonna stay awhile," Earl called and pointed around.

Al climbed into his truck and waved. "Call me if you need me, Earl. Really."

A few hours later, shortly before noon, after being barraged by calls about the fire all morning, Lenora sat at her desk and unwrapped her regular lunch, a chicken salad sandwich and tub of coleslaw. She planned on heading home as soon as she finished eating. As she took her first bite, the phone rang. She picked up the receiver. "Good afternoon, Coyote Brand."

"Lenora?" It was Erlene. Her voice was trembling.

"Yes, child."

"Daddy there?"

"No. At the fire."

"I heard about it," Erlene said. She wept over the phone. "Daddy OK?"

"Fine," Lenora said. "He's down there helpin'. What's the matter, dear?"

"They couldn't get him so they called me to the morgue at the hospital."

"Why on earth—"

"To collect Mama's things," Erlene said.

"Oh dear. Isn't death hard enough?"

"They found something and need him over there," Erlene said. "Can you get word to him? They're calling in the authorities."

For hours Earl kicked through charred bits of paper and mud, wondering if there was anything worth saving. He thought of Sheila: her visits to Coyote Brand, her summer dresses, her jewelry, and her fancy shoes.

Several hours later, by the sales office, he found two old file drawers that had been saved and put aside. They were still warm. He thumbed through a wad of memos in an open drawer. *Good times*, he thought. The sun was falling fast as he read them and dropped the crisp papers into the steaming mud.

He walked through the mud toward his old, dented Mercedes. As pre-dusk settled, Al pulled into the gate, splashing mud. He jumped out of his van and called urgently, "Say, Earl. Lenora called Shirley." He splashed closer in the mud. "Erlene's at the hospital morgue at Presbyterian. They found some kind of note from Sheila. The authorities are coming in. They want you up there right away."

"Huh? Authorities? Note?" Earl gulped. "Shoot, what now?"

When Earl emerged from the hospital elevator almost an hour later, he looked left, then right. Panicked from imagining what the urgency might be, he started to hurry down the blue-colored corridor. *What could possibly be the big deal now?* he wondered.

He stopped. Erlene sat there on a wooden bench against the wall, quietly weeping. Her hands covered her eyes. Above her, a small blue sign stuck out from the wall—MORGUE.

"Erlene! What is it?" He rushed to console her.

She looked up with reddened eyes. "Wait, Dad—uh, Earl."

Earl stopped and dropped his arms, nonplused at her address. She never called him by his first name.

"They let me read the letter she left behind," she sniffled.

"They didn't say anything about any letter before," he said.

"They didn't find it right away. It was in her shirt pocket. Now they're holdin' it for evidence. They might call this a suicide if the drug tests come back positive. Her pills weren't in the medicine cabinet at home."

"Shoot," he said and shook his head. "I'm not surprised. How she's been actin'— "

"Who in their right mind would've gone out on the lake with that storm comin' anyway . . . and then taken all her pills like that?" she asked. "Sounds crazy."

"I know, I know. I saw that coming, too," Earl said. "She hasn't been in a good way."

"That detective was here and said Mama only had enough gas to get to the

center of the lake. Like this could've
been planned by someone that knew her
habits. He's wantin' to ask you a bunch of
questions."

Earl froze. Guilt zapped through him.
If he had filled the tank like he'd planned,
Sheila would have been alive now.

"You OK, Dad? What is it?" she asked.

"Nothing. Just nothing." *I did this
thing to her,* he thought. He had ended
her life.

"You look miserable," she said.

"Well, Erlene, what do you expect?"
He turned away.

"You won't like the note, neither," she
said.

"What about it?" He turned back.

"Her lovers. Her dreams. Sit down,
Daddy. You look pale."

"What lovers?" he asked.

"You won't believe it," she said.

"What?" He sat down and trembled as
he tried to light a cigarette.

"I'm sorry, Dad," she said. "Someone
has to tell you this stuff." Erlene wiped
her eyes. "I know about Sven Larson."

"My old first mate?" Earl said and
forced a smile. "What's he got to do with
this? That old sea dog."

"He's my real father," she said.

"What?" He looked up.

"Sven was my father and Mark White was Bryan's," she said.

"Mark? My old boss?" Earl closed his eyes. "What are you saying?"

"It's true, Daddy," she said. "All of it." She sniffled.

"But, Erlene—"

"It's all in the note," Erlene said.

"But your mother wouldn't say all this. Where is this note? I don't believe it."

"They kept it. There's more."

Earl reached over to Erlene, but she held her hand up.

"James Post, Daddy! She spent five thousand dollars to have him killed so you could get his stupid job," she said.

Earl froze. *For all sorts of reasons this couldn't be,* he thought. "Jesus, Erlene, what are you saying?"

"You heard me. She paid Coy Duncan to slice his brakes."

Earl stared. "Oh, my God. I can't believe—"

"Coy raped her, too. Mother and daughter rape—nice guy, huh?" Erlene laughed a hard, dead laugh. "That asshole. He deserved to die."

"I have to—" Earl shook his head in slow motion, stood, and staggered toward the elevator.

Just then the door slid open. A serious, slightly built, pock-faced man in a trenchcoat emerged purposefully. He looked vaguely familiar to Earl. "Hi Hickman."

"Yep. What is it?" Earl stopped and asked.

"Remember, we met at your office that one morning. Detective Mike Adams, Dallas Police?" They shook hands. "We talked about Frank Benedict," he said.

"Of course," Earl said. His felt a pang in his gut. "What is it now, detective?"

"Daddy, you don't need to answer anything," Erlene called.

"Technically right, sir," Detective Adams said. "I'd like to talk to you down at headquarters, though. Get you printed. They found some latent prints on that gas can."

"Well, of course, the damn thing was mine," Earl said.

"Possibly ties you to your wife's death, sir. Sorry at a time like this, but I do need to print you right away. Routine."

"Me? Kill my wife?" Earl hung his head and mumbled, "Shoot."

Adams said, "I'm also workin' with the Corsicana force on this old Post case.

Your name," he said as he looked at a small spiral notebook, "and Frank Benedict's came up in a letter written by Coy Duncan. His wife gave it to us."

"Letter? Daisy?"

"That's right. Need to talk to y'all about that," he said.

"What would I know?" Ray asked.

"Have to see. For one thing, know anything about Mr. Benedict's whereabouts?"

"Nobody does." Earl couldn't believe how everything seemed to be unraveling before his eyes. He felt cold from the inside out and began shivering uncontrollably.

"Well, best we have a long chat, print you, and clear this thing up. How 'bout we go now. Won't take too long," Detective Adams said. The detective reached forward, took Earl firmly by the bicep, and led him into the waiting elevator.

Earl turned to Erlene: "Don't worry, baby. I'll call you."

"Er, Daddy, should I call someone?"

Earl glanced at the detective, then back at Erlene. "I'll call you later at the condo. I'm sure it's nothing, but get out

Art Fennel's number in case we need him."

26 *Corsicana, Texas   June 5, 1981*

Marcus Ramsay arrived at the Corsicana cemetery in the unusually neat taxi just as Sheila Hickman's funeral was ending. The pleasant, British cabby had driven him all the way to Corsicana from Dallas for a fixed fare of twenty dollars. The taxi had arrived at Marcus' house just two minutes after it was called.

Shoot, but I'm still late, Ramsay thought as he looked at his watch. "It certainly wasn't your fault, though, Mr. Waverly," Ramsay said, scanning the cabby's license mounted on the dashboard. They pulled into the cemetery.

The cabby looked over his shoulder. "I'll get you to the airport on time, sir," he said in a proper voice. It sounded vaguely familiar.

"Great. I'll just be a second," Ramsay said. He would pay his last respects, then head up to DFW airport to leave on an exploratory trip to California and a new life.

Ramsay stepped out of the taxi and walked across Corsicana's rolling old cemetery. According to Daisy, who had heard from Erlene, Sheila had insisted in her farewell note that she be buried there. Her time in the town was, after all, the highlight of her life, she had pointed out.

A small group of departing mourners passed Ramsay as he walked. It was surprising how many friends Sheila had accumulated. Given her strange suicide and boorish demeanor, though, Ramsay guessed they may have attended her funeral more out of curiosity than from some great devotion to the deceased.

As the mourners' cars rolled away, a sudden breeze rustled the sparse, early summer leaves. Before Ramsay walked to Sheila's canopied grave site, he stopped nearby at the cemetery's largest monument. A bed of daisies fluttered about its base. One of Margaret Post's last requests was to add "Dream sweetly tonight" to James' stone. Ramsay smiled, remembering her endearment and when she had told him about it.

On the ground, partially hidden by the fluttering flowers, Ramsay caught sight of a dull silver object. "I wonder how this got here," he said. He bent over and retrieved the fat, worn, silver pen. *I must've misplaced this,* he thought. Now a white note was crammed into its clip. He studied the inscription on the pen's body. He wished that sometime in his life he'd experience the love, trust, and commitment the Posts had shared. As he stowed the pen in his pants pocket, the partially folded note fluttered away on the ground. The note landed, danced twenty feet, and came to rest near Sheila Hickman's burial site.

Under the temporary, blue velvet awning, he saw Erlene Hickman, the last mourner, huddled inconspicuously beside her mother's casket. The "first lady of Coyote Brand," as she had liked to be called, lay sheathed in a copper casket, poised for final internment. It was strewn with a mixture of roses, some fresh, most wilted.

Nearby, two Hispanic cemetery workers whispered as they fiddled with their orange cemetery back hoe. Ramsay wandered over to Sheila's casket and up to Erlene.

"Hi, Marcus," she said.

"Man. This must be really crummy," Ramsay said to her. He couldn't imagine her loss.

"The worst," she said. "Mama's gone,
Daddy looks like he could get charged
with a bunch of stuff, maybe even her
murder. Shoot, he isn't even my daddy,
technically, you know?"

"Why?" Ramsay asked.

"Long story."

He nodded. "You hanging in there?"

"Yep. I guess." Erlene faced Ramsay.
Tears dripped down her cheeks. "You
mind?" she asked as she moved close to
him and wrapped her arms around his
waist. She lay her head on his chest.

"It's OK. It's OK," he whispered. He
rubbed her back as she continued to
weep. "A lot at one time, huh?" he said.

"I'll survive," she said and sniffled,
"once I get over the shock. It's so weird."

"Any plans?" he asked.

"Not yet," she said. "Maybe finish
school. Find some prince of a guy."

They pulled away from each other.

"You and Bryan didn't deserve this,"
Ramsay said, holding her shoulders.

She laughed and looked away,
squinting into the breeze. "What about
you?" she asked.

"I don't know. Start over, I guess. I've
been lookin' at opening a photography
studio in California. It's been my secret

love all along. I'm flying out there today to look at some possibilities. I think I owe Kathy a little bit of me, too. She's had a distracted Marcus for too long."

Erlene looked over his shoulder at the taxi. "She in the cab?"

Ramsay hung his head. "Naw, she got a job out there already, starting tomorrow."

Erlene looked back at him. "I feel so sorry 'bout you an' your dreams for Coyote," she said.

"They were fantasies. Daisy was right. I am a damned foreigner." Ramsay hung his head. "But I've learned a lot."

"Like what? A world full of takers self-destructs?" she asked.

"Something like that. It was stupid for me to try to push Coyote to buy the northern approach, like it was the only way to go. They got back at me pretty good, though. I guess I deserved it."

"Naw, you're a nice man, Marcus, really." Erlene gave him one last hug and smiled. "You damn Yankee." She leaned up, gave him a peck on the cheek, and walked away.

"Bye, Erlene," he said and waved. He called after her, "Say, doesn't family get a limo?"

She looked back. "I told Bryan to go ahead. Gotta get used to bein' on my own."

"Good luck. Should I check in on you in a month or so? The condo? Alamo Road, right?"

"Be nice. Hey, thanks." She shuffled away through the grass with her hands in her pockets. He watched her for a long time. Against the vast cemetery lawn, dotted with decades-worth of stone markers, she looked small and solitary. She climbed into her Acura, started the engine, and drove away.

Ramsay faced Sheila's casket. "So it's over?" he asked. He fiddled with the silver pen. He recalled frail, little Margaret Post and her affection for her James, killed by this woman. He welled up. "It's not right!" Then an involuntary voice resonated from deep inside him. "Y'all got what you deserved, ma'am!" He spat on the casket, then caught himself and wiped his mouth with the back of his hand.

He quickly glanced over at the cemetery workers, who had stopped their respectful mumbling to turn and point. "Say, you OK, mister?" one of the workers called.

"Me? Fine. Just fine." But when Ramsay turned back to Sheila's grave, something clicked inside of him. He rapidly scolded her, slobbering in tongues. It only lasted a few seconds before he caught himself again, stunned. *My God,* he thought. *What is going on inside of me? Isn't this over?*

One of the cemetery workers genuflected and called over. "Say mister, you possessed or something?"

Ramsay wiped his mouth with his forearm and whisked his hands up and down. Oddly, it did feel like he, in fact, had been possessed: Like he was the person who had just finished digging this woman's grave, like he had just fulfilled some great destiny by engineering putting Sheila and Coy deep in the ground and sending Earl and Frank far, far away. Perhaps, all along, his visit to Texas might have had a greater purpose than saving some old chili business.

As Ramsay stood there, the little white note that had dropped from the silver pen fluttered up to his feet. It was lightly wrinkled and had ink blotches here and there, but, besides the discolored old paper, looked in otherwise good condition. He picked it up and unfolded it. Its short message was scrawled in large, rolling blue strokes.

Ramsay scratched his temple and gaped at the verse, vaguely familiar:

In the lake ye shall find peace.

Have I see this before? he wondered and stuffed the note in his pocket. Just then his taxi's horn sung across the cemetery grounds.

The taxi crunched slowly over the gravel path and past the Navarro County Historical Society offices.

By the time the cabby was headed down Route 287 toward I-45, Ramsay realized that no matter how bad things had turned out in Corsicana, they now felt settled, like they had been set right for James and Margaret Post. He looked at the driver's meter and picture on the dashboard. "Say, Mister, uh, Waverly, can I ask you a stupid question, get your opinion on something?"

"Anything, sir."

"Well, do you think the spirit of a dead man can possess the body of a living man?"

The cabbie smiled in the mirror. "I've always believed that if there is a purpose for a living man to be possessed by some bygone spirit, if he is the perfect host, and will learn something from being occupied, as it were, he is likely to be the perfect vessel for some spirit that needs to finish tasks on earth."

Ramsay leaned forward. "You realize how spooky that sounds?"

The cabbie chuckled. "I think it's all part of a plan that most of us don't understand."

"I guess," Ramsay agreed. As he thought back, he pitied Earl Hickman a little. The man had lived to serve Sheila. Now, with her gone, he would serve no one, and was likely to spend his remaining years in prison. Earl had always wanted to leave a legacy; it was a shame this would be it.

After an hour or so, Ramsay looked out of the taxi at the homogeneous development of the Dallas Galleria at the toll road and I-635 in North Dallas. Soon they reached the grassy outskirts of the DFW airport. In another minute the taxi pulled up to the terminal's drop-off point. Ramsay climbed out and the cabby followed, fetching Ramsay's bag from the trunk. "Thank you, Mr. Marcus Ramsay," Mr. Waverly said properly. "For everything." He waved away Ramsay's offer of a tip and smiled. "Truly interesting ride, mate." He shook Ramsay's hand vigorously and winked. "Not quite over, though."

Ramsay nodded, but was confused at what the cabby meant. "Right. You're welcome, sir," he said. "I guess." Marcus pulled open the door to the terminal, then looked back at the sturdy little man with the crewcut and glasses standing alongside his cab, arms behind his back, rocking back and forth, whistling "God Save the Queen." Ramsay wondered what the cabby had meant and how he had known his first name was Marcus, for he had never told him that.

Ramsay lugged his bag to the American Airlines ticket counter, checked-in, and walked down the long, crowded aisle to Gate C-22. He felt relieved that he would finally be leaving Texas and laying the groundwork for a new life in California. Maybe he could make his marriage work, too, if it could survive the weird Texas experience, his dismissal, and the probable separation that Kathy seemed to be hinting she wanted.

Standing at his gate, her face bathed in spent tears and a sheepish grin, was a big surprise. Daisy was there, wearing cut-off jeans and a stretchy pink tank top, her hands jammed into well-washed pockets. "I had to see y'all once more," she said. "Couldn't leave it hangin'. I called your house and Kathy said you were booked out this afternoon. I've been sittin' here for a couple of hours."

"Oh, Daisy." He leaned forward and gently hugged her. She fell hard into his arms. They clung to each other for a minute.

"I don't know what to say," he whispered. "I thought you hated me after Coy—"

"Where is Kathy anyway? Separate flights?"

"Out in California already—her new job," he said.

"Exciting."

"Right," he said. "I'm looking at studios, she's still in the Abyss."

"Abyss?"

"The corporation, what else?"

She nodded.

"We might be separating for a while if she gets her way. I'd be in an apartment, she'd have the new house."

"Oh."

"I think her dad doesn't approve of me doin' the photo studio thing. Not good enough for his little executive girl."

She sniffed and wiped her nose.

"What're those tears for?" he asked. "Don't feel bad about that, Daisy."

"Naw, it's not that," she said and looked at her watch. "You just got to hear the truth before you go, Marcus," she said. "You deserve that." She wiped her eyes and sniffled.

"About what? What do you mean?" Ramsay shook his head, confused. "I thought I already heard the truth."

"Well, Sheila wasn't the only one that hired Coy to kill James Post."

"No?" he asked.

Daisy looked down and fiddled with her fingers.

"Erlene told me about Earl," he said.

"Yep. Coy was always braggin' about it during his damn drunks," she said. Daisy squirmed in place.

"Why didn't you ever tell me?" he asked.

She clenched her jaw.

"Coy threatened to beat you, didn't he?" Ramsay asked. "So you kept quiet."

She looked away. "I know I was wrong doin' that."

"Daisy, it's OK," he said. "It's all over."

She swept her hair back and said, "Coy played 'em all for suckers. He knew he'd clean up if he worked 'em separate. So he did—got twenty grand total out of it. That's how we got a new pickup and the addition on our double-wide."

"Man. A murder spree," Ramsay said.

"Yep. Earl's dream was to please Sheila," she said. "So, Frank talked him into joinin' forces and killin' Post—makin' Earl president, then givin' Frank Houston to broker."

"So, Coy was hired by both Hickmans and Frank? Man, how do you know this, Daisy?" he asked. "Didn't Earl and Sheila know about each other?"

"Nope. Nobody knew all that was involved 'cept my Coy," she said. "He was always gettin' drunk and laughin', 'Those greedy assholes'."

Ramsay thought back. He could easily imagine Coy being a guilty party, the center of it all. "But Daisy, if Coy was the point man for all this, why were you so pissed at me after they found him dead? I mean, he did some pretty bad stuff."

"Marcus!" Daisy hit him hard on the shoulder. "Remember, the man was the father of my little Shannon."

"But, I still don't get Earl," he said, shaking his head, looking at his watch. Earl hadn't seemed mentally capable of being a part of some complicated murder scheme.

"Sneaky cuss all along," she said. "Sure did want to make Sheila happy."

"But Oscar wasn't part of it, right?" he said.

"Naw. The man just wanted a lot," she said. "Always pissed at Allied."

"God. They each wanted something real bad," he said. "So they did what they needed to do to get it. That's greed."

"And, in the end, you're the one to go and lose your damn job," she said.

"Well, truth is, I wanted the glory at y'alls' expense," he said.

Again Daisy hit him hard on the shoulder and laughed.

"Ow!" he said.

"Say, Yankee, 'y'alls' expense' idn't bad Texas talk." She dusted off the spot where she had just hit him. "You'll recover from this. Give y'all a year."

"Sure." Ramsay shook his head dejectedly, leaned over, and kissed her lightly on the cheek. "Well, adios, Ms. Duncan."

"Oh, Marcus?" She raised her index finger. "By the by, I always hated it when y'all called me Ms. Duncan," she said. "Prissy Yankee shit."

He snickered, "Just trying to be genteel."

"Gentle?"

"Whatever."

"Damn straight," she said and punched him again.

"Ow! Hey, thanks." As he rubbed his arm, he thought of Daisy and her marriage, Coyote Brand and its resistance to him, and how he had unsuccessfully tried to tame them both. "You can help 'em, but you can't fix 'em," he muttered.

"Say what?" she asked.

"Somebody told me that." He looked at Daisy and paused for a long second. Then, without warning, he wound up and started to hit her hard on her left shoulder. At the last second, he stopped, just short of contact.

"Shoot!" she yelped. "That would've hurt!" She caught his fist and carefully lifted it to her mouth. She kissed and stroked it, looking up at him with only her eyes. "Marcus? Anyone ever tell you, you've got beautiful hands?"

"Just you, Ms. Duncan. Just you. Remember? Once when we were parked on a rainy road."

She smiled and nodded, recalling. "Always liked them hands," Daisy said.

He could tell she didn't necessarily mean it, but that was OK. Relief washed over him. He had been deeply wounded by getting tossed from his job, but Ramsay realized that accepting, even embracing, the diversity of the Corsicana people might have been one lesson he was meant to learn all along. Just then Daisy dropped his hand, toodled a wave, and sauntered away as if he wasn't there, and had never been.

Marcus watched her disappear into the airport crowd. Then he turned and walked down the ramp into the waiting Boeing 737, rubbing his shoulder.

**Other memoir and
contemporary drama titles
by Jack Eadon,
only from Eloquence Press**

order only these ISBNs . . .

GOT TO MAKE IT!

ISBN 09753300-6-3 - a sixties memoir. The collectors' edition with CD and photo gallery.

LATENT IMAGE

ISBN 0-9753300-4-7 - A story about loss, love, and recovery. The sensitive sequel to A CONSEQUENCE OF GREED.

THE ARMSTRONG SOLUTION

ISBN 0-9753300-1-2 - A corporate thriller in the ENRON tradition . . . and then some!

THE CHARM FROM DELHI

ISBN 0-9753300-2-0 - A contemporary story of karma.

"GIGOLO" ON THE ROW

ISBN 0-9753300-0-4 - A neighborhood mystery is slowly revealed after a young woman is killed by a hit-and-run driver, supposedly by accident.

LACEY'S DAY ISBN 0-9753300-5-5 An Internet love story that drips with realism.

Also see: http://www.eadonbooks.com

and http://www.eloquencepress.com